The Beardmore Relics

E.J. Lavoie

WHISKYJACK PUBLISHING
Greenstone●Canada

Library and Archives Canada Cataloguing in Publication

Lavoie, Edgar J. (Edgar Joseph), 1940-
The Beardmore relics / E.J. Lavoie.

ISBN 978-0-9809017-3-3

I. Title.

PS8623.A837B43 2011   C813'.6   C2011-902604-X

Acknowledgements

The author thanks the many people who encouraged him in this project and/or cooperated in his research. Special thanks to the first readers, who offered valuable feedback: Karen Dauphinais, Christina Stricker, and François Sarrazin.

Disclaimer

Typeset in Times New Roman by WhiskyJack Publishing, Canada
Printed and bound in the United States of America

WhiskyJack Publishing
PO Box 279
Geraldton, Ontario, Canada
P0T 1M0
www.whiskyjackpublishing.ca

*For our late father, Robert, who led his family
to a magnificent green country.*

MAP 1

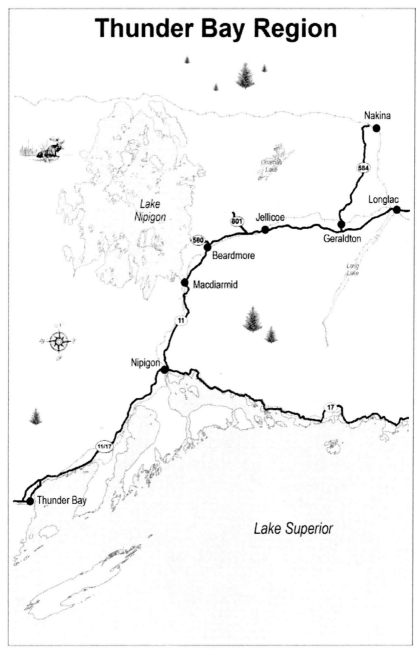

Thunder Bay Region

Nakina

Longlac

Jellicoe

Geraldton

Beardmore

Macdiarmid

Nipigon

Thunder Bay

Lake Superior

Lake Nipigon

MAP 2

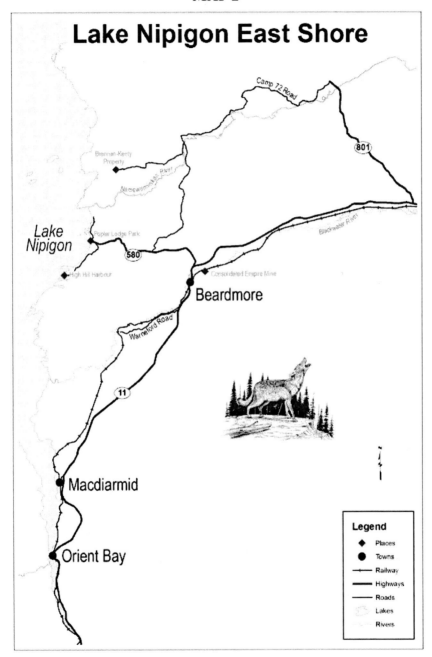

Lake Nipigon East Shore

v

Prologue

IIIIIIIIIIIIIIIIIIIIIIIIIIIIIIIIIIIIIIIIIIIIIIIIIIIIIIIIIIIIIIIIIIIIIIIIIIII THE BEARDMORE RELICS

The man dropped from the train when the sun was crowning the mountain to the east. The locomotive huffed and snorted, its nose pointed to the mountain. The man carried a khaki haversack slung from one shoulder, and from the other, a big-bore rifle. He glanced westward over the rooftops at the choppy waters of the big bay, and walked stiff-legged to the baggage car. The conductor waddled comically after him, like a penguin, cradling his vested paunch with one hand.

The conductor rapped on the door and hollered, and the door slid open. An exchange of words, and then the handler dragged an enormous off-white canvas pack from the dark interior and tipped it over. The man, all arms and legs, caught it and lowered it gently to the ground. A modest-sized canoe followed, a Peterborough, with red-painted canvas which matched the man's red flannel shirt. The handler jumped down, caught the bow as it left the door, and

1

the two of them set it upright on level ground well away from the train.

The little village sloped down from the track to the bay and the docks and the steam- and diesel-powered tugs. Dark-clad figures lounged about, some with distinctly lighter skin. Scruffy dogs slunk around. Occasionally a yelp or a flurry of barks marked a hostile encounter. Two horses burst from behind some buildings, pulling a fully loaded dray. Individual figures scattered, and with a flourish and a shout, the teamster brought the wagon to a stop neatly beside the door of the baggage car. Willing hands surged forward.

Someone leapt up into the car to assist the handler. A steady stream of trunk-sized wooden boxes disappeared into the interior. Some of the boards carried the dark patches of melting ice. The odor of fish wafted on the breeze.

The man adjusted his wide-brimmed hat and reached for his huge pack. He shouldered it and lifted the canoe over his head. He trudged down to the harbour, limping noticeably. When the train pulled out, headed to the big cities of the south, the man was squatting on the lakeshore between the docks, rummaging in his haversack.

He extracted an oilskin packet, fussed with the knotted twine, and removed a slim volume with dark blue covers. From a pocket on the inside back cover, he plucked a document, and unfolded it. It opened out into a good-sized map. He studied it for a long while, raising his chin from time to time to check the bay and sense the wind and gaze at the far green shore a good mile away.

After a time he pulled a dark lump from the haversack and gnawed on it. The sun had risen above the mountain and illuminated the entire bay. He arranged his pack as a backrest, and dozed a bit, and after upwards of an hour had passed, he rose to his full height. The chop had somewhat subsided. The waters gleamed blue.

He pulled a cartridge belt from his haversack and buckled it around his waist. The sun flashed from ranks of brass casings. He pushed the stern of the red canoe into the water, and unlashed the paddles that had formed a carrying yoke. He loose-tied the rifle and haversack to the front thwart. The pack with its accoutrements he stowed in the stern. He wedged the spare paddle between the pack and the cedar ribs. He pushed into the bay, folded his long legs into the canoe, and arranged himself on the bow seat, facing the stern. His good paddle bit the water.

He rounded the rocky promontory and headed north. A breeze caressed his left ear and cheek. On his right the rockbound shore rose to uneven terrain carpeted with the dark green of conifer and the lighter green of aspen and birch. The chop transformed into gentle swells. After an hour he reached the main lake, the far shore just a line on the horizon, the faraway big islands distinguished by their dark colour, the closer little islands a rich green. The canoe now breasted the gentle swells straight on, and the breeze cooled the back of his neck. He pulled on the floppy brim of his hat to shade the right side of his head and neck. He north steered from point to point, never cruising more than two to three hundred feet off shore.

Stretches of sandy beaches broke the monotony of rock. Behind the sand, swampy terrain strained to lift itself to the distant hills. Far to the west, banks of white cumulus, some tinged with gray, hovered over the big islands. Close to the islands, a single black plume walked slowly southward. He should have asked the commercial fishermen about anchorages. No doubt he was passing tiny creeks that would shelter a canoe in a storm, but the heavy forest disguised the openings. At one point he realized he was passing a river mouth. The map had called it the Blackwater.

From time to time he satisfied his thirst. He raised the paddle high, put the grip to his lips and caught the run-off down the shaft. Since leaving the great bay with its tiny fishing village, he had been steering north toward a nipple of land where the shore

3

dissolved into nothingness. The nipple had resolved itself into a breast, and then into an island just offshore. When he finally approached the fair-sized island, the breeze had picked up. He noted that it was now washing his left ear and cheek. The island loomed larger. He steered for the inside passage, and finally stopped on its leeside.

He eased himself forward to his knees, sighing gratefully, and plucked at the haversack. He extracted a lump of jerked moose and chewed meditatively. Now he could have used Chappy. Chappy would have thumped the canoe ribs with his heavy, brushy tail, and whined an inquiry. They would have had a conversation then.

He drank from his double-cupped hands, rearranged the haversack, and resumed paddling. Soon he was rounding the next point. The shoreline veered northeast. Glancing behind him, he could see rain falling at the north end of the big islands. As he studied the wide expanse of water, he caught the odd fleck of a whitecap. He glanced up at the blue vault, and then resumed the monotony of paddle.

When the wind whipped his hat, he snapped out of his reverie. He jammed the hat down. It was growing dark rapidly. The canoe was bucking. The swells had transformed in a matter of minutes to ranks of foam-topped rollers marching from the southwest. A blast of raindrops peppered his back and neck. There was an island ahead, close ahead. He dug his good paddle fiercely into the next swell.

It was a cobblestone island with steep banks. He steered to the inside. Even there the waves chopped at the boulders, dousing the stones two yards up the bank. He raced along the shore, steering around boulders that had been dropped offshore by invisible forces. The troughs of the waves revealed shingly reefs. He turned abruptly toward shore, toward the merest suggestion of a ledge jutting into the water for a few yards. He rounded it and eddied out behind the meagre shelter of the ledge. He jumped onto the

4

wet boulders, walked his hands along the gunnel, and picked up the stern. He wedged it higher in the boulders. In one motion he flung the pack high and over the bank. Both hands on the gunnel, he worked the canoe up the bank without scraping the red canvas, setting it down carefully whenever he had to take another step up.

At the top of the bank, he teetered in the blast. A wind-ravaged clump of trees offered little shelter. A few steps away, a circular pit beckoned. He inverted the canoe so that the stern rested on the rim of the pit on the leeward side, the bow on the bottom. He retrieved the pack and crawled under the canoe. The heavens released their burden. He was dry enough, he decided. The pit resembled an inverted igloo, constructed entirely of large roundish stones. Several yards wide at the top, it curved concentrically to the bottom. The cracks between the stones absorbed the deluge.

When he awoke, the squall had passed. He was sore in places from the cobbles. The sky was gray, but the whitecaps had retreated to centre lake. He resumed paddling. After he had rounded a long promontory, a sand beach stretched for a couple of miles. Further north, past the next point of land, a bright patch of shoreline leapt to the eye. The sky grew lighter, the sun a dull glow west of noon. It must have been three, three-thirty. The water rocked with gentle swells.

He approached the rocky point. Wisps of smoke floated over the poplars. Eventually he made out a bark lodge, maybe two, and the white canvas of a prospector's tent. A creek emerged from the forest just south of the point. He found himself steering further out. A child, features indistinguishable, wandered down to the shore and stared at him. Small islands ahead. When he glanced around, he could no longer see the child. He took the inside passage. The islands guarded a small bay with a sandy beach. He caught a glimpse of wooden crosses grouped together, some painted white.

Around the point, light-coloured sand bluffs reared up from the shore, rimmed with trees. His direction was more northerly now.

5

A major river sliced through the bluffs. The Namewaminikan, the map had said. A highway to the interior. If there were any guys like him around, they would be up that river. On the north side of the river, a rocky shoreline jutted into the main lake. He followed it west three-quarters of mile before he could turn north again.

Full sun now. Almost calm. He travelled close to shore now, breathing in the wilderness. The shoreline took him into a broad bay. There would be a creek here somewhere. There was always another creek.

To the northwest, where the big bay became the big lake, where it became the great lake, islands beckoned. Islands of calm.

He had always been enamoured of that phrase. Islands of calm. In the quiet hour before the big guns had thundered, before the furies of hell had been unleashed against the German lines, before he and his comrades had struggled out of their holes and staggered through the mud and the soupy craters and the blasted snags of the ravaged landscape, he had almost enjoyed the peace. The calm before the storm. The island of calm, in the ebb and flow of war and screams and horror and death. And noise. Always the noise.

He broke his own rule about crossing big water. He turned northwest and steered for the islands. An almost perfect calm reigned under the brilliant sun and the blue canopy. He quickened the pace, for he knew how unpredictable was the weather in big water. A wind burst on a perfectly calm day could bury him and his little canoe. A squall could track him down in mid-crossing and pelt him with thunderbolts. His good paddle churned up first the yards and then the chain-lengths and then the miles. He estimated it was three miles across. When he reached the first island, he was drenched in sweat. His arms heavy as lead. Hips and thighs aching from strain. He let the calm overwhelm him. He let the islands heal him.

He drank and he rested. He drank some more. He reached into the haversack and pulled out the oilskin packet and *unwrapped it. From the back pocket of the blue book he pulled out the map, issued by Canada's Department of Mines. The map was dated 1910. It was, so far as he knew, the only geological map ever produced of the great lake called Nipigon. He found the islands, standing out from a long shallow crescent carved out of the eastern shore. The crescent, he could see now, was really a bay reaching inland, a deep bay. The crude instruments of the old-time surveyors had misled them. He raised his eyes to the east.*

His eyes traveled down the northern shore of the big bay. The island he had reached was perhaps a mile off the eastern shore. His eyes traveled to the featureless terrain at the head of the bay, a green line, like a distant hedgerow. Beyond the shore the country rose into contours that drew the eyes. His eyes fastened on one contour, a ridge, a big hill. The sun, which was dropping in the west, illuminated the big hill. If he were standing at the bottom, he thought, it would be a mountain, perhaps an unscalable mountain. A mountain of greenstone. His eyes dropped to the map in his lap.

The cartographer had coloured that whole terrain green. Green for greenstone and iron formation. To the north a huge swath of red ran inland for miles and miles. Red for granite. Red did not hold the promise of gold. Green was promising. Very promising. The map was flat, no contour lines. Just north of the Namewaminkian, in the greenstone, a string of boxes drawn in black ink located the claims that had been staked during the rush of 1910.

They had not found gold, though, those colleagues of his. They had found iron. One can find all manner of interesting minerals in greenstone. One can even find gold. One most often finds gold in greenstone. They had missed it. The gold was there.

Chapter 1

Thursday, August 13th . . .

In winter a cruel wind blows every morning from the west and scours the streets. It's no fun for pedestrians nor is it for the hardy cyclist, and one does find the odd cyclist in Thunder Bay when the Sleeping Giant takes its first deep breath of a winter morning.

On a summer morning, though, the gentle giant exhales, and its sweet breath skips westward across the Bay of Thunder and up the slopes of the sleeping city and winds through the flats and creeps through every open window.

Even that summer Kennet Forbes had slept with his windows open. Summer had been slow in coming, and for days and even weeks at a time it had disappeared altogether. The usual hordes of flies – the mosquitoes, blackflies, and no-see-ums – never materialized. Now it was mid-August, a period when normally, north of Lake Superior, the botanical world was retrenching for the onslaught it knew was coming, and yet everything was still lush and green there. In Thunder Bay itself on Superior's western shore, summer prevailed.

It was the thumping that finally woke him up. He peered at the clock. 6:01. He swung his naked torso to the edge of the bed and reached for a dressing gown. It was barely light outside. He walked in a fog toward the door.

The thumping persisted. "I'm coming!" he said. "I'm coming."

Kennet cracked the door. A petite blonde swayed on the landing with knuckles raised. "I'm so sorry, Mr. Forbes," she said, her mouth twisting. "I rang and rang and . . . nothing."

Kennet mumbled something about a chiming dream and said, "Cindy. You're Cindy. Vander . . . Vander . . ."

"Horst," she said. "Vanderhorst. It's Alfie," she said. "He didn't come home."

From the bottom of the stairway a querulous voice arose. "What's going on up there? Are you alright, Mr. Forbes? What's that racket?"

Without moving, Kennet raised his own voice. "It's alright, Mrs. Sandberg. Just a visitor. Sorry we disturbed you."

Kennet swung the door wider. Conscious of the usual morning tightness in his groin, he used the door as a shield. "Come in," he said. "Come in, come in. No point standing there. I'll get dressed."

He spun on the balls of his feet and headed for the bedroom. He called over his shoulder, "Coffee's set up in the kitchen. Press the button. I'll be ten minutes."

Showered and shaved, dressed casually in tan trousers and a light brown print shirt, he looked in the mirror, first at the bad eye and then at the good eye. The left eye of the face in the mirror had a slightly drooping lid. A scar like a rapier cut slashed through the eyebrow at an angle. It started at the bridge of the nose, skipped to the eyebrow, and stopped precisely 2.7 centimetres further along the forehead. Scar tissue below the eye and around the outside edge puckered the skin. There were reddish streaks, the whole area peppered with black specks, giving him a permanent black eye.

He looked at the good right eye of the face in the mirror. Gray iris. Same colour as the left iris in the mirror. Coincidentally, Kennet Forbes had a good left eye and a bad right eye. Both gray.

He ran a hand over the thick black bristles on his scalp. Not a bad head of hair, he thought, not for the first time, for a man who'd never see forty again. To hell with the bad eye.

Cindy had two cups of coffee on the small table. She lifted her chin and chirped. "I didn't know how you liked it. It's black." She wore a mismatched skirt and blouse, bright red lipstick slightly awry, short blonde hair mussed. She was a pretty thing. Kennet wondered not for the first time how Alfred Vanderhorst had landed this goldfish.

"That's exactly how I like it. So, you're up early."

"I didn't know who else to call. Alfie never came home last night. He would've called. I couldn't sleep. At all. I thought of you. I rang you and rang you, there was a busy signal, so I thought you were up."

I was up, thought Kennet. "This is my phone-free day. I pulled the plug last night. I –"

"Your what?"

"Never mind, I'll explain later. Tell me, Cindy, what made you think of me?"

"Well, we did meet at Convocation, in May, you remember? We sat together, at the luncheon, Alfie was off somewhere, having a heavy discussion, as he usually does, and we got to talking, and anyhow, you mentioned you were born in Beardmore or something, and when Alfie didn't come home, or phone, I waited up all night, well, I thought of you, Ken."

"Born in Beardmore? Good Lord, no. I did go to school in Geraldton. A long time ago. That's what I must've said." Kennet remembered that Alfred Vanderhorst had cornered the head of Anthropology, Dr. Peter Sheridan, off to one side of the throng, and that there were a great many gesticulations and grimaces on the part of Vanderhorst and some grim shakes of the head and terse words mouthed by Sheridan. Vanderhorst was a lecturer, like him, except that Vanderhorst lectured on archaeology, not media studies.

"But that's next door to Beardmore, isn't it?" She was gripping the coffee cup with both hands. He hadn't seen her take a sip of the milky soup. The crystal sugar bowl sat uncovered.

Kennet let the black liquid slide down his throat. "A few doors down, actually. Anyway, what's Alfred doing in Beardmore, and how do you know he isn't just late? I got the impression over the past couple years that he gets tied up with things, forgets the time, misses appointments . . ."

"Oh Ken, he would never miss this one. It's Willem's birthday today, this morning, his fifth birthday, he'll start kindergarten in two weeks, and Alfie would never, never miss Willie's birthday, especially this one, so important to his educational career, Willie's, I mean, Alfie believes so strongly in education, and –"

Kennet raised his hand. "Okay, okay." He recalled his impressions of Vanderhorst. An intense character, middle thirties, with a greasy mop of brown hair, a beard that had been lightly trimmed with garden shears, coke-bottle glasses, clothes he had rescued from a laundry hamper, and very dirty white sneakers – and that was when he dressed up.

"And you remember, Ken, he wanted so much to examine that relics site, the one in Beardmore, where they found those Viking things, a sword and everything, they're in the Royal Canadian Museum now, authenticated – I think that's the word – authenticated genuine Viking relics, but no one's ever done a dig, you know, a proper dig at the site and Alfie, well, Alfie saw this opportunity – it's publish or perish, you know, Alfie's always saying that – he saw this opportunity, but the university, his boss, you know, he wasn't so keen, so Alfie decided to do an independent project, like, it wouldn't cost much, and he had vacation days this month, so –"

"Cindy. Cindy. What are you expecting me to do?"

"Can you look for him? I'm really, really worried."

"And where's your boy now? Willie. Willem."

"Kathy's looking after him. She's single. She's my best friend. But I can't leave Willie long. She works. She –"

"Okay. Okay. Let me think."

Kennet Forbes owed nothing to Cindy, pretty as she was. He certainly owed nothing to her brat. He owed even less to Alfred Vanderhorst. In fact, the longer Vanderhorst stayed lost, the better Kennet liked it and, he suspected, so would a lot of faculty. But Kennet knew Sheridan. He liked Peter Sheridan, and if Peter were missing a member of his teaching staff, then Peter might be concerned.

"Look," he said. "Do you have any idea where your husband might be? Where he was staying? Where the dig was? Anything."

"I have his cell number, but he doesn't answer. Hasn't answered all night. And Kyle's cell, but he doesn't answer either. Kyle's his assistant. As for where he's working, he did give me a piece of paper a couple weeks ago, with a bunch of numbers – GRS, is it? – they didn't mean a thing to me, and I ran them over to Dr. Sheridan, like he asked. Dr. Sheridan's his boss. But I don't know where Alfie's working. In the bush somewhere. That's why I thought of you. You would know the country."

"Yes, like the back of my neck." He drained the cup. Cindy hadn't touched hers. "Look, I'm not promising anything, but I'll go talk to Peter – Dr. Sheridan – and then I'll get back to you. Damn, I can't phone you. Leave me your e-mail. But I can't promise anything. Officially my vacation's over – I took my time in July. And I have to prepare for classes. My boss, now, she'll have a say in the matter. But I'll do what I can."

It was enough for Cindy. It was more than enough. She didn't know how to thank him. She would be eternally grateful. Alfie would be grateful. Alfie would –

By a combination of demurrals and deft management, Kennet herded her out and shut the door. He went to the bank of windows that overlooked the lower north side of the city and he looked over the harbour and the breakwater and across the dimpled surface of the great bay. Glorious light burst from the cloud bank hovering over the great lake that lay beyond the low-lying mountain barrier, the rock formation which the early indigenous people had named after a character in legend. The Sleeping Giant lay supine, head to the north, massive arms folded across its chest. In the streaks of light it dozed on oblivious.

He loved this apartment. He loved it for the view, winter and summer. He loved it for the hillside behind the pre-war two-story house, the hillside that rose steeply and greenly in this season to Hillcrest Park, a publicly maintained overlook where always there was somebody, at any time of night or day, who had either walked there or cycled there or driven there to gaze eastward and meditate upon the magnificent scene. Two years now he'd lived here, and he knew, as his independent daughter Susan kept reminding him, he'd have to find larger accommodation. He was accumulating stuff. His landlady, Mrs. Sandberg, had been gracious, had allowed the camping gear and the mountain bike and the kayak to command space in her garage, and had permitted the furniture and other heirlooms from his father's old house to gather dust in her basement, as well as several boxes of stuff that Diane had held dear.

Diane. Dear Diane. Dear wife. God I miss you, he thought. Oh God I miss you. They had had twenty-two years together. And a child. Susan.

Kennet prepared what he called his French breakfast. Black coffee. Corn flakes and milk. Buttered whole wheat toast with clots of camembert. A little toast and wild preserves, *les fruits de la campagne*, to cleanse the palate. But no rough red wine this morning. Just black coffee.

He rummaged in his office – what he called his office, a corner of the living-dining-kitchenette area that comprised two-thirds of his apartment – until he laid hands on a bundle of topographical maps for the region. He had acquired them to research rivers which offered a challenge to whitewater kayaking. There was no Beardmore map.

He booted up the laptop. He googled "Beardmore" and "Ontario", immediately getting over 800,000 hits. He selected a travel site, clicked on the only offering for accommodation and read about the Chalet Lodge. Among other things the Chalet Lodge offered deluxe housekeeping cottages and kayaking. Right up his alley. The small print gave a phone number and an address in Jellicoe.

That didn't sound right for a location. Still, he couldn't phone to check on whether an Alfred Vanderhorst had returned to his room, if that's where he had booked it, because today was his phone-free day. When he had signed on two years ago to teach media studies at Thunder Bay University, he had embarked on a personal experiment. One day in every cycle of five days, he would live without one of the essential tools of the communications industry in the twenty-first century: the World Wide Web, television, radio, the Walkman-and-iPod genre, and phones. Reading he never gave up. Reading had been around for centuries. Reading predated the Common Era. Reading and writing were ancient and venerable forms of communication.

Another travel site listed bed and breakfast sites for Beardmore, none of which listed Beardmore as an address. In fact, most of them gave Thunder Bay as the locale. There were multiple references to the World's Largest Snowman in Beardmore, and to fishing, and Precambrian geology, and weather, and government websites, and interminable offerings of services and products which he suspected – which he knew from experience with the Web – had absolutely no connection to Beardmore, things such as bar/bat mitzvahs and florists and party planners – the trainloads of

14

trivia and misinformation which he willingly and eagerly sacrificed for one day out of five. He decided to pass on the remaining 800,000-plus results.

The references to Greenstone intrigued him. Wikipedia disclosed that Beardmore was one of several communities in the new Corporation of the Municipality of Greenstone, incorporated in 2001, and that the 2006 census gave the amalgamated communities a population of 4,906. Greenstone he had heard of, but he had assumed it was a geographical region, like Lake Superior's North Shore, not a new town. Geraldton, where he had graduated from high school, had been demoted from a town to a ward in the new municipality. Well, that's what they paid him for – his grasp of world affairs and the latest up-to-the-minute information.

He googled "Beardmore relics". Instantaneously, 544 results. God, what did it mean? Was Vanderhorst actually on to something? He selected one of the first results. It was a history forum item that dated to February of '04.

He read an extract from the literature that the first interlocutor had dredged up: *A Viking sword, axe, and shield handle were found in 1931 on a portage trail between Hudson Bay and Lake Superior, near Lake Nipigon. Known as the Beardmore Relics, the Royal Ontario Museum, Toronto, eventually acquired the artifacts and placed them on display in 1938. Curator of the museum, Dr. C.T. Currely, determined that they were genuine Viking weapons made in about 1000 . . .*

The Royal Ontario Museum, and not, as Cindy put it, the Canadian Museum. Other discussants dove in quickly. One suggested that the artifacts were a plant by a sometime prospector and full-time railway brakeman named James Edward Dodd. There were allusions to characters and incidents and cases, some of which Kennet recognized, but the relevance of most of them eluded him: La Verendrye, J.M. Hansen, Eli Ragotte, Julius Caesar, the Kensington rune stone, Farley Mowat, an unnamed

Ukrainian boy, and so on. The discussion, as these online colloquies were called, see-sawed and whipped about, jumping from serious commentary to mutual accusations of deception and ignorance and sinister personal agendas and then back to fairly intelligent exchanges.

A glance at other websites confirmed that the archaeology establishment treated the relics as a hoax, that the discovery site had never been revisited since the '30's, that no one knew where exactly the site was today, and that only amateur historians and kooks expressed the slightest interest in finding it again. Enter Alfie Vanderhorst.

Something, though, tugged at Kennet's mind. He hoped, he fervently hoped that it wasn't his investigative impulse. He had enough on his plate now. He didn't need a wild goose chase.

He fetched the newspaper from the box outside the door downstairs. Before he climbed the stairs, he experienced a tremor, an internal tremor, so brief that he almost missed it. He had trained himself to ignore it. He spread *The Lakehead Journal* on the kitchen table and scanned it quickly, efficiently, expertly. The wars and insurgencies and civil unrest in various hot spots of the globe were unfolding as they should. Afghanistan remained the focus of Canada's foreign policy and domestic concern. Ottawa was as messy and as maddening as before. Thunder Bay was weaving itself through the national economic downturn in its usual plodding fashion. Police had made a drug bust in Greenstone. Greenstone. He studied the article carefully. The Mayor of Greenstone made a comment to the press. Yes, Greenstone was a municipality.

The national television weather channel promised Thunder Bay a fair weather day. He clicked the tab for a regional forecast, and started to scroll through Ontario place names alphabetically. There was no Beardmore forecast. Thunder Bay looked forward to sunny and clear with a high of 21 degrees Celsius.

He extricated his bike from his landlady's garage, careful to avoid bumping her eight-year-old white Honda Civic. He popped on a helmet and pedaled swiftly south on Crown Street. As soon as the headset had wrapped up the 7:30 news, he pulled it down around his neck and switched off the radio.

At the intersection of John and High Streets, he breezed through on a green light. To his left he noted a yellow Yamaha motorcycle waiting for the light to change. The rider wore black chaps. Two bulging saddlebags draped behind the seat. A road warrior, thought Kennet. He'll pull into Hillcrest Park to survey a domain that no one'll ever conquer.

Kennet inhaled the breeze sweeping up from the bay. It was going to be a fine day.

Chapter 2

... Thursday morning

Kennet cycled across campus to the Fermi Building and chained the bike outside. He found Dr. Peter Sheridan in his office cum lab in the basement. A fire had swept through the basement complex last winter and forced a relocation of some lab accoutrements of the Anthropology Department.

Peter's long frame sprawled gracefully in an antique wooden swivel chair behind a scarred wooden table. He was flipping through images and diagrams on his desktop computer, facing twin monitors. Books and loose-leaf binders packed the shelving along the walls. There were several idle computers, photographs on the walls in cheap frames, articulated bones of rodents or reptiles, and stacks of paper everywhere. He glanced up at Kennet Forbes and smiled quickly. As befitted the head of a prestigious university department, Peter displayed carefully coiffed silver hair with black streaks, long and combed back on the sides, almost bristly on top, and a salt-and-pepper stubble. He must drive the ladies wild, thought Kennet.

"Kennet, what a pleasure."

"I have one word for you. Vanderhorst."

"Kennet, Kennet, Kennet. You are no longer a pleasure." Peter smiled briefly again. He swung away from the computer and rose to face his visitor.

Peter continued: "I've missed you at the Club. Do you know this one?" He came to attention and bowed slightly.

Kennet reciprocated. Peter assumed the ready stance, followed swiftly by the guard stance, left leg planted forward, body turned sideways, hands clenched at chest height. Kennet reciprocated.

Peter's left hand struck at Kennet's face, palm down, fingers stiff. Kennet blocked the punch easily, for it was a demonstration, not an assault.

Peter resumed the attention stance and bowed again. "Supposed to be good for street fighting," he said.

"The finger strike. Know it." Kennet continued: "Been away in July, Peter, so I haven't zoned into the Tae Kwon Do yet." He drew up a wooden chair as Peter sank back into his. "The reason I dropped in, Peter, I had a visit from Cindy, Alfie's Cindy." His intonation made Alfie's name a joke. "And apparently the star of the Anthropology Department has gone missing. Up Greenstone way. What can you tell me about it?"

Peter sighed. "Greenstone? Oh, you mean Beardmore. We told Alfred – I told Alfred that the Department could not sanction his project, that the object was dubious, that certainly in these tight times there was no funding available, and that if he wanted to pursue evidence that horned and helmeted warriors of a Scandinavian persuasion had voyaged in their clinker-built boats from the Polar Sea via Hudson's Bay to the moraine country of Northwestern Minnesota, he'd have to do it on his own time and at his own expense. He'd have to use his holidays. That's what I can tell you about it."

"What I thought. Cindy left you something?"

"Oh. Yes." He reached over to a corkboard and snatched a scrap of creased and smudged paper and handed it to Kennet.

"GPS coordinates, apparently. Maybe he lucked out. Maybe he did find the site where Eddie Dodd unearthed the relics, or claimed he did."

"Well, he never came home last night. Had an important appointment, apparently. Cindy wants me to look for him. Thinks I was born in Beardmore and know the country like the back of my neck."

"Yeah? Well, be my guest. I'm not going to look for him . . . yet." He bit his lower lip lightly. "Here . . ." He snatched the paper back. "Let me make a copy for you."

"Cindy said something about a Kyle assisting him."

"That would be Kyle Henderson. Undergrad. Worships at the feet of the master. Listen, you're the second person to bring up Beardmore in as many days. You remember the bones that the police brought into our forensics laboratory last fall? There was an item in *The Lakehead Journal* about it."

"Vaguely. An Indian burial, wasn't it? Or some unfortunate prospector from the gold rush era. You have information on them?"

"This is not for publication, Kennet. The lab has not officially released this, but they do have a preliminary finding. They are the remains of a young woman, a female adolescent about eighteen years of age. And here's the gut-kicker – they may have been in the ground only twenty, twenty-five years – thirty years tops. If you're going up there, keep your ear to the ground – damn, I hate lousy puns. Just nose around, discreetly. I trust your nose."

Kennet left with Peter's assurances that he, Peter, would officially appreciate a search and rescue operation for one of his department's most valued members. And it wouldn't hurt to validate the timetable's allocation of faculty members – the timetable he had already submitted it to Administration.

Kennet paused at the foot of the stairs leading to the second level of the English Department and to his boss's office. There it was again. That momentary sense of a weight descending upon him. A sense he sometimes got at the bottom of a staircase. Today there was a memory flash – he knew it was a false memory flash – of a white prom dress.

He rapped on the door and entered. "Dr. Sharpe, I presume?"

"Yes?" The forty-ish brunette looked up from her desk with a quick professional smile. Long straight black hair framed a Vogue face with a Mediterranean complexion, dark red lipstick, long eyelashes, and very dark eyes. "Oh. It's you, Kennet. I wish you wouldn't do that."

"Melissa, Melissa. I cannot help myself. You are so intimidating. So domineering. So devastatingly beaut –"

"Cut it out, Kennet. I'm busy. You should be too."

Kennet grinned. He was still standing. He turned his palms outwards. "I truly cannot help myself, Melissa. I need a favour."

"Have I ever denied you anything, Kennet?" Her demeanor changed. She smiled coquettishly and leaned back, twisted sideways and thrust out her chest. She tapped the desk impatiently with a silver-capped pen. He had no doubt that it was genuine silver. Her eyes turned steely: "Spit it out."

"I have to go out of town. Be back tomorrow, I expect. Friday."

"You haven't failed me yet, Kennet. You've always been prepared. The students like you. I've never regretted hiring you. I only wish you were making more progress on your thesis. You need a degree, Kennet, to go anywhere here. To go anywhere anywhere."

"I have degrees. Degrees up the wazoo."

"And a degree of charm. Yes, I know. You know I mean a doctorate. You could teach grad school. You could even have your own department where you could indulge that journalism stuff. Oh hell." She threw down her pen in disgust, and then picked it up quickly and examined it. "We've had this conversation before. Go, go. Just see that you're back Monday, 8:30 a.m. Sharpish. For the department meeting."

"Aye, aye, Doctor. Sharpish." She was bending over her desk again, scribbling, and shaking her head as Kennet ducked out the door.

In seven-and-a-half minutes he was back in his apartment. He e-mailed Cindy Vanderhorst. He checked Environment Canada. The forecast for Greenstone (it said "Geraldton" after the name) was sunny, a high of 20 degrees Celsius, a southwest breeze at 7 kilometres an hour. He threw together his outdoor travel kit, including his hiking boots and a hand-held global positioning system unit. He consulted the paper Peter had given him and programmed the GPS unit with the coordinates. The colour map on the tiny screen displayed a tiny flag, a waypoint, southwest of Beardmore. He packed his laptop and an overnight bag. He knocked on Mrs. Sandberg's door and let her know he'd probably be away overnight. She worried about things like that. He'd phone Susan, his daughter, later. She'd be at work now. No, he couldn't phone her, he'd e-mail her later.

He unlocked the compact red sports utility vehicle that he kept parked in the back yard, off the driveway. He loaded the luggage into the back seat of the SUV, careful to avoid the double-bladed paddle and the personal flotation device, the PFD. It would not be too much trouble to detach the twelve-foot amber-coloured whitewater-model kayak from the roof rack of the Kia Sportage, but he might find an opportunity for a quick paddle.

Traffic was light on the two-lane highway north to Nipigon. He measured the journey today by the rivers he had run during the freshets of the past two springs. At each river he slowed down and studied the moving waters, and each time he concluded that they were far too slow to pose a challenge this time of year. Not to say each river didn't have its year-round challenges, but they were few and far between. Occasionally a driver behind him reprimanded him by leaning on the horn. The mesa-like formation of Red Rock hove into view, and soon he was crawling through the highway commercial sector of Nipigon. He pulled off at the overlook before descending the long hill to the river.

He always stopped at this overlook on local jaunts as well as on journeys to and from the East. His father lived in Quebec now, the Province of Quebec, in the montagne region of the Eastern Townships. He'd moved there from Thunder Bay after Kennet's mother had passed. And after Diane had passed.

The houses of Nipigon tumbled down the hillside to the water and stopped at the point where the Nipigon River debouched into a great bay, a bay that stretched south and east and melted beyond the horizon into the great invisible lake. Great hills and small mountains dropped swiftly into the bay. In the old days pillars of smoke and steam had marked the little community of Red Rock on the far south shore. One had to look hard nowadays to make out the profile of the gigantic dormant mill. Sunlight bathed the textured expanse of waters.

Kennet sometimes glanced at the historical plaque posted at the cement-capped rock wall that discouraged tourists from tumbling after the houses. Father Joseph Allouez, Society of Jesus, had paddled up the great bay and the river in the year 1667 on his way to the sixth Great Lake. More accurately, the good father's aboriginal companions had done the paddling. On the return journey from Lake Nipigon, had they shot, Kennet wondered, had they shot the rapids between Lake Helen and Nipigon Bay in their fragile birchbark craft the way Kennet had done in his lightweight kayak?

Just beyond the bridge white letters on a dark green sign spelled BEARDMORE and COCHRANE and an arrow pointed north. He turned off the TransCanada onto Highway 11. The posted speed limit was 60. Another green sign spelled out the distances:

BEARDMORE 78
GERALDTON 162

LONGLAC 190
COCHRANE 619

Seventy-eight kilometres. In the old days he remembered it as an hour's drive. At the posted speed limit of 90, he would beat that time. At the speed he usually drove, he would beat it to death.

He paced himself through the First Nation reserve up to the lonely white frame church that overlooked Lake Helen, and the aboriginal cemetery with its white crosses. He accelerated to 115 and locked in the cruise control.

To his left a westerly breeze rippled the waters of Lake Helen, or perhaps it was a southwest breeze altered by the high rounded ridge of the far shore half a klick away. To his right rose the massive cliffs he recalled from his school days. Black and grey bulges of rock that tried to muscle the traffic off the road and into a watery grave. He passed a roadside park that projected into the lake. Five Mile Park, that was the name. It had no sign now. Moist dark patches on the rock walls marked the strain of holding back a hundred miles of water-laden peat bogs and black spruce swamp.

The highway straightened, rising and falling, bisecting miles and miles of greenery. He slipped a Neil Young CD into the player and slipped into reverie. Yes, at one point they were strangers and then they were lovers . . . Yes, he was still in love with her. He wanted to see her dance again . . . on this harvest moon . . .

He met traffic occasionally. Many transport trucks. A platoon of motorcyclists glided toward him in a diamond formation. He was startled when a biker passed him at breakneck speed. He was aboard a yellow Yamaha with full saddlebags. On the back of his black helmet Kennet distinguished a crown design.

The Pallisades leapt into view. He switched off the CD player. The Pallisades of some unpronounceable aboriginal name. The massive buttresses of rock marched up to the highway. The road rose and fell and descended further and further into the basin of the sixth Great Lake. A complex of white-grey buildings nestled in the folds of the intermontagne hills, and huge white pipes writhed like giant sandworms. The PanCanada Pipelines compressor station. Clouds of steam drifted up, clouds he never remembered seeing when he was younger. Then more evidence of human habitation, a resort off to the left on a small lake, roads melting into the bush, and then a long stretch of water. Orient Bay. Another resort, separated from the highway by heavily rusted railway tracks, and the long bay engorging itself as it prepared to become the sixth Great Lake. In the hazy distance on the east shore, suggestions of buildings. Macdiarmid.

He remembered the school bus laboring up the long hill as it had climbed out of Orient Bay. The whole basketball team knew then that they were only an hour and a half from home and their sweet beds. The road sign at the Macdiarmid turnoff was complicated by prominent references to a First Nation and a powwow – he didn't catch it all. He was gazing at the green sugarloaf mountain ahead, shorn of trees. Something was very different there. A few minutes later the hills fell away and he could see for miles and miles, a foamy green sea stippled with the masts of an armada of sunken ships. A burn. The aftermath of a forest fire. A massive fire had swept through there not many years before. On the faraway hills sentinel trees, some skinny as beanpoles, paced back and forth.

Flashing lights ahead. The flickering blues and whites resolved into an emergency vehicle of some sort. When it was three hundred metres away, Kennet pulled over on the shoulder. The ambulance whooshed by. He had a bad feeling. He had a very bad feeling. He put his foot down.

To his mind, the descent of the long S-curve signaled the proximity of Beardmore. He raised his eyes to the west where the rolling hills bore the scars of the big burn. At the bottom of the descent, to the left, a stretch of railway track, and beyond it, a glimpse of river. Up the short steep hill and over and down into

Beardmore. The Kia Sportage bumped over the rusty tracks. The highway became main street. There stood the World's Biggest Snowman in an empty green space, fishing rod cocked and ready, sunglasses on nose and a black porkpie hat on head. He pulled into the first place that looked busy, The Hook'n Bullet.

MAP 3

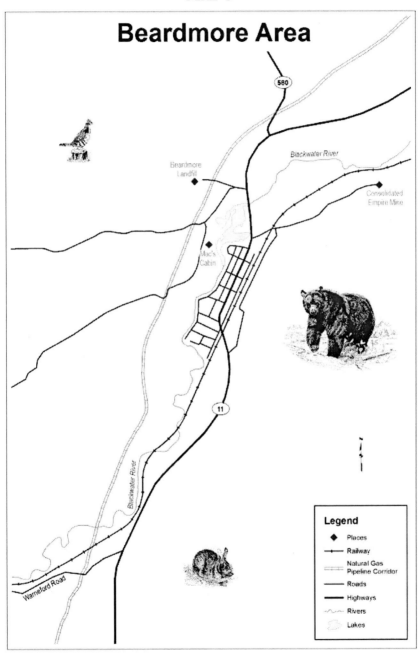

Beardmore Area

580

Beardmore River

Beardmore Landfill

Consolidated Empire Mine

Mac's Cabin

11

Blackwater River

Warneford Road

Legend
- ◆ Places
- —+— Railway
- Natural Gas Pipeline Corridor
- —— Roads
- —— Highways
- ～～ Rivers
- Lakes

Chapter 3

. . . Thursday mid-day

The dilapidated premises of The Hook'n Bullet stood well back from the main street. Artifacts of the sporting world littered the forecourt – a rusted-out fishing tug, an old snowmobile, a tripod for hanging moose, figurines of bear and wolf and trout carved by a chainsaw artist . . . Beside the doorway and elevated on a dais, a wooden captain's chair with cushioned seat and a hand-lettered sign:

The Grouch's Chair

Sit at your Peril

Kennet penetrated the dim interior, squeezing past a triad of customers whom the proprietor was ushering out the door with a great deal of bonhomie. The father, son, and – Kennet surmised – grandson clutched prizes of maps, fishing tackle, soft drinks, and dripping ice cream cones. The proprietor turned a bland face to Kennet. He was dressed in suspendered trousers, clunky boots, and a battered felt hat pinned indiscriminately with hand-tied flies. He might have been sixty or seventy. Or eighty. His left hand moved to fondly stroke his comfortable paunch. Back in the dim recesses a female figure with a head scarf puttered around.

"You're not The Grouch, surely." Kennet let a smile play on his lips.

"Walt Kellerman," said the man, sticking out his right hand. "My friends call me Bull. The ladies call me Brad Pitt's nemesis. And the wife calls me lazy good-for-nothin'." A grin cracked his stubbly jowls.

"Kennet Forbes." Kennet took the hand. "A pleasure. I just came from Nipigon. Met an ambulance on the road. No trouble here, I hope."

"Not here, nope. At the motel." Kellerman jerked his thumb to indicate a place up the street. "Sad, really. Badly beaten up. They found him this morning, late."

Kennet felt relief mingled with concern. "Gentleman of about thirty-five? Badly barbered beard?"

"Nope. Kid, really. Name of Henderson, I think. Nope, not that Vanderhorst. Nowhere to be found. Good riddance, most folks'd say. You know him, eh?" Kellerman eyed Kennet shrewdly.

"No friend of mine, but his wife asked me to look in on him. At the motel, you say?"

Kellerman jerked his thumb again. "Three doors down."

"I'll be back," said Kennet, stepping out the door. Kellerman followed. Kennet looked around the yard. "Place hasn't changed much in twenty-five years. Mind if I leave the truck here?" Kellerman waved him permission.

Kennet walked toward the windowless plaster wall of a long gray single-story building, past the brick facade, and came upon a broad parking area. Beyond it, a two-story building with a concrete facade faced the street, and an old-fashioned theatre marquee, sans lights, overhung the sidewalk. The marquee spelled out "Regency". The theatre-hall length of the Regency appeared to have been converted to apartments. Glancing down the parking slots, he spotted a neon sign which read "Open". It glowed from a window of the bottom L of the gray building. A few vehicles occupied the parking slots, including an Ontario Provincial Police black-and-white, a Ford Crown Victoria. He walked up the parking lot and entered a door near the sign. A tiny lobby led into a tiny restaurant.

A tiny crowd commandeered the few tiny tables, crowded against the grill area. Two people who looked like plainclothes officers hovered over a table, interrogating a customer. A uniformed officer was filling a cup from the automatic coffee maker. A harried-looking waitress confronted him.

"A seat, sir?" The tall blonde Amazon smiled, wiping her hands across her apron.

"I'm looking for the manager."

"That's me, sir. Come." She pointed to the lobby immediately behind Kennet.

Standing behind the narrow counter, she said, "What can I do you for, sir?"

Kennet smiled tentatively. "Actually, I'm looking for one of your customers. Alfred Vanderhorst."

"He's not in his room, sir. Actually, we haven't seen him since breakfast yesterday. Everyone's looking for him."

A voice boomed behind him. "You know this Vanderhorst?"

Kennet turned and looked down into the pugnacious features of a beefy individual in an ill-fitting suit. Behind him towered his female colleague, smiling nervously. She wore a dark tweedy business outfit.

"Excuse me?" Kennet's eyes dropped to the man's belt, where a silvery badge glinted.

"You know this Vanderhorst? You asked about him." The man's eyes squinted.

Kennet recognized the type. "Hello," he said animatedly, proffering his right hand. "My name's Kennet Forbes. To whom do I owe this pleasure?"

The detective, if that was who he was, glared. His broadly striped tie, loosened at the collar, was not compatible with his brown suit. "What are you doing here?"

Kennet could feel his dander rising. "Excuse me," he said in a controlled voice. "I was minding my own business."

Other heads framed themselves in the doorway to the restaurant. The detective glanced quickly around and back again. "Out," he said, peremptorily. "Outside." He gestured magisterially to the outside door. That suited Kennet's purposes. He swung leisurely about and sauntered out.

Outside, the officer glared at another customer as he sought to enter the lobby. He swiveled to confront Kennet. "Okay, spill it. What's your interest in this Vanderhorst?" A flush crept up his thick neck. A customer emerged from the lobby, glanced furtively at the detectives, and scurried away.

Kennet switched his attention to the willowy female officer. "How do you do. Constable, is it? Kennet Forbes." She took his hand.

"Detective Constable Kelly Armitage," she said. She nodded in the direction of her partner. "And this is Detective Constable Mueller. We work out of the Greenstone Detachment, headquartered in Geraldton. We're investigating an assault that occurred here at this motel. This Alfred Vanderhorst is a person of interest."

The colour in Detective Mueller's neck now suffused his face. "And we don't take kindly to obstruction," he blurted.

Kennet switched his gaze slowly to Mueller. "Who's obstructing?" he said mildly. "I do know Mr. Vanderhorst, but just slightly. His family is worried about him. Seems he missed an important appointment last night, and they asked me to check on him. There's not much else I can tell you."

"You know where he is?" Mueller thrust out his chin.

"No, detective," Kennet said carefully. "I do not know where he is. Why do you imagine I was inquiring after him?"

"Next time say so. And a lot quicker." Mueller stalked off to a black Tahoe truck which was parked facing the two-story Regency. Detective Armitage asked a few more questions, politely, and jotted in her notebook. She thanked him with a smile.

Kennet passed an open doorway barred with a police tape. There was a black Chevrolet Suburban parked in front, and beside it, a battered brown Dodge Grand Caravan. He peered into the dimly lit room. The front room had the sink, fridge, microwave oven and cupboards of a housekeeping unit, plus a table and chairs. An unmade bed stood to the right of the door in front of the curtained windows. On the rubber mat beside the door, a pair of mud-streaked boots. Beyond a narrow hallway he could see another room and part of a rumpled bed. His eyes switched back to the table. It was covered with tiny rusty objects. A swath of the collection had been wiped out and pieces littered the carpet, along with a number of transparent bags, all empty.

"Not for rent yet!" said a male voice behind him. A uniformed constable sidled up, nursing two styrofoam cups of steaming coffee. He was grinning.

"Oh. Sorry. Just curious. I guess nosy's the word."

Another voice behind him. "Curiosity killed the cat!" Another constable came down the hallway from the back bedroom. He had his face set in mock grimness. Both officers appeared young, groomed, and well proportioned.

"Excuse me," said the constable with the cups. "If you'll just unhook that tape for me, I'll duck in." Kennet unhooked the tape. Once inside, the constable looked back. "Sorry, sir, but this is not public business. If you'll excuse us."

Back at The Hook'n Bullet, he found Walt Kellerman perched on The Grouch's chair, surveying his domain. "You look familiar now," he said to Kennet, "in spite of the boo-boo you got there." Kellerman gestured to his own right eye.

"You were on TV," he continued. "Haven't seen you for a while."

"I'm a teacher now," said Kennet, "at TBU. Same place where Vanderhorst teaches. Just a minute." He walked over to his truck, clicking the remote key, and pulled out his GPS unit. He switched it on, tilted it skyward, and let it search for satellites. He came to stand by Kellerman during the search.

"And I may know you," he said. "Indirectly. You had a boy named Chris? Played right forward on the Geraldton High basketball team more than twenty-five years ago? Scrappy little guy?"

"That's our son alright!" Kellerman beamed. "Chris's a stockbroker now. Down in the Big Smoke. We rarely get to see him anymore. So you do remember this place."

"Yep. Passed it many a time on trips to Thunder Bay, or the North Shore. Maybe you can help me here." Kennet held the tiny GPS screen up to Kellerman's face. "See that little flag, the waypoint? Where is that, exactly?" The LCD display showed a street graph of Beardmore in one corner.

"Well, that's the highway you came in on. That's the river, the Blackwater, and the railway. And that red line, that's the Warneford Road. That's where Vanderhorst and his sidekick were fartin' around. Exactly where they were, I can't tell you, but there's someone who could."

"I think I can find it. What's the road like?"

"Before the fire, it was barely passable. After the fire, it was a mess, with the windfalls. But Beardmore Logging went in to salvage timber, and patch up the washouts, and I hear it's in good shape now. Fishermen use it, and hunters. But you still need a 4x4 for some of the old washouts and the odd mudhole. The Sportage should cope. And – " Kellerman slid off his perch and beckoned Kennet into the shop. "If you're going in the bush, you'll need this."

He lifted an orange fluorescent vest off a pile on a shelf. "Bear season. It's smart to look as little like a bear as you can. Got a banger?"

Kennet took the vest. "A what?"

"A bear banger. Warns 'em off real good." Kellerman showed him a pencil-like instrument and explained how the cartridges worked.

"And I'd better look at your maps," said Kennet. "I don't have any topos of this part of the world, and I'd like an overview of the country. And you must have whitewater paddling hereabouts?"

Kennet emerged from the shop with a bagful of purchases, followed by a smiling Kellerman. A large garishly painted Dodge Ram Quad Cab had parked on the shoulder of the main street and a roughly dressed man in cowboy boots was striding toward the shop. Another man with shoulder-length hair sat in the passenger seat, looking on with interest. Another face peered from the back seat. An aluminum boat sat in the truck box.

"Ah shit," said Kellerman softly.

Kennet stowed the bag in his passenger seat and shut the door. The newcomer stopped a few paces from Kellerman and placed his hands on his hips in gunfighter position. "Kellerman?" He thrust out his jaw. "You got leeches?"

Kellerman had paused in the doorway. "What's it to you, Fleming?"

"Ozzie's out of 'em," said the newcomer, truculently. "I need 'em."

Kellerman did not move. "Again, what's it to you?"

"You got some? I'll pay."

"You're goddamn right you'd pay for them," said Kellerman. "If I had some." He added, "To sell." And then more deliberately, "To you."

Fleming raised his voice, and raised his right arm in a gesture that might have been supplication or might have been contempt. "Fuck, Kellerman! I'm being friendly here."

"Friendly? And you say 'Fuck Kellerman'?"

"You goddamn well know what I mean. Well, what about it?"

Kellerman set his jaw. "I ain't got none." He added, "To sell". And again deliberately, "To you."

Fleming swung his gaze to Kennet Forbes, hard eyes glinting. "What are you looking at?"

Kennet had sensed his muscles tense. He breathed once deeply, letting the breath out slowly. "Nothing," he said, and then added, "Nothing I haven't seen before."

Fleming swung around to face Forbes across a distance of four or five paces. "What the hell's that mean?"

Kennet held his gaze. He assumed the ready stance, feet planted apart shoulder-width, hands at waist-height, as though he had hooked his thumbs behind his belt. "What would you like it to mean?" he said softly.

Fleming advanced two steps and raised his right hand, index finger and thumb poised to work an invisible hammer and trigger. "Well, fuck you and the boat you rode in on! What are you, a fucken granola-eater?"

Kennet had carefully assumed a modified guard stance, right hand loosely clenched at the waist, left hand raised casually to his shirt pocket. His eyes never left the aggressor.

Kellerman had moved quietly forward a few paces, fingers hooked around his suspenders. He spoke in a steady, steely voice. "Fleming, you don't come here and insult my customers. Get off my property. Now."

Fleming turned to face him. He sneered. "Or you'll what? You'll make me? You and –" he gestured toward Kennet – "granola-eater here?"

"It won't be the first time," said Kellerman quietly. "But maybe they'll make you." He nodded toward the street.

A black Chevy Tahoe with tinted windows was moving quietly past from the direction of the motel, driver's window down. The pugnacious features of Detective Mueller looked curiously at the scenario in front of The Hook'n Bullet.

Fleming wheeled toward his pickup and hurled over his shoulder, "Fuck you, Kellerman."

"That's what I thought you said," said Kellerman softly. "The first time." The Tahoe passed and turned down a side street. The Fleming pickup gunned away. Kellerman turned to Kennet, smiling apologetically. "Sorry about that. You have just met the dark side of Beardmore. The Fleming clan. Probably had his useless brothers in the truck waiting for the call."

"What sort of work do they do?"

"Work? That's a laugh. They're specialists. They specialize in troublemaking. When they aren't fishing or hunting. They carry guns in that truck year round."

"Guns? You can't be serious."

"You know, rifles. Encased, of course. Unloaded. But they've convinced the Ministry that they use them legally."

"You mean the Ministry of Natural Resources?"

"Yep." He gave Kennet a small wave. "Hope you find what you're looking for. Just don't bring it back here." He smiled. "Vanderhorst, I mean."

Kennet pulled into the motel/restaurant parking lot. The police Suburban still sat in front of the open door of Room 39. In the restaurant there was one lone customer. Kennet chose a tiny table that could accommodate two people in a pinch and ordered the lunch special from the blonde manager/waitress: green pea soup and a ham-and-cheese toasted sandwich on whole wheat. He chose black coffee for a beverage. The customer, an older man, a strikingly handsome man, with long white locks combed back, threw him sidelong glances as he supped a coffee murky with milk. He was dressed in working man's clothes.

While he waited for his order to arrive, Kennet made a decision to learn more about the community. The customer called himself Mac. A lifelong prospector, he said. He said that many of the folks thereabouts prospected, full or part-time. That the region was experiencing a boom in mining exploration, and that many prospectors had not only found lucrative work but had optioned their properties and were now flush for the first time in decades.

Kennet's order arrived and he set to work, finding himself inexplicably famished. And, yeah, Mac said, there had been a bit of excitement in town this morning. That most of the folks there were decent people but there were, as in any community, some galoots who broke the public peace. Beardmore had no bar as such, there was not enough custom to support one, but you could get a beer at Arlene's Tavern down the street. Still, you didn't see any drunks rolling home after an evening's carousing like you did in the old days. They didn't even have a resident officer there anymore. So the boys in blue were bored stiff with the Beardmore patrol. No, the forest industry was pretty well dead these days, and it was more than a regional problem, it was a goddamn national economic disgrace.

The waitress surprised Kennet with a jello and whipped cream dessert not listed on the lunch special menu. Some of the lads, said Mac, still made a living commercial fishing, on the lake, you know, Lake Nipigon, but the heyday of the fisher was long gone. So the future of the region seemed to rest with one of the many junior mining companies now poking around trying to find an economic resource. The Beardmore-Geraldton gold camp had once been the toast of Canada's mining fraternity. The camp would rise again from the ashes. And what was Kennet doing up in this neck of the woods?

"Just checking on a colleague," said Kennet, rising and heading for the lobby and the cash register. "A pleasure talking to you, Mac."

As he left town and topped the hill, he could see to the west the rolling green sea and the scattered gray masts that commemorated a graveyard of ghost ships. Climbing the long S-curve of the next hill, he slowed, looking for the Warneford Road. He still tooled past it. He glanced in the rear-view, braked, and reversed a few metres so that he could turn. It was a narrow, hard-packed trail except for the grassy centre between the wheel tracks. Leafy brush closed on it, reaching for the pristine red finish of the Sportage. The truck sloshed through puddles in a stretch of ruts and burst into a clearing, a utility corridor. Power lines hung from eiffel-tower structures. A small metal sign with the letters "PPL" signified that a natural gas pipeline was buried below.

The trail entered a stand of trees and dipped momentarily into a washout that had been expertly mended with crushed rock. A trickle of water ran across the gravel, headed down the slope to the right and through the mixed wood to the Blackwater River. The trail emerged into the sea of brush he had seen from the highway. He was driving dry shod – dry tired, he thought – along the bottom of a latter-day Red Sea.

Chapter 4

... **Thursday afternoon**

What was he going to find? he thought.

He allowed the Sportage to glide to a stop. Thick leafy shrubs crowded the boundaries of the trail and rose three and four and sometimes five metres in the air. He could see no ghostly masts. What the hell was he going to find?

Vanderhorst had not returned to his room yesterday, or so it seemed.   Kyle Henderson had returned, and Kyle had been assaulted, sometime during the evening or the night, for no one had seen anything, or was admitting anything.   Had Vanderhorst indeed returned and beaten up Kyle?

Vanderhorst? A scholar and, beneath the bohemian facade, no doubt a gentleman, a gentle man, who had married scatterbrain Cindy and fathered a child, Willem. Willie. A man whose child doted on him. A man who had impressed Dr. Peter Sheridan and the Board of Governors of Thunder Bay University to the degree that they had hired him, as they had hired Kennet, for his knowledge and his experience and his ability to relate to students, and for his passion. His passion in his chosen field. Did Alfred

Vanderhorst assault his student and then pull a runner? Had he abandoned his career and abandoned his family and was the penurious archaeologist now thumbing a ride to the Yucatan or to Pichu Machu or to the Rift Valley in Tanganyika?

Impenetrable green walls rose on either side. If he stuck an arm into the brush he might lose it. If he stepped into the brush he might lose himself. He had lost himself once in such a brush. Rwanda, 1994. The military convoy had paused to clear the road of some obstruction, probably of a body, or of a succession of bodies. He couldn't see up ahead, but he could see a wall of brush beside the trail, and he had felt an urgent need to relieve himself. He advised the driver that he was stepping out to take a leak. There were some nuns in the convoy – where, he wasn't sure, but they had evacuated a mission school an hour before, and the nuns were traveling with them – and so in a fit of modesty he had stepped off the trail into the brush. He had stepped on a body. Then he saw them.

Many, many bodies. Clothed, and semi-clothed, and naked, and bloody. Collected grotesquely. Collected into one neat pile. He looked down. He had stepped on a child. The child had no head. He had relieved himself then. In his pants. The familiar stench of corpses overwhelmed him. Maggots crawled everywhere. Flies swarmed.

He had seen plenty of bodies during the Rwandan genocide. He had seen hundreds, maybe thousands of bodies. When he had tried to analyze his mental and emotional distress, when after this macabre encounter with the casually disposed-of dead, and after he had pleaded with his producer to bring him home, and after he had resumed duties as relief anchor on CBC-TV's national news desk, then he had finally, he thought, he had finally put his finger on the proximate cause. It had been the one body. It had been the one body that he had personally violated.

Kennet stepped out of the Sportage and took a leak. He was

prepared to swat flies, but there were no flies this summer. No flies to speak of. Something to do with the late spring. He watched the yellow stream splash on the hard-packed sand and gravel of the trail. He stared into the vegetable maelstrom. No, Vanderhorst would not have run. Vanderhorst was still out there. Somewhere. It did not look good for Vanderhorst. Dead or alive.

He reached over to the passenger seat and retrieved the orange hunter's vest and put it on. He held the GPS to the sky and let it search. A few wispy clouds marred the deep blue. The map appeared with the waypoint he had programmed with the coordinates Peter Sheridan had supplied. He set the unit to track the waypoint.

The trail wound up and down slopes. Twice, topping a rise, he could see a long ridge stretching from west to east, beyond the unseen river. It was populated with the upright trunks of dead trees, snags left by the great fire. Sometimes the brush fell back from the trail, providing opportunities for parking. Small mounds of black turds he identified as bear scat. Occasionally water stood in the trail, or ran down a wheel track in a tiny stream. The unusually heavy and frequent rains of that summer were now seeking the sea. Sharp dips in the trail marked the points where culverts had been removed and the ditches filled with crushed rock.

Every once in a while he noted red flagging tape hanging from roadside branches. A few were faded to the point they had no colour. Near one fresh tape was a small pile of sawdust – someone, it appeared, has salvaged a snag for firewood. Twice he identified boot tracks in the muddy edges of puddles that had commenced to shrink in the sunlight. Three or four times he noted a single, very narrow tire track crossing a softer patch of ground between the double wheel tracks of the trail.

His track on the GPS screen was closing in on the waypoint, planted firmly to the south of the trail, the red line on the map. A small pond overwhelmed the trail. He drove carefully through and climbed a long hill, his left tires sloshing through a fast-moving stream coming down the wheel track. The stream left the track and tumbled down a channel beside the road, almost hidden in the brush. By the time he had reached the summit, the brush had swallowed the stream. The trail was level for a while. His map track moved past the waypoint. So. He would have to disembark and search on foot.

He pulled off the trail where the brush permitted. He extracted a kit bag from the back seat and, looking around first from pure habit, changed swiftly into light-coloured bushranging clothes and hiker's boots. He fitted a broad-brimmed hat, what he called his safari hat, snugly on his head, chin strap dangling loose. The GPS hung from his neck on a lanyard. He loaded a cartridge into the bear banger and slipped it into a deep pocket of his cargo pants, along with spare cartridges.

He locked the truck. He paced slowly down the south side of the trail the way he had come, studying the ground and the wall of brush. Faint impressions on the soft ground on the edge of the wheel track resolved into fragments of heel and toe marks, heading east. The wall of brush betrayed no entrance to a path. Then he was spotting marks of somebody, perhaps more than one body, walking west. The marks made sense if Vanderhorst and Henderson had parked some distance away from the path to the dig in order to disguise its location. They may even have parked the Grand Caravan where he was now parked.

As he was descending the long hill the footprints petered out. He returned to the crest and studied the brush. A spruce tree occupied a small opening beside the trail. It was a young spruce, a product of the great fire. The ground was gravelly. He poked around behind the tree and descended into a shallow brushy ditch from which at one time an excavator had scooped gravel for the roadbed. The brush seemed sparser behind the shallow ditch.

There was a distinct footprint. A scuffmark on a windfall log. And there it was. A trail carved out of the brush.

He hurried along a trail which was sometimes only shoulder-width. The LED screen told him he was headed due south. On a flat patch of sand he noted some tiny round balls, rabbit turds. The trail left the flat ground and climbed into a stand of trees the fire had skipped. Soon he was climbing in sunshine up a barren rocky hill spotted with snags and isolated clumps of brush. Knee-high bushes carried ripe blueberries. Some happy flies buzzed about a pile of bear scat. Here and there red flagging tape helped identify the trail. To his left he heard the gurgle of tumbling water, possibly the stream that crossed the road below.

The trail veered to the southwest, diving into heavy brush again. He stumbled a couple of times into shallow pits excavated in the soil, pits which his reason told him were made by the old-time prospectors looking for the bedrock and the quartz veins that hosted the gold. A low rocky ridge materialized. At his feet he noticed a rock shard, mud-stained, out of place. And then, purely by chance, he noticed a shard at eye level in a clump of brush, wedged between the trunk and a spray of branches.

The trail ended in a fairly large clearing. Small birch trees and brush had been tossed down slope. A low mound paralleled the rocky ridge closely, which rose three or four metres. An archaeologist's sifting screen, perhaps a metre square, sat in a wooden frame in the clearing.

The left portion of the mound was entangled in string and fresh wooden stakes. From the direction of the rock wall, a trench slashed through the mound, this depression also encompassed by string. He shifted his line of travel to the right and climbed up the mud-and-rock-shard mound that paralleled the rock wall. To his left the string and stakes resolved into an excavation grid. Several inches of the mound's crest had been removed, leaving a level tabletop.

In the shadow beneath the wall, he distinguished a narrow, shallow trench. The soil appeared undisturbed. He noted the stumps of brush recently hacked down.

A vein of white quartz drew his eyes. Like a lance it plunged down the cliff face into the shadowy trench. Simultaneously he saw the body. The body had no head.

The body sprawled with feet towards the mound. He had an impression of dirty white sneakers. The legs pointed to the cross-trench which cut through the mound, probably for drainage. The clothes of the body blended with the earth and shadow. The body lay on its face . . . if it had a face. Only the once-white sneakers stood out. He smelled the familiar smell. A few houseflies buzzed.

Kennet steeled himself to descend the mound. The body was truncated at the shoulders, and mere centimetres separated the shoulders from the cliff and the quartz vein. Beneath the shoulders, water pooled. A small pool of dirty water. Kennet moved closer and leaned over. The neck was there. And attached to the neck, wisps of thick brown hair. The head was there after all. It was submerged in the pool, a very deep pool.

Kennet sat back on his heels. His eyes rose up the white lance of quartz to the top of the cliff. Of course. A prospector – Eddie Dodd, Peter Sheridan had called him – any prospector worth his salt would have followed such a prominent vein down into the ground. There was a pit there, excavated in the rock and soil. A pit wide enough to admit the body of a man and God knows how deep now and now filled with water. And plugged with a dead body.

Kennet spun slowly on his heels, still squatting, and gazed through the drainage ditch to the green tangle beyond. There was no doubt that this was Alfred Vanderhorst. Dead. Not alive. Cindy's Alfie. Willie's dad. His colleague.

Damn. Goddamn. Goddamn, goddamn, goddamn.

Whoever had done this – whoever had done this –

44

But had somebody done this? Had somebody *else* done this? Or had Vanderhorst done this? In a fit of remorse.

Goddamn. Kennet rose slowly to his feet. A cloud shadow passed swiftly by. He started down the trail. His pace picked up. Soon he was trotting. Then he was running. He caught himself. No point in breaking a leg here, he thought. Then they'll be looking for me. He slowed to a brisk walk.

He unlocked the truck and pulled out his overnight bag and extracted his cell phone. No silly games today, he thought. When he got a signal, he punched in 911. "I want to report a death," he said.

A female voice responded. "A death? You mean an accidental death, sir?"

"A death. I don't know if it's accidental or not. I'm not qualified to pronounce."

"Where are you, sir? Give me your address, please. And your name."

"I'm on the Warneford Road – I'm near Beardmore, in the bush . . ."

"Beardmore, sir? And where exactly is Beardmore?"

"In Ontario!" he responded. "Christ, I'm calling the Ontario Provincial Police! Where are you now, exactly?"

"Calm down, sir. I'm in our Sudbury office. Now what is your name, sir?"

"Kennet Forbes. Look, I am reporting a dead body, in the bush, near Beardmore . . ."

"Beardmore. Now, what is the nearest large centre? A city perhaps."

"A city? Well, Thunder Bay is three hours away. That's the closest –"

"Thunder Bay. I'm transferring you right now, sir."

"Wait! That's too –" She had cut him off. He should have said Greenstone, he thought. Surely she had the Greenstone detachment in her directory.

A male voice came on line. "Yes, sir. How can I help you?"

Kennet was thinking fast. He did not look forward to meeting that oaf again, that Detective Constable Mueller. He had a better idea. "My name is Kennet Forbes. I'm reporting a body near Beardmore. I wish to speak to Inspector Robert Kenilworth, please."

"Sir. Mr. Forbes. This is not a private communication, sir. You called 911, an emergency response line. Please give me your exact position, and details of the emergency."

Kennet complied.

"And you will stay there until officers arrive?" asked the male voice.

"Yes. In fact, I will stay with the body. There is bear sign in the vicinity. It is about 700 metres off the road, south side. I will park my red SUV at the entrance to the path, which is hard to find. When can I expect the officers to arrive?"

"We will notify the Greenstone OPP immediately. It shouldn't be long."

Greenstone OPP. Damn, thought Kennet. "And will you pass this message on to Inspector Kenilworth in the Regional office? There is a Thunder Bay connection."

"I will do that, sir."

"And, oh, ask the responding officers to honk their horn. As I said, I'll be off trail."

Kennet moved the truck and parked it pointing east. He retrieved a compact digital camera from his kit bag and slipped it into a shirt pocket, and added a hunting knife to his belt. He locked the doors. He retraced his steps along the path, picking up the pace when he passed the bear marker. The sun still shone brilliantly. The body still lay partially in shadow. He looked the scene over carefully.

A brown wide-brimmed hat (*Shades of Indiana Jones*, he thought) lay beside the body. *Practically new*, he thought. He noted the implements of an archaeological dig – buckets, a couple of shovels, a mason's trowel, a gray Pelican camera case, a notebook resting on the case, pinned in place with a rock, a spool of heavy string, two or three measures, and several other items. The largest item was a long-handled metal detector, the kind used by treasure-hunting hobbyists. On the body, he thought, there would be a GPS, perhaps, a pen, even a cell phone. He would not touch the body. He was no detective. They would not be pleased if he did. Let the professionals do that.

He started snapping pictures. He covered the whole area. He walked back on the path and took pictures of the rock shards, including the one suspended in an alder. He put the camera back in his shirt pocket and buttoned the flap.

He made his way west along the rock wall until he could climb, and then he sat on the rock with legs dangling over the edge, the body four metres away. It was, his watch said, twenty minutes past two. Six hours ago he had been joking with Peter Sheridan about the star of the Anthropology Department. Alfred Vanderhorst was – had been the sort of person who attracted snide comments. He had somehow put Walter Kellerman's nose out of joint. Kellerman had indicated that he didn't know exactly where Vanderhorst was digging, but that he knew someone who did. Who else knew Vanderhorst's work site? Without the coordinates that Peter had supplied, by way of Vanderhorst and Cindy, he himself would have been hard pressed to find the site. He would, in fact, have never found the site without considerable help. So who knew about the site's location? And who had been mad enough at Vanderhorst to kill him?

There was no doubt in Kennet's mind, not any more, that Vanderhorst had been murdered. Suicide by drowning oneself in a mud puddle had not been Vanderhorst's style. If he had had a style of suicide. If he had wanted to commit suicide. If he –

Kennet ordered his mind to stop churning. He breathed deeply several times. He drew his legs up under him and assumed the lotus position, palms open to the sky and resting lightly on his knees.

Chapter 5

. . . Thursday afternoon, later

The faraway blast of a car horn broke his concentration. Kennet stood up and reached down into the deep pocket of his cargo pants and withdrew the bear banger. He released the safety. He canted the tube and aimed it toward the unseen road below and released the trigger.

The tube banged and bucked slightly and the cartridge exploded over the bushes several metres away. He climbed down from the ledge, climbed the low mound of debris from the trench, and started down the path. He studied the path more closely. He found three more pieces of rock on the leaf mould, pieces that had never been transported there by natural means. He returned to the mound and waited.

Soon he heard voices down the trail. The deeper voice was cursing. Detective Kelly Armitage appeared. When she saw Kennet she stopped and turned around and said something. Mueller came around the corner and stopped. Armitage advanced toward Kennet, Mueller following more slowly. Armitage put on a smile.

"Mr. Forbes! We meet again. Show us what you have." Mueller huffed. He had stopped behind her, the skirt of his suit jacket swept back and his hand on his right hip near his holstered weapon.

"This way," said Kennet, about to turn.

"What the hell was that shot!" barked Mueller.

"That was me. I was signaling my position."

Mueller's fingers tapped his holster. "Where's the gun?" he growled.

"This is my gun," said Kennet, and he held up the bear banger. "Did you not see the bear sign? I carry this as a precaution."

Mueller's features twisted in disgust. He waved his right arm peremptorily. "Show us the body." He added, "You better have a good story."

The detectives examined the body and the site without touching anything. From time to time each of them addressed questions to Kennet. After a few minutes, Armitage said, "What is this place anyway? What was the victim doing here?"

"If that is Vanderhorst, he was looking for evidence that Scandinavian sailors visited this area many centuries ago," said Kennet.

"Vikings?" said Mueller. "What kind of shit are you handing me?"

"If that is Vanderhorst and this is the right site, there is a scholarly consensus that Viking relics were recovered here in the 1930's by a prospector. As we speak, the relics repose in the Royal Ontario Museum."

"Never heard of them," said Mueller in exasperation. "And what do you mean, 'If this is Vanderhorst'? Don't you know him? And," Mueller stepped closer to Kennet, hands on hips, "you told us you didn't know where he was."

"I haven't seen the victim's face. And I may still not know where he is. All I had was a place to start looking, and I just followed directions."

"Who told you?" Mueller snarled.

"GPS." Kennet touched the unit suspended on the lanyard. "GPS told me."

"Well, fuck, smart ass" said Mueller, "I'm going to get to the bottom of this." Mueller turned to Armitage.

"Armitage, you take this – this," Mueller's face glowed red, "key witness to the Beardmore office and you sit with him until I arrive. I'll wait for the SOCOs. Go now."

Armitage straightened up and gave Mueller a hard look. "Detective Constable Mueller. I'll thank you to address me properly. And I don't take orders from you, Con. But I'll do it, because it's procedure. You stay here."

"Yeah, yeah," said Mueller with a dismissive gesture. "Just go."

Kennet preceded D.C. Armitage down the path. After a few steps they heard Mueller calling.

"There are bears around? Better leave me that banger, Forbes. It looks like a weapon to me, and you're in our custody now."

A few minutes down the trail, Kennet turned to Armitage and smiled. "He didn't ask me for a cartridge. The thing's not loaded."

"Just as well," she replied, smiling. "He won't hurt himself ."

Back at the vehicles, Armitage suggested that Kennet precede her with his truck. She gave directions to the town office. Kennet removed the hunter's vest and slipped his wallet back into his pocket. Armitage followed in the black Tahoe SUV. They met the unmarked OPP Suburban with the two officers who had been processing the motel room. It pulled over to let them pass. Kennet stopped, watching in the rear-view while Armitage stepped out to chat briefly with them.

In Beardmore he drove past the Regency to a new-looking structure with signs identifying it as property of the Municipality of Greenstone, housing the volunteer fire department, the public works garage, and the office of the Beardmore Ward. Two tall vehicle bays accessed the fire engines and two more, the garage. Kennet parked in front of the people-sized doorway.

Kennet walked into a tiny reception area and up to the service window. He addressed the gray-haired woman behind the small desk in the cubicle.

"Excuse me, ma'am. Do you know about the so-called Beardmore relics?"

The lady rose and approached, putting on her may-I-serve-you? smile. "Of course, sir. Call me Janet. Please. Would you like to see them?"

Kennet did a double take. "See them? I understood they were in the ROM."

"We have replicas. Just a minute, sir." She returned in less than a minute with a long wooden case, which she set on the countertop. She oriented the case so that when she lifted the lid, the contents lay there in their individual velvet-lined compartments.

"Good Lord!" said Kennet. The door opened and Armitage came up behind him. "What is it?" she said.

A heavy-looking antique-style sword rested in the longest compartment, the blade broken near the middle, and fragments preserved. "May I touch?" asked Kennet, and Janet nodded. He pushed a big blade fragment with one finger and it moved easily. It was synthetic material, rusty-looking, most likely fabricated from a mould. Another, smaller compartment held a disk-shaped object and a third, a bent rod affair.

"What are those?" he asked.

Janet reached under the counter and produced a newsprint tabloid, which she slid across. "This will help. This is all we know." It was a local historical society publication, complete with fuzzy photographs.

"May I have one too?" said Armitage. Janet produced another copy. "May we use the training centre, Janet?"

They exited the office, turned left, and entered another door. A huge yellow machine, a loader with a enormous tires and a bucket, occupied one half of the public works garage. Kennet scarcely hestitated before they climbed an open stairway to the second level. Behind the door lay a well-equipped room, with kitchenette, filing cabinets, a chalk board along one wall, long tables slid together, and upholstered chairs.

Armitage seated herself in a chair near Kennet's and pulled out her notebook.

"Okay," she sighed. "Let's begin with personal information – name, address, telephone, employer, et cetera." Kennet complied.

"Now start at the beginning. What brought you up here?"

Kennet filled in the picture, beginning with the visit from Cindy Vanderhorst that morning, moving on to his visits to Peter Sheridan and Melissa Sharp and to his meeting the ambulance. He supplied phone numbers.

"What is the status of Kyle Henderson? he asked. "Where is he?"

"Mr. Henderson is in the Nipigon hospital. His jaw is broken, he's in critical condition. We don't have a statement yet."

She snapped her notebook shut. "We'll have to remain here. Detective Mueller will leave the site to the scene-of-crime officers. He may have more questions".

Someone was climbing the stairs. The door opened and D.C. Mueller stepped in. He gestured to D.C. Armitage. "Come on. We're going to Geraldton."

Kennet said calmly, "Does that mean you're through with me?"

Mueller's eyes glinted. "Oh no. You're coming with us. I have more questions."

Kennet said reasonably, "You don't know what questions I've answered. Maybe I've answered them all."

Mueller smiled tightly. "You are coming with us, or I am placing you under arrest for obstructing an investigation. What will it be?"

"I'm coming, " said Kennet quietly. "But I have to look after my truck and kayak. I'll leave it at the motel."

At the motel Kennet parked facing the two-story section and strode quickly to the office. The blonde warrior was defending the desk in the tiny lobby, or perhaps she was just sorting through some receipts.

"I'd like a room, please. Looks like I won't be going home anytime soon."

"Oh I'm sorry, sir. It's Thursday, and we're all booked up. There's a paving crew patching the highway, and another crew mending guard rails, and we just don't have any rooms."

The two detectives crowded in behind him.

"But, sir," she continued, "you're a friend of Mr. Vanderhorst, aren't you? And that poor boy, Kyle Henderson? "

"Well –"

"There's a third bed in that unit. The maid's not made up the room yet – she won't today. Jennifer found that poor boy this morning, and it's been quite a shock. But the police have gone, the other officers, I mean," she said, glancing at the detectives, "and they took down the tape. I don't see why you can't stay there." She concluded by glancing at Mueller defiantly.

"Let's get on with it, Forbes. Mr. Forbes." Mueller put a sarcastic twist on the title.

"Here's a key," said the manager. "Now, I'm about to close shop here, but if you need anything, there's a phone on the wall outside, with a direct line to my place. Good luck," she said, handing the key over and glancing significantly at Mueller.

"I almost forgot," said Kennet. "Do you have Internet access?"

"Yes sir." She plucked a scrap of paper from under the desk and handed it to him. "Here's today's password for the wireless connection."

As they turned to leave, the manager said, "Oh sir, sign here, will you? For the record." She slid a ledger over to him.

Kennet signed. "And what's your name?" he said.

"I'm Alice, and this is my restaurant." As they shook hands, they both grinned.

Kenneth rode in the rear seat of the Tahoe. Mueller drove. There being no panel separating front from rear, he could hear everything they said, but they spoke in monosyllables. The radio emitted human-like sounds from time to time, sounds that Kennet struggled with little success to interpret. The scenery whizzed by but he paid little attention to it. This was not the way he had imagined he would be revisiting his old stomping grounds. He was working up a slow burn. His tongue had got him into jackpots before, and he had learned from painful experience to get a grip on his temper. He had learned to suffer fools, not always gladly, but with minimal grace.

The speedometer needle had hovered around 120 for the first while but slowly it crept up. At one point a terrific jolt shook them up. A railway crossing. The needle subsided to 90 as they crept through the scattered community of Jellicoe. A speed limit sign with the number 70 flashed by. The needle crept up again, trying to decide between 140 and 150 and finally settling on 147. After a time, when the vehicle had topped a long hill and entered a level straightaway, the speed dropped dramatically. Kennet could see infrastructure ahead. Street light standards. Then a familiar landmark, the headframe of the old MacLeod-Cockshutt mine.

Mueller braked sharply and swung left. A short paved drive led to a long single-story brick edifice with darkened windows and an institutional feel. Mueller followed the drive around to the rear where a number of vehicles, police and private, were parked.

Mueller was first out of the car. He opened the rear door and motioned to Kennet. When Kennet emerged Mueller grasped Kennet's upper arm.

"This way," he grunted.

Kennet stepped away, breaking his grasp. "Do not," he said evenly, "put your hands on me."

Armitage spoke across the roof of the SUV. "Con, follow the protocol. You don't want to mess this one up."

Mueller scowled and gestured towards the single door in the rear wall of the OPP detachment office. Armitage beat them to it, punched a code into the keypad, and held the door open as they entered. They passed through a mud room with a coat rack and lockers. Mueller pushed past Kennet and pulled the inside door open and started punching a keypad on a door leading left.

"Detective Mueller," said Armitage in a steady voice. "What are you doing?"

Mueller looked up. "The interview room. What do you think?"

"I think the soft interview room is more appropriate, don't you think? We're debriefing a witness."

Mueller made a sound of disgust and led off down the corridor to the right. They passed a couple of offices and then an open area behind a privacy panel where some officers worked away at desks. Near the ceiling a row of one-way windows let in the daylight.

They turned a corner and just before they reached an open area with a couple of civilian employees – women – whom Kennet assumed were receptionists, Mueller opened a door leading to a cubicle.

"Have a seat," said Mueller, gesturing to the furthest of the two padded chairs. "Detective," he continued, "you take the monitor. I'll question him."

Armitage left. Kennet took a seat, glancing around. He spotted a video camera near the ceiling and a microphone on the narrow table jammed against one wall. Mueller took a seat facing him, left arm on the table. Kennet put his right arm on the table. Mueller fiddled with some switches on a module and then looked at the microphone.

"Okay, I am interviewing a person of interest in the homicide reported today just outside of Beardmore." He glanced at his watch and related the time and date. "The victim is possibly an

Alfred Vanderhorst, a professor at Thunder Bay University, and the SOCOs are checking the scene at this very moment, and the idents are arriving soon from Thunder Bay."

Mueller turned to Kennet. "Okay, give your full name and address and occupation."

"Kennet J. Forbes. 936 Bay Street, Thunder Bay, Ontario. Teacher at Thunder Bay University."

"Kennet? Or Kenneth? Spell that."

Kennet spelled it.

"What kind of name is that?"

"Is that relevant?"

"Bay Street? Isn't that the part of town where the rummies hang out?"

"I live in a quiet residential area. Do you get to the city much?"

"Let's get one thing straight. I'm asking the questions here." Mueller looked Kennet over, upper lip drawn back in a sneer. "Where'd you get that shiner? It's a beaut." Involuntarily Kennet jerked his hand, as if he had been about to touch his bad eye.

"None of your business."

Mueller smiled mirthlessly. "How do you know this Vanderhorst? And what's your interest in him?"

Kennet repeated what he had told Armitage, and added, "All this information I gave your partner earlier."

"Now you're giving it to me. Why did you deny knowing where Vanderhorst was when I asked you earlier? What were you hiding?"

"I did not know where he was. I did not deny knowing where he was. I simply did not know where he was."

"You had directions! You had GPS coordinates."

"I did not know exactly what they signified. I certainly did not know if they identified the location of Vanderhorst. So is the body now positively identified as Vanderhorst?"

"I'm asking the questions! Why didn't you give me those coordinates when I asked?"

"You did not ask for the coordinates. You asked if I knew where Vanderhorst was. I did not know where he was. I still don't know where he is, positively. Do you?"

"Listen, smart —" The flush was climbing into Mueller's cheeks. "Listen, I'm getting to the bottom of this if it takes all day. How did you get those coordinates?"

"I gave that information to Detective Armitage."

"Are you getting smart with me?"

"I have always been smart. I gave a full statement to Detective Constable Armitage, and it seems to me," Kennet canted his head to look straight at the video camera, "if you were to read her official notes, you would be saving yourself a lot of time and the taxpayer a lot of money in paying both your salaries —"

Mueller half rose from his seat, his face beet red now. "I'm not paid to take anybody's crap!" he shouted.

"Sure you are," said Kennet. "But I am not giving you crap. I am, however, suggesting that D.C. Armitage's notes would be an excellent starting point for this interview. I am —"

Mueller brought his left fist down hard on the table and stalked out, slamming the door shut. Kennet glanced at his watch. He cooled his heels for a good twenty minutes before Mueller returned. He had a notebook, presumably Armitage's notebook, and he took his seat again, visibly calmer and lighter in colour. He consulted it frequently over the next hour.

The interrogation – Kennet did not imagine for a moment it was an interview – the interrogation continued with thrusts and parries. Privately he felt that he had cooperated fully with the authorities and that he was now indulging the bullying temperament and limited intelligence of a cop who had somehow achieved a position of power and prestige in the provincial police force. Right. He would play the game. He would not lose his temper. Meanwhile his mind drifted to the green bush and brilliant sunlight beyond Beardmore, to a lonely hillside in a ravaged landscape, to flies buzzing about a body that lay with its head in a water-filled hole in the ground. Perhaps, however, the body of Alfred Vanderhorst was even now being spirited away to chilly white chambers in the cellar of the Thunder Bay regional hospital. Perhaps Cindy, his loving wife, and Willie, his loving son, were being apprised of the mortal end of her husband and his father. Perhaps . . .

Mueller arose abruptly and exited the interview room. He left the door ajar.

Chapter 6

. . . Thursday evening, early

Kennet rose and tucked one leg under him and then the other so that he was sitting in the chair in the Buddha posture. He closed his eyes and breathed in deeply and let the breath out slowly. He concentrated on the breath, in, and out. In. And out. In . . .

After a time, while still in full awareness behind his closed eyelids, he heard a female voice.

"Sir?"

Slowly, with a final deep breath, he raised his arms aloft and, exhaling slowly, lowered them, ending with hands in the prayer position on his chest.

"Sir? Are you alright?"

Kennet opened his eyes. "Of course I'm alright. Never felt better." He unwound his legs and rose to a standing position. "Where's Detective Mueller?"

"Gone home, I think. It's the end of his shift. He asked me to tell you that you may leave." She wore a constable's uniform, a petite woman with a thin face and long brown hair in.

Kennet gritted his teeth. "Gone home, has he? Then where is

60

my ride? He transported me from Beardmore. My truck is in Beardmore."

"I don't know, sir. " She bit her lip. "Perhaps you'd like to speak with the Staff-Sergeant?"

"Yes, I would like."

She led him past the administrative area where full windows looked out on the front parking lot and the highway. She paused at an open door and rapped lightly on the frame. A voice said "Yes?"

"A gentleman to see you, ma'am."

Kennet advanced, and met a woman in uniform dress tunic and pants coming to meet him. She held her hand out.

"Ah, yes. You must be Professor Forbes. I understand that Detective Mueller was interviewing you." They shook hands.

"I'm Staff-Sergeant Jillian Halvorsen," she said. "Detachment commander. Have a seat. Please." She waved to a padded chair and seated herself behind the big desk. She was a full-bodied woman with curves in the right places, black hair in bob fashion, dark red lipstick, and she emanated a hard, brittle beauty.

"The interview," said Kennet carefully," is apparently terminated, and I am stuck here without a ride. My truck is in Beardmore. And," he continued, "I may have a complaint to lodge."

"Well, we'll have to do something about that. The ride, I mean. Now, what is the nature of your complaint?" She sat upright, squaring her shoulders and shifting her feet. The smile faded.

"I was whisked here, for no good reason, apparently, at high speeds, putting my life and limb at risk, not to mention those of your officers, at speeds that reached 150 klicks an hour. There was no emergency. There was no siren. There were no flashing lights. Just a pleasure trip, apparently. For Detective Mueller's pleasure."

"I see." She rose, lips pursed. "Let me check into this. Will you wait, please, Mr. Forbes?" Then she was gone.

Kennet looked around the office. It was a spartan space. A computer on the desk and a few scattered letters. A filing cabinet. Wood-paneled walls. Carpet on the floor. Vertical blinds on the tall windows. Shelving behind the desk with a few books and loose-leaf binders. A framed black-and-white photograph. A few knickknacks.

Kennet glanced at the open door and then sauntered over to the photo. It looked familiar. It was a modest brick building with bars on the windows and a classic black-and-white Ford patrol car parked in front. He remembered that place. It was the crowbar motel, as he and his buddies used to call it. The cop shop. The old police station on Main Street, Geraldton.

He sauntered back to his seat, noticing a small pile of magazines near the padded bench seat by the door. On top was the latest copy of *Motorcyle Mojo*.

Staff-Sergeant Halvorsen returned, smiling. She seated herself and looked up brightly. "Well, Mr. Forbes. I spoke to Detective Kelly Armitage, and she reports that the trip was brisk, but she says she did not monitor the speed continuously. Still," she said, smiling tentatively, "if you wish to file a complaint, I will bring a clerk in, and we will have an official investigation of Detective Mueller's actions and, of course, Detective Armitage's role in it."

Kennet let his gaze wander to the shelving behind her and over to the padded bench and to the open door. "I am prepared," he said slowly, "to let matters rest. What I really want is a ride."

"Of course!" said the Staff-Sergeant, rising. "Actually, you have an acquaintance here who has offered to give you a lift. Follow me, please."

"An acquaintance?" Halvorsen smiled mysteriously, moving toward the door. Kennet continued, "By the way, who's interested in *Motorcycle Mojo*?"

"That would be me!"

"Oh. You ride?"

"Yes," she said brightly. "Is that so unusual?"

"What are you riding? If I may be so bold."

"Right now, an '06 Honda Roadrunner, but I want to get something bigger. You know bikes, Mr. Forbes?"

"I know cars better. But, lead on."

Halvorsen led him down a corridor that bisected the premises, east from west. They emerged near the mud room door, where they met Kelly Armitage in civilian dress, a colourful flouncy skirt and pink blouse and a white clutch purse in one hand and car keys in the other.

"Ah, Detective," said Halvorsen. "Professor Forbes has decided to let the matter rest. Have a good evening."

Kelly nodded and smiled. Halvorsen was rapping on a door frame to a glass-walled office. She looked back. "This way, Professor."

A big-framed man in an expensive black pinstripe was sprawled in a chair behind the cluttered desk. He was holding a document file that hid his face. A deep voice rumbled.

"Well, Forbes, stirring it up again, eh? Thought you'd left those days behind you."

The document file lowered as the black suit stood up, thrusting a big paw at Kennet. Kennet broke into a smile and grasped the paw with both hands.

"Robert! How good to see you!"

"I'll leave you gentlemen to it," said Halvorsen, backing out.

Robert Kenilworth topped Kennet's six-foot height by three inches. Under the short, clipped moustache of his handsome square-cut features he also was grinning. A full head of black hair, curling at the tips, completed the picture.

"How are you, Kennet. I got your message – came right away. I'm going to look into a Thunder Bay connection – that's the story I'm going with. And besides," he said, his grin widening, "I might provide some balance in the investigation."

"Well, it's been weighted against me so far, and I'm not even a suspect. I think."

"Yes, I've seen –" Kenilworth glanced around quickly. "Let's get out of here. You must be famished. I am. Dinner's on me."

Kennet glanced at his watch. Seven o'clock. As he followed Robert's broad back, Kennet said, "What, exactly, is behind that door?" It was the door behind which was Mueller's first choice of interview room.

"That's the lockup, my son. For cops and bad guys only."

"Oh. So that's where you keep the hoses and truncheons."

"Oh no. We are a modern and enlightened law enforcement agency. We have enhanced our techniques – we have sleep deprivation, waterboarding, a continuous loop of Céline Dion – that sort of thing. Come on, come on."

Outside, the shadows had lengthened. A car door opened. A flash of a brown nyloned leg. Kelly Armitage emerged from a compact mauve Ford Focus. "Mr. Forbes? May I have a word?"

Kennet met her by the car. "Detective Armitage," he said equitably.

"It's Kelly, please. I'm off the clock now. Listen, Mr. Forbes, I sound like a real shit, I know, but I cannot shop a fellow officer with a hasty word. I –"

"I understand, Kelly. And call me Kennet. If everyone were a whistleblower, all our institutions would collapse. They survive on deceit and deception. On looking the other way. On cover-your-bum on a massive and systemic scale. Believe me, I know. From experience."

"Thanks . . . Kennet. Oh, gosh!" She glanced frantically at her watch. "I've got to run. Rod's expecting me."

"Husband? Son? Lover?"

"Friend," she said, smiling broadly. "I hope we meet under different circumstances, Kennet." She turned to leave.

"We will."

Robert Kenilworth was driving an unmarked car, a gray Chrysler sedan. They pulled onto the highway and turned east. The headframe grew larger, its ancient walls re-clad in a

64

presentable siding for the tourists. A boxy structure sat close by, with a tall metal tower slanting down into it. *That's a diamond drill rig,* he thought. *Must be.* They turned sharp left at the crossroad, Highway 584, and proceeded north. The old garage that Kennet remembered, surrounded by a graveyard of derelicts, no longer offended the eyes. On the hilltop behind where it used to squat, stood a modern building with eye-catching architecture, with long wooden arms projecting over the hillside, like the jump poles of an old-time Mississippi River steamboat.

Robert was silent as they drove the straight stretch, past the golf course, through the scattered buildings of Rosedale Point and across the causeway and bridge that spanned the west arm of Kenogamisis Lake. Jonesville had had a facelift, the shacky buildings on Main Street having been razed. Jonesville was the local name for this suburb.

Main Street stretched for a half kilometre through a stringy subdivision of modern homes until the back streets began to fill with clustered houses. They passed a vast parking lot on the left, vast for Geraldton, backstopped by a large green building with the gigantic letters of "Family Food Court" painted on the wall. The old crowbar motel on the right, deserted. Garages, the stretch of wartime houses, as they were called, built for returning veterans after the Second World War, a church, some false-fronted buildings reminiscent of the Old West, and they were downtown.

It looked sharper and cleaner than Kennet remembered. He counted three pedestrians and about the same number of parked cars. Then the familiar brick post office in front of them as they bumped across the railway tracks, the heavily rusted tracks, and turned sharp right, following the main street.

"So," said Robert. "Nostalgic? Or sick to the stomach?" He pulled into a parking lot next to the old brick theatre where a two-story building used to stand.

"I'm not sure yet," said Kennet, slowly. "It's been a long time. What's with the railway tracks? Aren't there any trains anymore?"

"The line's been decommissioned. They're ripping up the tracks. They've started at the Thunder Bay end. Don't you read the papers?

"Oh. The Kinghorn Subdivision."

"And this," said Robert, gesturing to the building alongside, "is the Cowboys Bar & Grill. Best watering hole in town, maybe the only watering hole in town. The economy's shattered here. No mining. No forestry. Minimal tourism. There is exploration, of course, mineral exploration, lots of hype but nothing guaranteed yet. Come on."

Kennet looked at Robert's suit. "I'm not dressed for a fancy restaurant."

"For Geraldton you're dressed."

The high ceiling of the Cowboys Bar & Grill was the main evidence of its movie theatre history. A long brightly lit bar, a food counter with steaming Oriental cuisine, and a floor space with faux wooden tables that accommodated two chairs apiece, and a handful of diners. Luxurious armchairs, upholstered in faux leather, pampered the customers. Kennet noted the empty band stage up front, the postage-stamp dance floor, the upholstered benches along the wall, and two modest-sized billiard tables.

Robert led them to a table, pulled out his chair, and said, "What're you having? Mine's a cold Bud."

"Canadian Lite. Thank you."

Robert placed the order at the bar, chatting up the young male bartender. When he returned, he suggested they fill their plates and get started.

The food had a Vietnamese flavour. After a few minutes, Robert said, "As I was saying back at the station. When I came in, Kelly played back the first few minutes." Robert munched between takes. "Mueller had already left. You gave him a rough time, Kennet. Some of your ambush interview technique, I reckon."

"Me, rough?"

66

"It was classic C.J. crap."

"C.J.?" Kennet raised the Canadian Lite bottle to his lips again.

"Constance Jerome Mueller. He's at the core of many a story. Or should I say butt. Some of the stories reach even us in the ivory towers. Yeah, C.J. is what he urges everyone to call him, until they get to know him."

"I'm worried, Robert."

Robert grinned as he tore off a bite of egg roll. "As I said, I'll provide the balance. And we have a highly competent forensics identification unit on scene. We call them the idents. Why, you sticking around?"

"I'm not sure what to do. I've got the time off. From Melissa, you know."

Rob gave him a steady look. "You'll stick around, professor."

"Yes, inspector." A minute or two later, he continued, "How does a C.J. get to play detective?"

"Constance Jerome got lucky, seven or eight years back. He patrolled in the London region, haunting the donut shops, fraternizing with the mall cops, that sort of thing, when he became instrumental in solving a merchant's murder. A few years as detective, however, and his superiors pulled the strings to get him transported to the boonies. Here. No offence, Kennet."

"None taken."

"Hell, I was posted here myself, early '90s. Constable 1st Class. A SOCO. We competed with the spiders for space in the basement of the old station down the road there. I know a lot of the people yet. And, I keep in touch."

"What do you know of the Fleming family? Beardmore."

"The Greenstone Mafia. We've busted them for you-name-it. Assault, B&E, theft, vandalism, drugs . . . Not murder yet. So you've met them already?"

"I met a big rough character who drives a Ram diesel 3500, painted like a circus wagon."

"That's Rawl. Rawling Fleming. A hard one. A hard character. He's served time in Stony Mountain for possession and distribution."

They returned to the food bar to pick over the desserts.

"So," said Kennet, seated again. "Who's the rest of the gang?"

"There's brother Lanny. A brother Ritch. Not a brother, really, a cousin on the mother's side, but he lives with the Flemings, joined at the hip. Another brother, Storm, doing time in the Thunder Bay lockup for a Saturday night dustup in the street. And there're other hangers-on. And there's a brother in the military – he got out of Beardmore. And I heard there was another brother, the youngest at the time. Left in the '80s and never came back. The father died about that time." He pointed to his chest. "Heart."

Robert Kenilworth leaned back in his chair and drained the bottle of Bud. "Enough of this shop talk, Kennet. Let's talk the other shop talk. Why haven't we seen you at Frank's for two months?"

"Six weeks. It's been six weeks. I spent some time in Quebec, visiting Dad. And, I stopped off in Toronto, talking to the guys at 250 Front Street West, and caught up on the industry gossip over a few lunches and dinners."

"The CBC, eh? The Canadian Bloody Corporation. Ah," said Robert, with a deprecating gesture. "Ignore me. I'm just bloody-minded tonight. CBC's still got the most intelligent programming on TV, even since you left. This murder, if it is murder, in Beardmore. It'll be a high profile case, I'm thinking, with a university professor involved. And they'll expect me to handle the political ramifications."

"We're not professors, you know, Vanderhorst and I. You need a Ph.D. to be a professor, and even then, some don't have the title. We were – well, I still am, a lecturer. A teacher."

"Still," said Robert, "it's the university. The only one in Northwestern Ontario. The regional bank where we keep our intellectual capital." Robert's black moustache twitched.

"Your office, Robert," said Kennet with a straight face, "by that analogy, would be rated, at the least, as a credit union."

Rob wagged his finger mockingly. "Don't you underestimate the underdog, Kennet. I've solved many a crime with the help of small fry."

When they left the Cowboys Bar & Grill, the brightness had faded from the sky. It occurred to Kennet that Robert had checked his BlackBerry only once, so unusual for a high-level official.

"Drive by the high school, will you, Robert?"

Robert drove down the deserted business section, the three or four blocks that qualified as the business section, and turned right. The high school lay quiet and dark, a security light burning here and there. Only the shop wing and the gymnasium broke the sprawling one-story profile of the brick structure.

"I wonder if any of the old staff are still here?" Kennet mused.

They turned east again, past the two-story brick structure that was, or used to be, the Ministry of Natural Resources. "There was one teacher," said Kennet, "who taught an introductory journalism course once. It kind of got me interested."

"Remember his name?"

"Yes. Boyce. Mr. Jared Boyce. Taught English."

"Boyce. There was a Boyce who wrote the local history book just before I came. And I still see his name in the local paper. I like to keep abreast of district news."

"History, eh? I wasn't aware he was into history. And that relics – that Beardmore relics angle. I wonder if that's what got Vanderhorst killed. If he got killed. Listen, Robert, can we get an update on that case?"

Robert plucked his BlackBerry from an inside pocket and punched a button. "Hi, who's this?" He listened. "Listen, Sherry, it's Inspector Kenilworth. Will you patch me through to the coroner's office? To a Dr. Newgate, or his assistant? Thanks."

They crossed the bridge and drove south. The sodium vapour lights lining the highway flicked on. "Hello. Dr. Newgate?" Robert turned right onto Highway 11.

"Morty, what's the story on that body from Beardmore?" Then, "Yeah, yeah. I know when office hours are. But you don't. Else why are you still there? Quit pissing around. What's the story, Morty?"

Robert listened. After a while, "And the family's been notified?" After a long pause, "Thank you, Morty. See you at the club."

Robert laid the phone on the console. He glanced at Kennet and grinned. "Play golf with him. Half of police work is having the connections. You know that, from your own career. Superiors, subordinates, informants, the couples with the .9 children and the white picket fences . . ."

They had passed the OPP detachment office and were descending the first long hill. The red sun burned on the horizon over the dark trees. It would be burning in Beardmore, thought Kennet. "Can you get Jared Boyce's address? It may be important." *The wall of the old prospect trench burned red.*

Robert picked up the phone again. "Sherry? Okay, sorry, Cathy. Inspector Kenilworth here. Can you get me a Geraldton address for a Mr. Jared Boyce? Thank you. I'll wait."

"What did you learn?" said Kennet. *Red flames licked the waters of the great lake beyond the burning forest.*

"Oh. Yes, it was Alfred Vanderhorst. Had his driver's licence on him. His wife – Cindy is her name? – was notified under twenty minutes ago. And here's the kicker. There was trauma to the base of the skull. Not likely self-inflicted. I'll get more detail tomorrow, they're still doing post-mortem."

He spoke into the phone. "Yes, Cathy." He listened. "Thank you, Cathy. You're a – you've been very helpful." He hung up.

"I almost said 'You're a doll!' Old habits are hard to break."

He accelerated a bit, the needle climbing to 110. "Jared Boyce lives on Creelman Creek Road, Wildgoose Lake, just ahead. Want to drop in?"

Chapter 7

... Thursday evening, later

A heavy-set man opened the inside wood-paneled door. Through the outer glass-paned storm door Kennet could see he was balding, with gray stubble over the ears, wearing gold-rimmed bifocals. Well, as long as he'd known him, he'd worn bifocals.

"Mr. Boyce? I'm a former student. May I speak with you?"

Boyce opened the storm door and invited him in. "You look very familiar."

"Kennet Forbes, sir." Kennet offered his hand and Boyce accepted it.

Boyce smacked his forehead. "Stupid of me! Another brain fart! Kennet! And for God's sake call me Jared. You're the teacher now. At TBU now, aren't you?"

Cupboards and counters cluttered the foyer, if that's what it was, of the A-frame home. Big timbers supporting the roof stopped at a low ceiling, probably a loft above. Behind Jared Boyce the ceiling quit, and Kennet could see a wall of windows and timbers climbing skyward. A couple of tween girls had the volume cranked up on the wide-screen TV. Boyce turned around.

"Céline. Would you and Sky mind watching downstairs for a bit? I want to talk to this man." The TV clicked dead. The two petite girls with brown complexions advanced. They gave Kennet the eye and flashed two sets of white teeth. They turned to Kennet's right as they descended the staircase that he hadn't yet noticed. Giggling drifted up the staircase.

"Come in! Come in. My granddaughter Céline, and her friend."

"Uh, Jared. I can't stay, really. I have a ride waiting. I'm helping the police investigate a case in Beardmore." At that point he realized that he had made a decision to help. "I hear that you're into local history, and I have a question."

"Fire away. But won't you sit down for a moment?"

"No, thanks. It's about the Beardmore relics. Heard of them?"

Jared's hand rose to grip his chin, and through bifocals he regarded Kennet with gray eyes that glistened. "I should say, Kennet. I rediscovered the site in the fall of 1990, using a grid pattern search. And one of your colleagues, a Vander-something, was asking me about that recently."

"Alfred Vanderhorst. Yes. The case is about him. He's been found dead. At the site."

"Good Lord! What happened?"

"I can't tell you, Mr. – uh, Jared. Actually, we don't know anything to tell yet. So you gave him the GPS coordinates?"

"Well, no. That handy little instrument was a military secret back then. No, but I keep detailed notes on my field research, and so I was able to lead him to the site. But the whole area has been transformed. A helluva lot of bushwhacking it took. That was two weeks or so ago. I advised him to cut a trail in. I was so happy that someone professional was going to examine the site again. I had told no one of that rediscovery, to protect it from vandals and souvenir hunters. But Walter Kellerman – you know Kellerman?" Kennet nodded. "Kellerman told him if anyone could help him it would be me. So he tracked me down."

"Jared, do you know of any reason why someone who was not an archaeologist would believe the site was valuable?"

"It is valuable, and not just to academics. Properly excavated and written up in the journals, and with a good road and an interpretive centre and promotion, it could become a tourist destination. In this economy, every tourist dollar counts."

"What do you think an archaeologist might find there?"

"Aside from a few metal slivers, not much. But it could be evidence that the relics actually reposed there at one time. It could disprove a hoax."

Out on the back deck, Kennet remarked, "You've got a fine home. You're on the lake here?" He peered around the corner. A fireball filtered through the trees on the lakeside of the Boyce residence. His eyes traced a blood trail that stretched across a narrow bay and led directly to the red metal roof of the A-frame.

"Thanks. That's my new roof. Cost a small fortune. Well, a big fortune for a pensioner."

Back on the highway, they sped through a dark forest, broken occasionally by the entrance to a road that the forest soon swallowed. On some stretches they could see the red fireball dropping into the darkness.

"You should have come in," said Kennet.

"I find," said Robert, "that my presence tends to inhibit conversation. Sometimes."

"He didn't say much. Just that he showed Vanderhorst where the relics were found."

"Okay. That answers one question."

"And," Robert continued, "I think you can find other answers that the police can't. Are you sticking around?"

"Yes."

They rode together in companionable silence until some scattered structures materialized at roadside. Jellicoe. Robert slowed to 70. A pair of gas pumps in front of a log building. The Jellicoe Trading Post, Kennet remembered. Soft lighting glowed within, and an OPEN sign blinked. Robert slowed significantly to cross the railway track. His speed crept up again.

Robert spoke. "Are you coming back, then? To Frank's?"

"Why, of course. Why wouldn't I? What's the latest project?"

"A '69 Dodge Swinger. Four-barrel. V-8."

"Yeah? Really? Wow."

"Yeah, the guys have the idea of restoring it as a race car. And then taking it to Minneapolis in the spring to compete in the vintage car racing meet."

"Wow." Kennet was silent for a while. Then, "Well, I won't be there this Saturday. Nor you, probably. But tell me about it. What's been done, and what we have to do."

They chatted animatedly about the project until they pulled into the Regency Motel. "Coming in?" said Kennet.

"Naw. I need my beauty sleep. I'm at a B & B in Geraldton. See you tomorrow."

Kennet looked around. Vehicles jammed the parking lots of both the one-story units and the two-story building across the way. They included some heavy-duty trucks.

He scraped away a fragment of yellow tape on the frame before turning the key to No. 39. He flicked on the lights. Nothing had changed. The messy beds. The disarray of clothing. The debris on the floor near the only table. The contents of a briefcase dumped on the master bed. He walked swiftly through to the back bedroom and checked. Yes, there was a made-up bed. He returned to the living room/bedroom cum kitchenette.

He had left the door open. He went to his truck, unlocked it, and retrieved the overnight bag and the clothing he had neatly arranged on the back seat when he had changed in the bush. He also snatched up the shoes and the laptop case.

The first order of business was a shower. After he had toweled off, he paraded around in fresh skivvies and bare feet, avoiding the particles on the floor. He flicked on the TV to catch the CBC news. Peter Mansbridge was assuring the nation that everything was more or less under control. Only the normal round of fraud, scandal, violence, and mayhem. Kennet heard a rapping sound. He turned the TV off. Someone was knocking tentatively at the door.

He had not brought a bathrobe. He hastily threw on trousers and shirt and padded in bare feet over to the door. A slightly built man stood there, blinking. "Can I come in?"

"I don't know. Can't this wait?"

The man glanced around furtively. "It's about the guy who was beat up."

"Come in." Kennet closed the door. "What's your name?"

Beneath a mop of sweat-dried brown hair, the man's face displayed his strain. "I'd rather not say."

"Come on. Everyone knows everybody here. It'll be easy to find out."

The man wrung the cap he held in his hands. "Yeah, I guess. Alfred. Al Cummings. Ol' Bull told me you're Forbes. Mr. Forbes."

"Ol' Bull?"

"Bull Kellerman. It's Bullshit Kellerman, really." He flashed a nervous smile. "He told me what you did today. How you made Rawl back down."

"What information do you have on the beating of Henderson, Al?"

"The police talked to me," he said. "Can I sit down?" Kennet gestured to an armchair. It dawned on him that this was the man whom the detectives had been questioning in the restaurant.

"The police talked to me, but I ain't saying nothin' to Mueller. That son of a bitch. He'd put the blame on me. You can tell the police if you want. Just don't say it was me."

"Tell them what, Al? It's getting late."

He gave an up-from-under look. "I know why they beat up that kid, that Henderson."

"Tell me."

Al Cummings launched into a convoluted story. It seemed that Vanderhorst had very quickly achieved a local reputation as a scrounger and a deadbeat. He'd charged items at The Hook'n Bullet and never made good on them. He'd tried to enlist free labour for his project. He'd bummed a bucket here, a shovel there, and scrap lumber elsewhere. Two days ago he'd shown up at the Con Empire mine where Al Cummings worked as a casual labourer. The property was gated, but he'd found the gate dummy-locked, so he had driven up in his panel truck, alone, and been confronted by Cummings. He'd wanted to borrow a Wajak.

"A Wajak?"

"It's a water pump. You know, a portable pump. The Ministry uses them, to fight fires. Forest fires. And they're using them all over the bush here, to wash down the rock after they've stripped the dirt off."

Cummings did not have the authority to lend a Wajak. So he had escorted Vanderhorst underground to talk to the foreman where he was supervising the removal of some loose, as Cummings called it, and the insertion of rock bolts to secure the ceiling. The foreman, Christie, had chewed Cummings' ear off, told him to get the fuck back to work, and to throw that bum off the property. Cummings led the way back, and as he was trotting down the drift towards the shaft, he noticed Vanderhorst wasn't behind him. He found him squatting in front of an ore car, beside a muck pile beneath a stope – the terminology baffled Kennet – and in the dim light of the bare incandescent bulbs, he saw Cummings tuck something shiny in his shirt pocket.

Yesterday, Cummings had been in the restaurant – he didn't work every day, or all day – only when they called him in. "Do you have a drink?" he asked Kennet.

"I'll get you a glass of water."

"Nothing harder?" said Cummings, hopefully.

"Just water." After Cummings had taken a swallow, he continued.

CORRECTION on p.77
CHANGE he saw Cummings tuck
TO he saw Vanderhorst tuck

The Flemings, Lanny and Ritch, who never seemed to work, had been killing time, and had diverted themselves by ragging Cummings. They asked to see the high-grade he had smuggled out of the mine.

"Well," said Cummings, "I never even seen any high-grade there, but I told them Vanderhorst had, that I seen him put a nugget in his pocket."

Later, the Flemings had accosted him, had come knocking on his back door. His mother was out, she was a custodian at the school, and they had wormed it out of him that he had seen, not a nugget, but a silver star.

"A silver star?" said Kennet.

"Yeah. I don't know what else to call it. Like a marshall's badge, you know, like the one in *3:10 to Yuma*, the one starring Russell Crowe. And boy, did that Lanny go crazy then! He wanted to know every detail then, but I had nothing more to tell him. He treated me pretty rough. Slapped me around, tore some buttons off my shirt."

Cummings set the water glass down. "So I figure they went after Vanderhorst then. Maybe they killed him. Then they went after that poor kid Henderson. And," he said, rising, "if they find out I told anybody, they'll be after me, or they'll get Rawl after me. He always sticks up for them. He done time, you know. He's one ugly son of a bitch." The strain had returned to his face. "You can't let it slip that I told you. You can tell the police, though. I don't trust that Mueller not to say it come from me."

"I'm going to have to tell the police about you, Al. You're a witness." Fear stabbed through Cummings' eyes. "But I won't be talking to Mueller." Cummings' shoulders slumped, and his eyes cleared.

After Cummings left, Kennet booted up the laptop as he balanced it on his lap. He checked his mailbox – nothing urgent. He e-mailed Susan, explaining that he'd be a day or two out of town, and that he'd phone tomorrow. He checked the weather forecast – Thunder Bay sunny, Geraldton rainy.

He closed the laptop. His eyes settled on the debris littering the carpet. He got down on his knees and fingered the rusty-brown pieces. Some seemed to be same sort of shards he had seen on the path and on the excavation mound. Most looked metallic. He picked out a rusted nail with a square shaft, obviously hand-forged. He fingered a three-inch length of a Swede saw blade – his father had proudly displayed a complete Swede saw on his den wall. The remnant of a bottle cap. A chunk of charcoal . . .

Tomorrow the maid would sweep up the litter and it would never be seen again. He did not feel qualified to judge what should and should not be saved. The pieces on the tabletop were laid out helter-skelter, in no particular order that he could see. The empty plastic bags had codes inscribed with a felt-pen marker. At one point the artifacts had been sorted.

He poked around in the cupboard below the sink and came up with a dustpan and short-handled brush and disposable white plastic bags. He selected two bags and arranged one inside the other. He swept the tabletop first and then the carpet, and deposited the mess, including the collection bags, in the white plastic bags and knotted them tight. His eyes swept the room. The clothing and personal items – he'd pack them up.

The stuff in the main room he crammed into the suitcase he found lying on a shelf above the open-sided wardrobe. The stuff in the back bedroom he relegated to the two gym bags he found there. In them he also tucked away the personal items from the bathroom. He had made the assumption that the back room was Henderson's territory, that Vanderhorst would have commandeered the main room and the artifact display. Henderson, when he recovered, could identify his former partner's personal items.

During the night he woke up. Rain was drumming on the roof. It would put out the fire, he thought, illogically. It would put out the fire that was burning up the country. He didn't remember dozing off again.

MAP 4

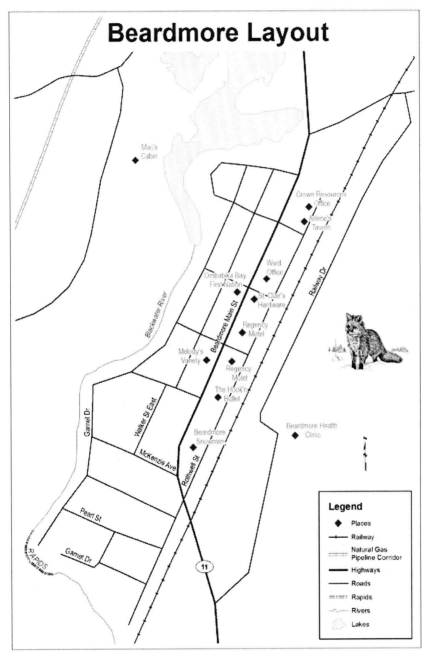

Beardmore Layout

Chapter 8

Friday, August 14th . . .

Kennet realized that he had been turning restlessly for a while. He opened his eyes. The travel alarm said 5:41.

Shaved and dressed, he flicked on the television and found CNN. He made himself coffee and watched the news for a while. He took the white plastic bags and opened the door. Dawn was well advanced. Alice's Restaurant was open and busy and some of the parking spaces were already free. He opened the hatch of his truck and deposited the bags.

He returned to the room, turned his cell on and slipped it into his shirt pocket, put the room key and his wallet into his trousers pocket, switched off the TV and closed the door behind him. He tried the knob. It had locked. Across the highway cum main street the business signs identified a variety store, a branch bank, a post office, and a liquor store. Behind them to the west stood a few houses and beyond them a bank of mist hovered, catching the sun. The river's there, thought Kennet. To his left, down main street, across from The Hook'n Bullet and the big snowman, stood a line of houses that reflected their histories, and a derelict garage.

He set off at a brisk pace, taking the sidewalk north past the concrete facade of the Regency. Large empty lots separated the scattered structures, the grass closely clipped. Fires or demolitions would have created the emptiness, and apparently the municipality maintained appearances. Several structures displayed painted steel-clad exteriors, no doubt covering a multitude of blemishes. On the west side, a large new building displayed a sign with an unpronounceable aboriginal word. He passed a hardware store and the municipal building. Arlene's Tavern sat back from the street behind a large unpaved parking area. It proved to be a blocky two-story building with a covered veranda. Hours ran from 9:00 to 7:00. Arlene had little desire, apparently, to capture the breakfast crowd. Except at Alice's Restaurant, the breakfast crowd was still abed. The last building on the east side was another steel-clad one with the sign for ambulance service. Across from it stood a tiny wooden church. Thereafter the bush began. The highway curved left and crossed the river.

He passed a rock cut and turned east up a gravel road. A dull, rhythmic motor noise which emanated from beyond the bushes to his left suddenly increased in speed and intensity. The ear-battering sound rose in pitch as a bright red helicopter rose into the sky. Beneath it hung a gigantic butterfly net, the net pinched below the belly of the chopper, the hoop open to the ground.

Through the bushes he noted a sprawling structure in a vast field that, he recalled, housed both the ice rink and curling rink. In a hundred metres the railway crossed the road. He looked north up the rusting tracks; the tracks scurried around a curve. He looked south. The tracks stretched between trees and brush that threatened to engulf them. The town had disappeared. The chopper had disappeared.

Beyond the tracks, a large sign proclaimed Crown Resources Inc., and in smaller letters beneath, Consolidated Empire Property. A few metres beyond, a gate barred the road. He turned south, following a gravel road labeled Railway Drive. At the corner on the west side, junky trucks and rusting machines and rotting wood structures littered a lot upon which the bush was encroaching. On the east side a few structures stood, or in some cases, leaned. Some offered evidences of vacancy. In many cases the bush was colonizing the yards. On the west side a green space occupied the area between the road and the railway, with manicured fields and a long narrow stand of young poplar.

He came across a small house with a large yard surrounded by a picket fence. Some of the slats of the fence, once painted white, leaned askew. Some were missing, all were scored deeply with rot. Two dormers projected from a south-facing roof covered with deteriorating asphalt shingles. Heavily weathered clapboard walls supported the roof.

Beside a cinder driveway in the unmowed grass sat a battered dark green Chevy pickup. Dispersed among some crumbling outbuildings were derelict vehicles, assorted junk, old lumber, a pile of scabby firewood, aluminum boats, and three snowmobiles covered with clear polyethylene plastic. Between the castoffs, the grass and weeds rioted. At the end of the long cinder driveway sat an unpainted wooden garage, doors gaping. Inside the dark interior a slim figure leaned over a gleaming yellow machine.

Kennet paused. The cinders crunched as he approached the doors. *Cinders from the steam train era.* The figure looked up. "Howdy," said Kennet. The dirt floor of the garage held assorted junk, a work bench, and three mud-spattered dirt bikes.

A dark-haired young man looked at him with steady eyes. "Looking for trouble?" he said quietly.

"Nope. Looking at your machine. I'll leave if that's a problem."

"You ride?" said the young man.

"Used to. That's a Yamaha V-Star. What is it, a 650 Cruiser?"

"An 1100 Classic, actually." He patted the chrome front fender. "I made a few changes too."

"You passed me yesterday," said Kennet pleasantly. "On the road from Nipigon."

"I never passed no bike. Met some, though."

"No, no. I was driving a truck. I recognize the helmet." Kennet gestured to the helmet perched behind the padded saddle. "And you passed Hillcrest Park that morning, didn't you?"

"Yeah. You a detective or something?"

"My name's Kennet." He extended his hand.

The owner of the motorcycle looked down at the hand, and after two heartbeats, gripped it firmly. "Saxon," he said, face giving nothing away.

Kennet continued, "That's the insignia of the Princess Patricia's Canadian Light Infantry. Are you serving?"

"Yeh. Out of Edmonton. Just rotated out of Kandahar. Got a short furlough. How do you know the Pats?"

"I worked alongside them from Kandahar airfield. That was in '06. No, no," Kennet held up a hand, "I was never a soldier. I was attached to the CBC news service."

"A reporter!" Kennet detected a sneer. "So you're chasing that story of the dead prof, eh?"

"Actually, I had no idea he would be dead. I was the one who I found him. And no, I am not a practicing journalist. Not anymore. I've changed professions. I'm a teacher."

Saxon looked at him speculatively. "Well, I guess you seen dead bodies before, if you were in Kandahar."

"Yes. Too many. Almost joined them, one time." Kennet touched the skin lightly beneath his right eye.

"Yeah? You got that –?" Saxon broke off and looked over Kennet's shoulder. A big garishly painted pickup was pulling into the driveway.

Saxon's tone changed. "I guess you know my brother," he said evenly. "Rawl?"

Rawling Fleming braked sharply beside the house and leapt out. He strode toward them, fury in every step.

"What the fuck's *he* doing here?" He stopped one pace from Kennet, hands on hips, anger rippling through him. "You're trespassing. Get the fuck off my property!"

Kennet looked him in the eyes. Then, turning his head carefully to look at Saxon, he said, "Your brother here . . . " He knew what was coming. When Rawling swung he was ready, leaning his head and upper body sharply back. The wind from Rawling's blow fanned his face. The momentum of the blow propelled Rawling forward. Rawling lost his balance and stepped into the side of the Yamaha Classic 1100. As the machine toppled, Saxon grabbed the forks and handlebars and by main force, stopped the machine from falling.

Immediately he was on his big brother, stiff fingers of his left hand jabbing Rawling's chest. Each jab sent Rawling backward.

"I warned you, Rawl," he said with quiet fury, "never, never, never," each 'never' reinforced by a jab, "touch my bike!" Rawling's face exhibited a pained surprise.

When Rawling's backside hit the work bench, Saxon dropped his arm. Rawling's face contorted. "Goddamn you, Sax! I can still give you a licking!"

Saxon looked at him cooly. "Yes, Rawl, you could try. You could sucker punch me too, and you'd be winning. For about four seconds. But then," Saxon took a step backward, "my training would kick in, and I'd probably kill you."

Rawling looked stunned. Suddenly he grinned. "Damn it, Sax. You sounded just like Pa there. He'd've been proud." His face darkened again. He waved his arm toward Kennet. "I want that son of a bitch off my property!"

"Last time I looked, it was mother's property." Saxon turned his head and looked at Kennet without expression.

Kennet raised his hands, palms outward. "I don't want to make trouble, Saxon. We'll talk later." Saxon nodded. Kennet spun on his heels and walked swiftly up the drive. From the garage came the raised voice of Rawling.

"What the fuck's he doing here?"

"We were talking." Saxon's voice was still cool. "About the Yamaha."

"And where the fuck's Lanny and Ritch? I told them to be ready. The lazy bastards still in bed?"

The house door slammed. Looking back, Kennet saw a gangly man with greasy blond hair stretching and yawning on the tiny porch. "What the fuck's the racket?" he said, looking toward the garage. "And who scooped the last of the coffee? The jar's empty."

Kennet walked south again, toward a wall of trees. Houses now clustered together, houses with painted fences and sun decks and occasionally an RV in the yard or a canopied motorboat on a trailer. Beyond them, to the east, appeared to be more homes. A large sign standing on the lawn of a large two-story building proclaimed Beardmore Health Clinic. At the tree line, a cross-road headed west across the tracks, and he took it. He was a block from the motel. He turned north on the gravel road that paralleled the railway.

In the restaurant he ordered the breakfast special – two eggs, hash browns, bacon, toast, and coffee. He placed a side order of orange juice, which arrived in a bottle. There were three other customers. Looking around, he determined that a dozen people could be seated, in a pinch. And it would pinch.

His phone rang. It was Robert Kenilworth. "Oh hi, Robert. I would've called you earlier but I didn't have your number. Can I get back to you in twenty minutes? . . . Fine." He programmed in Robert's number.

One customer had his nose buried in a newspaper. The other two studied their coffee cups. As he ate, Kennet addressed the reader. "Excuse me, sir. Is that *The Lakehead Journal*?"

"Yes," said the man, lowering the paper. It was the handsome Mac, the man he'd met in the restaurant yesterday.

"I was just wondering where you got it. That today's?"

"Yes. At Melody's, across the road." He raised the paper again and resumed reading.

Kennet left a loonie tip. As he was paying Alice in the motel lobby, she volunteered that his room would be cleaned before lunch. He asked her who Mac was.

She lowered her voice. "That's Mac King. The Beardmore Hermit. He's a civil guy, but he lives alone in a log shack back in the bush and he loves his privacy. He's been known to run off trail bikers and sledders with a gun." Then, in an elevated voice, "Thank you, Mr. Forbes."

In his room, Kennet pulled out the local telephone directory. There was no listing for King. There was for Kellerman and for Fleming and for Cummings. He speed-dialed Robert Kenilworth on his cell.

"Hi, Robert. Got something for you." He relayed what Al Cummings had told him about the Flemings' interest in Vanderhorst, skipping over the "marshall's badge" reference, for he discounted Cummings' description of the item.

"Christ, Kennet. Good work. The day's just begun and you have a lead for us already?"

"I lead an active life. Hell, just this morning Rawling Fleming threw a punch at me."

"Christ, Kennet. I hope he's not badly hurt."

"Nobody got hurt."

"Sorry to hear that."

"That's no way for an inspector of police to talk."

"Ah, *mea culpa*. Sometimes I'm just too human."

Kennet walked over to The Hook'n Bullet. He waited as Kellerman and an older woman with a kerchief around her hair – Mrs. Kellerman, he guessed – served a half dozen customers.

Walter Kellerman finally turned to him. "And what can I do you for this morning, professor?"

"Good morning. And is this your good wife, Walter?"

"Yes, indeed. Marta, this is Kennet I was telling you about." Marta nodded and grinned. She had dark good looks even at her age.

"Walter, you were telling me that someone could have shown me where Vanderhorst was working. Who was that?"

"Reg Laroque. Bushworker. Currently unemployed. Like most of Beardmore, more's the pity. He did a job for that guy. Marta?" He turned to his wife. "Reg lives on Garnet. What's the number?"

"I don't memorize house numbers, Bull," she shot back, tempered with a smile. "Look it up."

Kellerman picked up a softcover volume from a stack of similar volumes and thumbed through it. "Here it is. Réjean Laroque. 396 Garnet Drive. Know where Garnet is?" Kennet shook his head.

"Come outside." Kellerman picked up a stick and sketched a street map in the dirt. "Here we are. Here's the main street. Over there," he pointed south, and then continued drawing, "is McKenzie Avenue. Follow it past the school, here, to the river road. That's Garnet. Turn left, for about two blocks. 396 Garnet. Reg's an early riser. Like me."

From the doorway, Marta grunted in disgust. "No one gets up at four in the morning, *except* you."

"By the way," said Kennet. "You know Mac King? Of course you do. He's not listed. I was just curious."

"King," said Kellerman expansively, "is K-u-e-n-g. Everyone pronounces it 'king'. And no, K-u-e-n-g is not in the book either. Mac lives off the grid – no power, no telephone, no TV. He's a throwback to the pre-Industrial Age. Got a battery radio though. And he reads. Got quite a library. He's a character. Like me."

Marta snorted.

"By the way," said Kennet. "I saw a chopper take off at the Community Centre. It was supporting the biggest butterfly net I've ever seen. Do they grow that big here?"

"Ah. You saw the LongRanger 207 with a dream-catcher. The pilot will fly a grid pattern and capture electronic signals that bounce back from the bedrock. It's a geophysical tool the mining companies use."

As Kennet was leaving, Kellerman passed him the directory. "They're free," he said. "Got a stack of 'em to dispense."

McKenzie Avenue ran two blocks toward the river, past older homes and a modern brick-and-stone facility that had to be the school. A gravel street ran along the bank of the river. No fence or guard rails separated the street from the bank, about two metres high, that dropped quickly to the river. Mist clung in small clouds to the water. There were no houses on the bank. He passed a house with a hand-lettered sign, OZZIES BAITS. Laroque's home was a modest bungalow with a dark blue older model GMC pickup in the drive. A man was sitting on the tailgate, a cigarette dangling from his lips.

"'Ello," he said. He was a dark, small-framed man, unshaven, probably in his fifties, in slippers and checked flannel shirt. The shirt pocket had a bulge under the flap.

"Mr. Laroque? I was just talking to Bull Kellerman. Said you could help me?"

"Ah yes? Maybe he bullshit you." He grinned as he tugged the stub of a roll-your-own from his mouth and expelled a cloud.

"I'm Kennet." Kennet extended his hand. Laroque grasped it limply and dropped his hand.

"*Réjean.* Dey call me Reg. Nice day, eh?" He waved his fag toward the river. "My wife," he continued, "she make me smoke outside. *Câlisse!*"

"Bull tells me you did a job for that professor guy."

"Yah, yah. I cut trail for him. Use my own saw, my own gas, my own oil. Use my own truck to get dere. And den de son of a bitch," he threw down his butt and then jumped on it with one slipper, "he don' wan' pay me! Say I'm doing service for *l'université. Câlisse!*"

"You tell anyone else?"

"Sure I tell ever'one!" He gesticulated wildly. "Tell ever'one he's son of a bitch! Fin'lly he pay me a few bucks. 'Nough for maybe gas."

"Did you tell anyone else where the trail was?"

Laroque seated himself again. He looked at Kennet slyly. "Dat guy got himself dead, eh? Not too many people sorry. Not me anyway." He paused. "Why you wan' know?"

"I worked with the guy. I had no great love for him, but he's dead. I'd like to find who did it."

Laroque dropped his eyes. "No. No. Not me, sir. I don' know not'ing."

Kennet tried another tactic. *"Vous êtes citoyen, monsieur? Vous êtes un homme responsable? Vous êtes canadien, n'est-ce pas? Fier? Honnête?"* He added in a confidential tone, *"Courageux?"*

Laroque sat up straight. His eyes popped wide. *"Oui!"* he said fiercely. *"J'suis canadien! J'ai des grandes boules!"* The tension drained from his body, and a smile broke out. *"Ouin, monsieur. Il faut poser cette question à ma femme."*

"I believe you!" Kennet laughed. "But I still need to know."

"Ah Chriss." Laroque gave Kennet a straight look. "You de guy who tol' dat Raw-ling to fuck off, eh?"

Kennet said nothing.

Laroque sighed. "It was dat Ritch fellow. He come 'round here, ask me dat question, Where da trail? Where da trail? I know dose guys, dey run all over d' country 'ere, wit' dere bike, dere truck, dere boat, dere sled, make trouble all d' time. I don' wan' no trouble. He could slash m' tires, eh? He don't say dat, but he look at dem when he ask me. I know he know dat road, so I tell him where, exactly, da trail is." He paused. "I do wrong, eh?"

"You're not responsible for his actions. Thank *you*, Reg." Kennet offered his hand again. Reg took it and squeezed. "I'm going to have to pass this on to the police, Reg."

91

Laroque shrugged. "Dat don' worry me," he said, extracting a tobacco pouch from his shirt pocket and rolling another fag.

Kennet returned to the main street by way of Pearl Street, noting some newer residences and several well-kept yards. The sun was peeping over the hills on the town's eastern border. He punched the speed dial and relayed the new information to Robert Kenilworth. Robert said he was at the Greenstone detachment office. At Melody's Variety, across from the motel, he bought a newspaper. The grinning matron behind the counter, well fleshed out, was dying to speak. "You're Professor Forbes, aren't you! From the university?"

"Kennet Forbes, yes. Don't tell me. You are Melody, right?"

She tittered, and then said, in a voice that cracked on the high notes, "Yes I am! Do you remember my daughter, Mr. Forbes? Crystal Gayle Mallory. We named her after the singer. You know, Loretta Lynn's sister. She took your class this year."

"Crystal? Certainly. A bright student. I didn't know she was from Beardmore?"

"Yes she is!" said Melody brightly. "She's cook assistant this summer, at the Buffalo Grass Gold camp up the 801. She'll be in this afternoon. She'd love to say hello, I'm sure."

"And I'd love to say hello back. See you again, Mrs. Mallory."

"Melody."

"Melody."

Chapter 9

|||||||||||||||||||||||||||||||||||||||||||||||||||||||||||||||||| THE BEARDMORE RELICS

. . . Friday morning

Kennet walked across the highway to The Hook'n Bullet. This time Kellerman was ensconced on The Grouch's Chair. "Bull," said Kennet. "Do you mind if I call you Bull?"

"Everybody does."

"Bull, I see that the Crown Resources property is gated off. How do I talk to whoever's in charge."

"You do get around!" Kellerman shifted his weight. "Well, that would be Daegal Nordstrom. Everybody calls him Dan. He's staff geologist, and the project manager. His office is next door to Arlene's – Arlene's Tavern. That two-story building, just before the ambulance, that used to be the mine office out at Leitch. You know the Leitch? Used to be the richest gold mine in Canada, richer than Croesus, richer than King Midas, who played checkers with him, before he opened the string of muffler shops. They moved nuggets around the board as big as hen's eggs. Round eggs, they were, and flat. The Leitch's up the 580 road. You know it – the road to the lake, to Poplar Lodge Park. Closed in '65, just after

I come here. I came for the fishing one summer, and I never left. Will never leave, I guess. Fine country. Excellent country. You done any fishing?"

"I have, as a matter of fact. I see by your hat," Kennet nodded to the fedora with the hand-tied flies, "you're a fly fisherman. I've done that. Haven't for ages, though."

"Well, stick around. There's a stream I've been meaning to try. Never seem to find much free time in spring or the summer. But I take a week off after the spawning in September, and go for the wily trout on the North Shore streams. Between Dorion and Wawa. Marta's good at handling things when I'm away."

"About that Dan Nordstrom –"

"Yeah, yeah. You might find him at the office. Else, he's at the mine. They don't like unauthorized people at the mine, might give you a hassle."

"Another thing I've been meaning to ask, Bull," said Kennet, tapping the rolled up newspaper on his thigh. "Who's the oldest miner around here? Who might've worked at the Consolidated Empire in the old days."

"Now that," said Kellerman, straightening himself perceptibly, "is a question. Never been asked that. Let me see." Kellerman stroked his chin in the time-honoured gesture of the thinker.

"Most of the fellows I know, were prospectors. Still *are* prospectors. The ones who haven't moved away, to condos in Arizona, or condos in the sky. Hardrock miners, I've never asked about. There's Mac Kueng, of course, who was here when Christ left Jellicoe. Don't know if he worked underground. Wait a minute."

He dropped his hand and wagged a finger at Kennet. "The oldest prospector has got to be old man Carlson. Wes Carlson. Might be he mined too. A prospector does a lot of things to earn his daily biscuits. Yep," he said reminiscently, "old man Carlson. In his nineties now. A real relic. Pushing a hundred. Haven't seen him for ages."

"Still live around here?"

"He lives down the road." Kellerman jerked his thumb toward the north. "You follow the road, maybe twenty klicks, you'll see a *Lakehead Journal* box on the shoulder. That's old man Carlson. Just past the 801."

He looked at Kennet speculatively. "This all about Vanderhorst?"

"I feel a certain responsibility, Bull. I'm just nosing around. That's what I do best. And I'd appreciate your discretion. I don't want to become an object of curiosity."

Kellerman gave him a slow wink. "That's my job," he said.

Kennet returned to his motel room. It was still messy. He opened the newspaper, scanned the heads, and found a small item about a body recovered from the bush near Beardmore. The item was buried in a regional community notes column. The police, it said, were not releasing the name of the victim pending notification of family. There were five lines. *Five Lines for Vanderhorst.* That could well be his epitaph.

He dug into his kit bag and pulled out the historical newsletter the lady at the Ward Office had given him. It was a publication of the Nipigon Museum in 1982. On page 3 was a reproduction of a booklet put out by the Royal Ontario Museum in 1966, titled *The Beardmore Relics: Hoax or History?* The article described each of the three artifacts – a sword, an axehead, and an object described as either a shield handle or a rattle – and there were photographs of each. There seemed to be no question about their authenticity. There was a question about the veracity of the finder, a prospector named James Edward Dodd. Eddie Dodd had lived in Port Arthur – the city that amalgamated with Fort William to become the City of Thunder Bay. Dodd worked for the Canadian National Railway and prospected in his spare time.

Dodd brought the relics to the ROM in 1936. He claimed to have retrieved them while working on his claim. *He had been sampling an exposed nearly vertical quartz vein,* the article said, *on a claim near Beardmore on May 24, 1931.* After blasting through a tangle of roots, the relics had been exposed lying on the bedrock. Thereafter the relics wove a tangled tale until they ended up at the ROM, and the investigation that followed wove the tangle more tightly. Kennet skimmed that section. The article concluded by saying the artifacts lay in limbo in the ROM, the evidence to support their being found near Beardmore being so questionable. Perhaps Norsemen did reach Lake Nipigon at one point, the author said. *Perhaps some day,* the article ended, *unequivocal evidence will be uncovered to support that theory. At present, there is none.*

If Dodd were prospecting in that area, the old Warneford Road, presumably for gold, perhaps a motive for Vanderhorst's murder lay in that direction. He would sound out Nordstrom, the geologist. He pulled out his laptop, booted up, and dashed off a note to Peter Sheridan: "Expect you know about our colleague from the OPP. Cindy's been notified. Am nosing things out." Daughter Susan told him she was going to join an athletic club. When she pinched her waist, she could feel the fat. That was unacceptable. And not to forget dinner on Sunday night. Alexei would be there. There were a few e-mails dealing with matters related to his work at the university, and some junk mail that had slipped through the filters, which he assigned to the trash.

Someone knocked lightly on the door and turned a key in the lock. A middle-aged woman in a maid's apron pushed the door open.

"Oh, I'm sorry, sir. I'll come back."

"No, come in. Please." She entered, leaving the door open. "You must be Jennifer. Alice told me."

She stood there with towels folded across her bent arm. "Yes, sir. I don't want to interrupt, sir."

"Listen, I'm assisting the police. Can you tell me how you found the vic – . . . that poor man?"

"I told the police all that, sir." She was biting her lip.

"I'd be very grateful."

"Well," she said, glancing around, "I guess it's alright. You're staying here, right? Living here?"

"Yes."

She described entering the room about the same time yesterday morning. She had heard snoring from the back room, which was highly unusual. Usually the occupants had gone for the day. And Vanderhorst's bed was made up. She had noticed she was stepping on rocky debris on the floor. The snoring sounded wrong, so she tiptoed to the bedroom. Henderson was lying on his back, fully clothed, in the bed that was still made up. She could see blood on the pillow. He was breathing really heavily, through his mouth, jaws slack. She immediately ran to the office to report.

"Was there anything about the room that was unusual? Or about the victim?"

"About the mess on the floor, you mean? Well, I see someone's cleaned that up, sir. That Mr. Henderson, now, there was something peculiar. All his pockets were turned out. And the stuff in his luggage scattered. As if they were dumped. Even the other gentleman's. His suitcase, I mean. And briefcase."

The scene-of-crime officers, thought Kennet, had sifted through the mess and then left it in further disarray. "Thank you, Jennifer. I'm leaving for now." As he left, he placed a five-dollar bill discreetly on the side table.

He took the gravel road that ran behind the motel – Rothwell Street, according to the sign. He walked north, paralleling the railway track. On the left very few buildings lined the street. Some appeared to be facing Main Street across long empty lots. In a bunch of trees on the right he came upon a graveyard. It was a graveyard for worn-out snow machines. They were the granddaddies of the modern snowmobile, products of Bombardier factories, looking like giant, legless beetles. Kennet remembered his father telling him about these snow buses, for they had been used in the logging industry in the forties and fifties to navigate unplowed bush roads. The steering apparatus guided a set of skis at the front of the machine, and an engine located in the rear powered an axle with a pair of sprocket wheels that drove rubber belts that resembled bulldozer treads. Inside the treads were rubber-tired wheels. The junked machines he encountered had no skis or treads.

There were four nearly intact machine bodies lined up, noses oriented to the street. Kennet approached the one which still retained a battered coat of orange paint. He tried the passenger door of the cab section. It opened. He peered inside. The interior had been gutted.

The Crown Resources office sat back from the street, like Arlene's Tavern, except that it was oriented to the gravel street behind it. He paused at the bottom of a short flight of stairs. A piece of cake. He climbed easily, and entered an enclosed porch, and knocked on the inner door. Someone sang out, "Come in!"

He was standing in a long lobby. In front of him, an open door to a living room. To his right, a counter piled high with documents. There was no one around.

"Can I help you?" a female voice said.

He stepped up to the counter and peered over. A woman with long auburn hair was tapping away on a keyboard in front of a monitor.

"Yes. I'd like to see Mr. Nordstrom."

Without turning her head, the woman shouted, "Dan!"

A well-built man in a short-sleeved tan shirt filled the office doorway, sandy hair and square-cut features. "Yes, Ioanna?"

"Someone to see you." She kept typing.

Kennet moved forward, extending his hand. "Hello. Mr. Nordstrom? Kennet Forbes. I'm hoping you can help me."

Nordstrom had a firm grip. "Come in. Don't mind the mess. And don't mind Ioanna. She's barely office broken." Ioanna flashed him a smile.

Nordstrom offered him a seat on a settee, and sat beside him. An open laptop sat on his desk. The multi-paned window beyond admitted the sunlight. "Just call me Dan. Kennet, is it?"

"Yes. I came up from the university looking for Alfred Vanderhorst, who hadn't reported in. I guess you've heard."

Dan sighed. "Oh yeah. It's all around town. Unfortunate, that. Drowned in an old pit?"

"Possibly. I understand he paid the mine a visit."

"Oh yeah. He got Fergie's shirt in a knot! Ferguson Christie, he's our foreman. We're in process of dewatering the workings of the old Con Empire, and rehabilitating the drifts. We discourage visitors. A liability issue, you know. An old mine is a dangerous place, a very dangerous place. Even an operating mine is, for that matter."

"Just how old is the mine?"

"Well, now," said Dan, making himself more comfortable, "don't get me started. This is my baby. I've been here since '06. The Consolidated Empire poured its first brick in 1934, and its last one in '41. Then nothing much happened till 1979, when an entrepreneur started dewatering the mine and extracting some high-grade ore. There were no superstructures then – just a shaft and an adit that the guy used to access the workings. It wasn't too profitable, I guess, because he soon optioned the property to a big company, which had plans to make the mine operational. It built a modified headframe, and even a mill. Both are still standing. But that dream faded. Water, the ground water, flooded the workings again. Then we came along. I work for Crown Resources. We've got a few properties in this gold camp. We're a junior company. So far."

"A junior?"

"A junior mining company. Juniors do exploration. We bring a property along to the point where a major will invest tons of money to develop a mine. With the Con Empire, we just might raise the money ourselves. But we're always open to partnerships."

Dan grinned at Kennet. "Would you be an investor, by any chance?"

"I invested in Bre-X in '96. But I employed a poor tactic." Kennet winced internally as he recalled the Bre-X Minerals Ltd. fiasco from 1997. The Calgary-based company had boomed a gold discovery in Busang, Indonesia, and stock worth a few cents in 1993 reached a high of $286.50 a share in 1996. The next year, the stock collapsed, ruining thousands of investors. Massive fraud had been detected. No one was ever successfully prosecuted.

Nordstrom said, "Poor tactic?"

"I bought high, sold low."

"Yeah, you and everybody else. Well, what can I do for you, Kennet?"

"I'd really like a tour underground."

"What the hell for? It's not a pleasant place. It's not a place for tourists."

"I'll be frank with you. I believe that Vanderhorst picked up something in one of the tunnels – drifts, you call them? It may have a bearing on his death. And on the beating of his partner. I'd really like to look around."

Dan gathered himself and rose to his feet and walked the few steps to his desk. He turned around. His features assumed an official mien. "That, I'm afraid, is out of the question."

He sat down, and closed the lid of the laptop. "Bill Markowitz, that's the President, Bill would have my guts for garters. We don't need that kind of publicity." His fingers drummed on the desktop. "You're from TBU, eh? I heard you're a journalist too."

"I'm a teacher, strictly a teacher. I write a few things, to keep my hand in, but I'm not a reporter. I certainly won't be writing about your operation, or about a tour, if I'm granted one."

"Why's a teacher want to poke around underground? No," Dan said firmly, "no can do. Sorry."

"I see your point. Will you answer another question? Unrelated."

"Sure." He leaned back in his chair.

"You know where Vanderhorst was working? South of Beardmore? He was excavating an old prospector's trench. What're the chances he struck gold there? I know," Kennet said, flipping a palm outward, "it's a dumb question, but I'm no geologist."

"The chances? Zero to none. There are," said Dan, opening his hands to encompass the region, "maybe fifteen juniors with interests in this camp – west of here, north of here, east all the way to Geraldton and beyond. No one's found a mine yet, that is, a property that has the prospect of becoming a new mine. Old mines we have in abundance. Fifteen, or some such number. The last one around here closed in '65."

"The Leitch," Kennet interjected.

"The Leitch. At one point it was producing the highest grade ore in the whole of Canada. Crown Resources, by the way, now owns that property outright, and we'll be taking a hard look at it. Many a new mine's been found in the shadow of an old mine's headframe. That's why we're here at the old Con Empire. Now as to your question." He leaned forward and placed his muscular forearms on the desktop.

"South of here, the geology's not right for gold. Not a single junior is exploring there. The old-timers, now, they chipped every rock they could see with a hammer, for miles and miles in every direction, and thanks to them, we're a lot smarter. They found hundreds, hundreds, maybe thousands of prospects, but only a few mines. And the old miners missed a lot – there's gold galore yet at the Con Empire. We've found lots of it – enough for a mine, we don't know yet. We're going to begin long-hole drilling underground. Now that's a long-winded answer to a short question." He leaned back again.

"So it was a dumb question."

"There are no dumb questions. Time and again a prospector or an exploration company has found gold where others swore there would be none. The Hemlo at Marathon. Brown Bear Explorations," he waved his hand to the north, "north of Jellicoe, has found it, for God's sake, in a granodiorite intrusive! Priority Gold Inc. in Geraldton is finding it practically on surface around the old shafts of the MacLeod-Cockshutt and the Hardrock and the Little Long Lac – mines where the bulk of the gold in this camp came from. Everyone thought the ore was exhausted."

"So there's a chance that south of here –"

"Not a chance. That's my story and I'm sticking to it. Mind you, they did limnological studies in Orient Bay recently, found gold particles in lake sediments. The gold had to come from somewhere. So I'd love to be proved wrong. Want to try?" He grinned.

"I'll stick to teaching. I find it very rewarding."

As Dan showed Kennet out of his office, he introduced him properly to the secretary. She was Ioanna Mallory.

"Really?" said Kennet. "So Melody is –"

"My mother-in-law. Not my mother. Please." She rolled her eyes.

Back at the motel, his room was clean, and empty. There was a note where he had left the five-dollar bill. "Thank you so much, Mr. Forbes."

Suddenly he thought of Diane, his late wife. It was the handwriting, he thought. He had met Diane Rochambault in Beirut in the fall of '86. In the spring of '86, the globe had erupted with world-shaking events. He was finishing his last year at Ryerson U. In April a bomb exploded in a West Berlin discotheque, killing some, injuring hundreds. The United States President ordered air strikes against Libya, killing Gadhafi's daughter. In Beirut, Lebanon, Islamic terrorists kidnapped a British journalist, John McCarthy. A nuclear plant in Chernobyl, Ukraine, self-destructed.

Since those days Kennet had learned that the globe was always erupting. But it was in April of '86 that he resolved his journalism career would embrace the globe, and not just anywhere on the globe, but in the hotspots of the globe.

In the fall of '86 he was a freelance in Beirut. The ongoing hostage crisis had drawn him to the Levant. Multiple hostage situations dominated the headlines. It was in Beirut he had met Diane, a journalist working for the same service that John McCarthy was. McCarthy would spend five and a half years as a hostage. Kennet and Diane shared a few moments in a bar over drinks after a hard-driving day.

In January '87, the jihadists captured another British citizen, Terry Waite. By that time Kennet knew his beat thoroughly. It helped that he spoke French, and had picked up some Arabic. His reports on the kidnapping were timely and accurate and professional. He attracted the attention of several news organizations, and they began soliciting him. He met Diane again. He learned she was an expatriate Frenchwoman who had spent her childhood in Normandy before her family moved to Britain. She spoke excellent English. Their paths crossed more frequently, and they became lovers. In the fall of '87, they married. She applied for Canadian citizenship.

In 2004 Diane contracted breast cancer. They were living in Thunder Bay at the time, close to Kennet's parents. They wanted to give Susan a stable adolescent life. They had cut back their commitments to travel and still made a decent living. Diane passed in November of '05. A few weeks later, Kennet's mother died suddenly of a ventral aortic aneurysm. A few months later, Kennet offered his services to CBC to cover the Afghan war. Susan stayed with his father as she started college.

He crossed his legs and sank to the carpet in lotus posture and breathed deeply for a quarter hour. The refrigerator hummed away.

He rose and checked the phone book. There was a W. Carlson listed for Highway 11, Jellicoe. On second thought, what could he accomplish over the phone? The old geezer likely had lousy hearing anyway. He'd have to call on him.

After he crossed the Blackwater River, the highway curved right. On the left he noted the sign for a cemetery. He passed the intersection with Secondary Highway 580. It was hard-topped. Soon he was sailing in bright sunlight through a healthy green forest set back from the highway. He met a black Tahoe truck. The privacy glass obscured the occupants. Not far behind was a gray Chrysler 300. Robert Kenilworth was speaking into his phone, eyes on the road, and did not see him.

In twenty klicks he passed the sign for Secondary Highway 801. It was unpaved. He spotted the yellow plastic newspaper box and turned right on a rutted track in a grassy clearing. To his left lay a river, still the Blackwater, for he knew that it flowed from Jellicoe. He crossed the rusty rails, which in turn ran north across the river on a dark metal bridge. An older building stood under the trees where the clearing ended. It was painted a muddy chocolate brown, like old railway buildings he had seen. Except that the paint was new.

He pulled up behind a late model truck, a light blue Chevy Silverado. Crumbling outbuildings appeared to hold split and stacked firewood. Power lines swooped down to the house. A satellite television dish clung high up on one of the hydro poles.

The door opened and a tall, raw-boned man with mussy white hair strode out. Wide shoulders stretched a workshirt. As Kennet opened the driver's side door, the man's voice thundered:

"Climb down! Welcome to Pisa. Kettle's on." He turned abruptly and stepped inside, leaving the door ajar.

Inside, an electric kettle boiled on a kitchen counter. Carlson had set two plain white pyrex cups on the kitchen table. He gestured to the bowls and jars and packages occupying the middle of the table. "Help yourself. Tea or coffee. Sugar there. Spoons. Do you take cream?" Kennet detected a slight Scandinavian accent.

"Black. Thank you." He sat on a wooden rail-backed chair. Carlson returned from the fridge with a small bowl. He poured a thick cream into his own cup and returned the bowl to the fridge. He returned with the steaming kettle.

"Did you say this was Pisa?" said Kennet, pushing the cup forward into which he had spooned some dark grains of instant coffee.

"Nezah." Carlson replaced the kettle and sat down, plucking a greenish tea bag from the clutter and popping it into his cup.

"Nezah. Nezah is a ghost town, and I'm the only living ghost." He grinned with a set of almost perfect white teeth. His sunken cheeks were suffused with a permanent blush under high cheekbones. His eyes were green, a South Sea green.

"This was once a thriving community," he continued, "named for a big shot who helped build the railway. Hazen was his name. Hazen. Nezah. Get it?"

Kennet nodded. *No signs of senility yet*, he thought.

"When I first saw it in the '30's, it was the only way to get into the backcountry, north of here." He gestured toward the highway. Unless you went by the big lake, or by the river." He gestured northward.

"The Blackwater?"

"No, no, no. The Sturgeon. It's got some Indian name that I can never pronounce. The railway crosses the Sturgeon the other side of Jellicoe, and the Sturgeon was the aqueous highway to the gold fields. That 801 road? That was the overland wagon trail to the gold fields."

"You worked there?"

"No, no, no. Too young at that time. I was going to school at Beardmore."

"You lived in Beardmore?"

"No, no. At Empire. The Con Empire had a townsite then, long before Beardmore. My father worked there. We had a house there, way up on the hill, above the headframe and above the mill

105

complex. We got letters from the old country addressed to Empire. My father was a mine captain."

"Underground?"

"Of course underground. There's no jobs for a captain on surface." He chuckled. "Yes, I am enjoying this." He leaned back, stretching out his long legs, supporting the tea cup with a thick wrist. "No one's asked me about those days for a long time. I don't think I've seen you before."

"I'm in Beardmore temporarily. Bull Kellerman told me where you live."

"Ah yah, Kellerman. He still living? Given his sedentary lifestyle, I'm expecting to read about that old fossil's final cardiac arrest any time. He's had a few attacks."

"You look healthy. Very healthy."

He thumped his chest. "Waiting for my first arrhythmia. It will be an experience. So you hunted me down, eh?"

"Yes. Let me introduce myself. Kennet Forbes." Carlson gave his hand a strong shake.

"Call me Wes. Or call me Carlson. I like both names."

"I had questions, and you've answered some already. You know the old Con Empire, eh?"

"I should say. And from '39 until it closed, I worked there. Underground. Following in my father's footsteps. Let me find some cookies."

As Carlson rummaged in the cupboard, Kennet looked around. The large area contained living room furniture and a black wood stove on a red brick hearth, with a shiny insulated chimney rising to the ceiling. The ceiling was a board one, as was the floor. There was surprisingly little clutter. Along one wall an array of bookshelves, crammed full. On a smaller table sat a stack of books.

"These," said Carlson, sliding a plateful of cookies across the tablecloth, "I made myself. Can't seem to find decent cookies in the stores anymore."

They looked like shortbread, but had a distinctive flavour. He had tasted that spice in Denmark and Iceland.

"So, Wes, how did you miners get underground? From surface, I mean."

"The cage, of course. The steam hoist operated the cage, and the cage rose and fell vertically in the shaft under the headframe. You really are a novice when it comes to mines, eh? Come here, let me show you."

Carlson led him to a very large framed photograph. A large disjointed building tumbled in stages down a steep hill to a railway track. Carlson pointed to the tower-like structure near the top of the hill. "That's the headframe of the Con Empire." He pointed to the multi-staged building. "That's the mill. It operated on the gravity principle to concentrate the ore. A primary crusher processed the ore underground, and conveyed it to the mill, where it was pulverized and concentrated." His finger moved up the hill and beyond the headframe to a line of buildings on a higher ridge. "And there's our house." His finger rested on a fuzzy building with a peaked roof. "We had a grand view of the whole operation!"

"Fascinating. So, there was only one way into the mine – to go, you know, underground."

Carlson looked at him shrewdly. "Planning a reconnaissance, are we, Forbes?" He turned back to the photo, and spoke deliberately. "Right about there," he stabbed the photo with his middle finger, "is an adit. Into the hillside." The finger moved up to a spot just left of the headframe. "There was a manway, all the way to the first level. And another, farther east." His finger moved left, moving off the photo. He turned to face Kennet. "When I worked there in '79, Aaron Scharf pulled the ore out through the adit, which accessed the shaft. Come, let's finish our tea." They moved back to the table.

"You've got me baffled," said Kennet. "Adit? Manway? Level?"

"Ah, you youngsters know nothing. An adit is what the man in the street calls a tunnel. It's a horizontal corridor in the rock that begins on surface, often in a hill or a cliff. The one I showed you, actually sloped down to the shaft.

"Now, a manway is a way for a man to climb, up or down, on a ladder. Every mining operation mandates escape routes for its underground personnel in cases of emergency. Even in those days they were careful. A level is – come on," he curled his fingers in the come-hither gesture, "you tell me."

"It's a horizontal corridor in the rock that begins at the vertical shaft. It's also called a drift."

"You learn fast. Learn this, too. An old mine is not a picnic site. I know geologists who plan every step before they set foot on an old mine site. There are man-traps everywhere. And to penetrate underground? Well." He left the rest unspoken.

"I have no intentions of penetrating anywhere. I'm just curious."

"Yah. Well, when Scharf was opening up the Con Empire, he knew I had special knowledge. I knew where we had left some rich ore, between the first and fourth levels. The adit I pointed out, it declines, it ramps down to meet the shaft, 80 feet below the headframe. A conveyor system pulled the ore out and fed it to the mill in the old days. Scharf utilized the adit to pull out his high grade to surface."

"Where was this high grade?"

"Lots of it, right next to the shaft. And there were ore reserves, between stopes. What's a stope? A stope is a working space for the hardrock miners. It's usually a chamber above a drift, chasing the gold-bearing vein, so that the blasted ore can be funneled down to an ore car in the drift. The gravity principle again."

"Ore cars? Like, little trains on tracks?"

"In the '30s, yes. In '79, no. Scarf's crew hand-cobbed. It was a shoestring operation. They broke the ore out with hammers and hand-steel and sticks of dynamite, and then broke it up. There was no headframe in '79, no hoist, no cage, so Scharf had to improvise them. It was a two-compartment shaft – one compartment for a manway, and one for a cage. We rigged a bucket to lift the ore to the adit, and a windlass to lower the submersible pump into the depths . They were scary contraptions. The crew accessed the workings by the manway."

"You inched down hundred-foot-plus ladders?"

"In stages, yah. You couldn't fall far, before you hit a landing, made of timber. In other manways, you might have hundred-foot ladders. Those old ladders, now, they were just accidents waiting to happen. More coffee?"

"I'm fine, thanks."

"Curiosity satisfied?"

"For the time being, yes. I may call you again. You have a phone, right?

"And a fax. And a computer." He rose and walked to a desk near the bookshelves and whipped off a dust sheet to expose a monitor and keyboard. "I check on my investments, daily."

Kennet followed him. "You have quite a library." A quick glance took in classics and modern best-sellers and reams of titles from various disciplines.

"In late '41, I signed up for king and country. Did my bit overseas. When I got back, the government paid for college, but I could never settle on a single career. Too boring. I should really say, everything's so interesting. And I love the outdoors. I've been a miner and a lumberman and a surveyor and a mechanic and a few other things. Never married. Lots of girlfriends, though. Even now." His eyes twinkled.

"Prospector?"

"Of course! It goes with the territory. Prospectors have prowled this whole country, mostly on their hands and knees. They were the original explorers."

"Have you ever found anything interesting?"

"Interesting? Let me think." Carlson pursed his lips. Then he said, "One time, wandering in the backcountry, near the lake, I found some iron."

"Iron?"

"Buried in a tree trunk. Sunk to the eye. Handle had rotted out." He grinned at Kennet expectantly. "It was an axehead."

"Ever figure it out?"

"It's a mystery. Some bloke may still be looking for it."

Kennet's eyes wandered to the books on the table. There were two volumes of James Frazier's *The Golden Bough*. Carlson volunteered, "Dropped off yesterday by a friend. Going away, he says. So he's cleaning house. Are you going to look at the falls?"

"The falls?"

"Just down the hill there. I leave my bedroom window open so I can hear the grandfathers talking. That's what the Indians call the sounds of rushing water. Indians. That's my name for them. It was good enough for Columbus. My indigenous friends can't decide on what to call themselves – Natives or Native people or First Nations people or Aboriginals. Myself, I long ago decided I was Canadian."

As Kennet stepped outside, Carlson said, "If you're going to see the falls, watch your step. I have a water line running from the river. In winter I carry buckets. And year round I use the shithouse. I believe that shit belongs outside, don't you?"

He laughed at Kennet's expression. "Take care, Forbes."

Chapter 10

. . . Friday mid-day

As he crossed the bridge in Beardmore, it was 12:11 by the dashboard clock. He had taken a rain check on the sightseeing tour of the waterfalls. At Arlene's Tavern he noted the black Tahoe and Robert's Chrysler. At the Regency motel, four vehicles appeared to belong to Alice's diners. He unlocked the door to his room.

There was an e-mail acknowledgement from Peter Sheridan. His e-mail signature included phone numbers for his office, home, and cell. Kennet programmed them into his cell. A circular memo from Melissa Sharp reminded members of the English Department of the meeting on Monday at 8:30 a.m., sharp. He sent back a confirmation, as requested. A professor from U of T, whom he knew, asked Kennet if he were attending the seminar on citizen journalism at Ryerson U in October. Kennet replied that he would let him know when his calendar firmed up.

A knock on the door. Kennet opened the door to Robert, who ducked in quickly.

"Just me," he said. "We can't find the Flemings anywhere. So

I suggested the crime unit try again this evening. They've gone to Nipigon, to talk to that Henderson – I didn't think it advisable for people to see the police vehicle here. The less you are associated with the police, the better. For your investigations, I mean." He sank into a chair.

"Good thinking. You saw Cummings? And Laroque?"

"Laroque, yes. Cummings, his mother said they'd called him in for half a shift at noon. The detectives will interview him later this afternoon. If they went to the mine site and disrupted the routine, word would get out. Don't want to alert the Flemings until we have to. Got anything else for us?"

"Just gathering background. Now here's a piece of news, quite unrelated. You know those bones they found last fall near Lake Nipigon? And the TBU forensics lab was examining them? Well, they're about to release a report."

"I've seen no report."

"I said they're *about* to release one. So this is an unofficial communication. The victim was a young female, late teens, and the remains may have lain there twenty to thirty years."

"How do you know about it?"

Kennet remained silent.

"Do you think there's a connection with the case?"

"I see none at all. But I promised to make discreet inquiries, and those inquiries may come to the attention of the authorities. Like a Detective Mueller."

"Here's a piece of news for you. Detective Mueller is no longer the primary in this case. Detective Armistead is. It seems that Jillian – Staff-Sergeant Halvorsen – reviewed the tape of your interview, and she ripped Mueller a new one. He's walking very gingerly nowadays. And I have something else for you."

Robert reached inside a breast pocket and produced an unloaded bear banger and handed it over. "I got it from Kelly. She got it from Mueller. He wanted her to return it. He said it didn't work and he wanted nothing more to do with it. Kelly knew I'd be seeing you. How *does* it work?"

"It works with a cartridge that you screw in here." Kennet pointed to the tip of the banger.

Robert heaved himself out of the chair. "Well, I'm off. I've got paperwork at the home office. But I'll be back tomorrow."

"Tomorrow's Saturday."

"Think you're the only one who can claim overtime?"

"No one's paying me."

"Oh. That's right, isn't it." Robert grinned.

"Any more news on the body?"

"That'll be part of my paperwork. I hope."

Kennet paused with his hand on the doorknob. "There's one more thing. Anything you can tell me about the discovery of those bones will be very useful."

"Of course. Right." Robert cogitated for a moment. "When I was posted in Geraldton, I worked with guys who had been there since the early '80s. There's one guy, Dale Marchuk . . . He was posted to Beardmore when we had an office here. We've sort of kept in touch." Robert pointed a finger at Kennet. "Tell you what. I'll ask him to call you. And while I think of it, have you a card?"

Kennet pulled out a business card from his wallet and printed on the back. "Here's my home number too. I have to be back Sunday night, and I have a meeting Monday early."

Robert had pulled out his own card and reciprocated.

After Robert drove off, Kennet pulled out the maps he had bought at Kellerman's. He checked the location of the Con Empire in the context of local geography. Not far from the railway that extended north and east of Beardmore, symbols indicated buildings at the mine site. And at some points, the railway skirted the Blackwater River, not far from town.

Kennet checked that the door had locked and strolled up the main street to Arlene's Tavern. It was starting to cloud over.

113

He paused at the bottom of the steps and composed himself before climbing to the veranda and opening the glass-paned door. Picture windows on either side of the door looked over and through the veranda. There were three customers at the scattering of tables in a modest L-shaped room. A fieldstone fireplace graced the north wall. Beside it, a small television screen hung from the ceiling, tuned to a sports channel. He seated himself at a table beside a picture window where he could observe the fireplace, the counter, and the kitchen door in the top of the L.

A waitress in uniform emerged from the kitchen and hurried over. "Can I get you something to drink, sir?" Stiff light-coloured hair, streaked with grey, threatened to escape her cap.

"Coffee, please."

"We have beer," she said hopefully.

"Just coffee. And the lunch special." A slate on the wall, beside a doorway leading to the rear and, he assumed, the restrooms, offered cabbage soup and a Reuben sandwich. "Toasted," he added.

"Fries with that?" She scribbled away.

"Only if it's part of the special." She went away, head down, still scribbling.

Ioanna Mallory came flouncing up the veranda steps and through the door. She gave him a smile and a greeting and yelled toward the back, "Is it ready yet, Marge?" The waitress sang out, "Coming!"

She turned to Kennet. "I eat on the run."

"You did look busy."

"They give me eleven hours' work in a seven-and-a-half-hour day. But I get it done. There aren't too many jobs going here."

"Why do you stay? Is this your home town?"

"Hah. I'm a city girl. Born in Fort Frances, went to school there, but I love the city. Curtis was born here. He loves it here. We met at Superior North College, in Thunder Bay. He's a certified millwright, and he looks after the mill at the mine. But I keep telling him he could work anywhere – Calgary, Toronto, Montreal – as soon as the economy improves, of course. Okay, here's my lunch." She accepted a brown bag from the waitress in exchange for some large coins.

His soup and sandwich were quite satisfactory. Sans fries. When he left, he stood on the veranda and surveyed the scene toward the river. He could see for blocks, there being so much empty green space. Directly across, a block to the west, there was a cluster of houses. A bay of the river seemed to come in behind them and the little wooden church, which fronted the highway, the last building on that side. It may be a good launch site, he thought.

Rawling Fleming's pickup powered down Main Street, entering from the north, sound system blaring, dual rear wheels churning. The truck still had the aluminum boat in the box. Fleming's left arm extended from the window and his palm slapped the door, keeping time to the music, if it could be called that. He had passengers. Fleming turned his head to look at him, and his hand curled into a fist with the middle finger extended but he never raised it.

Kennet stopped in at the ward office. The gray-haired Janet was alone. He asked her how to locate Mac Kueng's cabin. "One thing I'll say for him," she said, "he pays his taxes on time." Kennet wondered if she should be volunteering such information. As he was leaving, she volunteered again. "Toot your horn where you get there, and wait. He doesn't like surprises."

Kennet drove north across the bridge and took the first left, before the cemetery road. It was a gravel road. To the right a sign announced a landfill site. A well-used gravel road forked left off the main road, and he took that. Very soon he took another left, driving through a mature jack pine stand. He guessed that he was paralleling the river. He stopped beside an ancient gray Chevrolet truck parked in a small clearing. He beeped the horn twice, paused, and then gave another short beep. He cut the engine and waited.

In two minutes Mac Kueng emerged from a footpath in the direction of the river. He walked over to Kennet, who rolled down his window.

Kueng flashed a set of yellow dentures. "Good day, sir. Are you lost?"

Kennet had thought about his response. "I hear you're an authority on local history, Mac. I wonder if you can help me."

Kueng leaned his forearms on the window lip. "Well," he drawled, "I just might be able to do that." His blue eyes studied Kennet keenly. "What's keeping you around? That archaeologist you found?"

"I have some explaining to do to his wife. She sent me to look for him. My name's Kennet, by the way." He thrust his right hand forward. Kueng lifted his right hand and waved it vaguely.

"Yes, yes. Everybody knows that. You've caused quite a stir. You've even got the Flemings trash-talking you. They take an immediate dislike to any stranger, but you, you set a record. Well, climb down. We can't talk here. The flies are out." He waved a hand around his head, batting imaginary flies.

Kennet followed him down the footpath through well-spaced jack pine. Kueng glanced over his shoulder. "You," he said, "are one of the privileged few. I can't abide tourists."

They emerged in a small clearing. The gray-walled log cabin was capped with a tin roof streaked with rust. There were a few piles of four-foot logs and at one of them, a bucksaw leaned against a sawhorse. A large open-sided shed appeared to be stocked with ironmongery and ancient leather harness and old machines. A huge anvil dominated the floor space, mounted on blocks of wood, and a long metal chimney climbed from the hooded furnace to the slanted roof.

"What've you got there, Mac?" Kennet pointed to the shed.

"That's my forge. You wanted history? Well, that's history. I acquired it when the last horse-logging camp closed in this neck of the woods. I still find it useful. I've made many a machine part on that anvil. Well, welcome to my abode."

He gestured toward the cabin, a blocky structure whose bottom logs seemed to be melting into the ground. Two small windows with six panes apiece were located on either side of the door. "That's the last building from the old Buffalo Beardmore mine. I took it over when I came into this country, back in '53. Come on in."

Kueng unlatched the plank door with its flaking red paint and stepped into the semi-dark interior. Kennet heard him fumbling, then a match striking, and saw the twin globes of a gas lantern lighting up. "Come in, come in."

Kennet stepped inside.

Kueng said, "I don't normally light this till dark, but I know you city folk are fussy. You seem to be half-blind. Must be the city lights that spoil you."

The room, about five by five metres, grew brighter as Kueng pumped up the lantern. Small-diameter peeled log rafters supported a plank roof. A clothesline with a single shirt and a pair of trousers and long underwear ran from side to side. Against the back wall stood a glass-fronted bookcase and beside it, another door. On either side, a six-paned window. On the walls clothes hung from pegs, as did a number of interesting artifacts. On the west side supplies crowded roughly built shelves and cupboards illuminated by another six-paned window. The plank counter held a simple metal sink, sans faucet. A plastic drain led down into the floorboards. A large galvanized water pail stood on the counter and a five-gallon bucket on the floor.

Kueng set the lantern on a small table covered with oilcloth. "Sit." He pointed to one of the three chairs. "I'm not firing up the stove just for the kettle." He gestured to the old-fashioned upright wood heater occupying the centre of the room on a loose fieldstone hearth. Black stovepipes rose to the roof. "I use it for breakfast and supper this time of year. I can offer you a soda."

"Soda's fine."

"Orange, cream soda, Pepsi, root beer?"

"Pepsi, please."

Kueng stooped in front of the kitchen counter and lifted a door in the floor. On the counter Kennet noticed an old-fashioned alarm clock with double gongs. Next to it was a tabletop radio. Kueng quickly descended a ladder and reappeared a few seconds later with two canned drinks. He lowered the door. "My cool room," he said.

Kennet grasped the can and pulled the tab. It *was* cool.

Mac Kueng took a great gulp of his Pepsi. Kennet gestured toward the alarm clock. "That's quite a timepiece. But it's five minutes fast."

"That's the way I like it. There are certain programs on radio that I listen to, religiously. I don't like to miss the beginnings."

Kennet raised his eyes to the roof. "You live here year round?" he said.

"Of course I live here year round."

"I was just wondering. There doesn't seem to be insulation in the ceiling."

"Of course not. That's the way they built in those days. The tin is new, though. I tore off the old planks and shingles, because they leaked. Nailed down new planks. Got two layers of tin on now. In some places, three. Not a single leak."

"Doesn't it get cold? In winter?"

"Sure it gets cold. But cold builds character. I bring in a heavier gauge stove for the winter, keep it going all the time. Ever see a trapper's line shack?"

"No."

"Same principle. Only they use a lighter gauge stove year round. A Queen's heater, they call it. In winter it's only used a half dozen times, so the metal lasts. In my case I'd burn out a lighter gauge in less than a month. Ever hear of a trapper freezing to death in his shack?"

"Not lately."

"Not ever. So. Is that the kind of history you wanted?"

Kennet took another sip. "I'm on a steep learning curve. I'm trying to figure out the geography and sociology and the lifestyle of the region. I went to school in Geraldton –"

"You lived in Geraldton? And you don't know the country?"

"Amazing, isn't it? Fifty miles away, and it's another world. I thought that happened only in Thomas Hardy novels."

"In Hardy's books, five miles was a world away."

Kennet looked at him sharply. "I heard you were well read."

Kueng grinned, his yellow teeth in contrast with his thatch of white hair. "You heard that about me, eh? Well, I guess they've got a right to talk about me. I talk about them. To strangers. And you still qualify. I don't have any truck with the villagers, as a rule. Keep to myself. But I listen very hard."

"I've seen you a couple of times now, in the village." Kennet smiled on the last word.

"I go three, four times a day. After breakfast, for morning coffee and the paper. Around noon, when I go to the post office. Late afternoon, if I want to mail a letter. And maybe later in the evening, if I want to shoot the shit with someone, usually at Kellerman's. Some hermit, eh?" Kueng grinned again.

"You used to prospect, I hear. Is that the word – prospect?"

"I still do. And here's a thing about prospectors, since you're in a learning mode. A prospector is not just a guy with a little hammer who goes around chipping rocks. A prospector is a jack-of-all-trades. He can cut timber like a lumberjack and blast rock like an engineer and drive a machine like Stirling Moss, only it's a drill rig or a backhoe or a bulldozer, and he can drink like a sailor. I've done it all. I've made three fortunes, blew most of them on whiskey and women, and the rest I spent darn foolishly."

Kennet grinned his appreciation. "Right now, I presume, you're between fortunes?"

Kueng's face tightened. "Judge not this book by its cover. This is the life I have elected. If I chose to, I could buy out Beardmore. When I go to town, I also drop by the bank to check my investments. I am past the age of sixty-five, how far past I'll not say, but I haven't applied for the old age pension these past fourteen years. And I never will. I'll not take a cent from the government. I only wish they had the same scruples. Look. I'm paying the Municipality the same taxes as someone who's got a lovely cottage on the lake. And I don't even get a garbage pickup. Not that I want one. I pay my taxes on time so that there's no excuse for some meddling government arse to pay me a visit. I've even got a smoke detector," he pointed to a white plastic capsule over the kitchen window, "to boggle the fire police if they should drop in."

"Good thinking. Look, I apologize," said Kennet. "I did not mean to be rude." Searching for a way to ease the tension, Kennet looked around and said, "Thoreau – Henry David Thoreau – would admire your lifestyle."

"And I admire his *Walden*. Don't care much for his other stuff. And I doubt he'd approve of electricity, which I have."

"I didn't see any power lines coming in."

"I've got a wind generator, there's a tower out back. And storage batteries, under my feet here," he stamped a foot, "so they don't freeze. If I go away for a day or two in winter, I plug in a couple of heaters and keep my books warm, and direct them at my cupboards here, because there's some stuff that'll freeze, like jam jars and pickles. Or if I want to thaw a carcass fast." He gestured toward the east wall, where an oval-shaped frame held a beaver skin, and some leg-hold traps hung from chains. "Trapping is something I keep up."

"And you hunt," said Kennet, pointing to the bearskin rug.

"And I guide, when the spirit moves me."

"So you know bears. Tell me, what do you do when you see one in the bush?"

"Most bears you never see. They see you first. When you do startle one, it's likely to take off. It doesn't like most people, which shows good sense. Other times, a bear will take it in mind to challenge you, and then you have two choices: fight or flight. I've done both."

"You'd outrun a bear?"

"Never. But I've beat it to a nearby tree, or climbed on my cab."

"So, you hunt on your trapline?"

"I trap on my trapline. But the fire burnt over most of my line. No marten any more. Lots of rabbits, though, so I get a few lynx."

"Ah yes. The Fire of '99. How did that start anyway?"

"Some idiot in Macdiarmid. He was burning trash in his yard and let the fire get away from him. It burned all the country west of the highway, clear to the lake. It just about converted those lovely lake cottages into cinders. Burned clear across the river, the Sturgeon, until the rains extinguished it. It burned a path to my back door, up to the pipeline right-of-way. And the son of a gun got off scot-free."

"No charges laid?"

"Charges, no conviction. What's the point of the law if the criminals get off? I've had break-ins here, and not even charges laid. Where's the justice?"

Kennet prompted him. "It doesn't sound fair. Did you have any suspects?"

Kueng looked at him shrewdly. "Oh yes. They'll not fool with me again."

"Any thoughts on the Vanderhorst case?"

"None. I don't put my nose in where it doesn't belong. But there is a criminal element here. Hell, criminals run the country! I just have to look at my tax bills."

"Would you include the Flemings in that category?"

"I'm not saying that. It's none of my business. I don't invite trouble. And they know enough not to mess with me." He rolled his eyes meaningfully to the doorway. Kennet turned his head. Above the door an old-style heavy-calibre rifle sat on wooden pegs.

"Is that a Garand? The American military rifle?"

"Second-best rifle ever made. An M1."

"It's a relic now. But I've seen it used around the world. In areas of conflict. Also the .303. Though the belligerents prefer more advanced weaponry nowadays, like AK-47s and RPGs."

"I thought you were a professor at the college?"

"I used to be a journalist. I covered a lot of conflicts. But the last one I attended, sort of put me off the business." Kennet pointed to his right eye.

"I wondered about that," said Kueng, smiling thinly. "It looked more serious than the outcome of a disagreement in a bar. And I've had those."

"That area where they found Vanderhorst, do you know it?"

"I know this whole country. I walked over most of it. Canoed the rest of it. In winter I favour snowshoes. People nowadays don't use the racquets, they've got their skidoos – their snowmobiles, their sleds, they call them. And I have no ambition to imitate the galoots you find on sleds."

"Is there any prospect of a gold strike where Vanderhorst was working?"

"Is the Pope Protestant? You think that archaeologist died in a dispute over gold? I thought it was an accident. He stumbled into a pit and drowned, didn't he?"

"It looked like an accident to me. But if it wasn't an accident, can you think of a motive for murder?"

Kueng rose to his feet, crushing the empty can in his fist. "You disappoint me, sir. You come to me as a student of the country, and now it seems you're just looking for dirt. A scandal to sell to some yellow rag."

Kennet stood up. "Mac, I'm sorry. I'm sorry I'm giving you the wrong impression. I am not a journalist. Not anymore. I am not writing a single line about this unfortunate death. I am trying to understand it. And you're right, it's premature to talk of anything but of a death by misadventure."

Kueng tossed his can into a large garbage bin in the corner. "Ah, forget it. I'm just on edge. Have you seen that new kid in town, on a motorcycle? Another Fleming. Another troublemaker. Just what the village needs."

"I talked to him briefly. He sounded normal." Kennet sat down again.

"Ah," he said disgustedly. "So did Al Capone." He started pacing.

"Mac, something maybe you can help me with. You're a prospector. Did you ever do any actual mining?"

"Underground? Never. Scares me to death. Why do you ask?"

"I'm curious. The region seems to be crawling with exploration companies, but I can't get past the gate of the Con Empire. I'd like to see the layout. Get a feel for it."

"You're asking the wrong person." Kueng paused in his pacing. "There's no better feeling than finding a mine that nature did its best to conceal. It's a battle of wits." Kueng wagged his finger lecture-style. "But working in one? That's unnatural. A man doesn't belong in a hole in the ground."

"Still, I'd like to see one."

"The Con Empire, so I hear, is full of holes. The stopes are collapsing. There are crevasses right up to surface. It's a long way to fall, sir. They've got no business rehabilitating that property. They'll kill someone."

"Yet, mines are the holy grail of prospecting, aren't they?"

Kueng stopped pacing and glared at him. "Prospectors made this country. Nobody'd be here now if it weren't for the prospectors. The Con Empire was the first real mine. And there are still a thousand – heck, ten thousand – holes in the bush that might become mines yet. How's that for history?"

Kennet drained the last of his drink and rose. "Thank you, Mac. One more favour. May I peek at your library?"

"My pleasure." Kueng strode over to the bookcase and threw open the glass doors. "I keep them behind glass because the smoke and the damp, you know, are not good for the paper." He plucked a hardcover book and thrust it at Kennet. "Do you know this author?" It was a copy of Friedrich Nietzsche's *Man and Superman.*

"Only by reputation." Kennet glanced at other titles on display. Some volumes by Ayn Rand leapt out: *Atlas Shrugged, The Fountainhead . . .* Other titles included George Orwell's *1984*, Charles Dickens' *A Tale of Two Cities*, Plato's *The Republic*, Leo Tolstoy's *War and Peace*,

"I keep titles," said Kueng, "that I want to consult again. But I'm not strictly elitist. I'm a fan of certain Western authors too." He indicated the east wall where a low-height glassed-in bookshelf held paperback copies . "I've got Louis Lamour, Luke Short, Clay Fisher . . . When I finish re-reading one series, I start another. And," he indicated some cardboard boxes stacked in the corner, "there's my collection of *Popular Mechanics.* Goes back to the '40's. I'm keeping only the more recent issues handy. Donated the others to the library. I can always read a back issue there if I need to. My taxes are paying for the heat and light there anyway."

"Are you reading contemporary literature as well?"

"As little as possible. It's all been said before. I belong to mail-order book clubs and I place orders all the time. But I pay by money order. I don't believe in plastic. Plastic means debt."

Kennet eased a hardcover volume of Hardy's *The Return of the Native* off the shelf and feathered the pages. There were a lot of dog-eared pages. Kueng remarked, "I can't get very far in that one – not at one sitting. Such a weight of detail. Such a heavy sense of place. It's . . . oppressive."

Returning to the table, Kueng plucked a softcover book from a chair. It was *Dark Journey: The Last Expedition of Henry Hudson,* by an author named Larsson. "This, on the other hand," he said, "depicts far horizons. Vast emptiness. It stretches the mind."

Outside, Kennet gestured toward the forge. "Use it much?"

"Nope. Used to, when I was operating machinery. I could make a part faster than having it delivered from Winnipeg or wherever. Still got a good stock of Pennsylvannia coal – see those bags there? And I had some lovely machines for working metal. Had a welding outfit too, but I let them all go. I'm no pack rat. When something's no longer useful, I sell it. Or give it away."

Mac Kueng walked him to his truck. Kennet nodded to the ancient Chevrolet pickup. "That's an old-timer there. A Silverado? What year?"

"That's an '82. They could build trucks in those days. I know how to keep it running, so I see no reason to trade it for a gewgaw with fresher paint and computer innards so delicate that the first big thunderstorm off the lake will addle them."

"No plug-in for the winter though."

"If it's dropping below 40, I take the battery inside. Never had a problem." As Kennet drove away, he could see Kueng in the rear-view, arm raised in farewell.

He parked at the motel and crossed the road to Melody's Variety. Melody's face lit up. She was serving another customer as Kennet grabbed a hand-basket. He browsed the shelves and coolers as he selected bread, non-hydrogenated margarine, a tin of pickled herring, cheddar cheese, two tins of soup, a small jar of dill pickles, a carton of orange juice, and a package of fig newtons which, as he determined by pinching the package, were less than board stiff. If he finished his business that afternoon too late to take advantage of the early closing of Arlene's Tavern, he would not starve.

As Melody punched in the prices, she grinned inanely. After Kennet paid, she said, "Crystal's here. She's in the back. Want me to call her?"

"By all means."

Crystal was the pretty and petite flaxen-haired girl he remembered, with her hair tied off in a pony tail. "Professor Forbes!" she enthused. "So good to see you!"

"Crystal. Likewise." Kennet smiled as he shook her hand. "Are you coming back this fall?"

"Try to keep me away! I loved your course. But I won't have you this semester. Listen, I have the rest of the day off. How would you like a home-cooked meal?"

"I hear you're a cook. Are you any good?" Kennet teased.

"Just wait and see. I'm cooking for my brother, Curtis, and my sister-in-law, Ioanna. You met her today. They live just a block away," she pointed behind her, "at 282 Walker Street East. Across from the school."

"I'd be delighted, but I'm afraid I'll have to decline. I figured to do a bit of paddling, and I may not be back till 7:00 or 8:00."

"We'll wait. They always eat late anyways. They're always so tired when they come home, they just throw anything together. So they'll have no problem waiting for one of my meals. Please come."

"It would be churlish of me to refuse."

Back in his room, Kennet stored his supplies in cupboard and refrigerator. He walked over to the LCBO and picked up a bottle of red wine. Down the street near the Snowman, he noted the presence of Fleming's Ram 3500. It just sat there, dark windows brooding.

Chapter 11

... Friday afternoon

Kennet turned at the wooden church. A large grassy area sloped down to a quiet backwater of the river. He portaged the amber-coloured kayak down a narrow trail used by all-terrain vehicles. Fleming's circus wagon paraded past, headed for the bridge. Rawling craned his neck for a look.

Kennet wore a paddling wet suit – pants and short-sleeved vest – and completed the outfit with his safari hat, a short-sleeved bush shirt, and hiking boots, which he had left unlaced. He slid the kayak gently into the water, removed the boots, and stowed them in the stern hatch along with a waterproof camera case. He picked up the paddle and stepped into the kayak.

His wristwatch read 3:53 p.m. He patted his left shirt pocket, where his GPS sat, attached to an extra-long lanyard around his neck, and he touched his right pocket, which held the truck keys under the buttoned-down flap. He tightened the skirt around his waist. As he took the first strokes he noted the Fleming pickup driving very slowly toward the downtown.

127

Something was wrong. The cool sensation on his feet and calves portended ill. He pulled quickly into shore and stepped out. The backsides of his calves were wet. The craft had a leak. He lifted it out and turned it over on the bank and examined the bottom carefully. Near the bow he found a small slit, like a knife slash. The pickup, which had stopped on the highway shoulder, accelerated away in a spray of gravel. Someone gave a war whoop.

He retrieved a roll of gray duct tape from the truck and mended the leak. He threw the roll into the rear hatch and launched again.

In the main river he turned south, cruising with the current past the flood plain on which the community sat. The high bank cut off most of the view of the town. If anyone were watching, he was on a pleasure jaunt. Where the buildings ended, the river turned sharply eastward at a set of rapids. He turned around. On the west shore where the wilderness began, in a tiny backwater of the river, a small jetty identified Mac Kueng's property.

He paddled north against the current of the Blackwater, rather strong for the time of year, and passed under the highway bridge. Once past the recreation complex on the east bank, and the private buildings on the west bank, the river angled northeast. The trappings of civilization gave way to dense bush. The dark waters swirled under overhanging brush and nudged the closely crowded cedar trunks on either bank. Kennet estimated the river was about three kayak-lengths wide – perhaps twenty metres.

He experienced a small shock. He had glanced left and spotted a bloody spear. It was a picket that someone had erected in a cleared corridor and sprayed the sharp exposed end with red paint. The corridor, perhaps a metre wide, came down to the river bank from the west.

He activated the GPS, propping it on the deck in front of him. Soon the map appeared, tracking his progress on the water. He settled into a steady rhythm. To his right a creek, practically invisible, emerged from a small lake. To his left another creek, also unnavigable, drained a smaller lake between the river and the highway to the west.

The GPS told him that he had reached the point where the tracks almost touched the river. A screen of trees prevented his seeing the tracks. He pulled into the east bank where an embankment and some ancient timbers suggested a bridge had once spanned the river. He tucked the unit back into his pocket.

He pulled the kayak well out of the water. He swatted half-heartedly at the one lone mosquito he had seen. He retrieved his camera from its waterproof case and looped the lanyard around his neck. He retrieved his boots and laced them on tightly. In a few steps he emerged on the right-of-way, a corridor about forty metres wide. Before him, across the tracks, the concrete foundations of the old mill climbed the steep hill, creating a series of small chambers intermingled with standing trees, brush, and debris. It looked climbable, but hardly safe. The railway stretched north and south for a distance before disappearing around curves. He snapped a number of frames.

He walked west, examining the heavily timbered hillside. After a couple hundred metres there was no evidence of a path or a break in the forest cover. He turned around and walked past the old mill site and continued east. He came upon a wooden conduit, a long box-like structure that emerged from beneath the rail bed and snaked across the ditch and climbed the hill. It was covered with ancient asphalt roll roofing to weatherproof it. Kennet surmised that it protected a line that drew water from the river. Whatever it was, it followed the path of least resistance up the hillside.

The conduit was a half-metre side. He walked on it across the ditch, and then dropped down beside it on a faint footpath when the pitch grew extreme. After a short climb through the trees he found the pitch of the conduit had decreased. He jumped on it again, the tread of his boots gripping the shingle tightly. He climbed easily. The conduit summited on a long wide bench of the hill, clear except for patches of brush. An old tote road ran down the centre of it. He left the conduit and walked west until he found the upper walls of the old mill. It looked like an even more dangerous way to descend. At each new locale, he snapped pictures.

He faced around, looking at another steep slope above the bench, also wooded. Further left, the woods gave way to brush, and on top of the slope, he discerned the top of an open steel structure surmounted by a huge wheel. It looked like a pulley. No doubt miners had a special term for it. He advanced to the base of the slope and in the brush he discovered a small wooden structure built into the hillside. It resembled the truncated front end of a shack, its wide double doors secured with a large padlock. It had to be the entrance to the adit, the tunnel extending into the hill. He walked along the base of the hill towards the conduit.

Kennet could not discern any footpath ascending the hillside, which was dominated by brush and loose rocks. He tested the ascent in several places, placing each foot deliberately, fearful that the ground could collapse at any moment as the skein of dirt over a hidden pit or a crevasse gave way. He found himself approaching the wooden conduit again. *Of course.* The conduit was the path.

He leapt on the conduit and walked confidently up the hillside as it wormed itself around shallow pits and patches of brush. As he approached the crest, he began crouching forward. The steel pillars of the modified headframe loomed. The conduit leveled out, and he found himself peering through a brush screen past the headframe to a clearing that held buildings. The conduit veered sharply right at the crest and headed down slope. To advance further would be to risk discovery. It was then he noticed the dog.

The German shepherd crouched by the corner of the headframe, poised to leap. From five metres away the beast fixed him with a steely gaze. Kennet froze in place. The animal's forelegs twitched in anticipation, its tail curved over its hindquarters. For the space of a long minute each held his pose.

Then it dawned on Kennet . . . that a guard dog would have already done one of two things. It would have barked its heart out, or it would have silently ripped his throat out. He bent his knees slowly and sank down to bring himself closer to the dog's level. He extended his left hand tentatively and whispered, "Here, pooch. Come here, boy."

The German shepherd's tail whipped, and then the dog bounded toward him, tail wagging. It sniffed his fingers and licked them. Kennet stroked its fur, talking to it softly.

He stood again and looked carefully around. Beyond the screening brush and the clearing, another hill rose. It was heavily forested. On that hill many decades ago had stood the townsite of Empire, for Wes Carlson had said his family had had a front-seat view of the whole mine complex.

He began his retreat. The dog followed. It ignored his command to stay. He picked up a stick and heaved it over the bushes into the clearing, realizing too late that he might be alerting someone to his presence. The dog whipped around and chased it.

A few metres east he could distinguish some security fencing in the brush. He was sorely tempted to investigate it, but good sense prevailed. If he remained on the conduit he was assured of safe footing. Off the conduit and he could be on the down slope to a bottomless pit. According to Carlson's description, that would be the manway, the narrow escape shaft accessed by ladders, or it could be a crevasse beneath which a stope, a chamber in the rock, had collapsed far underground and brought the roof down. Carlson had also located a manway further east. Kennet was not inclined to investigate. In fact, the sooner he was in his kayak, the safer he would feel.

He descended the conduit quickly. The dog did not return. Back on the railway track, he walked to the mill site. To the west, at the bend in the track, a flock of songbirds burst from the trees on the river side. He crossed the shallow ditch and poked his head through a portal, its sill about a metre off the ground. The portal must have given access to the mill at this level. He placed his hands on either side of the portal as he leaned forward. He felt the sting of concrete chips in his left hand and arm at the same time as he heard the shot. He dove inside.

Another shot, and the sound of the bullet striking and ricocheting off the wall. *What the hell!* Fear washed through him. He felt his bowels loosening and he struggled to contract his sphincter. His gut felt as if it had received a karate kick. He was prone on a concrete floor, safe behind concrete walls. Except for the open portal. But the shots had come from down the track, toward town. He took long deep breaths, forcing his heart rate down. Tremors ran the length of his body. He listened hard. After a few minutes he lifted himself up and worked his way into a corner where the broken foundation permitted him to peer out. He could see nothing, there were too many obstructions.

He examined his elbows. Both were skinned. On his left arm and the back of his hand, small flecks of blood indicated where concrete chips had peppered him. It was nothing serious. If the sniper had been any good, or if the sniper had been serious, he would be a dead man. He stood up and walked to the portal and leaned out, looking west along the track. He could see nothing. He jumped down, and looked at the gashes in the concrete where the bullets had struck. They were a good metre above the level of his head. So the sniper hadn't been serious. He couldn't have been that lousy a shot. He looked down the track again. The sniper must have stationed himself at the curve, in position to make a getaway without being observed. He would not investigate. Only if the sniper were a fool would he have left evidence such as shell casings. It had been a high-powered rifle. Besides, Kennet felt his curiosity satisfied for the day.

He returned to his kayak, becoming aware of his limp and of pain in his right leg. And of dampness in the seat of his pants. He had banged his knee good, but the wet suit had absorbed most of the shock. At riverside, he pulled down his pants. He looked distastefully at the excrement stains. He removed his boots and his pants, and rinsed the pants in the river. He plucked some leaves from poplar bushes and wiped himself. He pulled the pants on again.

Back on the water, he felt a slow burn ignite within him. It had been years since he had been a target for gunmen. And the list of suspects was short. Mighty short. In Indian country, you suspect the Indians. Metaphorically speaking.

What was he doing here, in Indian country? It was a term that he'd heard Canadian soldiers in Kandahar Province employ to describe the territory outside the wire, outside the security of Kandahar Air Field or outside the perimeter of a forward operating base. Outside, where ambuscades and firefights could happen anytime.

Today, he could have been inside, inside the perimeter of a city, inside the walls of a university, far from here, indulging in a peacetime activity. Two days ago he had felt no inclination to depart from his predictable existence. He'd had no reason to. Then yesterday morning Cindy Vanderhorst had come knocking on his door before it was full light. She wanted his assistance to find her husband, who had departed to another region as part of his job as an academic archaeologist. He agreed to help . . . because he was still groggy with sleep. Or because she had been pretty. Or because Vanderhorst was a colleague.

Until then, he had never really regarded Alfred Vanderhorst as a colleague. Alfie was a strange creature who squirreled himself away in another department in other recesses of the campus and when he left the campus for extended periods of time, mucked about in the dirt like a gopher. He had had one brief contact with him earlier that spring when Vanderhorst had been babbling incoherently about a project he intended to carry out in spite of the discouragement of his department head. Kennet knew Alfie's boss, Peter Sheridan, and respected him. Sheridan he thought of as a colleague. Their association had begun off campus, in the martial arts club. Members of the English Department were his colleagues. A few other faculty members he regarded as colleagues. He respected them, and he sought their respect. As for the rest of the faculty, they worked under the same roof, but they had nothing to do with him, nor he with them. They felt no attraction nor responsibility toward him, nor he toward them. Two years on staff himself, he felt no deep loyalty to the faculty as a whole, nor to the university itself.

So his interest in the mission to locate Vanderhorst had sprung from his friendship with Peter Sheridan. There was another reason. The search required him to rediscover a region where he had spent the prime of his youth, but it was a region he had never cared to revisit. And he still wasn't prepared to examine his reasons for avoiding the Geraldton district. In his youth it had been called the Geraldton district. Today it was called the Greenstone region. So when he had accepted the mission he had also acknowledged that it might be time to stir up his personal demons.

And then there was the third reason. Perhaps it was, after all, the first reason. He had devoted a career, his whole adult life, to investigative journalism. He was answering the call, the siren call of a story in dangerous territory. Sometimes the territory was geographical. And sometimes it was social. And always, always the territory was emotional.

The volcanic red Sportage was waiting patiently for him. Normal traffic whisked along the highway, but he recognized no vehicles. He drove up the access road toward the Con Empire and turned south on Railway Drive. Yes, he thought. No one would be looking for a parked vehicle in the junk-cluttered corner lot. There was no vehicle there now.

Back at the motel he peeled off the wet suit and jumped into the shower. It was almost seven o'clock. Pulling on boxer shorts, he meditated for twenty minutes.

He tuned the TV to the weather channel. It forecast intermittent showers for that night and the following day. He powered up the cell phone. One voice message, from Robert Kenilworth, a simple statement: *A suspicious death. Official cause: drowning.*

He checked his e-mail. Peter Sheridan advised him that the forensics lab had officially released the report on the remains of the unidentified female found last fall near Lake Nipigon. He could expect the media to pick it up soon. Sheridan had attached the digitized report. He closed his e-mail.

Impulsively he clicked on the Google Earth icon. Soon he was looking at a satellite image of Beardmore from 14,506 feet above the earth's surface. He traced the route his kayak had taken to the river bank below the ridge on which the Con Empire headframe stood.

At the south end of the image, the Warneford Road ran west from the highway. One could also walk down the railway line from town and cross the river twice, once to the west side, and again to the east side, and find oneself paralleling the Warneford Road just two or three hundred metres to the south.

West of the river a corridor in the bush identified the natural gas pipeline. A man on foot who didn't want to be seen, could have walked, or driven, down the corridor starting in the vicinity of the landfill site. He could have accessed the rail line where it crossed to the east side. There was more than one route to the Beardmore relics discovery site. There was even the river itself. Which, supposedly, the Vikings took.

He dressed quickly in casual clothes and stepped out the door. He glanced up at the cloud cover moving in. He had questions to ask. Alice's Restaurant was closed. He crossed the street to Melody's Variety. Instead of Melody a young woman was looking after the till. She was alone. Had she been on duty last night? Yes. Had she noticed any suspicious characters near his truck, the red SUV with the kayak? No. He bought a can of Pepsi. He noted the closing time for the store: 9:00 p.m. He looked up and down the street. Not a soul. Beardmore was closed for the night. A light burned in The Hook'n Bullet, and the door stood open. He returned to the motel and retrieved the bottle of merlot.

Chapter 12

. . . Friday evening

The meal had been superb – stuffed chicken breasts, vegetables that melted in the mouth, the merlot, a bottle of zinfandel supplied by the hosts, and an airy dessert concocted of fluffy cakes and fruit and whipped cream.

In the living room, sipping his zinfandel, Kennet sighed. "Crystal, I fear the world of broadcast journalism may have to share you with the culinary arts. But that may not be a bad thing."

Crystal laughed, her generous mouth flashing white teeth. "You mean I'd make a lousy journalist? Thanks a lot, Kennet." Kennet had laboured during the first few minutes of his arrival to get everyone to address him by his first name.

Kennet laughed. "It sounded like that, didn't it? What I meant is, we might have to invent a new category for you. The Gourmet News Anchor, or something. You'd wind up a newscast by drugging the weatherman with a stuffed mushroom, or seducing the guest with a French pastry."

Curtis Mallory chimed in. Curtis, about thirty years old with strong good looks, had proved the genial host. "When I was a kid," he said, "I tried to convince Mom and Dad that I didn't need a sister. I told them to take her back to the store where they got her. But," he grinned, "I may change my mind. That was a yummy meal, sis. As usual."

Curtis Mallory sat on a kitchen chair in the tiny living room. Crystal and Ioanna sat on the couch, Kennet, in the only stuffed chair. A young woman sat on the carpeted floor, along with the Mallorys' dog. Kaiser, the German shepherd, lay with his head between his paws, eyes fixed on Kennet.

Crystal had invited the girl next door, Gracie Elder, apparently her best friend. She had said that Conrad couldn't make it. She had made no further comment.

Crystal addressed Gracie, a rather plain, pudgy girl with long dark tresses. "Gracie, you must remind me tomorrow to return that cup of sugar to your mom." She turned to Kennet, her pony tail bobbing. "By the way, Kennet, that phone call earlier? That was a message for you. That was Barb – she works at the store? She phoned my Mom, who told her to phone here. You asked her something, apparently?"

"Yes, I asked her if she had seen anyone suspicious hanging around my truck."

Curtis burst out laughing. "The motel has been full of suspicious characters all week! Jennifer 's been talking about the sorry state of the rooms, and she's got to clean up. Bozos tramping over the carpet with oily boots. Vomit that missed the toilet bowl. Dirty underwear lying around."

"Well," Crystal continued, "when Barb was going home – last night, not tonight – she remembers the two Fleming boys – they're not boys anymore, they're men, they're in their forties, but they just act like boys – Lanny and Ritch? She remembers them crossing the railway track towards the motel. She lives in that area, near the Health Clinic? What was so unusual was to see the Flemings

138

walking. And, of course, there was nothing open downtown. Not that time of night. Anyway, that was the message."

"Thanks, Crystal."

"They do something to your truck?" asked Curtis.

"Nothing serious. Just some mischief."

"I heard the police were looking for them today."

"Not on my account," said Kennet. "I haven't reported any mischief."

"Anytime any crime goes down in this community," said Curtis, "the Flemings are the usual suspects."

Ioanna piped up. "Curtis, you'll give Kennet a bad impression of Beardmore. It's a lovely little place. Great people." She smiled. "Not like Calgary, mind you. But then, what is?"

"You saw Calgary for, what? Two minutes? At the height of the Stampede? And it's now the most exciting place in the world?"

Ioanna grimaced. "Ah, spare me."

"I agree with Ioanna," said Kennet, "from what I've seen. Beardmore is not the crime capital of Canada. But crime does happen here, does it?"

Ioanna replied. "We've had a break-in at the mine – the mill. And one at the office. I've only been here a couple of years, so I'm no authority."

Curtis filled in. "I've lived here all my life – well, till I was nineteen. I'm thirty-one now. And I remember break-ins, vandalism, people getting beat up, drunks – domestic disputes, the police call them. Lots of camps get broken into, especially in winter. Outpost camps, people's camps on Lake Nipigon, and on Windigokan Lake. Boats and motors disappear. Bicycles, too. Quads. Bushworkers report things missing. And then there's the usual kid stuff – lawn ornaments missing, Hallowe'eners mugged, gardens raided. Heck, I did some of that myself. But no murders. At least not by me," he chuckled.

"Drugs?" asked Kennet.

"Oh yeah, drugs," said Curtis. "There's the odd wild party at one of the camps, like the end-of-high-school celebration the grads always have. There's booze, of course, and maybe some pot. Nothing serious. Where would you get money for serious drugs in this town?"

Ioanna said, "You told me the Flemings were drug dealers."

"Yeah, but not around here. There's no market here. They leave town for long periods of time. They have no steady jobs. Everyone thinks they're selling. Probably stealing too. Like copper wire. Big bucks in selling used copper wire. They always seem to have money."

"But no murders, eh?" Kennet grinned.

"None that we know of. I can't remember a murder in Beardmore, in fact. Except, maybe, that archaeologist. How did he die, I wonder?"

Kennet shrugged. "I'd like to be able to tell his wife that. That's sort of why I'm sticking around."

Ionna laughed. "Yes. We kind of wondered about that."

"So, Curtis," said Kennet, "do a lot of young people come back here to work, like you?"

"No," said Ioanna, smiling. "Curtis is the exception. I married an exceptional man." Kennet detected sarcasm.

Curtis said, "Ioanna thinks my skills are wasted here. She thinks we should move to Calgary – lots of work for millwrights there. And," he glanced at Ioanna, "we will. Soon. I don't want to be accused of keeping my bride in a hell-hole like Beardmore." He grinned wryly.

"Anywhere without you is a hell-hole, dear," said Ioanna sweetly. Kennet noticed that Gracie sat with her head down, glancing up occasionally at some remark. Kaiser still had his eyes fixed on him.

"I grew up here," said Curtis. "I love the place. But not everyone feels the same. You asked about young people – most of them leave, of course. They go where the work is. I might be able to name six people that still live here that grew up with me, within two or three years of my age, I mean. Crystal's Conrad is one of them."

"And do you ever hear from them again? The ones who leave, I mean."

Crystal said, "Sure. If they've got friends or family still here."

"That's true," said Curtis. "But friends and family also leave."

At this point, Gracie Elder, who hadn't uttered three words all evening to anyone but Crystal, stood up and walked out. Crystal jumped up and followed Gracie's long dark tresses into the kitchen.

Curtis lifted his shoulders, palms open in question mode. He said softly, "Was it something I said?"

Crystal returned. "Gracie's gone home. She's not feeling well."

"Was it something I said?"

"You know what it is. We'll talk about it later."

A half hour later, Kennet said that it had been a long day and he was ready to hit the hay. When he stood up, so did Kaiser.

Curtis remarked, "You've made a friend there. He's waiting for you to throw something. I take him to work every day, but I've got no time to play with him. Have you met before, by any chance?"

"Never seen him before in my life."

"He's a rescue dog."

"Excuse me?"

"We rescued him. As a pup. Someone found him at the landfill gates. His brother had been shot but was still alive. The mother was guarding them both. Someone adopted the mother, we got the pup."

"And the injured pup?"

Crystal said, "Had to be put down. It was a crime, abandoning those animals, and leaving the pup to die. Wolves visit that dump. And bears. The community got together, raised funds, offered a reward for the villains, put posters up all around town. But . . . nothing."

Interesting, thought Kennet. No such concern for Vanderhorst's killers.

At the door, Kennet asked Crystal, "Will your friend be alright?"

"Oh, it's nothing." She made a brushing motion. "Nothing new, I mean. It's something personal."

"And will I get to meet your friend Conrad?"

Crystal coloured slightly. "He worked overtime tonight. They're dewatering the mine, you know. And the guy who was supposed to do it, didn't report for work. They run three shifts underground. That's two strikes against him now. Just this week."

"Would you be talking about Al Cummings?"

"Yes! How did you know?"

"I heard that he was in the foreman's bad books for admitting an unauthorized visitor."

Crystal said, "You hear a lot of things fast in a small town. Well, I hope we didn't bore you."

"On the contrary. I love gossip. So Conrad works underground at the Con Empire? Any chance I can meet him?"

"Well, he'll sleep till ten. He has the rest of the day off. I'm leaving then, got to get back to work. Here, I'll give you his phone number."

Once outside, Kennet encountered a light rain. Crystal called on her brother to give him a ride to the motel.

At the motel, he checked his cell for messages – he had left the cell on and plugged in. A Dale Marchuk had called, no message. That was the policeman that Robert Kenilworth said had worked in Beardmore yea these many years ago. It was almost 10:30. He would take a chance and call. Probably a retired cop by now anyway.

It was a 905 area code. A female voice answered after a single ring. Yes, Dale was still up. He was watching *Mantracker*, she said. A male voice came on the line.

142

"Hello," said Dale Marchuk. "It's just a re-run. Is this Kennet Forbes?"

"Hello. Yes. I apologize for bothering you so late. I just got in."

"No problem. I don't work anymore. I just run the department." He chuckled. "I thought it might be you. This is an unlisted number, and Robert said it was rather important. Robert said you teach at the university, and that you could be discreet. How can I help you?"

Kennet explained about the bones of a young female that were perhaps twenty-five years old, unearthed on a mining claim near Lake Nipigon. "I wondered," said Kennet, "if you recalled any reports of a disappearance in the early eighties in Beardmore."

"Okay," said Marchuk. "Robert filled me in to that extent. I pulled my old notebooks from that period, from '79 to '84, and I can tell you there was no one reported missing that we didn't find within a few hours. Sometimes, of course, he was found in the drunk tank. I'm sorry, Kennet. If you can pin the date down more precisely, I might be able to help."

"I'll work on it. So, Dale, where are you working now, if I may ask?"

"I'm in the London area. I run the crime unit. For another year or so. Then I will sip gin and tonics all day. I'll be retired." A woman's voice protested in the background.

"Margery says," Dale continued, "I will be gardening all day. Little does she know."

Kennet said, "If you're near London, then we know someone else in common. Detective Constable Mueller."

Dale laughed. "Robert said you had been introduced. That's partly my fault, I'm afraid. Con wasn't getting along with the squad, and he requested a transfer. I approved it, and I suggested to Region, unofficially of course, that he be posted where he would annoy the fewest people. Turns out it was Greenstone."

"I'll forgive you, but thousands wouldn't. Dale, I'm dying of curiosity. Robert said Detective Mueller broke a big case when he was a beat policeman. Can you fill me in?"

"If you never heard it from me."

"Heard what?"

"That's the right answer. Okay, Con found a corner shop owner on the floor beside an empty cash register in the small hours. He'd been stabbed to death. Now, Con knew that beat like the back of his hand. Knew all the characters. He leaned on a few, in his inimitable way, and finally accosted an addict who, with minimum persuasion, because he was dying for his next fix, gave it up. His bosses were ecstatic. There'd been political pressure to solve the murder of the businessman, an important figure in the community, and Con lucked out. He had that ace-in-the-hole when he applied for promotion. To my squad. Lucky me."

"And now, lucky us. Dale, when you were in Beardmore, what was the nature of the police work?"

"Violations of the Highway Traffic Act. And attendance at traffic accidents. But the bulk of the work, in the quiet and unassuming hamlet of Beardmore, was drunk and disorderly. Domestic disputes. A lot of them. No fun at all. But there was occasionally more interesting stuff. B & E's. The odd drug bust. Occasionally I got out on the lake, Lake Nipigon, with a patrol boat. Crack-downs on illegal drinking. But it was the lake itself that was interesting. And snowmobiling in winter. I helped the CO's with the ice fishermen."

"The Conservation Officers. The fish and game police."

"Right. Listen, tell you what I'll do. I'll vet my notebook line by line, and if there's anything remotely connected with a missing person, I'll send you the page. Give me your e-mail."

After hanging up, Kennet booted up the laptop. Some junk mail, and several e-mails that could wait till he got back to the office. He opened the forensics report on the mystery bones.

Chapter 13

ıı **THE BEARDMORE RELICS**

. . . Friday evening, later

In the fall of '08, the operator of a bulldozer had been stripping overburden on a promontory in the Brennan-Kenty claim group two miles from Lake Nipigon. The area he was working, the northern portion of the property, was being explored as a gold prospect, although the most abundant known mineral happened to be molybdenite, and considerable trenching had occurred on the south end of the property at that moly occurrence.

The property, owned by Crown Resources Inc., was accessed by a bush road linked to Highway 580, a hard-surfaced secondary highway that gave Beardmore access to Lake Nipigon. Crown Resources had commenced work in the spring of '05, but the claim group had been explored by different owners since the 1930's.

On October 16th, the blade of the bulldozer had dug into a bank of soil. The operator, Conrad B. Parker, said that he had disturbed a burrow that he believed was a bear's den. When he backed off, he could see some peculiar lumpy objects strewn behind the strip that he was back-blading in order to move the soil. He got down from the machine and identified the objects as bones, extremely weathered bones, which at first he took to be animal bones, those of a bear or other large animal. As he walked about, kicking the loose soil to unearth more bones, he turned up a skull. A human skull.

Parker notified the foreman, Ferguson S. Christie, who was supervising the excavation of a cut in the molydenite deposit. Christie agreed that the authorities had to be notified. Officers from the Greenstone Detachment had attended the scene, taken statements, recovered the bones, and taken them to the Paleo-Forensics Laboratory of Thunder Bay University. The site was returned to the jurisdiction of Crown Resources.

Next, Kennet turned to the osteological analysis. The bones belonged to a young female, possibly Caucasian, in good health, aged seventeen to nineteen, height 161 centimetres. One of the pelvic bones exhibited a fracture. Severe trauma to the patellas or knee caps. A fracture in the frontal bone of the skull. Three cracked ribs and two broken ones. All of the injuries suggested perimortem trauma. All of the bones, including the skull, exhibited marks consistent with the tooth marks of a large animal, probably a bear. There were smaller marks consistent with rodents. Many of the victim's teeth had been recovered intact, but loose. The teeth showed a pattern of regular dental care, including fillings.

A swatch of black hair had also been recovered. Very little clothing had survived, with the singular exception of the major portion of a plastic belt, colour red, and denim rags that might have been jeans, and a mostly intact dark rubberized coat, sized for a large adult. Scene-of-crime officers had also recovered miscellaneous artifacts by sifting the soil, a list of which followed, and included:

Fragments of plastic belt, colour red, 5.5 cm, 2.3 cm, 1.2 cm, .8 cm

    1 belt buckle, white metal

    4 white buttons, plastic

7 brass studs (probably from jeans)

1 ring, 14K white gold, size 6 (with setting for a jewel)

1 cut stone, aluminum oxide, blue, 0.27 carat (commonly known as corundum or sapphire)

No evidence of footwear.

Evidence suggested the body/bones had been reposing on site for twenty-five years, with a margin of error of three years, plus or minus.

An addendum to the report alluded to concerns of a local aboriginal group, Ombabika Bay First Nation, headquartered in Beardmore. If the age of the bones suggested an ancient burial, the First Nation reserved the right to claim the remains and to provide a decent burial with appropriate ceremonies in a place of their choosing.

Twenty-six years ago, thought Kennet, *I graduated from Geraldton District High School. I might have known the decedent.* It was a disturbing thought.

An appendix listed the full names and addresses of people mentioned in the body of the report, including the officers involved, the scientists engaged in the investigations, and the contact person for Ombabika Bay First Nation. The employees of Crown Resources Inc. who had reported the find were Ferguson Simon Christie and Conrad Blake Parker.

Kennet created a document folder titled Beardmore, and saved the report. Next, he conducted a Google search with the terms "Brennan-Kenty" and "Beardmore". He struck gold. The first hit was a long document in PDF format. It turned out to be an 8-megabyte file. With the wireless broadband connection, it took only a few minutes to download.

He clicked on *CBC/The National* under Favorites, and scanned the headlines. He repeated the process for *CNN International News*. Satisfied that he was current with world events, he conducted a search using the exact phrase "how to unlock" and the essential words "dodge" and "ram". At the very top of the responses was a website titled *How to Pick a Door Lock On a Dodge Ram.*

He studied the content. He needed a lock pick set. They were necessary tools for any car thief, which he was not, or for any restorer of vintage cars, which he was. The article directed the thief, or the restorer, to the driver's door lock. A total of seven discs or wafers had to be aligned before the lock could operate. Then the lock had to be turned in the right direction. It looked easy enough.

Kennet booted down. Amazing, he thought. What a marvelous compendium of information the Internet was. A boon to any thief or embezzler or fraudster or scammer – to a crook of any description. And a boon to the honest scholar. Which he was. Mostly.

He brushed his teeth. It was 11:27. He set the travel alarm for 2:27. He could hear the water splashing as it dropped from the eaves.

At 2:24 he arose and switched off the alarm. He dressed quickly in his wet suit. He opened the door and stepped out, holding his palm open to the sky. A few raindrops moistened it. Lightning flashed, followed by a rumble. The motel windows were dark. He stepped back inside. He rummaged under the sink and extracted a large black plastic garbage bag. He had neglected to bring rain gear this trip. He fashioned two armholes and a neck hole and slipped the bag over his head. The bag disguised his body outline. The last thing he wanted was a report of a ninja marauder prowling the streets of Beardmore after midnight.

From the truck he retrieved the lock pick set he kept in the console. He found a dark ball cap in the back seat and jammed it on his head. He sensed a misty rain on his face. The sky was pitch black. He walked wide of the security light at the office. It was rather a pointless manoeuvre because he had to walk, fully exposed, under a streetlight as he found the walking trail and headed east over the tracks. As he approached the line of houses, a dog started barking furiously, but it was reacting to other marauders. He stood still, cocking an ear to the distant sound of a pack of hunting wolves.

The Fleming homestead stood dark. The nose of the Dodge Ram 3500 faced the garage. He would have to work with his back to the house. He hoped that the Flemings slept soundly.

He removed a small tool from his lock pick set, a small rigid tension tool that he had manufactured himself from a piece of steel. It looked like a very tiny old-fashioned hand crank. Before electric starters became de rigueur, car operators had had to crank their engines by hand. His back to the darkened house, he inserted the tool into the very bottom of the lock. Holding it with his left hand, he pressed gently to the rear of the truck. He operated by touch, not willing to risk a light, even if he had had one.

With his right hand he inserted another steel tool, a pick, with the pick facing down. He pushed it all the way in. He pressed it gently downwards, and withdrew it steadily. He re-inserted the pick with the pick facing up, and pushed it all the way in. Applying a gentle pleasure he withdrew it steadily. According to the instructions the inner mechanism should have rotated. He had heard no clicking. With the tension tool still in place, he inserted the pick again, pick facing up, and repeated the procedure. He heard the inner plug of the lock rotating. He removed both tools and glanced toward the house. Silence and darkness. He pocketed the tools.

The rain picked up. He squeezed the door handle release and slowly opened the driver's door. The cab light popped on. He glanced around. No reaction from the house. He opened the door wide. He pressed the button to electronically open all the doors, and then opened the rear door and climbed quietly in and fumbled for the lever to release the back of the bench seat. Half the seat folded forward. In the dim recess he felt around until he identified three encased long guns. He extracted one, carefully, and lay it on the floor of the back seat. He extracted a second one.

Behind him a light popped on. Through the truck's rain-streaked glass he saw that someone had switched on a light on the ground floor of the house. Judging by the size of the window, someone was utilizing the bathroom. There was a tremendous lightning flash, followed by a roll of thunder. The sound-and-light show, he thought, might prompt somebody to peer out a window.

Kennet snapped the rear seat back, grabbed the two gun cases, and stepped down. He closed the rear door, and clutching the cases with his right hand, hit the lock switch on the front door with his left hand and closed the door carefully. The cab light went out.

As he crept across the cinders, the heavens unleashed a downpour. He poked the two cases up under his makeshift raincoat, holding them in place with both hands. If he should encounter anyone in the darkness, he might cut an awkward figure but he would not give the impression of a walking arsenal. He took the trail west across the tracks, and once he reached Rothwell Street, behind the motel, he walked north along the road until he came to the snow machine graveyard. He pried open the door of the orange derelict and tucked the two encased guns inside out of sight.

No one would be poking around the junkyard except tourists like him. Or kids. It was Saturday, and kids might be roaming on their day off school. Okay, what was he thinking? This was summer vacation. The likelihood of kids locating the cache was slim to none. Still, there was a chance and it worried him. He had decided against stashing the loot in the Sportage in the event that the Flemings reported the theft, and the finger pointed to him. But the irony of a gang of thieves reporting a theft of their own property might be too rich even for the Flemings. Besides, he suspected that they redressed their own wrongs. He would have to move the guns at the earliest opportunity. And implement Phase 2 of the operation.

Back in his room he stripped off his wet outfit and hung it to dry over the bathtub. The garbage bag he stuffed in his kit bag.

He would not risk the chambermaid finding it. It was 3:04. He set the alarm for 7:00.

Chapter 14

THE BEARDMORE RELICS |||||||||||||||||||||||||||||||||||||||||||||||||||||

Saturday, August 15th . . .

Just after 7:30 a.m. he walked into Alice's Restaurant. It was buzzing with a small crowd of locals. No sign of the highway maintenance crews. He noted the familiar white locks peeping over the widespread newspaper at a tiny table, and approached the reader.

"Good morning, Mac. Do you mind company?"

Mac Kueng lowered *The Lakehead Journal* and gestured to the empty chair, still grasping the edges of the paper. "Help yourself. It's a free country."

Kueng lifted the paper and resumed reading. Alice arrived almost immediately and Kennet ordered the special. "Anything interesting?" he asked the paper.

Kueng lowered the paper and folded it. "Excuse my manners. I just wanted to finish what I started." He took a slurp of his milky coffee. "Nope, nothing new. The country's still going to hell."

Kennet glanced around. The customers, most of them male, engrossed themselves in eating and/or carrying on animated conversations. Kennet returned his attention to Kueng. "So," he said, "which circle of hell gets the front page today?"

Kueng responded quickly. "The fourth," he said. "Greed. Those Wall Street bastards are paying themselves fat bonuses again. I guess they deserve it."

"Deserve it? How, pray tell?"

"Hell, they convinced the country they were poor, and got billions for their trouble. I should be so clever. But Dante got it wrong, you know."

"Explain."

"Avarice should be ascribed to a lower circle of hell. The eighth, perhaps. Along with the crooked politicians. Without them, Wall Street and Bay Street might operate honestly. Devil forbid."

They chatted in desultory fashion about the state of the world until Kennet's breakfast arrived. Kueng excused himself and rose. Kennet said, "If you're finished with that, I'd like to read it."

Kueng clutched the paper to his chest. "Nope. Sorry. That's tomorrow morning's fire-starter. All it's good for now."

"Understood. Listen, Mac. I've got a little chore you might like. Mind if I drop by in an hour?"

"You're welcome. Just toot."

After breakfast, Kennet strolled across the street to Melody's and picked up *The Lakehead Journal*. Back in his room, he checked the telephone directory. He looked up the name Parker. On McKenzie Avenue there was a listing for a B. Parker, with the number Crystal Mallory had given him for her Conrad.

He opened the newspaper and scanned the articles. On page 5, under Regional Briefs, the following item appeared:

Beardmore remains

A news release from the Paleo-Forensics Laboratory of Thunder Bay University states that the human remains found last October near Lake Nipigon belonged to a young female in her late teens. The victim may have been lying there for twenty-five years.

The statement gave no indication there was any suspicion of foul play. It was originally believed the remains belonged to an ancient aboriginal burial or to the victim of a prospecting accident in more recent times.

Now, mused Kennet, why didn't Mac Kueng mention this item, so close to home?

On his way to The Hook'n Bullet, Kennet held out a hand, palm up. A heavy overcast shrouded the community. Puddles stood around. He imagined he could feel an occasional raindrop. Bull Kellerman loitered behind the counter of his shop as some customers picked over his stock. "Good morning, sir," he said. "Still around, I see."

"Going home tomorrow sometime." said Kennet. "Thought I'd see some of the country. Not having much luck with that other thing."

"No news, then."

"Well, there is some. Unofficial. I'll tell you about it." Kennet nodded in the direction of the customers.

"Right." Kellerman raised his voice to address the customers. "Anything in particular you're looking for?"

A bearded man in a hunting vest looked up from his examination of a glass-topped counter. "Any 10-gauge slugs?" he asked.

"10-gauge! We got black bears, sir. Not grizzlies." Kellerman unlocked the rear of the counter and pulled out a box of cartridges. "Did you ever hear about our cinnamon bear? Big as a silvertip." He launched into a tale that might have had elements of truth. Kennet browsed the shelves and racks until the customers left.

"Right," said Kellerman, bracing himself on the countertop, palms downward and angled outward.

"This is not for public consumption," said Kennet. He had considered this move carefully. The description of Vanderhorst's

154

death as a suspicious homicide would soon come out. He had half expected to find it in that morning's paper. He needed to test Kellerman's capacity to be discreet.

"Agreed," said Kellerman.

"I have learned, unofficially, that the police will be treating Vanderhorst's case as a suspicious death. Someone thumped him on the back of the head."

"Christ!" Kellerman screwed up his face. "I don't like to hear that. We've had assaults before – there's that Henderson boy, of course. But cold-blooded murder? That's rare. That," he said, twisting his lips, "as far as I know, has never happened here."

"You can't tell anyone."

"I agreed." After a pause he said, "Any suspects?"

"Not that I'm aware of."

Kellerman hung his head and pondered. After a while he said, "Maybe it did happen before."

"What do you mean?"

"You saw the paper today? The remains they found last fall on the Brennan-Kenty property. They belonged to a teenager. A girl. Died twenty-five years ago".

"I read that."

"I've been racking my brains. How could she die out there? There'd be no reason for her to be out there. She had to be deliberately buried there. Died someplace else, and then buried there. Christ, that place is thirty-five light years from anywhere else, and no one goes there, unless he's hunting. Or mining. Crown Resources has been taking bulk samples of molybdenite off and on now for three years. Mind you, twenty-five years ago or thereabouts, there was a company exploring that property. But there'd've been no call for a girl to be traipsing about there."

"You know the people here, Bull. Any young people from that era go missing?"

"Loads of 'em. Almost all of 'em. There wasn't much to hold a young person in Beardmore in those days. Unless they found a niche in the forest industry, or followed their dads into the commercial fishery or into tourist service. Prospecting was mostly a sideline, not a career. And that's mostly the boys. For girls there were even fewer opportunities. Christ, come to think of it, nothing's changed. Everything's a sunset industry, except mining today. And that's barely off the ground."

"If you think of anyone . . ."

"I've been racking my brains . . ."

"Won't take much racking," said a female voice from the doorway. Marta walked in, smiling.

"I'll have you know, dear," said Kellerman, pointing a finger at his cranium, "that this here is fertile territory."

"Well, it's well manured, that's for sure," said Marta, still smiling. She handed her husband a thermos. "Here's your tea." She turned to Kennet. "We keep the coffee hot here, for the customers. But Bull likes his tea. Black. How are you this morning?"

"In fine fettle, Mrs. Kellerman."

"Everyone calls me Marta. Nice to see you again."

"Likewise, Marta. And I'm Kennet, in case you've forgotten." He turned to Kellerman. "It looks like more rain today. Where can a person pick up a rain suit?"

"Try St. Clair's. Down the street." He jerked his thumb in the direction of the motel. "Opens at 9:00."

"One more thing. In my wanderings I found some derelict snow buses, on Rothwell, next to the tracks. What's the history there?"

"Would you believe that Joseph-Armand Bombardier once had a factory there? Filled orders from here all the way to Aklavik and Iqaluit and King George's Island?"

"No."

"Okay. The commercial fishermen used them on the lake. Now they use those runty little snowsleds. Would you believe they start using them right after Labour Day?"

"No."

"You're no fun. Git on with yuh."

"Oh, one more thing, Bull. When I went for a paddle yesterday, on the river, I noticed a recently cleared trail, straight as an arrow, heading west. And there was a red-tipped picket."

"Claim line," said Kellerman. "Or a grid line, for running geophysical surveys. The bush is cross-hatched with 'em."

As he walked back to his room, his cell rang. "Hello, chum," said Robert Kenilworth. "You up yet?"

"Since the crack of dawn. You coming up, or are you here already?"

"I'm not coming today. I wouldn't be useful. Our intrepid detectives did speak to Al Cummings yesterday. He worked a partial day shift, and they caught him at home. He confirmed your story. But the Flemings are proving elusive."

"The Flemings are strutting around Beardmore, large as life."

"Well, that's policing in Greenstone. It's a big area and we have limited manpower. We can't post a man on their doorstep unless it's a life-and-death situation. And Henderson's no longer on the critical list. He can't talk, though. His jaw is wired shut, he's on heavy medication, and to cap the cake, he can't write – got a broken bone in his writing hand, and a badly bruised left wrist. He could give yes or no responses, though, by blinking. He didn't know his assailants. There were two of them. And when Detective Armistead showed him pictures of the Flemings, he closed his eyes and went to sleep. They waited an hour till he woke up, and when he went into respiratory distress, the nurses shooed them out. They waited another hour and then the doctor advised them to come back tomorrow. That's today. We'll get the Nipigon detachment to interview him."

Kennet unlocked his door and stepped inside. "So, nothing new from Cummings?"

"Kelly said she struggled to get a confirmation of what he had told you. It's almost as if there were an intimidating presence hovering nearby. I can't say more."

"Cummings may have been unnerved. He didn't show up for a stint on night shift."

"Now how would you know that?"

"It's a small town." Kennet continued, "Robert, what did the SOCOs make of the stony debris on the path near Vanderhorst's body?"

"What debris? I didn't hear anything about any goddamn debris."

"Hey, keep your shirt on. There were some loose rocks that appeared to come from the dig. They were lying on the path about ten metres from the body. One piece was suspended in the branches of an alder."

Robert unleashed a string of curses.

"Robert, I am not the enemy."

Robert paused, breathing heavily. "Kennet, I apologize. You just happened to be within the orbit of my wrath. Now tell me, exactly, what did this debris look like?"

"I took pictures, Robert. I always carry a camera. Force of habit. I'll send them to you. By phone. I'm not using the Internet today. Okay?"

Robert thanked him.

"And you can do something for me. In the SOCOs' report, anything that I can follow up?"

"I'll look into it. Meanwhile, I'll roust out the SOCOs, and get their asses in gear. We'll need official images."

After he had hung up, Kennet downloaded the camera images into the laptop, and then copied the ones in question into the cell phone, and sent them.

Kennet drove the short distance along Rothwell Street and stopped at the snow bus graveyard. He saw no one around. He quickly extracted the gun cases from the orange machine and stowed them in the back seat on the floor. Over them he spread the newspaper pages that he had brought for that purpose. He drove slowly out of town and turned at the landfill site road. He stopped beside Mac Kueng's Chevy pickup and honked twice, paused, and then beeped again.

Kueng came striding down the path, beckoning to him. Kennet got down and beckoned to him in turn. He opened the rear door and removed the newspapers.

Kueng came up. "What's up?"

"I'd like to commission your smithy services," said Kennet. He looked meaningfully up and down the road and then pulled out a red gun case and unzipped it.

Kueng's eyes widened. "What d'yuh got there?"

"I'm not sure. Let's take a look." He eased out the long gun, a lovingly pampered .308 Winchester. It had a mounted scope and it was fitted with a trigger lock.

"That's a beauty! Where did that come from?"

"Let's just say, it fell into my hands." Kennet handed the Winchester to Kueng and pulled out the second case, a green one. It was a .30/06 Springfield, also with scope.

Kueng eyed him with interest. "Am I getting into something illegal here?"

"Let's just say," said Kennet, "that what the law doesn't know about, the law doesn't care about."

"What do you want from me?"

"Some corrective engineering. As it is now, that –" Kennet indicated the Winchester that Kueng was holding, "doesn't shoot around corners. It needs correcting."

Kueng smiled grimly. "Do these belong to the galoots I think they belong to?"

"If I told you, I'd have to kill you."

Kueng's jaw dropped. Kennet added hastily, "Hey, that's just a manner of speaking! It's a throwaway line in situation comedies!"

"Television! I avoid it like I avoid the politicians. Last time I watched, it was that Twin Towers thing. In New York. Political bullshit."

"Yes, 9/11. Listen, this is between you and me."

"Okay. And the .30/06? What re-engineering does it require?"

"This," said Kennet, "shoots only in the direction you point it. It . . . needs to become more . . . adaptable."

Kueng spoke slowly. "It is amazing how heat can adapt the toughest girder."

"How much time do you need?"

"I'm going to fire up now. Why don't you call back around, say, suppertime? This will be a pleasure."

On the way out, Kennet stopped at the padlocked gate of the landfill site. A cyclone fence ran around the extensive dumping ground. Ravens flitted about. There was no one around. He took the red and green gun sheaths, folded them into a bundle, and walked over to a stationary dumpster. He lifted the heavy half-lid. He picked up a stick from the ground and poked a hole in the garbage and stuffed in the cases, covering them as best he could. He lowered the lid. Some ravens clucked from the surrounding trees.

He parked at the motel and glanced at his watch. 9:07. As he walked up the street to St. Clair's Hardware, it started to spit rain. He pushed open the glass door and looked around, stupefied. He couldn't remember when he had shopped in an establishment crammed so full of stuff. He had a memory flash of shops in Istanbul.

He found a small counter with a cash register but no one in attendance. "Hello!" he said, raising his voice. "Can I get some assistance?"

"Be right with you!" The male voice came from somewhere deep in the rear. Kennet waited a moment and then started down one aisle, or rather, a space between rows of stock that suggested it had once been an aisle. He came up against handles of rakes and mops which had collapsed and now barricaded the passage. He retreated.

"Yes sir!" A bespectacled man with thinning gray hair in a shopkeeper's apron appeared before him. "I was just stowing away some new hibachis. Big demand for them! How can I help you?"

"I'm looking for rain gear."

"Right this way, sir!" His lips stretched in a pencil-thin smile below a pencil-thin spackled moustache. He led the way through another crowded aisle to a rack of clothing. "Look for yourself, on the far end."

Kennet pawed through some rain jackets and rain suits and selected a red suit made in Hong Kong. It had some openings to allow it to breathe, but it was hardly top-of-the-line gear. He had top-of-the-line gear at home. This would do.

"I'll take this." He handed the suit to the shopkeeper.

Back at the register, the man rang it up, and Kennet paid with plastic. The man held out his hand and said, "I'm St. Clair. Gerald St. Clair. You can call me Gerry. This is my establishment. Haven't seen you before."

Kennet shook his hand and introduced himself.

"Ah yes," St. Clair sighed knowledgeably. His eyes glinted behind the spectacles. "I thought at first you might be with the mining companies. We do a lot of business with the mining companies."

"You've been here a long time, haven't you, Gerry," said Kennet.

"Grew up with the town," he said, expansively.

"I used to know a St. Clair boy. In high school, around '80, '82?"

"My son. Cameron. Had a daughter, too, just three years older than Cam. And our youngest daughter, Colleen, she came late to Beatrice and me. She's going to college now."

"Cam. I remember Cam St. Clair. Big star in the drama club. I reported on performances in the school newspaper."

"That's our Cam."

"Is Cam still around?"

"Long gone. Not even in the country anymore. We're lucky to see him every couple, three years. He's a, waddyacallit, a cinematographer. He makes movies. For Hollywood and places like that. He always loved taking pictures."

"I remember that about him. Would you still have some of his old pictures?"

"Boxes full. But they're twenty-five, thirty years old. You wouldn't be interested. He did his best work after that."

"On the contrary, Gerry, I'd be very interested. It'd bring back old times."

St. Clair responded eagerly. "I was just thinking about those boxes the other day. I'll dig them up. When would you like to see them?"

"Would tonight be convenient?"

Kennet agreed to drop by the St. Clair residence about 8:00 p.m. When he opened the door to exit, it was raining steadily. He stood on the concrete step under the overhang and slipped into the rain suit.

He used the room phone to call Conrad Parker's number. It was early, but he might get lucky. A cheerful male voice said hello.

"May I speak to Conrad, please."

"That's me. Is this Mr. Forbes?"

"Hi. Kennet here. I'd like to talk to you. May I buy you breakfast?"

"Just a minute." There were muffled voices. Conrad came back on the line. "Does that include Crystal?"

"Of course. And anyone else there . . ."

"My parents have eaten, but we'll come, Crystal and me. I have to jump in the shower."

"Shall we say ten o'clock, at Arlene's?"

He booted up the laptop so that he could study the report on the Brennan-Kenty property. It had a hefty title: *Qualifying Report on the Brennan-Kenty Molybdenite and Gold Property in Dorothea Township, N.W. Ontario (NTS 52H9/NE) – Prepared for Crown Resources Inc.* A professional mining engineer had submitted the report in April of '06.

The report covered a wide spectrum of information on the property, including the location, a history of exploration, the geological setting, the mineralization, the activities of Crown Resources since '05, and the engineer's recommendations. Kennet noted that the road link to Beardmore included Highway 580, the 72 Road, and an unnamed bush road. As for the property location, it was north of the Namewaminikan River *(old name Sturgeon River)*, 3 kilometres from Lake Nipigon, in the area of, quote, *the 1999 forest fire*, unquote, that had burned 30,350 hectares. The fire had spared a 2-kilometre corridor bordering the river, which flowed into the big lake.

In the early '30's, two prospecting syndicates had held adjoining claim groups, one of which was named Brennan-Kenty Bros. Prospecting Company Limited. Since 1935, different companies had explored the claim groups, sometimes re-staking them and sometimes optioning them (which Kennet took to mean, paying a fee for the right to work them and to earn an interest in them). Sometimes the work focused on the molybdenite occurrence, and sometimes on the gold. In 1964 and '65, there had been a program of *geological mapping, trenching, stripping, sampling, and diamond drilling*, and then no work until 1983, when a similar program had been undertaken by a different company for one season.

Kennet glanced at his watch – six minutes before 10 o'clock. He arrived at Arlene's Tavern at exactly 10:00. Another short flight of stairs. He ducked his head and bounded up them. Inside, he headed for the table where Crystal Mallory was seated with a male companion. He carried the folded-up *The Lakehead Journal* in his hand.

Chapter 15

... Saturday morning

Kennet nursed a coffee while Conrad and Crystal ate a full breakfast of eggs, sausage, home fries, and toast.

Conrad Parker sat across the table from Kennet, beside Crystal, and kept a running commentary as he shoveled the food in. He kept Crystal in stitches. There was a scattering of freckles on his pleasant face beneath a thatch of reddish hair. He was a well-built man with strong hands.

"Sure beats Crystal's cooking," he said.

Crystal punched him in the shoulder and laughed. "You haven't tasted my cooking for ages."

"That must be the problem," said Conrad. "I've forgotten."

"Next week," she said, "try to get home on time."

"Yes, dear." Crystal giggled.

She glanced over at Kennet as she said, "If you could slow down a minute, I think Kennet wanted to talk to you."

Kennet said, "I was fairly curious about the man who could capture the fair Crystal."

Crystal glowed. "We've known each other for, what?"

"All my life," said Conrad.

"I mean, we've been going out for five years. He was always so much more mature than the other boys, and a gentleman." She giggled.

"Don't forget handsome," said Conrad.

"I didn't forget."

Conrad clutched his stomach and groaned. "A low blow!" He quickly finished the remnants of his meal and wiped up the grease with a piece of toast.

Crystal resumed her meal at a more leisurely pace. "I'm expecting my ride in twenty minutes. Someone's got to work."

Kennet jumped into the opening. "What sort of work do you do, Conrad?"

"Right now I'm rehabilitating the drifts that have been pumped dry. But you know that. I think of myself as a professional prospector. When I'm not staking ground, or optioning it, or working it, I fill in time with other jobs. That's what I'm doing now. That's what my father did, all his life." Conrad accompanied his spiel with an infectious smile.

'What's it like underground?"

"Dark," he said. Crystal giggled again.

"I mean, are the drifts in good shape? Any cave-ins?"

"Excellent shape. We're only on the first level, and the spaghetti rail is still in place, even a couple of ore cars, and you know what? You lean on one of those cars, and it moves. It's incredible, but the grease in those wheels has held up for, what? Sixty, seventy years? Cold, stagnant water is a great preservative. The timbers are sound, though we insert some rock bolts to guard against rock bursts."

"So the roofs are intact?"

"Pretty much. There's been some leakage from the chutes. You know what I mean? The stopes, the working chambers above the drifts where the ore was blasted out – the ore dropped down the chutes into the cars. There's been some accumulation of old ore beneath chutes, because the chute doors were constructed of wood, and some have weakened under the pressure from above."

"I get the picture." Crystal had given up on her meal and pushed it aside to concentrate on her coffee. Kennet said, "So, what properties have you optioned?"

"Many. The old Spider property. The Murphy. The Caliper-Sturgeon. Those names won't mean anything to you, but there's one I'm most proud of, which has been in the family, off and on, for years. The Brennan-Kenty."

"That one I know. And I'll tell you why." Kennet unfolded the newspaper and pushed it across the table with his finger on the item *Beardmore remains.*

Conrad studied it, Crystal leaning towards him. He ran a finger under each short paragraph as he read. He leaned back, a strange look on his face.

Crystal said, "Let me see that," and grabbed the page. "That," she said a moment later, "refers to the bones you found." She looked intensely at Conrad. "It was a young woman."

"I know," he said. "I mean, I know it's the bones I found." He looked dazed.

Crystal released the page and sat back. "That was just before I was born. She died just before I was born."

They looked at each other. The waitress approached the table. "One check or two, Blackie?"

Conrad looked at her uncomprehendingly. Kennet spoke up, "One check, please. Let me come with you." Kennet rose and followed her to the till.

As he paid, he could see Crystal and Conrad exchanging a few words. He returned to the table. "Who's Blackie?" he asked.

"Eh?" said Conrad. "Oh, that's me. My nickname. My middle name's Blake, same as my dad. But the kids in high school used to call me Blackie, after Conrad Black, you know. Big joke, you know. 'Where'd you hide the money, Blackie?', and "Why'd you shred the documents, Blackie?'" It was an unsubtle reference to the lordly Canadian wheeler-dealer who had been sentenced to six-and-a-half years in an American prison for fraud and obstruction of justice. Conrad Parker smiled wanly.

"I sense it's been a shock to you," Kennet said. "That article."

"Yes," said Crystal slowly. "Conrad may have known her. I may have known the family."

"Stupid of me. I should have been more sensitive."

"We would've read it ourselves soon enough," said Crystal. She looked aimlessly out the bay window. "Where's my ride?"

"But it's more than idle curiosity on my part." He had their attention now. "The university asked me to make enquiries while I was up here. There will be an investigation now, to identify the remains." It was a lie, but a white one. The university had asked him no such thing. Peter Sheridan had incidentally, and probably indiscreetly, asked him to poke around. To follow his nose. The problem with noses, they sometimes encountered bad smells. Kennet wrinkled his nose. It was the police now who would launch an investigation, and he'd have nothing to do with it.

Conrad said, "When I found those – those remains – the guys kidded me, saying maybe I could get a job playing the son of Harrison Ford. You know, the son of – in that movie series, *Raiders of the Lost Ark* and all that. They were just old bones, you know." He added, "I feel awful now."

Crystal massaged his arm with both hands. "Don't you dare, sweetie. Don't you dare. None of it's your fault."

"When I showed that to you," said Kennet, "I should have known you might have some feelings for the victim. It's a small town. It was a really, really dumb move on my part."

Conrad straightened up. "As Crystal said, we would've heard about it anyway. Besides, it may not even be anybody from around here."

"It's still a tragedy," said Crystal. "Someone so young. Younger than me. Do you think she was . . . " She couldn't say the words.

Kennet said, "It's too early to tell. In fact, we may never know. But if it was someone who lived around here, you could help me . . . identify the remains." There. He'd said it again. That he was investigating the victim. He wasn't. Not officially. He had another victim on his agenda. Vanderhorst. And he was getting nowhere fast with that.

Crystal and Conrad spoke together: "How?"

"You know the people here, the families. Who went missing here twenty-five years or so ago?"

Crystal cast her eyes out the window again and murmured, "Where *is* my ride?" Then very softly, "O my God."

Conrad looked at her curiously and then back to Kennet. "I suppose I could help in some way. But a lot of people have left and never come back. How would we start?"

"With pictures. As it happens, I am going to look at a whole bunch tonight. Gerry St. Clair said his son, Cam, has loads of pictures from that time, and I'm going to look at them, eight o'clock tonight."

"I'll come too," said Conrad eagerly.

"Here's my ride!" said Crystal suddenly. She stood up, snatching her handbag from where she'd left it on the floor. She turned to Conrad, giving him a peck on the cheek. "I'm coming too. Tonight. You pick me up at Buffalo Grass's kitchen."

"You can leave?" said Conrad, astonished.

"Bertha owes me. I filled in for her a while back. I'm taking a few hours off. Let them fire me, if they dare. Come get me." Then she was out the door.

Kennet and Conrad sat in silence for a few minutes. Kennet drained his cup. Marge appeared with a decanter and a large smile. He had left a healthy tip. He allowed her to fill the cup.

Kennet broke the silence. "What are you up to today?"

"Oh. Dad will have some little chores for me. Nothing much."

"I want to see the spot where you found the remains, Conrad. Are you up for it?" Conrad looked at him apprehensively. "There

I go again," said Kennet, "being insensitive. I'll ask someone else, of course."

"No, no," said Conrad. "I was just thinking, Crown Resources wants me to do more stripping on the Brennan-Kenty, starting sometime next week. I was just thinking, I'll have to spend a lot of time out there, so I'd better get used to it. Besides, there's a locked gate. You need permission to get on the property. And I have a key."

"What's involved in stripping, exactly?"

"Stripping overburden. Removing the trees and the brush and the soil and boulders that lay on the bedrock. The rock has to be exposed so that the geologists can do their work. I've used a dozer for that. But this time I'll use a backhoe, equipped with a blade."

"You can operate a lot of machinery."

"Oh yeah. Dad taught me. Plus, I've got papers for heavy equipment operator. In fact, Dad was stripping the Brennan-Kenty way back in '64, '65. He owned the property back then, and when he optioned it, he got the contract for stripping."

"So prospecting really does run in the family."

"Oh yeah. And you have to be versatile. I'm somewhat of a mechanic too."

"Mac Kueng, he was telling me he used to fabricate machine parts in his backyard."

"Ol' Mac. Dad's told me loads of stories about Mac Kueng. He was a hotshot operator of machinery too. Mac was working with Dad back in '65, and on a few other projects."

"Mac said he's made his fortune more than once."

"You better believe him. There's been more than one millionaire in Beardmore, but you'd never know it by their lifestyle. Once the rocks flow in their veins, they're hooked for life, and even if they can afford a condo in Toronto, they prefer living here. Modestly."

Kennet signaled to Marge. He said to Conrad, "You like BLT? We better take a sandwich."

Conrad nodded, and said, "You got a hunter's vest? Bear season opens today. Better safe than sorry."

"Yes, I have. I thought the season opened two days ago."

"Nope. Always on a Saturday."

Kennet arranged to pick up Conrad at his home. He drove to the motel and parked. He walked across to Melody's and picked up a case of bottled water. In his room he changed into his bush kit and ran down a mental check list of things to take. He slipped the bear banger into a pocket of his cargo pants.

Chapter 16

. . . Saturday mid-day

Following Conrad's directions, Kennet drove up Hwy. 580, a winding, hard-surfaced road with the shoulder barely wide enough to accommodate the wheels on the passenger side before they would drop into a deep ditch. They drove through a country recovering from the great fire of '99, a country now drenched with a steady rain. The hilly terrain rarely permitted vistas. Here and there a tote road wound away into the brush. The wipers worked constantly.

After a few kilometres Conrad directed him to turn right. The double-lane gravel road was unsigned. They drove north, eventually hitting a belt of mature bush. The natural growth gave way to stands of tall, majestic pines. A large sign informed visitors that they were touring the Tyrol Lake Demonstration Forest. The sign flashed by, but Kennet caught a reference to logging in the '40s.

He broke the silence. "What road are we on now?"

"The Camp 72 road," said Conrad. "I've never seen a camp, but that's what they call it. This whole area has been logged over – Dad remembers those days. Camp 72 was a bush camp, with a kitchen and bunkhouses and horse barns and all that."

"And they spared these lovely trees?"

"This is a plantation. A forester in Beardmore started it. He wanted to show that red pine, which is not a tree that you'd normally find up here – the red pine is a viable conifer for this climate. So, this area has been logged once before."

They met a dark Ford pickup. Conrad said, "Stop a minute."

Kennet stopped and rolled down his window. The battered '97 Ford Ranger coasted up and stopped. The middle-aged driver sported a heavy gray stubble. He had rolled down his window. He looked puzzled until he spotted Conrad. There was an aluminum car-topper in the truck's box. Conrad leaned over, raising his voice.

"Any luck today, Bill?"

"Got two. That was hours ago. They're not biting now. Where're you folks off to? You're not fishing from *that* thing?" He pointed up to the roof of the Sportage where the kayak sat.

Conrad laughed. "Naw. This is Mr. Forbes. He caught that thing in Lake Superior. Cleaned it, now he wants to mount it."

Bill smiled his appreciation of the joke. "Well, it's poor fishing right now, in this neck of the woods." Kennet felt his left sleeve getting damp from stray raindrops.

"We're going up to the Brennan-Kenty," said Conrad. "I'm showing him where I'll be working next week."

"Well, good luck. There's a washout on that road now." Bill waved and coasted off.

As Kennet drove off, he asked, "That's Bill who?"

"Bill Meyers. Used to have the service station in town. We don't have any garages anymore. Now he's a backyard mechanic and general contractor. Got all kinds of machines."

173

"I noticed that Melody sells gas."

"Yeah. Thank God for that."

"What do you suppose he caught?"

"Eh?" said Conrad.

"Bill. Bill Meyers."

"Why, walleye, of course. If it was something else, he'd've said so."

"Have you ever fished Lake Nipigon?"

"Why, of course. Dad loves to chase lake trout. He keeps an eighteen-footer at High Hill Harbour. We often go out."

"Catch any speckles?"

"Incidentally we do. We don't target them. Not us, anyway."

When they passed a road heading west, Conrad volunteered that it was the road to the dam and power plant on the Namewaminikan. It was the first time Kennet had heard the river's name pronounced. He asked Conrad to repeat it: *naw-may-waw-min-ih-kun.*

Soon they arrived at a narrow bridge over the river. Ten metres below, the Namewaminikan tumbled down a long series of rapids as it headed for Lake Nipigon. Immediately after the bridge, Conrad directed him to turn left on a narrow bush road.

"This road got a name? Or a number?" asked Kennet.

"Not that I know of. I just call it the Brennan-Kenty road."

The single-lane road, rough in spots, ran west. A barrier of brush on either side separated the bush from the road. After a time Conrad said, "We'd better check that out."

Kennet braked, then spotted a ditch that ran across the road from one alder swamp into another. Conrad was already out of the truck to check it out. He climbed back in. "Just take it easy," he said. He added, "The rain's letting up."

Kennet put the truck into four-wheel drive and eased the Sportage through the collapsed culvert. He put the wipers on intermittent sweeps.

"Something I've been meaning to ask," said Kennet. "I see flagging tape every once in a while. What's it mean?"

"Could be prospectors. Claim-stakers. If you look behind the flag, look hard, you might see a narrow claim line or a grid line cut out. Or it could be a trapper, marking a set. Could be someone's trail to a fishing hole. Lots of reasons."

The bush soon gave way to billows of green brush punctuated by isolate dark snags that stretched to the horizon. Grassy tote roads spun off the main road. At a small rise in the terrain they came to a metal pipe that barred the road. Conrad got down and opened the padlock and swung the gate open as Kennet drove through. Conrad closed the gate but did not lock it. Just over the rise the terrain dropped away and they could see a promontory about a kilometre away dominating the burnscape.

"That's the Brennan-Kenty," said Conrad. "Wait till you see the cuts, you won't believe them."

As they closed in on the prominence, Kennet noted exposed rock on the south side. Eventually he could see that it had been worked over by machinery. A double-track trail climbed the face of the steeply plunging hillside.

Kennet said, "Tell me we're not climbing that."

Conrad laughed. "Whatsa matta? Kia not up to it?"

They crossed a narrow bridge over a stream and skirted the bottom of the hill to the south. Kennet glanced up the steep hillside. They came to the industrial zone where the steep track climbed the ravaged rock. They passed it, the bush road continuing to skirt the hill and turning west. To their left, water lay in a stream or ditch. Beyond the thick brush the terrain rose to the south.

Conrad motioned to a rocky track that climbed the hillside at a precipitous angle. ""We'll go up here."

"Sure we will."

"Use four-wheel. I've done it lots of times."

Again Kennet switched to four-wheel drive, geared down, and gunned the motor. On the right he caught a glimpse of a huge trench gouged out of the hillside. The tires gripped the loose rocks of the steep trail and pulled the truck upward. The truck tilted back at a hair-raising angle. The trail leveled off and petered out. They were facing a brushy barrier that continued to climb. Kennet cut the engine.

"Come on," said Conrad. "I'll give you the tour. We'd better take rain gear, though."

Kennet slipped the camera into a shirt pocket. They stepped out of the cab and struggled into their rain suits. Conrad wore heavy-duty yellow pants and hooded jacket, a working man's outfit. The precipitation had resolved into a misty rain beneath a low gray ceiling. Kennet followed the yellow suit as Conrad walked westward on the ledge of rocky rubble. Soon they were looking down on several huge trenches that stretched over several hundred metres to the forest in the distance. The cloud ceiling sank into the top of the distant trees.

Conrad stretched his arm over the worksite. "See? They're following the strike of the moly veins. More or less east-west." He turned around and motioned eastward. "Let's look at one close up."

Conrad led him past the Sportage on a two-track trail over the rubble. A floppy net fence of red plastic lined the drop-off. A sign spelled out "Danger". Conrad said, "Don't lean on the fence." It was an unnecessary caution.

Approaching the fence as close as they could, they leaned forward and peered into a deep trench. From their angle they couldn't see the bottom. "This is a cut they did," said Conrad, "starting back in '06. Drilling and blasting, real miner's work. They wanted to see how continuous the quartz-moly vein is, and how deep it goes, and it goes – down, down, down." He simulated a steep angle with the flat of his hand. "The next phase should be a decline – you know, an underground ramp, so they can approach the vein farther down and take a bulk sample."

"Couldn't they just drill and find that out?"

"The vein is narrow, and easy to miss. Those old prospectors knew what was on surface. Now we have to find out what's below surface. The old-timers never got more than a metre or two below surface. There used to be old pits spotted all along here, on strike."

Conrad walked a few paces east along the fence. "Wait here. Be right back." The fence curved around the head of the trench, and Conrad descended into a neck of solid rock that separated that trench with another further eastward.

"What are you doing?" Kennet called.

"Getting you a sample," he called back. "This is an old prospector's pit."

Conrad picked over a few loose pieces of rock and returned with one of them. He thrust it at Kennet. "This is molybdenite."

The cake-sized piece of rock was shot through with a silvery gray metallic mineral. Kennet turned the rock over and over. "And this is molybdenum?" he said.

"Molybdenite. It's a sulphide of molybdenum. M^1S^1."

"Sort of looks like lead. A shiny lead. And it's heavy."

"It does look a lot like galena, the ore of lead. Pb^1S^1."

"What's it used for?"

"This, my friend, is an essential element for the manufacture of high-grade steel. If they find enough of it here, they'll have a gold mine." Conrad's eyes danced.

"And the gold? Is there real gold here?"

"This way." Kennet dropped the rock. Conrad led him past the truck and uphill on a grassy tote road, overgrown and rutted with washouts. Damp branches and knee-high grass and weeds brushed their rain suits. They came upon a narrow trench, sunk through overburden down to bedrock. In places the undulating rock surface was three or four metres below the original ground level.

"How did they dig that out?" Kennet asked Conrad's back.

Conrad stopped and turned around. "A backhoe. The bucket of an excavator is the only way to scoop that deep. I think my dad did some of that."

"They were looking for moly here?"

"Gold. They found gold here."

They continued climbing, crossing a wide shallow trench that had likely been stripped by bulldozer. Finally, at the top of the hill they came upon a shallow trench about twenty metres wide. On the north side of it bedrock lay exposed, running east over the crest, and west until it sank below the rim.

Conrad turned west, treading a wide, flat gravelly surface that paralleled the narrow strip of bedrock. "Over this way, is where I was working." He grinned at Kennet. "Nice sidewalk, eh?"

"Who'd've thought?" Kennet threw back his hood. "Rain's stopped." The ceiling to the west seemed to have risen, for he could see further across the green belt. The sheen of a small lake had emerged. Beneath the cheap rain suit Kennet could feel the perspiration soaking his clothes.

The gentle slope they were descending turned precipitous, at which point Conrad cut to the left away from the bedrock exposure. He stopped in front of a stretch of worked-over ground that had been reclaimed from the surrounding brush. He threw back his yellow hood.

Conrad stood there motionless, head canted forward, looking at a gravelly stretch of ground on the lip of the slope. A minute stretched into two and then three. Then he spoke.

"I was looking for an offshoot of the main vein. There was a bank here, topsoil and gravel. And I could see a burrow, a big burrow, this size." He held his hands a little more than a half-metre apart. "It didn't belong to a fox. Probably a bear. But it was too early for a bear to be hibernating."

"This was October 16th?"

"Yeah. Exactly. Three days after my birthday. And it was a beautiful day. Could see far out into the lake." He gestured westward toward the distant cloudbank.

"I started to back-blade the bank, pulling the dirt towards me, so I could push it down the hill there. And then I noticed the lumps there, not rocks, not pieces of wood, which would fall apart and leave dark tracks if they were rotting in the dirt that far under the ground. So I got down for a closer look."

He glanced at Kennet with a wry smile. "I kicked at them. I didn't realize they were bones till I kicked two or three of them, and saw the dead white colour, and their lightness. They had no weight. No weight at all. My first thought: they're the bones of a bear. Some large mammal."

Conrad faced away, turning west, turning toward the great lake shrouded in mist. His voice was muffled. "When I kicked up the skull, I knew." Kennet looked at the wide back of the yellow raincoat. He saw the shoulders hunch, give a little shudder. He stepped up and laid his hand on Conrad's right shoulder.

"Conrad, I know. Believe me, I know."

Conrad did not look at him. "How could you know?"

"It's a horrible story, but I'll tell you. Later." He released Conrad's shoulder and stood by him gazing toward the lake. "What did you do next?"

Conrad's voice became animated. "What I did next, was run like hell! Left the machine idling there, and ran like hell. I don't know why I didn't break a leg. Down that track we just come up," he glanced at Kennet quickly, "down to the bottom, over to where Fergie was overseeing the excavation of the last cut."

Conrad took a deep breath. "Fergie wouldn't believe me at first. Thought I'd found a bear skull. But I dragged him away. Fergie doesn't like to walk if he can help it. We took his pickup to where you left your Kia, and we climbed back up here, and then he believed me."

"That's when you told the police?"

"Well, that's the official story. The truth is, Fergie argued with me. Said it was likely an Indian skull, that some hunter had had an accident here, hundreds of years ago, broke a leg, maybe, had crawled into the den for shelter and never crawled out. Or his carcass had been dragged in, dragged in by a bear. And there was no point in making a fuss about it now, 'cause the company wouldn't thank me. They'd have to close the work site, during the investigation, you know. And I'd be laid off. God knows how long."

"It's a powerful argument," Kennet said, noncommittally.

Conrad looked at Kennet strangely. "It was a body! Well, bones, anyway. It was a human being. Once. There was no way I was running over human bones. And I wasn't about to push them over the edge!"

"I understand," said Kennet softy. "You did the right thing."

"Fergie was mad, but he called it in. Talked to Dan – first – who talked to *his* boss, and then Dan called the OPP. I wasn't here when the cops came. They assigned me another job, and I was damn glad. So I didn't see them recover the bones. Well, it was getting late in the season anyway, and I'd pretty well finished the job. Haven't been back since."

Conrad paused. "Now Dan has laid out a strip farther back, over there." Conrad pointed to the northeast, to a tangle of brush and snags. "There's a drop-off there, so I'll be using the backhoe, 'cause it works from a stationary position. I'll be moving it carefully so's not to back off a cliff."

Kennet turned his gaze westward. "Look," he said. "Is that the lake?"

The ceiling had risen further, and the horizon was a uniform gray, but a small dark mound in the distance had broken through the mist, as though a ray of sun had reached down to illuminate it.

"Yeh," said Conrad. "You can't see the lake proper, but that's an island off Bish Bay. We've fished around it, Dad and me. You can see this mountain from there."

"So we're not far from the lake."

"Three klicks, maybe. But if you tried it on foot, you'd still be walking when it got dark. There's an awful lot of burn between us and the lake."

Conrad looked back at the bulldozed ground, and said musingly, "You know, when I saw the bones, I didn't feel anything for them, I didn't feel as if they belonged to a person. I was scared, you know. Terrified, really. It was like . . . like a sword . . . like a sword had been buried in my chest. But now . . ."

"Now you know they belonged to a real person."

"Yeah," he said slowly. "Now I feel . . . pity, I guess. Like a real tragedy has happened here."

"And you may have known that girl. Or her family."

Conrad was still looking at his old work site. He hesitated before he answered. "Yeah."

"You have someone in mind, don't you."

Conrad glanced at him furtively. "It's just a crazy idea. A really, really crazy idea." He said nothing for a minute, then, "Are you ready to go?"

Kennet sensed that Conrad would not appreciate his taking pictures of the site, so he left his camera in his pocket. They spoke very little on the way down the trail. Back at the truck, Kennet said, "Hungry yet?"

"Sure. I could use a sandwich."

Each took a bottle of water and, at Conrad's suggestion, they walked down the steep track to the open cut and walked right into the trench. The walls stood fifteen metres apart and stretched for perhaps forty metres. Near the top of the walls, fifteen metres above the rubble floor, miners had drilled holes for rock bolts and strung wire netting to catch rock slabs that might be inclined to peel off and hurtle downward. Human skulls would offer little resistance.

Each chose a boulder for a seat and tackled his lunch. Having demolished one sandwich, Conrad pointed to a quartz vein about a quarter-metre wide that ran raggedly along the north wall from west to east. "That's the vein with the moly."

"And it just keeps going down, down, down, right?"

"Right. That's what the geologist says."

"No gold, though."

"Oh, there's gold in it too. But the moly is the paydirt."

Kennet raised his eyes to the top of the north wall. In the gray ceiling beyond he thought he detected a wash of blue.

"There's one hell of a lot of country up here," said Kennet, chewing thoughtfully. "All rock and water. And trees. Where it hasn't burned. And chockful of minerals. Treasures, waiting to be scooped. How many companies do you figure are exploring up here, just in Greenstone?"

"Last year, fifteen, maybe twenty companies. This year, just a handful, with the economy the way it is. And God knows how many prospectors, each with their own little claims, trying to get the bigger outfits interested."

"And you have your own little claims."

"Big ones, too. This was one of 'em."

"The Brennan-Kenty. I wonder who found it first. Brennan and Kenty, I guess. They staked it. But I wonder if anyone found it before them. And how the hell did he get here in the middle of a roadless wilderness to find it?"

"Well, I know one thing."

"Eh?"

"He walked the last two, three miles."

Entr'acte

Using his compass, he took a bearing on the ridge. He folded the map and stowed it away. He looked at the island behind him. From across the bay it had looked smaller and flatter. It was actually big and tall. Several hundred yards across. Water lapped gently at the rocky shore, which climbed rapidly to a summit two hundred feet above the water. A poor camping place.

He steered the canoe east. In a quarter hour he had reached islets offshore, and then he was coasting the north shore of the bay. He found a sand beach for a camping spot. He pitched a pup tent and gathered rocks for a hearth. Bacon and oatmeal porridge. He didn't have much else. He lay under the blanket, head and shoulders outside the open doorway of the tent, so that he could feed the small flames with sticks and watch the sun die. He dug a small pouch from his shirt pocket and stuffed the bowl of his pipe and struck a match. He smoked contentedly. A small breeze had sprung up. Later the sandflies woke him up. A half moon was drenching the landscape. He burrowed into his blanket to escape the flies.

Before full light he was up. Big mosquitoes drifted about. From his haversack he took out the McKirdy's ointment and applied it liberally to exposed skin. He dug the dutch oven out of the sand under the hearth and tested the biscuits. Perfect. He dressed the biscuits with lard and cold strips of bacon and washed the lot down with steaming coffee. He cooled the oven and the billy can in the water. Solitary cumulus drifted across the sky.

He steered toward the head of the bay. The map showed no streams flowing from the interior, but he knew there'd be a creek there. He found it, a shallow stream with a gravelly bottom. He could touch both banks by extending his paddle. The blackflies found him. The bush enfolded him.

Before he had traveled a half mile he found himself walking a great deal, pulling the canoe by the stern rope. The banks closed in, brush and branches barring the passage. They were a mere nuisance to a man who had traversed coils of barbed wire under fire. An occasional rocky bank, exposed by the stream over the centuries, confirmed that he was in greenstone country. The rocks displayed few interesting features. There came a point when the canoe no longer floated. The stream had jogged north for a while before straightening out, and he figured a bearing just north of east would bring him to the ridge. The line of the stream now angled well north of east, so he abandoned it. He calculated that he had come a mile. He had perhaps a mile to go, two at most. The flies were swarming him, so he applied more McKirdy's. It was going to be a hot day.

He abandoned his canoe. He carried some larded biscuits and bacon in the haversack, along with a full canteen and a few other items. He extracted some cartridges from the heavy belt and put them in a shirt pocket and buttoned the flap. He left the belt in the packsack. The less weight, the better. He would also have to take a single-jack and a couple of steel rods and some hand-drilling supplies. The rock hammer he stuck into his trousers behind one suspender strap. The sledge and set of steels he suspended as best he could to his waist with strong cord. As long as he felt them thumping his hips and upper legs, he knew he still had them. The Lee-Enfield he slung over his right shoulder, the haversack over his left. In his right hand he carried the axe. The compass dangled from a lanyard. He checked his railway pocket watch before tucking it away inside his shirt. He patted the shirt pocket with the glass magnifier.

Ten steps into the bush and he could no longer see the canoe. He cut a white gash about fifteen inches long on the east side of a large spruce, head height. He chipped a smaller patch on the west side. It was essential that he find the way back to his canoe. If he wished to find the mountain again, it was not essential to use the same route. He would probably find a better route anyway.

As he progressed, he consulted the compass frequently. He paused every few steps to blaze another tree. He also checked that he had a line of sight to the previous blaze. He was traversing flat, heavily wooded terrain. His boots sank into a floor carpeted with moss. From time to time he fought through clumps of alder saplings, and clambered over windfalls. A brush-choked corridor identified an intermittent stream, now dry or flowing underground, probably flowing north to join the stream he had followed up. After a half hour he noted that the terrain was higher and drier, and that poplar and some birch had joined the mix. The old wound in his right hip now let him know it was still there. He paused for a swig from the canteen.

The terrain became distinctly uneven, punctuated by rock outcrops. He chipped some of them, examining the chunks with the glass magnifier. He ignored the float, the rounded boulders that the ancient continental glacier had dropped in his path. His eyes searched ahead and to the sides, seeking to penetrate the thick forest cover. The sunlight filtered down through the canopy and dappled the forest floor. He crossed a couple of gullies, gouged out of bedrock by the glacier and worn down by water and covered with soil and small plants. Then he encountered the sharp-angled boulder.

It was a boulder that had not traveled far. It was covered entirely with ancient lichens and moss. There was no ledge or rocky knoll in the vicinity that would account for it. The terrain for some time now had seemed to slope up almost imperceptibly to his right. He selected a big poplar and blazed all four sides, with a double blaze on the south side. He departed from his easterly course and veered sharply to the south. Wading through the greenery he encountered another sharp-angled boulder. Within a matter of yards he was facing a scree of sharp-angled boulders at the foot of steeply rising ground. Widely spaced jack pine and poplar trees sprang from the cracks. He clambered over the scree. His right leg protested loudly now. Where the big hammer and the drills constantly thumped him, the flesh was tender. He drew up at the bottom of a rock wall.

He gazed upward. This was the ridge he had spotted from the lake. It was indeed a mountain. But he would think of it as a ridge. He had scaled ridges before. He had been up and down The Mound at Sanctuary Wood. He had scaled Vimy. He had charged up the Meetcheele Ridge at Passchendaele. As always, he experienced a moment of dread. Of foreboding. He swatted at a mosquito. Most of the flies had abandoned him now, although a few had persisted. On top of the ridge he would no doubt find a breeze that would discourage a few more. Then he would rest.

The wall was steep but it was far from perpendicular. He made out rock pillars where huge slivers of the wall leaned out. Gravity and the action of frost had levered the pillars away from the wall. His eyes traced a jumble of angular boulders up the wall, tumbling from various ledges and angling between the wall and the pillars. This was his path.

He sought out the nearest big poplar and blazed all four sides. He buried the axe in the trunk, head up, handle down. He would find this tree again and retrieve the axe. Sitting on a boulder, he took another drink. The sun beat down. He was soaked in sweat. His hip and leg ached constantly now.

He stood up, adjusting the haversack so that it rested on his left buttock and snugging down the strap on the Lee-Enfield. He started up the ridge, using his hands for leverage. The boulders ranged in size, many smaller than a breadbox, a few larger than a packhorse. Once he looked around from habit to see if Chappy was keeping up. Of course Chappy was not there. He had buried Chappy in the frozen ground last winter.

Chappy had been a scrapper, a real scrapper. When the half-starved dogs that prowled the alleyways of Timmins had set upon him, Chappy had fought bravely. It had taken Lanky three or four minutes to beat off the pack with a stick of lumber he had found to hand. In the course of the battle he had been nipped and slashed several times himself. Chappy had been bleeding too.

Lanky had given up the idea of a leisurely afternoon in the bars. He had already loaded his fresh supplies on the toboggan, so he started off home. He had let Chappy walk freely, although normally Chappy would have willingly carried his share strapped to his back. Before they had reached their camp in the bush, Chappy had been staggering and reeling. After Lanky had built up a big fire, Chappy had stretched out beside the flames on a bed of balsam boughs.

He had kept the blaze going all night, dozing in a sitting position. Sometime before morning a hand on Chappy's chest told him that the dog had stopped breathing. He kept the blaze going. In the morning light he took his pick and attacked the ground in a fury. It took upwards of an hour to dig a proper hole. Everyone, in the end, should have a proper hole.

Lanky. His buddies had first called him that as he stood on the fire step of the trenches. Even when he discharged the Lee-Enfield

187

Mark IV, he had to crouch slightly, so as not to expose himself unduly. After he made traverses of No Man's Land, they kidded him again. Claimed he must be running sideways so as to present a narrow target. A bullet did not so much as clip his clothing. When a shell burst had finally clipped him, fragments had lodged in his right hip, but the surgeons believed they had found most of them. The trauma had also fractured his thighbone. He always limped after that.

He saw the lance of quartz in the wall behind a pillar. For several minutes he glassed the quartz, but he could see no mineralization. The quartz vein in greenstone was promising. He continued to climb. The last few steps he trod a natural staircase. The forest crowded up to the lip of the cliff. White spruce and jack pine, paper birch, trembling aspen – all vied for a toehold on the mountain. They were not particularly tall trees, implying a shallow soil base. For a prospector that was good news. A tangle of brush and windfall stitched the forest together. He could see a lot of windfall. Winds off the big lake must play havoc from time to time.

He turned so that he faced north, and let his heaving chest subside. The forest stretched away, climbing distant rises. To the northwest he spotted the vapoury blue of the big lake as it melded with the sky. He faced west, and began making his way through the tangle along the cliff edge. Occasionally a patch of bare rock relieved the chaos. Each time he dropped to his knees and examined the ground carefully. He found some shears in the greenstone, some evidences that these rocks had undergone tremendous stresses in the course of their history. In a quarter hour he reached an outcrop that sloped west, and through a narrow gap in the bush he saw the lake, and he saw the islands. The blessed isles.

He eased himself to the bare rock and stretched his legs before him. He adjusted the tools tied to his waist to positions beside him. The pain in his right hip and leg had grown intense. He had asked too much of them. It would be better when he climbed down the mountain, but not too much better. He had to take care of himself. No one else could. He adjusted the haversack and rifle and lay back and let the sun massage his body. He had been right. Scarcely any flies, though only the faintest breeze reached him. A breeze, and the pleasant odours of the northern bush. A bee whizzed by him. Then another. There was the absence of stink.

That's what he had noticed when he had left the battlefield. The absence of stink. There had been the pleasant smells of green vegetation, and cooking food, and soap, and the normal smells of gasoline, and horses, and well-ordered latrines. The miasma of death had hung over the trenches. Fear and numbness. And invisible bodies disintegrating in the mud. No graves for them. And the stink of human shit. Everywhere the stink of shit.

He sat up abruptly. The sun stood high and strong in the heavens. He had to use his time wisely. He was prepared to overnight on the mountain, if he found something interesting. If he found something interesting, he would find a better path down, and he would establish a proper camp, while he carried on his exploration. But first he had to find something interesting.

He rose to his feet and retraced his steps. He passed the stone staircase he had ascended and plunged eastward into the bush. His right leg bothered him, but it was a bearable pain. He burst into a clearing, another rocky outcrop, but this outcrop extended southward for twenty or twenty-five yards. The rock exposure was gently mounded, longtitudinally, like an ocean swell. Moss blanketed the ground, with the odd bare patch and loose boulder. He crept south, crouched over. A swirl of contorted rock announced a shear zone, and he dropped to his knees, the hammer and the chisels thudding on the rock. With his naked eye he saw glints of mineralization embedded in quartz. The glass revealed the sheen of sulphides and mica and – he leaned closer, forehead touching the rock – a duller sheen. A speck of raw gold. Tinier than a pinhead.

He rose quickly. With bare hands he tore away the moss that carpeted the showing and determined that a quartz vein was striking east. He stripped the vein until he encountered the bush, a distance of only five or six yards. A north-south fault line interrupted the gentle slope of the rock, and the ground dropped abruptly, eighteen to twenty inches. He loosed his rock hammer and chipped at the lip of the vein where it dropped and brought a fistful of quartz up to his face. Under the glass it was plain as day.

It was peppered with gold. Tiny grains of gold. This was the gold he could see. He hefted the rock, trying to gauge its weight. It was definitely heavy. It might be, for all he knew, shot through with gold. Invisible gold. When he made camp, he would pulverize this chunk and pan it and weigh it and he would have a better idea of its richness. And it was definitely rich.

He drew his lanky body up straight and he cocked his head back so that he was gazing straight up at the sun through slitted eyelids and a veil of lashes. He raised the fistful of quartz and presented it to the heavens and he said softly thank you. Thank you.

He dropped the chunk into his haversack. He looked at the bush in front of him, choked with brush and windfall. He shrugged the haversack and the rifle into position and then he plunged forward, hammer in hand. He would follow the line of strike. He gave his gimpy leg no thought.

When he clambered over a windfall, he put his bad leg down first. That was a mistake. The leg folded under him. He plunged forward, and he heard a branch crack as his bad leg struck it. He fell, right shoulder hitting the ground, and then he was rolling. He came to a stop at the foot of a ledge, a wall of rock perhaps nine feet high. He was gazing up at the forest canopy.

His breath came back with a rush. The Lee-Enfield angled under his back, arching it and causing great discomfort. He tried to sit up, but his legs would not give him leverage. He clutched with the fingers of both hands at the ledge on his left side, finding cracks and bumps in the uneven surface. He pulled himself to a sitting position and shucked off the rifle, propping it up against the ledge.

His bad leg was sore. It was more than the usual soreness. A throb of pain made him gasp. A fierce aching rush of pain ran up his bad leg and thumped him in the brain. Oh no. O God no.

Chapter 17

. . . Saturday afternoon

As they sat in the trench on the old Brennan-Kenty property, Conrad had demolished two sandwiches and then accepted the offer of one of Kennet's.

"Tell me, Conrad," said Kennet, "what're your thoughts on the bones?"

Conrad countered. "You said you understood how I felt up there. How could you?"

Kennet sighed and shifted his backside on the boulder. "This is not a pretty story, Conrad. I was in Rwanda in '94. I was a correspondent, and I saw the genocide of the Tutsi population. Some of it, anyway." Kennet described his experience of discovering a body dump, and of stepping on the corpse of a Tutsi child."

"Jeez!" said Conrad, shaking his head. After a minute or so: "Did they catch 'em? I mean, the ones responsible?"

"In the case of this kill site, so far as I know, no, nobody was ever brought to justice. And as for the 800,000 others, very few.

Very damn few."

"Eight hundred thousand?" Conrad was aghast.

"You must've heard of it."

"Oh yeah. Of course." Conrad looked embarrassed. "I didn't pay much attention at the time. I was in high school. Trying to get laid. That was my burning issue at the time." He paused. "But how could those Hoodoos –"

"Hutus."

"– those Hutus get away with it?"

"People get away with murder all the time. As we speak, soldiers somewhere are beating or gunning down unarmed civilians, or some ethnic or religious faction is butchering its neighbours. It's a staple item in almost every country's national newscast."

"God! I never thought of it that way."

"And those bones you found, we may never know the story of how they got there, if we can't identify the remains."

"Oh yeah. That." Conrad studied his boots. "It's just a stab in the dark. I mean –" Conrad glanced at him, reddening.

"I know what you mean. Go on."

"I think –" He stopped, and then resumed. "I don't even think it, it's just a feeling I have, a horrible feeling."

Kennet waited.

"There's a name that keeps coming to me. Gracie."

"Gracie. The only Gracie I know is Crystal's friend."

"Yeah. Gracie Elder. I think it might be Gracie's sister . . . Georgie. I was just a kid, might've been five or six when I saw her last. Gracie never saw her, 'cause she wasn't even born yet. Georgie graduated and then she left town. She never came back. They said she was in Calgary or somewhere. But she never came back. And Gracie never saw her big sister. Ever."

"Georgie Elder."

"Yeah. It's just a feeling. Probably nothing to it."

Kenneth rose and shook out his cramped legs. "When we get back to town, there's something I'd like you to do for me."

"Yeah?"

"Introduce me to Mr. and Mrs. Elder."

Conrad was horrified. "You can't say any – !"

Kennet cut him off. "Give me more credit, Conrad. I just want to meet them."

Conrad stood up, crumpling the sandwich wrappings. "Well, you can't. Not Mr. Elder, anyway. He left home, too. Abandoned his family, you might say. But I'll take you to Mrs. Elder, if you'll say nothing. About my feeling, I mean."

"Good man. I won't betray your confidence."

At the gate, Conrad swung the bar back into place. He climbed back into the truck. "I'm coming back this week so I didn't lock it. Someone will be bringing my machine out first."

They rode in silence for a while. Conrad finally spoke. "I can't bear the thought that Mrs. Elder and Gracie will think I treated the remains disrespectfully. If it's Georgie, I mean."

"You didn't. You found them, and you reported them. That's the first step in giving any remains due respect."

They left the burn and entered the bush. After several turns in the narrow road, Kennet spotted a vehicle up ahead. It soon became apparent that it was stopped, blocking passage. Kennet swore under his breath.

"What's the matter?" asked Conrad.

"The Flemings."

"That's where the washout is. No way of getting around them."

"I was thinking that."

"I'll talk to them," said Conrad.

"No, I'll talk to them. They want to talk to me, not you. You stay in the truck. Please."

The three Flemings stood in front of the garishly painted Dodge Ram, in line across the road. In a caricature of cowboys, all three wore denim jackets and jeans and scruffy cowboy boots, except that Rawling wore dungarees rather than jeans. The Dodge's passenger door yawned open. Kennet stopped ten metres away and stepped down, leaving the engine idling. Conrad opened his door. Kennet looked at him. "Please, as a favour, leave this to me."

Conrad stepped down and held his door open. "Okay. I'm just watching your back."

Kennet closed his door and strode toward the trio. Kennet gazed straight at Rawling, who stood on the right-hand side of the road, hands on hips. "Rawling, we need to get past you."

Rawling grinned. "I know."

"Will you move your truck, then?"

Ritch, the lanky Fleming cousin, who was standing beside Lanny on the left-hand side of the road, took a couple of steps toward Rawling and passed him a roll-your-own. Rawling accepted it, grinning. He took a deep drag and held it, never taking his eyes off Kennet.

"I'm asking nicely," said Kennet.

Rawling handed the reefer back to Ritch, savoured the moment, and then exhaled a cloud. "I know," he said. Ritch moved back and passed the joint to a stone-faced Lanny. Ritch was also grinning broadly.

"Now. Please," said Kennet.

Rawling's grin faded. "I'm busy right now."

"Okay." Kennet looked at Rawling's two companions. He moved casually toward them, smiling as he crossed the washout. "Let's have a drag."

Ritch looked his surprise. He extended the cigarette to Kennet. "Well, why not?" he drawled. Kennet accepted it and drew it up to his nostrils and sniffed.

"Mexican dirt weed," he said, contemptuously.

Ritch's features hardened. "That's BC Bud. Best shit around."

"Not for me, thanks." Kennet extended the joint back to Ritch, releasing it prematurely. "Oops," said Kennet, stooping to retrieve it. Ritch also stooped, and at that moment, Kennet slipped past him, shouldering Lanny, who staggered backward toward the ditch. He moved quickly to the open passenger door. He pressed the door lock button and jumped up. Ritch was right behind him. Kennet bumped him back with the door before he slammed it shut. Kennet now commanded the cab of the Ram 3500 turbo diesel.

He checked the ignition. Yes, as he had anticipated , Rawling had left the keys. He positioned himself behind the steering wheel and turned the key. The turbo-jet engine powered up. Rawling was clutching the door handle with his right hand and slapping the window glass with his left. He was cussing a blue streak. The other two Flemings were slapping the hood with both hands as they screamed.

Kennet threw the transmission into reverse and started backing up slowly, guiding himself in the rear-view mirror. Lanny and Ritch remained standing, shouting and waving their arms. Rawling gripped the door handle like a pit bull, following the truck. Kennet saw Conrad jumping into the cab of the Sportage and shutting the door.

Kennet pressed on the gas and Rawling released the door. Rage distorted his features. Glancing out the rear window, Kennet could see no viable turnaround nor any place to pull off the track. After fifty or sixty metres, he stopped. Rawling started to run toward him. Kennet revved the engine in neutral, and Rawling stopped.

He slipped into first gear, left foot on the brake, and pressed the accelerator. He would have to create a parking space. Conrad had not moved the Sportage, for Lanny and Ritch were still blocking the road and now spewing their rage at him. Kennet released the brake and the Ram shot forward, rear wheels spinning.

The Ram gathered speed. Rawling leapt aside, landing in the dry ditch and a tangle of brush. Lanny and Ritch had turned to face the speeding truck. They crowded left, maintaining a toehold on the track, for water filled the low ground on either side of the road. When he was about to hit the washout, Kennet jerked the wheel right and the Ram plowed into the swamp. The front end ate up the brush as the truck slowed dramatically and then stopped.

Cutting the engine, Kennet opened the door and pushed against the resisting brush. He stepped onto the running board and, his back to the swamp, maneuvred himself into the truck box, slamming the door shut. He walked the length of the box to the tailgate. Lanny and Ritch had remained in position and were now shaking their fists and yelling at him. Rawling came running up.

At that moment the Sportage bounced into the washout. Horn blaring, the truck roared past the Flemings, and Rawling gave the fender a thump with his hand as it sped by. The truck stopped a few metres away.

Kennet stepped over the tailgate onto the trailer hitch and and then leapt to the high ground of the track, confronting the Flemings. Rawling stepped up, delivering a roundhouse swing. Kennet blocked it and a succession of follow-up blows from Rawling's flailing arms. Rawling lowered his head and lunged at his waist. Kennet easily sidestepped and assisted Rawling to flop face down in the shallow swamp. He stepped into the water and planted his right foot between Rawling's shoulder blades. He looked at Rawling's two companions, now silent, who had not moved. With the cupped fingers of his left hand, he invited them to advance.

Lanny looked at him stolidly. "I'm not afraid of you," he said.

"I believe you," said Kennet. "You're not smart enough to be afraid."

"Fuck you."

"You should be so lucky."

Ritch said nothing. He just glared. Kennet removed his foot from Rawling's back. Rawling pushed himself up. He was sputtering and gasping. Water streamed from his clothes. He struggled to a kneeling position.

"Hold that pose," said Kennet. He plucked the camera from his shirt pocket, and when Rawling craned his neck around, he snapped the picture.

"Ritch!" Rawling shouted. "Get the Winchester."

Ritch called back. "Why the fuck should I get wet too?"

"Well, fuck *you*!"

"No, fuck *you*."

"Well," said Kennet, "while the three of you are diddling each other, I'll move on." He stepped back on the road. He bent down and scooped up the cigarette, which was barely smouldering. He strode purposefully over to Ritch and extended it to him. Ritch flinched.

"Sorry about that," Kennet said.

"Fuck you," Ritch muttered.

"As I told your cousin here, I'm not that easy." He tucked the fag into Ritch's shirt pocket, looking Ritch in the eye. Ritch looked behind him wildly, it dawning on him that he could not step back out of reach.

Kennet looked at Lanny. "Isn't that right . . . Lancelot?"

A peculiar expression overtook Lanny. "How did you know my name?" he asked.

"You look like the kind of guy who would screw his best friend's wife. And if anything else happens to my kayak, the only one who'll be screwed is *you*."

Lanny scowled but he said nothing. Rawling was struggling with the door of the Dodge truck. "Looking for these?" said Kennet. He dangled the truck keys at arm's length. "I'll leave them at the bridge. You'll want to flag down a ride anyway."

He moved quickly to the Sportage. Conrad was standing on the driver's side beside the open door. "Thanks, Conrad. I'll drive." Conrad jumped up and shifted himself to passenger seat. Kennet climbed behind the wheel and grinned at Conrad. "Thanks," he said, "for watching my back."

As they drove, Kennet voiced a question bothering him: "They have a quarrel with me. How did they know where I'd be?"

"Bill Meyers, I guess. Probably stopped him to ask about fishing."

"Of course.

At the bridge over the Namewaminikan, Kennet left the keys on the first post of the railing. Back in town Kennet glanced at his watch. It was mid-afternoon. "Still want to do this? Will she be home?"

"Sure," said Conrad. "She never goes anywhere."

Kennet drew up in front of the Elder residence, next door to the home of Curtis and Ioanna Mallory.

When an elderly woman opened the door, Conrad said, "Hi, Mrs. Elder. Am I still welcome for a cup of tea?"

"Of course, Connie," she said. "You're always welcome. It's been ages." The gray-haired dowager moved back, holding the door wider. "Who's your friend?"

"Mrs. Elder, this is Kennet Forbes. He knows Crystal. And he met Gracie last night, over to Curtis's."

"Ah! Dr. Forbes! Gracie was telling me. Gracie's out right now, but you're welcome. Come in!"

Mrs. Elder's face beamed. She was a small, bent woman, almost emaciated, with a narrow, seamed face, and dressed in a plain housedress and apron. On her feet she had bunny slippers. "Come into the kitchen," she said. "It's cozier."

Chapter 18

... Saturday afternoon, later

"This cake is delicious, Mrs. Elder," said Kennet. He and Conrad had been enjoying Mrs. Elder's hospitality for about twenty minutes.

At one point he had asked to use the bathroom. Once out of sight, he had scanned the poorly lit hallway for photographs. There was a large framed photo of a burly man posed with a rather slim, good-looking young fellow sporting a shock of dark hair. They appeared to be standing on a commercial fishing boat, and each was displaying an enormous trout, each man holding up his trophy with the straining muscles of both arms. Kennet leaned into the picture. The eyes of the burly man drew him in. They were dark eyes, spaced a little wider than the average person's.

Returning to the kitchen, he noted a small table in the living room with several framed pictures. There was a wedding photo of the burly man with the intense eyes, and a young woman with a narrow, pretty face, probably a young Mrs. Elder. In a little display box there was a silver medallion, probably in recognition of military service, with multiple spikes, suggestive of a sunburst. There were a number of pictures of girls, posed at ages varying from babyhood to adolescence. Each picture featured only one girl. A family picture showed the burly man, his wife, and a dark-haired girl of school age. A white wooden cross behind them suggested they were standing in a graveyard.

Mrs. Elder responded to Kennet's remark. "More tea, professor?" It had taken Kennet several attempts to convince Mrs. Elder that he preferred to be called Kennet. She had been making small talk, asking after Conrad's parents, about Kennet's position at the university, and divulging that Gracie had caught a ride to Nipigon to do some grocery shopping, and that Gracie was a teacher's aide at the public school and doing so well.

"Thank you," said Kennet, "no, but I'll have another piece of cake."

"Help yourselves, boys. Gracie and I will never eat it all." It had been ages since Kennet had been called "boy". He felt himself blushing.

Mrs. Elder was hovering over the table with a teapot. Kennet said, "Please, Mrs. Elder, have a seat. You're making me tired just watching you." He delivered what he believed was his charming smile. She sat down between him and Conrad.

"Kennet," said Conrad around a mouthful of cake, "is looking into the death of his friend, that archaeologist."

"My goodness, yes. Whatever happened to that poor man?"

"No one knows yet," said Kennet. "But I'm getting to know the country. And the people here." He looked at her directly with his charm smile. "I notice a lot of photographs in your living room. Family, are they?"

"Oh yes. You wouldn't recognize Gracie from her pictures."

"Would you mind showing me her picture?"

"Of course! Come with me." Mrs. Elder deposited the teapot on the cupboard. Kennet stuffed the last bite into his mouth. Conrad did the same, dusting his hands over his dessert plate.

In the living room the shades were drawn. Mrs. Elder flicked a light switch. It was a small room with a dark red brick fireplace on one wall. It held faux logs, powered by electricity or gas. Some heavy upholstered furniture with antimassacars. Old-fashioned lamps. Flowered wallpaper.

Mrs. Elder picked up a framed photo of a young girl in a white communion dress. She held it for Kennet. "This is Gracie. Age twelve."

"Yes, I recognize her. Very pretty."

"And this is her at age three." The child was standing on a rock mound with an expanse of water behind her.

"I'd never recognize her from that. What place is that?"

"Oh, that's the lake. Where the park is now."

"Lake Nipigon."

"Yes. Harold had a fishing tug there."

"Harold. That'd be Mr. Elder."

"Yes." Her face closed up.

"And these other pictures. Do they show Gracie too?" Kennet moved to the framed photo of Harold and his wife and the dark-haired girl. He noted her blue eyes. Kennet tapped the glass. "Is this Gracie?"

"No. She looks nothing like Gracie. That's Georgie." Mrs. Elder's face showed some strain.

"Another daughter, is she?"

"Yes. She doesn't live here anymore. She moved away."

"Ah yes. Children do." Kennet sensed they were losing their rapport. He looked back at the photo. "I can't help noticing the white cross. Were you visiting a relative?"

Mrs. Elder looked somewhat relieved. "Yes, Harold's grandfather. He's buried on the lake. He was a fisherman too. I don't even know if that cemetery's there anymore. Since the big fire. I don't get out much."

Conrad piped up. "Mrs. Elder, that's partly my fault. Why don't I take you and Gracie there someday? Tomorrow, if you want. I'm not working."

Mrs. Elder smiled wanly. "Thank you, Connie. You're a good boy. But it wouldn't be the same without Harold. Harold loved his grandfather. I never knew him. Can I get you more tea?"

Back at the Sportage, Conrad turned his freckled face to Kennet. "Thank you, Kennet. For keeping me out of it. Did you find out anything?" They were standing beside the truck.

"I don't know yet. At least I have an idea what Georgie looked like. Maybe we'll get more information when we go through the pictures tonight. You know where Gerald St. Clair lives?"

Conrad said yes. "Okay, why don't you pick me up at the motel when you come back with Crystal?"

"Okay. I'll walk from here. See you tonight."

Kennet stopped by the hardware store to confirm that Conrad and Crystal would be welcome. He drove across the bridge and turned in at the landfill road. Two honks of the horn and a beep brought no response from Mac Kueng. He waited a few minutes, honked again, and then started up the path.

Mac was emerging from the bush on the riverside of his cabin. There was apparently a path there. He was lugging a heavily laden burlap sack, gripping it with one hand. The sack still dripped water.

"Keeping my handiwork cool in the river," he said. "I heard you the first time."

Kennet just nodded. Mac set the bag down and drew out a mangled rifle. "I'm afraid the water may have compromised the firing mechanism."

"That's unfortunate," said Kennet. "How could the owner shoot straight now?"

Mac glanced at him sharply. "Oh. That's a joke, is it?"

Kennet took the .30/06 Springfield in his hands. "It's a beaut, Mac. A little oil in the breech and it will perform wonders." Toward the muzzle the rifle barrel curled upward. "Aim at a moose and bring down a duck."

"Sure." Mac smiled tightly. "Hold it upside down and pot a porcupine. Here's the Winchester." He drew out the other rifle and passed it to Kennet. He continued, "It's a shame to tamper with a product like that. I hope it's in a good cause."

The barrel of the Winchester deviated left a few degrees. Kennet sighted along it and smiled. "It's in the cause of education. You believe in education, don't you, Mac?"

"Spare the rod and spoil the child."

Kennet replaced the weapons in the sack and glanced over at the smithy. "That's the altar of Vulcan, is it, Mac?" He caressed the cold metal of the anvil and looked up at the metal chimney. There was no evidence that it had been used recently, for not a wisp of smoke escaped. As he held a palm over the dark coals of the forge, though, he detected heat. He turned back to Mac. "A fine job. What do I owe you, Mac?"

"An explanation. But it can wait. It was a pleasure to fire up the old forge. Reminded me of better times. What's your next move?"

"You'll be apprised, Mac, when you come for your morning coffee. It'll be good for a laugh." Kennet gestured to a coil of thin-gauge wire that hung from a nail. "I could use several metres of that.

"Help yourself. Pliers right there."

Kennet stored the heavy sack on the floor of the back seat, spreading newspaper pages over it. The damp material started to stain the paper, so Kennet removed the newspaper. The sack itself looked nondescript enough.

Back at the motel he booted up the laptop. He pulled up the mining consultant's report on the Brennan-Kenty. At lot of it was technical stuff, which he skipped over. Only several courses in geology would qualify him to read those sections. He tried to pin down the year that a summer road had accessed the property. In the '50s there'd been a trail to Beardmore. There was a reference to a bush road in the '80s. However, there were few details on the work performed in the early '80s, the time period associated with the caching of the remains.

He resisted the impulse to log on to the Internet and do another search. He had to respect his electronic regimen. It was doubtful, anyway, that he would turn up a more detailed report. If he found the time, he would use another approach.

On the sidewalk he paused while a dark green Chevy pickup drove by. He noticed that the driver's head swiveled as the truck passed him. Ritch glared at him from behind the wheel. He crossed over to the store. Mrs. Mallory greeted him warmly. He selected a packet of potato chips and paid for them.

"So," he said cheerfully. "Anything new and exciting today, Mrs. Mallory?"

"Melody. Please!"

"Melody. Of course. And call me Kennet. I was out in the bush today, so I was wondering if I missed anything."

Melody leaned forward and lowered her voice. There was no other customer. "Kennet. Do you know about those bones they found near here last fall? That they thought they might be Indian – excuse me, First Nation? Or some old prospector?"

Kennet nodded.

"Well, Kennet, it turns out they belonged to some young woman! And they weren't lying around that long either!"

"You don't say. And are there any ideas about the identity of that young woman?"

"You know, people have been talking about that all day! You wouldn't believe some of the names that have come up. I myself believe it must've been a hitchhiker."

"A hitchhiker? You mean, someone trying to hitch a ride on the highway here?"

"Yes! Exactly."

"And how would the body end up so far in the bush?"

"Was it far? I don't know. But, you know, some of these hitchhikers, they can sleep rough. They can sleep anywhere. I've seen them climbing out of a ditch!"

"So you don't think it was anyone from around here?"

"God forbid! No young woman around here has gone and got herself killed. We'd've heard about that!"

"Thank you for the chips, Melody."

So, any suggestion of Vanderhorst being the victim of foul play was not the subject of gossip. Kennet found himself getting hungry, so as he crossed the road to The Hook'n Bullet, he opened the packet. A Ford F-250 truck-camper and a light blue Jeep Cherokee sat in the parking lot. A Toyota Tundra pickup towing a twelve-foot boat sat at the curb. Kennet loitered in the aisles, popping chips, as Kellerman waited on customers.

As the last one was leaving, another customer entered and began pawing through fishing lures. "What are you looking for, Ambrose?" said Kellerman.

"No. 3 hooks." Ambrose, a fifty-something, unshaven, looked as if he had slept in his clothes.

"Sold the last one just now. Have more on Monday."

"You sure?"

"Never been more certain in my life. And, Ambrose, you remember Kathy Kerrigan?"

"Kathy? Kerrigan? Hell's bells, Bull, you're talking thirty years ago!"

"I know. I got to wondering . . . Whatever happened to her?"

"Whatever happened to most everyone here – she left."

"You were sweet on her, eh, at one time?"

"Sweet? Christ, Bull, I'd've married her but I was laid off at the time. After that incident with the skidder. No, she left . . . for greener pastures. Or fatter wallets."

"Ever hear about her?"

"Sure. Married to some slob in Saskatoon. Passle of kids. I ran into her once, in Winnipeg. Looked happy enough."

Ambrose left and Kennet approached Kellerman as he picked up the phone. Kellerman acknowledged his presence with a wink. As he spoke he ran his finger down a hand-printed list on the counter, placing orders for sporting goods. He concluded by saying, "And those'll be on the bus tonight? . . . Good man, Thomas." He hung up.

"And how was your day, Kennet?"

"Fascinating. I have to leave tomorrow, Bull, but I want to see the lake first. I expect I'll be back later in the week. Listen, I couldn't help overhearing. What was the incident with the skidder?"

"Oh that. Not worth mentioning. Happened years ago. Many years ago. The company claimed Ambrose had forgotten to service his skidder after his shift. So when the next operator used it, he ran out of gas. Ambrose caught shit for it, insisted he had serviced it, and the long and short of it is, he punched out the foreman. Got fired." Kellerman continued: "Any progress on you-know-what?"

"If you mean Vanderhorst, no. I'm waiting for developments. How about yourself – anything on the identity of you-know-who?"

"I must've had ten or a dozen names come to mind, but nothing's panned out. I'll keep asking."

"Now, Bull, that other favour I wanted to ask. I notice you have a ladder out back, an aluminum one. Twelve-foot?"

"Sixteen. It's an extension. It's yours. Just bring it back."

"And again, mum's the word. It'll be worth a laugh come morning."

"I see you like chips. I sell chips."

"Of course. Give me a dozen. How's the sale of hunting vests? And bear bangers? Season opened this morning, eh?"

Chapter 19

. . . Saturday evening

Back in his room, Kennet dumped the packets of chips on a chair. There'd been no calls on his cell, and he couldn't, or rather, wouldn't log on to his e-mail. He watched the CBC round-the-clock news channel for a while and then made a decision.

He assumed the lotus position on the carpet after setting the travel alarm for 7:30. Taking long measured breaths, he was soon in a meditative state. Sometimes he drifted into unconsciousness – in effect, taking a cat nap. When the alarm rang, he rose immediately. After using the bathroom, he pulled the cheddar cheese block from the fridge and cut a few chunks to adorn the crackers. He washed the whole down with tap water. There was a knock on the door.

He climbed into the back seat of Conrad's gray Ford F-150 truck, clutching six bags of chips. Crystal greeted him with a strained smile. She wore a kind of beige uniform tunic. The St. Clairs lived on Pearl Street in a rambling single-story house faced with off-white brick. A white cabin cruiser sat on a boat trailer in the driveway. Gerald answered the door to Conrad's knock.

"Hi, folks. Beatrice's at her bridge club. We have the house to ourselves." Conrad stepped out of his shoes and placed them on a mat in the hallway. Kennet and Crystal followed suit. As Gerald led the way in his slippers, Kennet dumped the packets on a chair.

In the basement a number of boxes sat on the furniture and floor of the recreation room. A billiard table dominated the space.

"I pulled these out of the back room," said Gerald. "They're all labeled. Cam was very meticulous in his hobby. Now, what are we looking for, exactly?"

Kennet replied. "I'll be honest with you, Gerry. This is more than a nostalgia trip for me. You saw the paper today?"

"Yes."

"You saw the piece about the bones that were found in the bush last fall? I've been asked to help identify the victim. She may have come from round here. And you and Crystal and Conrad know the people round here."

Gerald nodded sagely. "Yes. I thought it might be something like that. You being a journalist and all. So you're looking for a young woman. Where do we start?"

"Why don't we start with Cameron's last year of school? What year was that?"

" '83."

Crystal said, "I wasn't even born then. I won't be much help."

"Yes, you will," said Kennet.

"Kennet," said Crystal, "when did you graduate?"

" '82. So I was a year ahead of Cam."

Gerald said, "I have Cam's grad photo. He didn't take it, of course." He walked over to a shelf and hefted a group picture of young men and women in caps and gowns. He brought it back. "This here is Cam." Cameron St. Clair was a slim, serious-looking person with short dark hair.

"Of course. I remember him. And that's Chris Kellerman. And Gordie what's-his-name. Bobby Fisker. Allison Granger. Marianne . . . Marianne . . ."

Conrad leapt in. "I know some of those people. Some of them are still around. Marianne. She's a Brown now. Lives in Longlac. There's George Smithers. Irwin Polanski. Now, I know her. She married George. I don't remember hearing her name. He worked in the bush here, and they left a few years back, moved to Thunder Bay."

"Marge," said Gerald.

Conrad paused with his finger indicating a pretty young woman with bobbed black hair. He said quietly, "You know *her*, Crystal."

"Let me see." She studied the photo and then said in a soft voice, "Yes, that's Georgie. Georgie Elder. Gracie keeps her grad picture in her room, beside her bed. '83 . . . That was the year she left. Gracie never knew her sister, wasn't even born yet. And then her father left, when she was three. She never really knew him either."

"So," said Gerald, "is this being helpful? There are," and he started counting heads in the photo, "one . . . two . . . three. . . There are three graduates here who lived in Beardmore. Cam makes four."

"Who are the three, then?" asked Kennet.

"George Smithers. Elsie Newman. Georgie Elder. And Cam, of course."

"I don't remember any Elsie Newman," said Crystal.

"Neither do I," said Conrad.

Gerald said, "She went away to college, and got a job teaching, somewhere down east. Guelph, I think. And then her parents, John and Greta, they moved down there, to be closer to their grandchildren. Elsie married, you see."

"And Georgie Elder?" said Kennet. He glanced at Conrad, shaking his head almost imperceptibly, and then at Crystal. Crystal kept her head down, ostensibly studying the photo.

Gerald spoke up. "She left too, after graduation. Her folks said she moved out west, Vancouver or someplace. I don't recall her ever coming back. But Crystal should know, she's friends with Gracie."

Crystal looked pale. She lifted her head and responded quietly. "That's what I've always understood."

Kennet spoke up. "Okay, Gerry. What year is the last box?"

" '83. He left for college that fall. And that was Cam's most productive time. For pictures. He had a camcorder by that time, and he shot loads of cassettes. He had a 35 mm Konica SLR, too, and his own darkroom back there," Gerald indicated the back room, "and he blew up a lot of his black-and-whites."

Gerald lifted a cardboard file box up to the billiard table. Large manila envelopes organized the material, each envelope labeled by subject. He pulled out a loose-leaf binder. "Cam had a system. He recorded the prints from each roll of film and coded them. He kept the negatives in a master file, and the prints he stored according to subject matter. Here, let me show you."

He opened the binder at random. There was a ruled page, divided into columns, and all the data entries printed neatly in ink. "Okay. This is August, 1982. See the date?" At the top of a ruled page, divided into columns, was the notation "Film processed August 29, 1982". The column headings were "Neg. No.", "Print No.", "Subject", "Details".

Kennet scanned the "Subject" column. There were three subjects: "Industry – Charter Fishing" and "Industry – Commercial Fishing" and "Scenes – L. Nipigon". Kennet asked Gerald, "Did Cam work on the lake that summer?"

"Cam? No. Never. Let me see." He scanned the page. "In his free time, he could be anywhere. He was working that summer at a lodge, up the 801 road. But these look like he was taking pictures at Poplar Lodge Park. Let's look at one."

"Okay. How about '21-Aug-82 IND'?"

"Right. Now we go to the box . . ." He pulled out four envelopes labeled in block letters: INDUSTRY. Each had a subtitle. Gerald opened the flap of the one subtitled COMMERCIAL FISHING and drew out a single sheet. There were a dozen or so codes listed. The "21-Aug-82 IND" was the eighth one in the column. "It's in this envelope, see?"

He took some cotton gloves from another box and slipped them on. He looked at the group apologetically. "Cam insisted on the gloves. Said your fingers may look perfectly clean, but there are invisible oils and what-not, and they can start the process of breaking down a photograph."

He drew out the small stack of prints, most of them 5 by 7-inch size. Two were enlargements. "Oops. I almost forgot. Be right back." He scurried away, climbing the stairs.

Kennet helped himself to a pair of cotton gloves and slipped them on. Conrad did too. By that time Gerald had returned with a folded tea towel. "The felt might be a little dusty," he said. He spread it on the billiard table felt, and set the stack of prints on it so that the backs were exposed. Each print had the code printed neatly in pencil in the lower left-hand corner. Gerald extracted one of the 5 by 7s and handed it to Kennet. It was a black-and-white photo.

"Alright," said Kennet. "There's a fishing tug, moored at a long pier, and a big lake beyond. A gentleman standing on the pier. I can't read the boat's name without a magnifying glass."

"That's Charlie Nylund's boat. I recognize it. And him."

"Let's see what Cam wrote about it." Kennet took the master file page and read off the details: "Fishing tug 'Storm Chaser'. Owner: Charles D. Nylund, standing. Location: breakwater at Poplar Lodge Park, L. Nipigon." Kennet looked up at Gerald.

"Gerry, I'm impressed. These photos are a great record. I hope some local archive becomes the beneficiary."

"I've been thinking that. I'm going to talk to Cam."

"What year does Cam's collection begin?" asked Kennet.

" '79, I believe."

"Well, let's start there. We'll depend on your memory, Gerry, because Conrad and Crystal were little then."

"I wasn't born yet," said Crystal.

"I was barely born," said Conrad. "Ran around naked most days." He glanced at Crystal mischievously, and she smiled.

"Right," said Kennet. "Let's concentrate on the pictures with people, and we're looking for a young woman who no longer lives here and for whose whereabouts we cannot account. Gerry will vet what we pass to him."

Crystal opened the loose-life binder for 1979 and started naming off candidate pictures. The other three rummaged through the envelopes. Some photos with people showed no females. Kennet and Conrad passed photos with adolescent or young adult females over to Gerald. He displayed an excellent memory for faces.

In the case of pictures taken at school or outside of Beardmore, Gerald scrutinized them for faces he knew. Kennet noticed many Aboriginal faces, and commented on the fact.

"Well, sure," said Conrad. "A lot of Beardmore people have Native ancestry. I have."

"You?" said Kennet. "I'd never have guessed."

"I'm Métis. Mom's mother was Native. Her father was white. So far as she knows. He might have been Métis."

Crystal said, "Here's Gracie's family. It says, 'Family outing to graveyard.'" At her direction, Conrad plucked from the box the envelope labeled PEOPLE: NATIVE. He passed the colour print to Kennet as Crystal commented, "Gracie's Métis too."

Three figures stood among white wooden crosses and isolate gravestones crowded into a small area. There were traces of a once-white picket fence, now askew. Kennet said, "I think I recognize Harold and Mrs. Elder. But there's a third adult."

Crystal read from the file: "Harold and Edith Elder visit his grandfather's stone. David, Harold's brother, left." David stood back, hands in pockets, looking off to the left of the photographer.

"What's the location?" asked Kennet.

"Lake Nipigon." She added, "There's more. Here's one that names Georgie."

The print showed the small graveyard set back in the trees from a sand beach. Four adults stood among the grave markers. On the shore, seated on a driftwood log, a pretty adolescent girl gazed out over the water. She had bobbed dark hair.

"She doesn't look interested," said Kennet. "Or maybe she's unhappy. Where exactly is that cemetery, Gerry?"

"You know the Park? Well, there's a string of cottages north of it, along the shore. There's a couple of undeveloped lots, just bush, and that's where the cemetery is. Used to be a path from the road there, down to the shore. Probably never find it now, after the fire."

"And here's me," said Conrad, "offering to take Mrs. Elder out to it. I should've checked the access first."

"So," said Kennet, "it's a Native cemetery? What happened to the cottages during the big fire?"

Gerald responded. "The MNR fire crews did a first-rate job. Kept hoses playing on the roofs. Saved every building. Including ours. We have a camp there, just a stone's throw from the cemetery, actually."

In about forty minutes they were starting the 1981 file. The number of prints increased significantly. In the boxes for 1982 and 1983, there were more prints of Georgie Elder, many in a school or school bus setting, always in group shots. Gerald accounted for the whereabouts of every other young female adolescent that hailed from Beardmore. He suggested a coffee break.

"Fine with me," said Kennet. "I brought snacks. You say Cam had videos too?"

"Yep. In his last year of school. There's one file here in which he describes them."

"Bring it along, will you? We can examine it over coffee."

In the upstairs hallway, one packet of chips had been torn open and scattered across the carpet. Another one on the floor had a big rip in it.

Gerald raised his voice. "Tickles! Where are you, bad girl!" He said to Kennet, "Our little Pomeranian. I should've warned you. Don't worry, we have biscuits to go with the coffee."

Only the men drank coffee. Crystal had an orange juice. "I'll be getting up at 4:15," she said. "I'll never get to sleep with coffee." She and Conrad had each opened a packet of chips. Gerald had set a saucer of cookies on the table. Kennet opened the master file for videos and leafed through the pages. Each video was documented scene by scene. It had been a monumental labour.

"Incredible!" said Kennet. "How did Cameron find the time?"

"Young people," said Gerald, "in those days, had few options for recreation in the evening. The old school had no gym, so no organized indoor sports, or pickup games, volleyball and that kind of thing. There was the curling club slash arena – still is – but in winter only. Snowmobiling was popular. Still is. No satellite TV. No video games. To speak of, anyway. No Internet. Cam wasn't into drinking or drugs. So he had the time."

"For which I thank him. In fact, Gerry, I may want to talk to him. Would you have a number?"

"Sure. I'll give you his home. In New York. And his office."

"Now here's a video titled BEARDMORE FISHING DERBY."

"I remember that," said Gerald. "He showed Beatrice and me most of his work. He was pretty proud of it. He edited them inside the camera."

"And GRAD PARTY '83."

"That I've never seen. Let's see that." He took the binder from Kennet and ran his finger down the scene summaries. "Whoa! 'Camille with Harvey's Wallbanger'! And 'The Wild Bunch. Born naked?'! Here's more: 'Hide the weinie'! I'm not sure I want to see this!"

"I do. How do I screen it?"

"Cam's video camera is still here. But it'll be a small picture. Tell you what. It'll take time to screen even a couple of videos. Why don't you borrow the camera and the videos that interest you, and return them when you're ready."

"I will. Thank you, Gerry. I'll take good care of them. I want to return next week, and I'll bring them with me. And I'll leave you my number, just in case."

Kennet choose three videos to borrow. It was just after 10:00 when they left, Kennet with a loaded shopping bag. Conrad drove to the motel and stopped to let Kennet out. Sitting in the back seat, Kennet put his hand on Crystal's left shoulder. "Conrad's told you then?"

Crystal nodded, still facing front.

"It's still a wild idea," said Kennet. "But for me, it's a lead."

Crystal said quietly, "It wasn't a surprise. I mean, when Conrad told me. I had a suspicion." She turned her head to look at Kennet. "Mrs. Elder has never spoken to me about Georgie since I was a kid, when I asked her about it. She said Georgie had left home suddenly and all they ever heard from her was a postcard. Even as a kid, I could see the subject was painful, so I dropped it. She never told Gracie much more either."

"The subject has to be broached. With her. Them."

"I know." Crystal faced front again and dropped her chin. Then she said: "I'll see her tomorrow. And Gracie. I have a rest break after lunch. If Conrad will pick me up."

"Of course, doll. No question." He put his hand on her shoulder and then cupped the back of her neck under her pony tail.

Kennet said. "I'd like to drop over to see Mrs. Elder. After."

"Of course," Crystal said. "Two-thirty alright?"

Kennet let himself into the room as the truck drove off. He set the alarm for 2:00 a.m.

Chapter 20

Sunday, August 16th . . .

Heavy cloud cover blocked out the stars. Widely-spaced sodium vapour lamps cast pools on the streets, and scattered dim yellow light into the darkness. Kennet deposited the sack at the base of the Snowman, at the rear. He walked swiftly back to Kellerman's shop along Rothwell Street. He was wearing his wet suit, having concluded that his light-coloured clothes would make him too easy to spot if someone should happen by.

A transport lumbered past on the highway, heading south. Kennet hefted the aluminum ladder, which was lying on the ground at the rear of The Hook'n Bullet. In daylight it had been positioned upright against the wall. He rummaged through the junk in the yard and found a short piece of two-by-four lumber. Returning to the Snowman, he erected the ladder immediately behind the oversized fishing rod that projected on the north side, paralleling the highway. The ground-level spotlight illuminated the front side of the monument and left the rear in relative shadow.

He dumped the mangled rifles on the ground. He took the coil of wire and severed about ten metres from it by worrying it between his thumbs and fingers. He attached one end to the trigger guard of the Winchester, and the other to the block of wood. He climbed the ladder with the wood in his right hand. As he climbed, the monument narrowed at the second-tier "snowball", placing him further from the tip of the rod. He stopped. The tip hovered behind his right shoulder about two metres out and a metre higher.

He could see a vehicle approaching from the south as it descended the hill, and then the monument blocked his view. The engine throttled down and headlights played on the homes across the highway. He froze. The car passed and continued north. Even if the motorist were to see a ninja climbing the Snowman, what would he do? Stop and challenge it? Not likely.

He twisted around. He coiled about four metres of the wire, held it in his left hand, and then chucked the wood over the tip of the rod. It worked the first throw. He allowed the wire to uncoil as the wood dropped slowly to the ground. He released the wire, descended, and retrieved the wood. He tugged gently on the wire, and the rifle lifted off the ground. When it dangled about a metre below the tip, he detached the wood and brought the wire behind the monument and secured it.

He repeated the procedure with the Springfield. In a matter of minutes, two guns dangled from the fishing rod, intertwined. Kennet smiled. Who would spot the prank first?

Back in his room, he set his alarm for 7:30. For a long time he was talking to Vanderhorst. It was a one-sided conversation because Vanderhorst refused to look at him. Vanderhorst stood with his back to him and stared stolidly at the rock wall of the trench. Finally Kennet resorted to screaming. Soundlessly. *Goddamn you, Alfie. If you weren't so . . .! If you weren't so . . .!* And then the long-handled spade hit Alfie squarely between the shoulders at the base of the neck. The spade had a very long handle, a very long handle, and Kennet could not see who was wielding the spade. But Alfie just stood there. And the spade hit him again. And it hit him again. *My God but that Alfie was stubborn.* And then someone dropped the spade as Alfie just stood there. And then the culprit faded back down the trail, back behind Kennet, and the lonely upright figure of Alfred Vanderhorst shrank as Kennet was transported swiftly down the trail backwards, in the wake of the culprit. And then Kennet was on a motorcycle, a ridiculous little motorcycle, a circus clown's motorcycle, and he was moving backwards, backwards through the tunnel of the brush, backwards through a black tunnel, and the culprit was ahead of him, or rather behind him, moving, just out of sight, and the sky was rumbling, the black ceiling of the tunnel was rumbling, the ceiling cracked and tore apart and great rocks tumbled, crashed, an unstoppable avalanche . . .

His eyes sprang open. He reached for the alarm and switched it off. He had not been thinking of Alfred Vanderhorst's murder for a while now. That was a mistake. That was the reason for his foray into Indian country. That was the reason for abandoning Fort Academia, for leaving behind the safe stone-and-brick walls of Thunder Bay University to venture into the wilds of the Canadian Shield, into a territory that was emotionally dangerous for him. And it had been brought home that savages lived in that country, some racing around in painted pickups and others, others less obvious, lurking behind friendly faces.

There had been two deaths. One had been a murder: Vanderhorst's. The other he could not yet label. But the young female victim had been dropped into a bear's den on a lonely hilltop in the middle of a howling wilderness and left to disintegrate without a trace, without a memorial, without even a friend or a family member taking the trouble to report her missing. Still, he had no reason, no reason whatsoever, to believe there was any connection between the two deaths. But the death of a teenage girl on the verge of womanhood dredged up a memory from his own adolescence.

"Liliana," he said aloud. There, he'd said it. He'd said her name. Lili. She had preferred to be called Lili. He had not uttered her name, her full name, for twenty-nine years. Liliana Waterson. She had died, they said, in a fall. He could see her there, at the bottom of the stairs. Not see her. Imagine her. He had not seen her there at the bottom of the stairs. He had imagined her there. For twenty-nine years. Lying at the bottom of the stairs.

He had not seen her fall. He had been at home. He had been removing his white sports coat. Or perhaps he had been folding his charcoal gray slacks over the wire hanger. Perhaps he had been brushing his teeth. He knew, though, he had been in bed two hours when the call came. His mother answered the phone.

"We thought you'd like to know," Mr. Waterson had said. "Before you hear it at school. Liliana . . . passed away. After you left. She fell down the stairs." Kennet had said nothing. "It was an accident," said the voice. "It's nobody's fault." Still Kennet said nothing. He was still holding the receiver when it clicked in his ear.

Alice's Restaurant held only three customers. A man and woman had ordered the breakfast special, pancakes and sausage. The third customer hid behind a newspaper in Mac Kueng's customary seat.

"Good morning, Mac. Do you want company?"

The paper held steady, but it spoke. "Help yourself."

Kennet ordered the special from Alice as she filled his cup. Mac lowered the paper to expose his eyes. "No news yet," he said.

Kennet grasped his meaning. "Give it time. The day is young."

Another customer entered. It was Al Cummings, the labourer from the Crown Resources property. He flung the word "coffee" at Alice, who was behind the grill, and then slid into the first seat. "You'll never guess what I seen," he said, glancing around the small dining room. "It must've been a whopper!"

The man who had been about to stuff a whole sausage into his mouth said peevishly, "What're you gibbering about, Cummings?"

"It must've got away. No sign of it."

"No sign of what?" The man put his sausage down. His female companion put her utensils down and picked up her coffee cup.

"Lake trout. Sturgeon, maybe. A dolphin. You know, like a 'Free Willy' fish. Not a Great White Shark. We got none of them."

The diner was decidedly annoyed. "We got no 'Free Willies' neither, Cummings. And unless you spit it out proper, I'm coming over there and shake you good."

Cummings smiled broadly. "It's the Beardmore Snowman. It's got the biggest multi-barbed hook hanging from its rod that you ever seen. Must be a Number 163. But no fish."

"Jeez, Cummings. You interrupted my Sunday breakfast for that load of shit? I should've known better." He hoisted the sausage again.

"Hey, check it out yourself. I ain't lying."

Mac Kueng had lowered the newspaper. He drained his cup and set it down, looking at Kennet. "See you 'round," he said, and rose, taking his paper.

After breakfast Kennet crossed to the store and picked up *The Lakehead Journal*. The blue sky promised a lovely day. Back in his room he scanned the stories quickly. No mentions of Vanderhorst. No mentions of the mystery bones. He dug out Robert Kenilworth's business card and, using his cell, dialed the home number on the back.

A woman answered. "Ah," said Kennet, glancing at his watch. "I guess it's still early. I apologize, I wasn't thinking. It's Kennet Forbes. Is Robert up, by any chance?"

"Why, yes, Kennet. Robert's told me all about you. I'm Nancy, by the way. Robert's always up." Kennet heard a slap on naked flesh and a yelp muffled by a hand over the transmitter on the other end. Robert came on the line.

"Yes, Kennet, and an early good morning to you too."

"I'm expecting it to improve. The sun's out, and I'm going to the lake for a paddle, and since I'll be out of cell range, I wanted to touch base. I'll be home tonight. In Thunder Bay, I mean."

"Any news yet?"

"About Vanderhorst, no. I'm depending on you there. I'm at a dead end here. About the mystery bones, I'm following a good lead. Possibly a local girl. Have you caught up with the Flemings?"

"As a matter of fact, yes. A cruiser spotted Ritch in a green pickup yesterday, pulled him over. Claimed he was on an urgent mission, had to pick up a party in the bush. The constable brought him to the detachment for questioning, as a key witness. Gave him a berth for the night. So Detective Constable Armitage will question him, if they can find her. She's got Sunday off, and Lord knows where she'll be. Would you have knowledge of any emergency in the bush?"

"If I told you," said Kennet, "I'd have to –"

"Kill me. Yeah, I know. Shaddup."

Kennet checked his laptop for e-mail. A message from Robert conveyed essentially the same information he'd relayed by phone. Nothing yet from Dale Marchak. Two messages related to his work at the university. Susan, lovely daughter Susan, reminded him of dinner at 7:30 that night.

His cell rang. Dale Marchak said, "Might have something here. Or nothing."

"Fire away."

"On June 25th, 1983, a Saturday, I checked out a complaint at Poplar Lodge Park. At the camps, actually. I was following up a message left the night before, about a camp party, but I was otherwise occupied that Friday night."

"Yes?"

"Fellow was complaining about young people raising hell. Then he handed me a pair of shoes."

"Shoes?"

"Boots, actually. A woman's ankle-high black boots. Size small. Said he found them sitting on the road that morning. Right in the middle of the road. Side by side."

"And?"

"And nothing. Party was over. Participants dispersed. Mystery unsolved."

"Okay, thanks. Could be nothing. Or something. Thanks for persevering, Dale."

He was about to switch on the TV to check the weather channel when he remembered that his schedule called for a TV-free day. He pulled out the map of Nipigon's east shore that he had purchased from Kellerman and studied it for a while. Then he strolled over to The Hook'n Bullet. A few puffy cumulus drifted in the azure vault.

Two RVs had parked at the curb, one pulling a cabin cruiser. An SUV and a pickup had pulled into the parking area. Kids squeezed through the aisles, fingering the merchandise. Marta, answering a customer's questions, kept one eye peeled for trouble. At the counter, a ten-year-old boy in a yellow ball cap tugged on the sleeve of a pudgy man in a Tilley outfit, who hadn't shaved for days. "Dad, can we go see the Snowman again? Can we, huh? It's just over there." He pointed south. "We can't get lost. Huh?"

"Alright, alright," said the man. "Keep the others off the road." Yellow Ball Cap streaked outside followed by three younger siblings.

"As I was saying," said Kellerman, ringing up the sale for the pudgy tourist, "we've had no reports of sharks in the area, but you never know. What line will you be using?"

"Sixty-pound test. You think I should upgrade?"

"Sixty-pound. Should be alright. You catch anything bigger, you'd need a harpoon anyway."

Kennet caught Kellerman's eye between customers. "Al Cummings is spreading the word," he said.

"Yeah, he was in here for a while. Hung on my every word."

Kennet said, "I wondered where he'd found his wit. Bull, I'm going to the lake for a few hours. I'll catch up with you later."

Kellerman said, "Take care," and eyed him appraisingly. "You don't mind making enemies, son. I admire that."

"Enemies keep one strong," said Kennet.

Kennet strolled over to the monument. Another RV had pulled over to the curb and a family of four were standing under the fishing rod, gazing up. The four kids from The Hook'n Bullet were ducking around the Snowman and slapping it with the edges of their hands, miming the making of snowballs, which they threw at one another. The family man waved him over and asked if he would take their picture. Kennet complied.

Back at the motel, Kennet packed up. He attracted Alice's attention and left the key with her. Some of the highway construction crew would not be returning, she said, and she anticipated some vacancies later in the week if Kennet returned. He took a business card with him.

Chapter 21

. . . Sunday morning

From time to time as he headed west on Hwy. 580, he met a vehicle on the narrow road. He slowed down on the blind curves so that he was not crossing the faded yellow median. Sunlight bounced off the billows of green brush and brightened the faraway hills. He passed the graveled 72 Road. A large bulldozed clearing on the right-hand side featured rock shards and rock piles, which he guessed was the old Leitch mine that Dan Nordstrom had mentioned. He passed a man and woman in the ditch picking some kind of berries from the shrubs, their vehicle pulled into a side road.

A gravel road forked left, labeled by a sign for High Hill Harbour. A billboard announced Poplar Lodge Park straight ahead. Kennet drove into a flat area of manicured lawns and mature trees with recreational vehicles of every description spotted about. The lake sparkled beyond. Adults lounged about in deck chairs or strolled across the swards. Children ran or cycled about, some chased by dogs, or played in the shallow water off a sandy shore that bordered a large bay. The east shore ran exposed to the main lake for three or four kilometers all the way to a knob or knoll. On the west, a small rocky point with a clump of trees divided the head of the bay from the main lake, and a breakwater extended the point by thirty metres. A boardwalk ran along the breakwater. Someone had moored a motorboat there.

Kennet pulled into a parking area at the point where two other vehicles stood empty. There was also a yellow Yamaha 1100 Classic, but no sign of Saxon Fleming. He opened both front doors to allow the breeze off the lake to ventilate the interior. At the far end of a green, treeless area behind the beach, there were a few small structures, probably change houses and privies. He noted that most of the campers had parked near the trees where the terrain rose into the bush, away from the beach, leaving an unobstructed field of view of the water and the children. It was a well planned park.

The main lake glittered to the west of the point. Kennet removed his shoes and socks and walked to the small sandy beach that faced the main lake. Small waves approached from centre-lake and slapped playfully at his toes. Immediately to the north, islets just offshore constricted his view, as did another point of land. Far out to sea, hazy land masses under banks of cumulus signaled the presence of an archipelago.

"Hi, there!" The voice came from the water, just off the point. Two canoeists, a man and a woman, steered directly for him. "Fancy meeting you here."

Kelly Armitage grinned at him from the bow. She wore dark glasses. Kennet returned the greeting: "Kelly! What a pleasure! And isn't this a grand day to be alive!"

The canoe touched bottom and Kelly leapt out. She wore shorts and halter. She grabbed the bow and dragged it up the sloping beach. "Kennet, I want you to meet Rod. Roderick Campbell." With a gesture she presented him to Kennet. "Kennet Forbes. We met a couple days ago, Rod, when I was on call to Beardmore."

Rod unfolded long bare hairy legs and stepped into the water in sandals. He offered his hand. "A pleasure, Kennet. From what Kelly tells me, and she can't tell me much, you're a colleague of that unfortunate man."

Rod was a slim man, about thirty-five, with clean-cut tanned features and short dark hair. He wore polarized glasses and an Indiana Jones hat. "Yes," said Kennet. "Feeling pretty useless, I'm afraid. I'm heading home tonight, but I wanted to see the lake." He was pleased to note they had the good sense to wear PFDs, even on a calm day.

Kelly smiled broadly. "This is our first time too! We've just come from High Hill Harbour. We parked there. And the lake was so smooth, we couldn't resist an excursion. We followed the shore. The country's all burned over, Kennet. What a shame! But we saw hikers on the trail."

"Hikers?"

"Oh yes. There's a walking trail from the park to the harbour, and a lookout from a promontory. We're going to walk up, if we get back in time. Oh no!"

Kelly had been gazing toward the campers fifty metres away. Kennet turned. No one seemed to be taking an interest in them except one burly man in shorts and t-shirt, standing with a beer can in his right hand. A young boy and a girl cavorted around the camper-trailer.

Kennet looked again. It was Detective Constable Mueller. Mueller's left hand, dangling by his thigh, lifted slightly and waved without enthusiasm.

Kennet waved back in like fashion. Kelly raised her arm to wave more enthusiastically. She turned to her boy friend. "Rod, let's get out of here. I don't want to spoil the day. Kennet, what were you planning?"

"I just want to get on the water. But I thought I'd take a run up the shore," he gestured northward, "and look for an old cemetery I heard about."

"Wow! Do you want company? Sounds like an adventure! Is it far?"

"Perhaps a klick. And I'd love the company."

Back at the truck, Kennet removed his trousers, under which he wore the pants part of his wet suit. He stripped off his shirt and pulled on the upper vest and jammed the safari hat on his head. He slipped the lanyard of the GPS unit around his neck. He stored his boots and a knapsack in the compartment before he launched the kayak.

Kennet led the way between the islets and the shore, crossing a shallow crescent bay where three or four camps stood on the sandy shore. The mainland was fully wooded. Kennet aimed for the northern point and some scattered islands. It was a ten-minute run. He slackened his rhythm to allow the canoe to catch up.

"This," said Rod, "is more interesting country. I wonder how far across it is." He pointed with his paddle to the land masses out to sea.

"Too far for a canoe. I have some experience on big water. A wind or a storm can come up anytime. Even cruising offshore like this can be dangerous on big water."

"Really?" said Kelly. "It seems so calm. Mind you, we've been exploring small lakes and rivers up to now."

They passed a camp and outbuildings nestled in a grove. They negotiated the channel between islands and shore, Kennet warning them of underwater boulders. Just past another camp the shoreline indented. The burn had roared down to the sandy beach. There was no evidence of structures. At the north end, a long narrow point projected into the channel, dominated by exposed bedrock and snags and brush.

"I think this is it," said Kennet. "The cemetery's in here somewhere. Or used to be." They paddled into the bay and beached their watercraft.

"What a lovely spot!" said Kelly. "I mean, it must've been. It's a mess now. But it would've looked out over the islands and had a view of the setting sun. How appropriate."

"I could still paint this, looking west," said Rod.

"You're a painter?"

"Amateur. A professional CO by trade. I think Kelly was attracted to my gun." He grinned at his partner.

"So. Conservation Officers still wear sidearms?"

"Oh yeah. We're inseparable. We do meet gunslingers in this line of work. Where've you been?"

"Out of the country. I was a journalist. Chasing wars and other natural disasters."

They were standing on the narrow beach and gazing at the tangle of brush and windfall. "Oh. Kelly said you were a professor or something." Kelly was sitting on the bow of the canoe and pulling on running shoes. Kennet dropped to the sand and pulled on his boots.

"Yes, I'm something now. At TBU. Media studies." Kennet looked thoughtfully at the terrain. "Maybe if we each took a five-metre swath, and walked in ten or twelve metres, we could spot something. Most of the markers were wooden, I believe. So we'll have to get lucky. Let's start at the head of the beach."

Kennet led the way to the north end of the beach. They spaced themselves seven metres apart and walked in. Sometimes patches of marsh grass separated clumps of brush. Kennet bulled his way through most of the shrubbery. Clumps that proved too thick to penetrate, he circumnavigated. When he paused, he could hear Rod and Kelly thrashing about and making comments.

Kennet cut to the right, meeting Kelly. "I'm just moving over. I'll head for the beach now. Let's just keep the same search pattern working." Kelly followed him. He repeated his comments for Rod. Rod said, "Damn! I have to plan each step. Sandals aren't the appropriate footwear."

Kennet said, "I'll take the farthest swath, Rod. Just move seven metres over and head for the beach."

At the beach, they displaced themselves further south and repeated the pattern. In a little while they were back at the beach again. Kennet said, "Not a sign, eh? The fire was thorough."

"Look," said Kelly. "There's something in the sand. A rock. A slab."

There was a flat stone protruding from the sand near the alders. Kennet knelt down and brushed it with his hand. It was a fragment of headstone with markings on it. Tracing the grooves with a finger, he spelled out the epitaph the best he could:

A. FPA9FR

1-64 – 19_7

AGE 73 YR

"It looks like the name is 'Fraser'," said Kennet. He stepped back to the water and did some arithmetic in the wet sand. "Add 73 to 1864 and you get 1937." When he stood up he sensed that the breeze off the lake had freshened.

"What do we do with it?" asked Kelly.

"There's a Cemeteries Act, I'm sure," said Rod, "but I don't know if it applies to unofficial cemeteries."

"For the time being," said Kennet, "we'll leave it. There may be some family that will claim it."

"How will they know?" asked Kelly.

"Let me think about it," said Kennet. "Alright with you, Rod?"

"Sure. Not my jurisdiction."

"Wow," said Kelly. "I feel a little weird. Walking away from it, I mean. As if I'm leaving a body behind. Somebody's grandfather or grandmother."

"You agree," said Kennet, "that it's not police business?"

"No, no. Someone honoured the memory. It's not as if the deceased were abandoned. Left in the bush. Some family honoured the deceased." She paused, then continued. "But I'll have to look it up in the regs." She smiled apologetically at Kennet. "It's my job," she said.

"Of course. But give me a few days, will you? I don't want this stone transferred to some police locker and then to some trash pile when there's a housecleaning."

"Sure, we'll discuss it further," she said.

Kennet held his GPS unit up and scanned for satellites. He marked a waypoint for the location of the gravestone.

Kelly said, "I'd love to walk out to that point, while we're here."

Kennet said, "The weather's changing. Wind's coming up. I think we should go." They didn't argue.

Back on the water, stray locks of Kelly's hair streamed behind her. Rod removed his floppy hat, pulled out a chin strap, and replaced his headwear. The water in the channel proved choppy. They paddled south. When they broke into the main lake past the islands, the waves rolled toward them from the southwest.

"Jeez!" Rod shouted. "What a difference!"

Kennet shouted back, "Just ten minutes to the park! Follow my lead."

"Shouldn't we hug the shore?" Rod shouted.

Kennet dropped back to address them: "Waves are magnified in the shallows! Just follow me, keep to my right. Slice the waves at an angle. When you meet the wave, both paddle on the lee side, the landward side. Also, kneel down. Bum on the edge of the seat. One at a time, now."

Kennet kept pace with them as they knelt down, first Kelly, then Rod. Kennet quartered the waves, which advanced toward them about five metres apart. The trough between waves looked about a third of a metre deep. Out to sea he could see whitecaps.

The canoeists soon achieved a rhythm. As the bow rose on a swell, Kelly switched her paddle to the port side. Past the crest, she switched back again. They moved steadily southward, paralleling the shoreline. Kennet judged their course would take them outside the islets. The faces of the canoeists set in grim concentration.

As they approached the islets, Rod shouted: "Shouldn't we head in now?"

"Trust me! A little further." They paddled past the islets, pointing to the wide open reaches. When they stood about eighty metres off the point, Kennet shouted: "After the next wave, turn sharply for shore!"

The canoeists executed the maneuvre on cue, and Kennet followed. The waves picked up the watercraft and shot them toward the small sand beach. "Keep paddling!" Kennet shouted. "Go a little faster than the waves."

Rod was whooping. "Put the spurs to 'im, woman! Make 'im buck!" Kelly was grinning in delight.

Twenty metres from the beach, Rod threw both hands in the air and whoopee'd. Kennet shouted, "Keep paddling!"

"We're there! We're there!" Rod responded.

A wave washed over the stern. The stern sank deeper. The next wave washed over the gunnels and the whole canoe sank deeper. Kelly shrieked. Rod leapt out into water up to his armpits and grabbed the gunnel. The canoe beached itself, water slopping from one end to the other.

Kelly rose unsteadily and stepped into ankle-deep water in bare feet. "What happened?" she said. "Are you alright, Rod?"

Kennet had lifted the kayak up to grass verge. "What happened," he said, "is that Rod stopped paddling. It ain't over till it's over."

Rod waded in, dripping wet. " 'Waves are magnified in the shallows.' Someone said that to me once." He grinned wryly. "I guess we ain't there till we're there."

"This has been a teachable moment," said Kennet, grinning. "Tune in next canoe trip."

Kelly pointed to Rod's legs: "Rod, look at your knees!"

Rod looked down at his red knees. Dark circles the size of quarters indicated bruising. "I'd rather look at your knees," he said, looking up.

Kelly's knees, also red, showed no bruising. "I was kneeling on my runners," she said. She slapped at her knees. "This'll go away. Oh you poor thing!"

"You should see my ego," said Rod. "It's bleeding." He glanced at Kennet, who was extracting his boots and knapsack from the compartment. "You must think we're rank amateurs."

"Amateurs, yes. Rank, no. You did well, for amateurs. We all have to start somewhere. Now, if I painted a picture, that would be rank. It would stink to high heaven. Come on. I'll give you a lift to your vehicle. Just dump the water and drag it up here. No one'll bother it."

Kennet lifted the kayak over his head and headed for his truck. He deposited it on the roof rack and snapped the latches. He stripped off the PFD and dug the truck keys out of his waistband. Kelly and Rod came up and shucked their PFDs.

"I have to find a ladies' room," said Kelly.

"I think I saw one as I came in. Jump in." Kennet pulled on shirt and trousers. Kelly sat in front, Rod behind. Rod apologized for getting the seat damp. They drove past the campers to a cinder block washroom under the trees.

Kelly left, and the men lounged outside the truck. Three men nearby sprawled on canvas chairs beside a classy fifth-wheel RV with beers in their hands. One of them called across.

"Hey! Where you from? That's some submarine you got there."

Kennet strolled over to the group. "That?" he said, gesturing to the kayak. "That's unsinkable. Like the Titanic."

A large-framed guy with close-cropped sandy hair grinned at him in a good-natured way. "The Titanic? Last I heard, she sunk."

"Last I heard, no icebergs 'round here. So she'll never sink."
Rod had followed him over.

Rod said, "Marcus, you got nothing better to do than harass the public?"

Sandy Hair rose to his full six-foot plus. "Roderick! Come and have a beer. Your friend too."

Rod looked around. Kelly was emerging from the washroom. "Love to. But my other friend wants to do some hiking. By the way, this is Kennet Forbes."

"Kennet! Crikey, I know you! Last time I saw you, you were on the TV."

I know him, thought Kennet, as he grasped his outstretched hand. "Chambers. Marcus Chambers," he said. "Still into hockey?"

Chambers, Kennet remembered, had led Geraldton's Juniors to several victories on ice. It was a game Kennet had never got into seriously.

Chambers shook his hand vigorously, then squeezed his fingers and pushed Kennet's arm back in an Indian wrestling move. "Hey! You didn't get those arms holding a mike." He released his grip and continued, "Yes, I play old-timers' hockey. Live and work in Geraldton. I trained as a forester, but the industry is dead in these parts, so I retrained as a teacher. I'm at the high school now. What're you doing in these parts, Kennet?"

"Today, enjoying myself. Listen, I have to give these folks a lift to High Hill. If that offer still holds, I'll come back."

Chapter 22

. . . Sunday mid-day

The gravel road to High Hill Harbour wound through the burn. The brush enclosed the road. There were no glimpses of the lake, but from time to time Kennet observed a prominent hill to the south. After six kilometers the road ended at a complex of parking areas and piers. The place looked deserted.

Under Rod's direction, Kennet pulled up to a light blue Ford F-150 truck with a white cap. A few cabin cruisers and fishing tugs bobbed at their moorings. The scattering of vehicles in the parking lot overlooked an enclosed bay to the east. To the west, a burned-over ridge rose steeply, cutting off any view of the main lake.

Kelly and Rod thanked him.

"What're you up to now?" asked Kennet.

"There's a walking trail, starts just back there," said Rod. "We going to climb that hill," Rod gestured to the high ground, "to the lookout. Then we'll go pick up the canoe."

"Okay, kids. Have fun. And Kelly, I'll get back to you on that gravestone."

Back at the park, Kennet parked beside the twelve-metre recreational trailer. Marcus Chambers emerged from the doorway with two beers in his hands. His male companions had departed.

"Let's sit in the shade," said Chambers. They sat at a patio table under a sunshade. "Kay's making sandwiches, enough for all of us." He grinned at Kennet. "I never asked – why was Rod as wet as a mad hen? – I said that wrong, didn't I – Was he waterskiing behind your submarine?"

"Oh. The lake got a bit rough and their canoe dumped. Just offshore. I happened to be there." Kennet looked out over the bay. "It doesn't look bad from here, but for a canoe, it's rough. They'll be back to pick it up."

"So, how do you know them?"

Kennet explained briefly, about his colleague Vanderhorst, about the police investigation, and about meeting Kelly and Rod and their pleasure jaunt up the shore.

"A graveyard, eh? You can see it from the Kimberlys' camp."

"You've been up there?"

"Sure," said Chambers. "Once. When I was a kid. There was one hell of a bash there. A fuck-it-tomorrow's-Saturday kind of party. I was in Grade 12. Had a good year with the Miners team, and got invited to lots of stuff."

"I was three years ahead of you."

"Yep."

"So the party was in '83."

"Yep. June. Yes, you were the BMOC in those days, eh? Big Man on Campus. As I recall, you ran the school newspaper – what was it called? The Purple and Gold. Edited the yearbook. Belonged to the canoe club – God, you guys used to stink up the corridors when you came back from a trip! And captain of Senior Boys Basketball, right?"

"Assistant captain. I never got to be that good."

A tall ash-blonde in shorts brought out a tray of sandwiches. "Kay," said Chambers, "this is my buddy Kennet. Went to school together. You remember him on the news?"

Kay Chambers smiled as she shook his hand. "You didn't have that scar, Kennet. I remember hearing something about that."

"A pleasure to meet you, Kay."

"I've got to run," she said. "The kids are at the beach. I'm taking a picnic lunch to them. Nice meeting you, Kennet."

She returned to the RV. Kennet turned to Chambers: "I heard something about that party last night. Who was there?"

"Three of us came from Geraldton. Guys, of course. There were some women. From Beardmore. A couple from Thunder Bay. Guys outnumbered the gals, so most of us struck out. At one point the sauna was packed with naked flesh, and then everyone streaked for the lake. It was a real gas!"

"Who was from Geraldton?"

"Keith Salmon. Jay Dithers. Myself. There was even a guy from Beardmore there, taking videos. You remember Cam St. Clair, the guy who ran around school snapping photos?"

"Keith and Jay still around?"

"Keith is. Works for Bell. I don't know what happened to Jay."

"Remember any girls?"

"Faces and tits, mostly. Bye, dear, don't get wet." Kay Chambers had emerged from the trailer with a basket and started for the beach. They both watched Kay's lovely tanned legs take her to the beach. They both took bites of their sandwich.

"There was one little brunette, though," Chambers continued, munching. "Georgie. She was really spaced out. When I got her in a clinch, she threw up on me."

"Drugs?"

"I'm sure. But booze was my drug of choice. She must've left early, though. Never saw her after that."

"And that camp is just up the road?" asked Kennet.

"Sure. You can see the graveyard from there. Want to take a run up?"

Marcus Chambers gunned the black Toyota Tundra pickup up the hill from the park. The fire had skipped that stand of trees. At the top a private road melted into the jack pines. After a stretch another private road appeared where the fire had touched down and swept west down a slope. Chambers turned into the road. To their left stood an intact grove. The lake appeared. The narrow road divided, the left fork going to a cottage and outbuildings in the grove, and the right snaking through brush. Almost immediately a clearing materialized.

Chambers braked in a grassy yard overlooking the little bay the paddlers had visited earlier. A single-story camp with faux-log siding overlooked the channel and islands. A small hut, likely a sauna, perched on rocks sloping down to the cove in front of the camp.

"This is different!" said Chambers. "That cabin is new. So's that sauna. There was a frame building with asphalt siding, and a log sauna where that one is now. Come on." Chambers climbed down from the cab.

The place looked deserted. They walked a few paces north to the bank overlooking the little bay. On the far side the bare fire-ravaged point projected west. "Hell!" said Chambers. "Nothin' left. The fire got it all." He pointed to the head of the bay: "You could see a bunch of crosses over there."

He turned to face the cabin. "Let me show you where I skinned my nuts!" Chambers led him to the rocks sloping down to the lake.

"Everyone was diving off of that rock there," he said, pointing to a dolphin's hump below the sauna. "Me, smart ass, I skipped along the shore here and ran out on that ledge, all me flags flying and me spinnaker at half mast. Just advertising, you know. We were all naked as jaybirds, guys and gals, and it was dark, but the lake reflected back whatever light there was, so you got good silhouettes. I dove in and stripped off three layers of skin from chin to toes. It wasn't five inches deep."

"Ouch," said Kennet.

"It took a lot of rum-and-cokes to dull the pain, let me tell you. When I got home the next day and I removed my shirt and pants, I stuck like a squealed pig – well, you know what I mean. The blood had caked and I was pullin' off scabs!"

"Don't tell me. You gave up drinking that summer."

"For one whole week. Man, that was a party!"

"Any other excitement that night?"

"I can't remember half the stuff. There were a couple of bozos who were hunting trouble. Gate-crashers. I hear they're still raising hell in Beardmore."

"You're talking about the Flemings."

"Hell, you get around! You've heard of Rawling and Lanny, eh? There was a younger brother tagging along, I forget his name, but he was quiet. Well behaved. A gentleman. When the two rowdies got too obnoxious, he tried to intervene. 'Course, they just ignored him. But Rawling and Lanny, they seemed to want to corner a girl and give 'er what for, so finally a bunch of us surrounded them and kicked their asses out of camp."

"And the younger brother?"

"He was dead sober. He wasn't any trouble anyway. He said he'd drive his brothers home, and they left, under protest."

"And this Georgie you mentioned?"

"Oh, she was long gone too. I tried to look her up again, but she was nowhere to be found. Why, you remember her?"

"Yes. From school. She was a cutie."

"Damn straight. I never saw her again, though. Wonder what happened to her."

"Yes. I wonder." Kennet continued: "Do you remember at which point in the evening you saw last saw her?"

"Why," said Chambers, "do I get the feeling that is not a casual question?"

"You're right. It's not. I've learned she left home after that, quite suddenly. Maybe ran away."

"Ah." He looked at Kennet speculatively. "The investigative journalist is working, is he?" He grinned. "Well, as it happens I can tell you. It was during the graveyard rally."

"Excuse me?"

"We had a helluva bonfire going in the yard here – that was before the sauna adventure – marshmallows and weinies. After the sweat and the swim, someone had the idea of a torch parade, to visit the graveyard and scare ourselves silly, so away we went. Some of us had burning sticks, one guy lit a broom on fire, I and a couple others had flashlights. The water is shallow at the end of the bay, so we splashed through the water. We formed a ring around the cemetery and a few goofs danced around the graves. Now that I think on it, it was pretty childish. And disrespectful."

"And Georgie?"

"Georgie. Georgie didn't want to go. But Gron picked her up, slung her over his shoulder, and carried her over, screaming and kicking. You remember Gron?"

"A big galoot."

"Gigantic is the word. Anyway, he set her down over there, and I remember trying to hook up with her, but she had disappeared. I had the light, so I found a trail leading up to the road. I followed it. Near the top I was nearly bowled over by two bozos coming down, leather bent for hell. It was really dark, but I recognized Rawling by his jacket. Up on the road there was a pickup down a piece, facing towards the park. It was just sitting there, just putt-putting away, all quiet. But no Georgie. There was someone standing on the road by the driver's side door. Just a blur, really. And it looked like someone was in the cab, on the passenger side."

"Can you describe the pickup."

"Couldn't see much. But it had three rear windows. The headlights backlighted them."

"Three rear windows? Oh. The five-windows style. That was a feature on some really old models."

"Yeah. The outline of the cab was old-fashioned. So I just assumed she got a ride, and that the driver told the Flemings to fuck off."

"You saw nothing else?"

"I did. That bugger standing on the road – he turned a spot on me. Just on and off. It was blinding. I shielded my eyes and retreated down the trail. That's all I recall."

Back at the Chambers' campsite, they tackled the remainder of the sandwiches. Chambers explained that his holiday was just beginning, having just returned from a six-week course in Guelph, Ontario. Kay, his wife, worked at the hospital, day shift, and returned each evening. She had been taking their two boys, aged ten and twelve, to town for organized recreational programs while she worked.

"Any other Geraldtonians here?" Kennet asked.

"Yep. A couple. None that you'd know."

"I saw the OPP officer, Mueller, over yonder today."

"Oh yeah. Mueller. He comes out on his days off. Hopes no one'll recognize him here, I guess. Not a popular guy."

"You got the time, Marcus?"

Chambers glanced at his watch. "One-thirty-five, or thereabouts."

Kennet stood up. "I've got to shove off. It's been fun catching up." Chambers shook his hand warmly.

In Beardmore, Kennet stopped on the main street opposite The Hook'n Bullet. When Kellerman finished serving the lone customer, Kennet spoke up: "Bull, I'm leaving shortly. Some late-breaking news for you: The cops picked up Ritch yesterday for questioning in the Vanderhorst case."

"Very good news. And I've got some for you. A patrol car pulled over Rawling and Lanny in their circus wagon not an hour ago. Followed them to their house and, I'm told, took them into custody. I still hate to think, though," Kellerman continued, "there's a murderer in our community. A cold-blooded one."

"That other matter, Bull. The missing girl?"

"Right." Kellerman came around the counter and leaned in close to Kennet. "I must've gone through a couple dozen names. There's only one I can't account for. She'd just graduated high school, and left town immediately, and she's never been back, though her family said she wrote to them in the beginning. No one else has seen or heard from her. She had a best friend, Elsie, who lives in Thunder Bay now, but I don't know her married name. This girl's family still lives here, but I didn't want to approach them. I don't have the rep of being the most sensitive of guys."

"The name?"

"Georgiana Elder. Everyone called her Georgie. Left in the summer of '83."

"I've met Mrs. Elder," said Kennet. "I'm going to see her again, right now."

"So you're ahead of me."

"It's still all speculation, Bull. But you've provided an important piece of the puzzle. You've narrowed the options. On the other hand, we might not even be looking for a local girl. I have to ask a favour."

"Fire away. It won't be the first."

"Keep this under your hat? For the sake of the family. And I do disagree with you on one point."

"What's that."

"You *are* a sensitive guy."

"You keep *that* under your hat. I got a rep to maintain."

Chapter 23

. . . Sunday afternoon

Conrad Parker's truck sat outside the Elder residence. Crystal Mallory answered the door with a somber expression. "They're in the sitting room," she said. "They're in shock."

Kennet approached Mrs. Elder, who was sitting in an overstuffed chair in the dimly lit room. The drapes were closed, and two table lamps cast a sickly glow over the chintzy furniture. Kennet knelt beside Mrs. Elder and covered her right hand with his and stroked her upper arm.

"I know I'm a stranger to you, Mrs. Elder, but believe me, I know how hard this is for you." He reached over to Gracie and touched her knee. "For you too, Gracie."

He clasped Mrs. Elder's hand in both of his. "When the three of us formed this suspicion, we knew – we knew we had to break it to you. And *that* is just what it is at this point, Mrs. Elder – a suspicion. Not a fact."

For the first time she raised her eyes. Her eyes and the lines around them gleamed wet. "I know it's true," she said simply. "I guess I've always known it's true." She turned to her daughter:

"Gracie, it must be harder on you . . . Because I told you she was alive. I was doing what I thought was best. To cherish your sister's memory."

She withdrew her hand from Kennet's clasp and dabbed at her eyes with a tissue she had had bunched in her hand. "But the years passed," she continued, "and she never wrote and she never phoned, so I knew. I knew she loved us, and she would never, never hurt us by cutting us out of her life so cruelly." She gazed at her daughter again. "I tried to protect you, Gracie. You had a big sister that you never knew, but I knew she would have loved you. Just as we did – your father and me."

Gracie said softly, "I knew too, momma. I knew when you gave up. When you gave up hope. But I loved her too. I knew we would've been great together. We would've had great times together."

Kennet rose silently and took a seat facing the two grieving women. "This is a hard time for you," he said. "But if that is Georgie who was buried out there – and I'm not saying it is – we want to confirm her identity. We want to understand what happened. I'm working with the university, Mrs. Elder. They have the remains in their possession, and I need you to tell me what you remember about the last days you saw her. Can you do that?"

Mrs. Elder drew herself up. "I want to tell you. I want to tell someone about Georgie. For twenty-five years – twenty-six years, I've held it in, except for the good things I told Gracie about her sister. It's truth time now. That last year of school, Georgie became a different person."

Georgiana Florentine Elder had been an "A" student, had been active in school sports, had immersed herself in community activities of every description, and had helped out around the house with a minimum of encouragement. She had been a girl with a ready smile and a cheerful word for everybody. Until her last year of school, Grade 12, when she had grown sullen for long periods of time. She had sometimes not uttered a civil word for days, had lashed out from time to time at her parents, at her peers, even at her good friend Elsie Newman. One Saturday night in springtime, she had not come home. She had stayed out all night, and when she did return, after missing church service, she had refused to offer an explanation. She was a grown up now, she said, and accountable to no one but herself. She'd be leaving home after graduation, she said, and no one was stopping her.

"She wasn't always like that," said Mrs. Elder. "Sometimes she was just Georgie, her normal self. And she would smile and joke. She came up to me in the kitchen, about a week later after that night – she sort of sidled up to me, and she said to me, softly she said, 'Momma, I don't know what I'd've been without you and Daddy all this time, I'd've been lost, I guess. Thank you, Momma, for loving me.' She said that: 'Thank you for loving me.' And she added, 'And tell Daddy that for me, will you, Momma?' "

Harold Elder had been a commercial fisherman all his life. He'd spend days out on the lake, and when he returned, he'd sleep a lot, and maintain his boat and his gear, and sometimes his family didn't enjoy his presence for days. But he loved his only daughter, said Mrs. Elder. He'd started calling her Georgie when she was in diapers. And when Gracie came along, he loved her just as much. Maybe more.

Mrs. Elder glanced over at Gracie and smiled. For the first time Kennet noticed that Gracie was toying with a small hoop decorated with string, feathers, and bells.

"Mrs. Elder," said Kennet, "in that last year of school, George acted strangely. Did you ever notice her acting, well, really out of character?"

"What do you mean?"

"I mean, did she act sometimes as if she was in her own world, sort of detached from reality, oblivious to her surroundings."

"I'm not sure what you mean."

"He means," said Gracie, speaking for the first time, "was she on drugs?"

"Drugs?" Mrs. Elder reacted in horror. "Good Lord, no! Georgie on drugs? No. No. Never."

"I had to ask, Mrs. Elder."

"Of course. It's your job. And we want to find the truth." She tucked her chin into her chest and breathed deeply for a full minute. Then she mumbled, "To tell the truth, how would I know? Does any mother know the truth about their children these days?" She lifted her head and flashed a smile at Gracie: "Not you, Gracie. I know you, Gracie."

Gracie flashed a quick smile in return: "Maybe," she whispered.

"There were times – that year, I mean – when Georgie sparkled. Just out of the blue, she'd be really lively, she'd say things that seemed really brilliant though sometimes we couldn't really understand them, and she'd laugh and laugh. She seemed like the old Georgie, and we were happier. But now I don't know."

"Georgie graduated in June," said Kennet. "Did you attend the ceremony, Mrs. Elder?"

"Was I there? No. I was in Sioux Lookout. My sister was ill, deathly ill. She died a few months later. No, I missed Georgie's graduation, but I told Harold, I told Harold, You be sure to be there. You be there for both of us. She's our princess, and she's receiving her crown. You be there."

She paused and looked hard at Kennet. "He missed it too. Something about the lake being too rough, he couldn't get back in time. He got back too late that day to dress up and then drive to Geraldton." She dropped her eyes: "Neither of us . . . Neither of us was there for her." She mumbled: "I never saw her again."

"Did Harold see her?"

"Of course. Yes. The next day. She was in one of her moods. She was packing to leave. She was throwing stuff into her suitcase – Harold's suitcase, actually – and saying she was never coming back. Harold couldn't stop her."

"How did she leave? I mean, did she have a ride?"

"Harold drove her, he said."

"Mrs. Elder, I have a strange question. Do you recall what Harold was driving at that time?

"Goodness, no. I don't know anything about cars. But it was a good truck. He bought it new just the year before. Now, wait. He didn't drive her. He said his chum drove her. She wouldn't take anything from Harold. She had some money of her own, from working at the store. No, Mac drove her, to the bus depot, in Thunder Bay."

"Mac? Do you mean Mac Kueng?"

"Yes. His best friend. Mac." Her eyes drifted to the flowered wallpaper.

Kennet leaned back. He started to sink into the spongy upholstery, so he leaned forward again. He had never asked Mac Kueng anything. Mac was the last living link to the missing girl. He glanced at his watch. He wouldn't have a chance to ask him today.

"Mrs. Elder, I beg your indulgence. Can you supply me with photos of Georgie? The older she was, the better. Portrait shots, and full body shots?"

"Of course."

"And I understand you got a letter from her?"

"Postcards. Two postcards. Let me get those." Mrs. Elder rose and went into a bedroom.

Kennet turned to Gracie. "Gracie, you understand we're dealing with bones. It's possible that DNA can be extracted from them. Can you think of anything, anything that Georgie used or wore that might still contain a piece, an essence of her?"

"I found a hairbrush long ago," she said. "It had some strands of hair. It was in a cardboard box, tucked away in the closet. It held her things, I think. I never asked Momma."

"May I borrow that box?"

"Of course. Anything to help." She left and entered another bedroom.

Kennet turned to Conrad and Crystal. "Thanks for being so patient. We're getting somewhere, I think. Conrad, when Gracie brings that box, could you put it in my truck, discreetly?"

"You bet."

Mrs. Elder returned. She handed two postcards to Kennet. He noted they were hand-printed. One was dated August 13th, 1983. The other, March 21st, 1984."

"And I may borrow these?"

"Yes. I'd like them back. And here's some good pictures of Georgie."

Conrad had slipped behind Mrs. Elder to intercept Gracie and relieve her of a box. He exited quietly.

"One more thing, Mrs. Elder. Elsie Newman. Do you have an address for her?"

"Yes. I thought you might like to see this. It's a letter. From her. She has a married name." She passed over an envelope with a return address in Thunder Bay.

"Thank you. Good thinking. I have to run, Mrs. Elder. An appointment to keep. But I'll be back. And I'll keep you posted."

Mrs. Elder nodded. Crystal embraced her and murmured something in her ear. Then she embraced Gracie.

Outside, Conrad was standing beside the Sportage, holding the box. "It's locked," he said.

"Force of habit. I'm a product of the city."

"We rarely lock things up around here," said Conrad. "Someone might need something, or need to get in."

Kennet relieved him of the box. "Tell me, Conrad, when did Mr. Elder pass away?"

"He never did, far as I know. One day, when I was a kid, I noticed there was no more Mr. Elder, and Dad said he had left. Just up and left. For parts unknown. He had a problem," said Conrad, and made the tippling motion.

"Ah."

"Then when I was growing up, I overheard kids saying he had been spotted in Thunder Bay, living on the street."

Crystal emerged from the Elder residence. Kennet met her and thanked her for her intercession. "One question, Crystal. That thing Gracie had in her hand, they call that a dream-catcher, don't they?"

"Yes. She makes them. Has them everywhere in her bedroom."

"They're supposed to catch dreams, aren't they?"

"Yes. The bad ones. The good dreams pass on through."

Kennet made one more stop at The Hook'n Bullet. Kellerman was hovering as two customers prowled the aisles. Kennet drew him aside.

"Bull, what do you know about Harold Elder?"

"Sad. Sad case. Made a good living as a fisher. Now he's a rummy. A bum. At last report, he was walking Simpson Street clutching a paper bag. That was years ago."

"You mean in Thunder Bay?"

"The one and the same."

Chapter 24

Monday, August 17th . . .

"Robert," said Kennet, speaking into his office phone, "I knew you'd be at your desk. Any news?"

It was two minutes after eight, Monday morning. Kennet was sitting in his office in the Fermi Building.

"Detective Constable Armitage is on the job, and interviewing the Flemings as we speak. I don't have news yet. What's up, cock?" Superintendent Robert Kenilworth sounded as brisk as usual, with a hint of humour and good will flavouring his speech.

"A few things. I'll be working at the university all day, but I'll have my cell. So if you hear anything –"

"I'll call you. Thanks for your continuing interest, Kennet. So, you do have something for me?"

"Yes. It's about the bones at the university forensics lab. We may be close to an identification, but, my news'll have to wait. I've got to prepare for a meeting. I'll catch you up when you call."

Kennet hung up the phone and sat back in the swivel chair. He looked around his spartan quarters. His glance fell on a wall of shelving, packed with books and journals; a filing cabinet, a floor lamp, two extra chairs, a desk and a PC computer. Nothing homey about this place. Not even a carpet. Not even curtains on the window through which sunlight streamed. The small room filled with light to the extent that he had not switched on the overhead lighting. He pushed off with his feet, and the chair scooted on casters over to the window. The view was unchanged: a patch of grass, a concrete sidewalk, and a multi-story building.

He scooted back to the desk. With the tips of the fingers of one hand, he touched the cardboard box. An answer might lie within. One answer. First he had to get that damn meeting over with.

In the hallway, at the foot of the stairs, he glanced up. He squared his shoulders. He ran up the steps, taking two at a time. At the top he let out his breath.

Melissa Sharpe presided. About fifteen members of the English Department had assembled, all lecturers or assistant professors, and a smattering of associate professors new to the staff. The full professors, and the professors emeriti, had apparently been excused. All had chosen places around the lounge that served as coffee room, kitchenette, lunch room, and conversation pit. Melissa talked. And talked. Sheaves of handouts came around to him. Each time he scooped a copy for himself and passed the remainder on. He couldn't focus.

Last night Susan had remarked on his lack of attention. She had Diane's dark eyes. But she had blonde hair. Lovely hair. Lovely looks. A tune was racing through his mind . . . a Neil Young lyric: *I've been a miner for a heart of gold . . . And I'm getting old.* Keep me searching, he said, for a heart of gold . . . Keep me searching . . . I'm getting old.

To boyfriend Alexie he had addressed only a half dozen sentences. To Alexei's remarks or questions, he had made adequate responses. Alexei Marinovski, four years older than Susan's twenty-two years, interned in a lawyer's office. When Kennet had heard whom Susan was seriously dating, he had been

252

prepared to dislike the man. Marinovski? Sounded like some brutish Russian. A hockey player, perhaps, or an underworld type. But he had liked the man instantly. He had a heart of gold. And his looks complemented Susan's. Straw-coloured hair. Strong facial lines. And yes, an athletic body. Susan had chosen well. He had excused himself after supper, gone home early.

He had logged onto the Internet and looked up the Cemeteries Act. The legislation seemed to be designed for establishing an approved cemetery, and for closing an approved cemetery, and for managing an approved cemetery. Then, buried among thousands of words, he found reference to "an unapproved aboriginal people's cemetery". Anyone who discovered such a cemetery was obliged to report it to the police, so that the officials of a non-aboriginal government could regulate said cemetery. He retired for the night. For a restless night.

A hundred disconnected facts still swarmed through his brain. Someone poked him on the shoulder. Melissa had been speaking his name.

"Kennet," she was saying, "if you could bear with our company for a little longer."

"Yes! Of course. My apologies. A rough night."

A male voice from the somewhere behind him tittered: "Was it the night, or the woman?" There were a few titters.

Kennet gave his attention to Melissa. "You were saying?"

"Your syllabus for Introduction to Journalism. I need your updates by the end of the month. *This* month."

"Of course."

It was close to ten o'clock when the meeting broke up. Kennet hurried a few doors down to his office and scooped up the box. In the basement he rapped on the door of Dr. Peter Sheridan and pushed it open.

"You're here," said Kennet to the tall man in casual clothes and distinguished coiffure.

"Some of us work," said Peter. "Good to see you again. You have something for me?"

Kennet set the box down on an empty desk. "This is my candidate for the bones. The lab may be able to do something with this stuff. I haven't even opened it. It belonged to a young woman, age eighteen, who allegedly left Beardmore in 1983 and never returned. Except for two feeble attempts at communication, both suspect, she was never seen nor heard of again."

"Let's take a peek." Sheridan opened the flaps and stirred the contents with a wooden ruler. "Hair brush, jewelry, gloves . . . plastic-framed photo – looks like a young married couple . . ."

Kennet glanced inside. "The parents . . . I've seen the enlarged version."

Sheridan continued, "Make-up, combs . . ." He fished out a silver locket on a neck chain. "Looks like it may contain something." He pulled on latex gloves and worked the clasp of the silver heart. It was a tiny tinted portrait of a good-looking woman, hair pushed up, with a faux pearl necklace and the collar of an old-fashioned white blouse.

Sheridan said, "Does the family have a name?"

"You don't need a name. Yet. I talked to the family. They are devastated. The uncertainty about the victim's identity, that's the killer. I don't want a leak until we are sure. Damn sure."

"But, Kennet, there may be dental records."

"Of course. You're right. But let's take this one step at a time. When the lab needs a name, I'll supply it. I have photos too." Kennet handed over the prints in a manila envelope. "Can you just make copies? I must return them."

Peter flipped open a flatbed scanner and placed one photo on the platen face down. "I can get a very high resolution copy. I'll see the lab gets everything."

The machine hummed. Peter looked at Kennet. "You've said nothing about my colleague."

Kennet flopped down in a chair. He rubbed his forehead. "Nothing much I can say. I found him – the body. It looks like murder. The police are questioning prime suspects this morning."

"Murder? That's news to me. You didn't think that was news?" Peter kicked a plastic storage container lying on the floor and sent it sliding. "God, Kennet! What are you thinking?"

"Peter. Peter. I'm so sorry. I was sworn to secrecy. It's not official yet. Unless it's in the papers this morning. I haven't seen them yet. It wasn't on the radio, anyway. Me and my big mouth. I shouldn't have said anything."

Peter had been pacing. He pulled up a chair and flopped into it. "You say they have suspects."

"Even that is unofficial, Peter. I've been treading on eggshells, Peter. My investigations have no official sanction. Unofficially, I'm working with the police – well, one policeman. Who can't tell anyone he's using me as a dogsbody. It's complicated. But I'll tell you my suspicion. Again, not for publication. I'm beginning to think there is a connection. Between the two deaths. It's a mighty tenuous connection. Two homegrown thugs were among the last to have seen the young victim alive – if I've pointed to the right victim – and one of those thugs, along with his cousin, is connected to the Vanderhorst case."

"That's incredible."

"Yes. And I'm incredulous. I can't see motive anywhere."

Peter touched the box on the table. "I'll get this over to forensics immediately. And the photos back to you today. Are you still looking into this – these matters?"

"I want to. But it's time away from the duties for which I am being recompensed at this institution. I don't know if I can."

Peter said, "I'll talk to Melissa. Leave her to me."

"Gladly." Kennet rose to take his leave.

Peter rose too. "Kennet."

"Yes?"

Peter brushed his own nose with a forefinger and pointed to Kennet's. "Love your nose," he said.

"Oh. Just remembered. I drove here this morning. I have another package for you in the truck. The debris from the excavation that Vanderhorst had in his motel room. Look like trash to me. It would've been thrown out."

"Of course," said Peter. "There may be something in there that will shake the world of archaeology to its foundations. Turn North American history topsy-turvy." He made no effort to contain his smirk. "Let me get an assistant to haul it back."

Kennet had accompanied the assistant to his truck. At the same time he retrieved Cameron St. Clair's video cassettes of the grad party. He went directly to the Student Union office in the Unversity Centre where the student president had his office. It being a paid position, he hoped to find Malcolm Stevens there.

Malcolm was lolling in his swivel chair, a cup of coffee in one hand, launching a paper airplane through the doorway at his pretty secretary. It skipped across her desk and landed on the floor.

"Message incoming!" said Malcolm.

"Malcolm!" barked the peroxide blonde. "If it lands on the floor, it stays there! Grow up!"

Kennet picked it up and handed it to the secretary. "I gather that Malcolm isn't too busy," he said.

"Take him for coffee! Please!"

"Hi, Kennet. Come on in. You're welcome anytime." Malcolm Stevens, in t-shirt and jeans, ran his free hand through his short curly hair. "What can I do for you? Got another story for *The Pegasus*?"

Kennet sat in the only other chair. "I hope we can have the same arrangement for my classes this year? My students will cover specified events and submit copy for the student organ?"

"Of course. Goes without saying. Whatcha got there?"

Kennet passed him the cassettes. "I want to get this transferred to DVD format. It's from one of the first camcorders, very popular before your birth. You'll know someone in the AV department could do the job."

"*Pas d'problème*, as they say in Shawanigan," said Malcolm. "How soon do you need them?"

"Yesterday. Start with the 'Grad Party' one."

"See me in the morning. There's a goofus that owes me one."

Kennet spent the time till lunchtime responding to e-mails. Lunch was a brown bag and bottle of water. He dialed Peter Sheridan's number. No answer. Dining in the faculty lounge, the bugger.

He brought up the journalism syllabus on the desktop. He was going to use one new book, so he tinkered with the outline until he had integrated the book's contents into it. He called the campus bookstore. No, they had not received the title yet. Yes, they expected it to arrive shortly. No, there was no guarantee. There was never a guarantee. Okay, okay, they would query the publisher again about the delivery time. Yes, yes, they would do it today. Within the hour. Okay, right away. Yes, they would look forward to his call later that afternoon. What was that title again?

He got up from his chair and stretched. He performed a few tai chi moves. His office was losing the sunlight from the eastern-facing window. His only window. He switched on the floor lamp. He reached up to a shelf and plucked out a book. It was the new book: *Journalism and Eight W's*.

He sat in one of the padded chairs, making notes on a pad. He called Sheridan again. Sheridan said, "Yes, Kennet."

"Finished with those photos?"

"Yes, Kennet."

"I'll come down. I forgot to ask you something."

"I know, Kennet. Come on down."

Peter was perched on his favourite chair in front of the double monitors. He did not take his eyes from the screens. "They're there," he said, pointing to a desk.

"You know, this case – these cases are taking a toll on me. I thought I'd left that all behind."

Peter swung around to face him. "You mean, when you left the CBC."

"When I left journalism – the practice of journalism – for this job, I thought my sleepless nights were over."

"Well," said Peter, "there's journalism, and then there's journalism. What you were doing, out there in various nefarious and barbarous corners of the world, flying on a hope and a prayer, and getting shot at and blown up, that was public service. Hell, that was humanitarian service. There are easier ways to make a living. And," he continued, "this has dredged it all up, has it?"

"And pieces of my former life, Peter. The bones in my own closet are rattling. I have some inkling now what drives an archaeologist to dig up the dirt."

"What you came back for," said Peter, "I mean, what you came to see me about, was the funeral arrangements for Vanderhorst."

Kennet sank into a chair. "Yes. How could I have forgotten? And I haven't even talked to Cindy."

"Anne is talking to Cindy." Anne was Peter's spouse. "And Cindy's not ready to talk to anyone."

"How could I be so insensitive? What happened to my feelings?"

"They have been considerably bruised, I suspect. Do you want to talk about it?"

Kennet did want to talk about it. He wanted to talk about a colleague who'd been indulging a personal passion, who'd been on a mission to change the world as we know it, however mistaken and self-indulgent that mission might have been, and he had been brutally murdered. His legacy was a grieving widow and a fatherless son and the patronizing attitude of his colleagues. He talked about a young girl on the verge of realizing the adult world's promise, who'd spent her last months on earth wallowing in distress and depression and cynicism, and then had had the promise irrevocably snuffed out. And finally he talked about a girl from his high school days, in the flower of youth, an unstained blossom, whose soft, trembling lips he had kissed, who had gently brushed away his hand as it sought the white breast beneath the white gown. Her father said she fell down the stairs. She had tripped and she had fallen and she had broken her neck. That was the story that circulated next day. That was the story. There was no investigation of the story that the public ever knew about. But the story never changed. That was the story which was now history. That he had kissed her, that he had tried to touch her breast, and she had died. Period. End of story.

"I don't know what to say, Kennet."

Kennet realized he had stopped talking. "Your job," he said, "was to listen. And you did a superb job."

"Anytime." Peter rose and walked over and squeezed Kennet's shoulder. "I took the pictures, and the box, to the lab. Dr. Koenig – she runs the lab – Dr. Koenig got a call this morning. From the OPP. Some big shot asked her to make our bones a priority. Promised some financial assistance. Like every department, the lab guys stretch their resources. So they were glad to see me. They'll be giving our bones priority attention."

"Great!" Kennet immediately tempered his delight. "Which brings me to the other matter I forgot. How is Kyle Henderson?"

"On the mend. He's still not talking, but he's been transported to the hospital here, so he's getting visitors, and his parents flew in from Fredrickton. He's a much happier lad."

"That's good to hear. And the funeral –?"

"Wednesday, 10:00 a.m. At Revelation Lutheran Church. Interment at Riverview Cemetery."

"I'll be there."

In his office again, Kennet called the bookstore. The book was on the loading dock at the publishers. Should arrive in five business days. Kennet promised to call in five business days. It was actually a promise with an edge. Not a threat, exactly, but a promise that left no doubt he would follow through. Long years of experience in the media had made him expert at such promises.

A colleague dropped into his office – a fellow lecturer named Brandon. Brandon, as he suspected, had made the snarky remark at the department meeting. Brandon enquired about Kennet's love life. Nothing there, said Kennet. Same here, said Brandon. Did Kennet think that Rosa, that sizzling brunette in fourth year, majoring in English and History, would be returning to pursue a master's thesis? Kennet had no opinion. Was it kosher, wondered Brandon, to date a grad if she wasn't studying under you? Kennet referred him to Ann Landers for advice. Oh, said Brandon. You're busy. Got that syllabus to do, eh? Brandon left.

It was two-thirty when his cell rang. Robert said, "I have something for you. We should meet."

"Can we meet here? I'll spring for coffee."

"Good idea. I have to meet a Dr. – a Dr. K-something, at the forensics lab. So, give me directions. Long time since I've been on campus."

Kennet was sitting on a bench outside the University Centre when Robert Kenilworth came striding up in a gray pinstripe and patent leather shoes. "Are you sure," he said, "security will let me park there?"

"Where are you parked, exactly?"

"Just around the corner there." He indicated the west side of the Fermi Building. They were looking at the south side of the Fermi Building across the broad walkway.

"Did you leave your handicap sign on the dash?"

"What the hell are you talking about?"

"Never mind," said Kennet. He put a hand on Robert's upper back to guide him. "The fine is minimal. I'll throw in a doughnut to compensate."

They entered the University Centre and crossed the cathedral-like space of the agora. Robert looked Kennet up and down. "This the way you dress for business? For class?" Kennet glanced down at his jeans, sports shirt, and runners.

"Sometimes. Other times, I dress down. We don't have classes just now, remember?"

Seated in the faculty dining room, Robert sipped a coffee, double-double. He had declined the doughnut. Kennet sipped a black brew.

"We might be getting someplace on the case," said Robert. "D.C. Armitage got Lanny and Ritchie to admit they'd seen Vanderhorst, at the dig. But they denied assaulting him. And they categorically denied any knowledge of the assault on Kyle Henderson. Kelly sent their mug shots to Thunder Bay – Henderson is recuperating at the Health Sciences Centre – and our people gave the patient a photo array, and he picked the two Flemings. Not Rawlings, just Lanny and Ritchie. Henderson confirmed by signals that there were only two aggressors. When confronted with that evidence, our suspects lawyered up."

"Rawling not involved? I'm surprised."

"Rawling claims he was visiting a lady friend in Thunder Bay, that whole day. And the day before. Claims he got back to Beardmore late Wednesday night. Of course we're looking into it."

He took a sip of his coffee and smiled smugly. "We have charged Lanny and Ritchie with the assault on Henderson. And they're looking good for the murder too."

"How did they get out to the archaeological site?"

"Said they used their trail bikes. Said they wanted to know if Vanderhorst had found any precious metals – that's the term Kelly said they used – precious metals. Said Vanderhorst told them to bugger off, and showered them with rocks. Claimed they didn't stick around. This was around suppertime, Wednesday last, they said. Robert looked at Kennet expectantly.

"You sent the scene-of-crime guys back after I talked to you?"

"Yes. And they found those rock shards on the trail. But we have only their word that Vanderhorst scared them off."

Kennet thought hard for a moment. "Precious metals," he said. "Are you sure that's the term – the exact phrase?"

"You think it's important?"

"Could be."

"I'll find out." Robert withdrew his cell from his inside breast pocket and used speed dial. "Detective Superintendent Kenilworth. May I talk to D. C. Armitage, please? . . . Right." He held the phone to his ear, looking at Kennet. Almost immediately someone came on the line. "Kelly," he said. "That comment the Flemings made about precious metals, can you pull up the transcript? . . . Okay, I understand. Call me at this number ASAP. Appreciate it, d– . . . Kelly." Robert gave his cell number and rang off.

Robert spoke to Kennet. "She's looking it up, on the tape. There's been no transcription yet." He swallowed the remainder of his coffee in two large gulps. "Now show me this forensics lab." He pulled out a scrap of paper from a jacket side pocket. "Dr. Allison Koenig, that's the name. I have an appointment for 3:40."

Kennet escorted Robert outside. He had never had any reason to visit before, but after Robert had called earlier, he had looked up Dr. Koenig's office location. An old gentleman lolled on the bench he had recently vacated. Thrift-store chic draped his skinny frame. His cadaverous face studied the two passers-by. His wide-set eyes rooted in pain.

Chapter 25

. . . Monday afternoon

Robert drove his Chrysler north to Oliver Road and then east. He sputtered: "Where the hell are we going?"

"Trust me."

They turned south on Balmoral Street and drove past two traffic lights and another entrance to the campus. After passing a long stretch of bush, Kennet directed him to pull into a drive with a three-story white building.

"The lab is operating out of this Boreal Technology Centre. We're still on campus."

"You're not staying, are you?"

"I'm curious about the lab. Never seen it operating. Then I'll walk back. I know a shortcut."

"Why didn't we take it?"

"It's not kind to patent leather shoes."

The receptionist took them directly to Dr. Koenig's office down the hall. A well-dressed woman rose from behind a large synthetic desk. It looked as if it had been recently vacuumed. She looked at Kennet first.

"You're the detective?" she said doubtfully.

Robert brushed by him and extended his hand. "Superintendent Robert Kenilworth, at your service, ma'am."

She shook his hand and smiled graciously. A tweedy business jacket and skirt encased her trim body. Her handsome face was framed by light-coloured, ear-lobe-length hair streaked with black. Light glinted from contact lenses. "Dr. Allison Koenig. How do you do?"

"I was expecting," said Robert, "a stained lab coat and coke-bottle lenses. What a delight!"

She continued smiling, turning to Kennet: "And this is . . .?"

"Oh," said Robert. "Excuse me. My partner in crime. Dr. Kennet Forbes. He's assisting me in this investigation. He's on the faculty here. He helped me find this place."

"I'm not a –" Kennet began, but she cut him off.

"Delighted, I'm sure," she said. She dropped his hand quickly and turned to Robert. "But we have business to discuss, don't we, Superintendent?"

"Call me Robert."

"Have a seat, Robert. I'm Allison." There was only one seat.

Kennet gave Robert a little wave. "I'll see you later, Superintendent."

Kennet followed a paved footpath at the back of the building. He had been aware of the existence of a path, but had assumed it would be a dirt one. It emerged into the compound of student residences about two hundred metres south of the university centre. To the east stretched a gargantuan snakes-and-ladders board of parking lots interlinked by cleverly camouflaged entrances and exits.

A hundred and fifty metres away, he spied a shabby figure shuffling across the vast empty area, heading toward the bush that bordered Balmoral Street.

Back among the university centre buildings, he noticed a security guard prowling the cobbled walkway. He approached him.

"Hello. I'm Kennet Forbes. I work here, in the English Department." He gestured toward the Fermi Building. "Did you notice an elderly gentleman loitering here earlier?"

"Sure did." The guard, dressed in a dark blue uniform with a peaked cap, sported a pencil-thin moustache. "And he wasn't no gentleman. He was spooking some of the secretaries and cleaning staff. Have you seen him again?"

"Did he say anything?"

"He wasn't easy to understand. Crazy as a loon. Wanted to know where the dead people were kept."

"Did you direct him to Administration?"

"Pardon?"

"Sorry. Poor joke."

"He was leering at some of the ladies. They complained to us. So I chased him off. Threatened him with criminal trespass."

"He wanted to know where the dead people were kept?"

"Something like that. Muttered something about his daughter being here somewhere. And he needed to see the bones. Loony, like I said."

The scarecrow had not looked like the bulky Harold Elder of the photographs. But the eyes had. Kennet hurried to a green mound that overlooked the parking lot area where he had seen the shabby figure walking. Nothing.

As soon as he sat down in his office, the phone rang. It was Melissa Sharpe.

"Where have you been?" she demanded.

"Around. Checked on the bookstore, for one thing." And he had, earlier in the day.

"I had a visit from Dr. Peter Sheridan. He says you've been extremely helpful with one of his projects – something about identifying old bones. Are you changing jobs, by any chance, Kennet?"

"No, no. Nothing like that. It's just that my little trip up north yielded some useful information."

"Dr. Sheridan says you probably could use more time. To pursue an investigation."

"Yes. That would be very helpful."

"If someone should ask, I'll be saying you are researching material for your courses. Something along the lines of a case study in investigative journalism. Actually, Peter suggested that. Just let me know when you leave campus, will you?"

Before Kennet could respond, she hung up.

Kennet dragged out the Thunder Bay telephone directory. He feathered the pages of the tome until he found the E's. There was no Elder listed. Not a single one. He looked up the directory for the city and found a number for Social Services. He dialed. He navigated the menu until he got a living person. He was redirected to another menu, and after some number punching, he once again found a living person. He was redirected to another menu, and eventually reached another living person, a woman, who connected him with another woman, apparently living, who was prepared to listen to his request.

"I'm trying to contact a Harold Elder."

"Yes?"

"Do have a record of a Harold Elder?"

"Possibly."

"Can you help me contact him?"

"May I have your employee number?"

"I don't work for Social Services. Can you help me?

"And who are you?"

"Dr. Forbes." Kennet mentally kicked himself.

"Are you a relative?"

"No."

"Are you the family physician?"

"No."

"Then I can't help you."

"Can you tell me one way or the other if you have a Harold Elder in your system?"

"No. We cannot give out that information."

"By 'we', whom do you mean?"

"I mean 'us'. We cannot give out that information."

"May I speak to your supervisor?"

"My supervisor referred your call to me. That would be a dead end."

"So you're another dead end."

"I beg your pardon?"

"Dead. As in 'end'."

"I have work to do." She hung up.

My tax dollars at work, thought Kennet. He rang all the social aid organizations he could think of, including the Sally Ann, Homeless Outreach Services, church-sponsored groups, and the food banks. Always the same answer: "We cannot give out that information."

It was five minutes to five. He locked the office door behind him. He exited the parking lot on Balmoral and drove south. He studied the tree cover. His familiarity with cityscapes told him that green spaces harboured a network of trails, some of them unauthorized. A person who employed shank's mare rather than a motor vehicle or the municipal transit system would soon ferret them out.

Before he reached the forensics lab, he surveyed the cityscape to the east and noted the pattern of trees populating the spaces between apartment complexes and private residences. He turned east into Jasper Drive, following an ill-defined belt of tall elms, at the same time descending the slope into the sector known as Intercity, a commercial/industrial zone.

Kennet entered the Intercity street system, keeping an eye on treetops that trended southward. To the east, beyond the compound of buildings servicing the city's telephone system, a thick band of bush marched southward.

A man who had grown up in the boreal forest, he thought, a man who had breathed the heady air of a freshwater sea as he caught his daily bread, that man would keep to the green belts and the open spaces. He would if he were finished with slumming. If he were leaving skid row behind him. If he were prepared, as far as it was within his power, to avoid the dirt and grime and ugliness and despair of the inner city. The man he had seen on campus had looked clean and sober.

He turned east on Central Avenue. The band of bush, now to the north, enclosed a stream or ditch, but the bush and ditch stopped well short of Central Avenue. He turned south on Carrick Street, his eye attracted to a block of thick bush. Behind it towered the concrete-block walls of The Super Stack Store, coated with a thick goupy green paint. The Super Stack was the city's largest department store, its biggest department being foodstuffs. He drove east down the alley between the store and the bush. Faint trails penetrated the tangle of trees and brush. He passed one well-defined trail. He continued driving and pulled into the Kia Sales & Service lot. He parked and entered the office.

He spotted the salesman who had sold him the Sportage.

"Jerry," he said. "I was just in the neighbourhood."

Jerry, a small, dapper man with mere wisps decorating the top of his pate, took his hand. He looked surprised.

"Kennet! Good to see you! Anything wrong?"

"Not a thing. I'm very happy with the Sportage. But I've got a question that's entirely unrelated to trucks and cars."

"Sure! Shoot! What can I do?"

"You work next door every day to a piece of wild country. That bush behind The Super Stack. Do you know anything about it?"

"Sure! It's a hangout for bums. Crack open their cheap liquor there. Sometimes we find an empty bottle sitting on the hood of one of our vehicles. Why do you ask?"

"I'm looking for a friend. Actually, a father of a friend of a friend. It's complicated. I'm thinking of exploring it."

"Jeez, Kennet! That'll take nerve. But you got nerve, eh?" He gestured toward his own right eye. "In that case, Kennet, go bearing gifts. The natives may be restless."

"That's a very astute suggestion," said Kennet, and Jerry beamed.

Kennet drove to the expansive parking lot that fronted The Super Stack Store. Inside, he loaded a cart with bags of chips and cookies and assorted snack foods, and several different fruits. He paid the extra charge for plastic bags, and toted the five bags outside. He walked around the enormous building to the back alley and chose the well-defined path. Before he proceeded, he switched off his cell – he didn't want to startle anyone.

A secondary path veered left. He continued on the main path, turned a corner, and found himself amongst a group of loungers – two men and a woman. He walked into their midst, set his load on the ground, and squatted down.

"Hi!" he said cheerily, glancing around.

"What can we do for you, sir?" The speaker was an older man with gray hair and a threadbare vest covering a paunch. He wore a fedora, a shabby business suit jacket, and shoes that had been recently polished. He sat in the one upholstered chair, a captain's chair, scavenged from God-knows-where. On the ground beside him was an open whiskey bottle in a paper bag.

"I'm looking for information," said Kennet.

"And a picnic?" It was the woman. She held a plastic glass. In her mid-fifties, maybe older, she wore slacks and a man's shirt. Kennet noted that Mr. Paunch held a tough plastic cup, and the younger man what looked like a large white bottle cap.

"I don't want to carry this stuff any farther. I'll leave it here if you'll help me out."

"What do you mean, help you?" The younger man had wild brown hair and wispy brown whiskers on his face. "We got nothin'. You can see that." He was sitting on a small uprooted tree trunk, the tree long dead. On the ground Kennet noticed several large plastic bottles, all empty. The label of one of them was readable: Listerine.

Kennet glanced around at all three. "I'm looking for a man."

"Not here, sonny," the woman giggled. "These guys are straight as arrows."

"This man has a name. His family is looking for him." That was not strictly true. It was not true at all. But it might serve the purpose.

"What's his name?" said Mr. Paunch.

"Harold Elder. He may not be a regular here anymore."

The three looked at one another. Mr. Paunch spoke up: "We've never heard of him. I apologize, but we can't help."

Just then a crackling of twigs announced the arrival of another visitor, coming along a path from the west. A skinny man with an enormous goiter staggered into the circle. He was clutching a wine bottle to his chest with both hands.

"Guess who I seen." His speech was slurred.

Mr. Paunch said, "Who did you see, Cornelius?"

"A pink elephant," said the young man. The woman giggled.

"I seen Harry," said the man named Cornelius.

"Harry Fisher?" said Mr. Paunch. "I haven't seen Harry for ages."

"Harry Fisher?" asked Kennet. "What's he look like."

"Actually," said Mr. Paunch, "we called him Harry the fisher. Had a lot of stories about catching monster trout and sea dragons. Harry the fisher."

"What's he look like?" Kennet repeated.

"Harry's a big man," said Mr. Paunch. "Must weigh two-thirty, two-forty. But he's moves easily."

"No, no," said Cornelius, swaying on his feet. "Harry's like me." One hand clutching the bottle, he raised his arms, and flapped them like wings. "As light as a fairy," he said.

"Harry's no fairy," said the woman.

"No, no. Harry's changed. But he rec'nized me. Wouldn't take a drink, though. He's changed. Harry's changed."

"Harry the fisher may be my man," said Kennet, rising to his feet. He addressed Cornelius: "How long since you saw him?"

"I seen him," said Cornelius, somewhat truculently, his goiter working.

Mr. Paunch intervened, "When did you see him, Cornelius? How long ago?"

"I dunno. Five minutes. Five hours. It was –" He brought the bottle upright to his eyes and spread the fingers of his free hand to gauge the level that his beverage had dropped. He thrust the hand out, thumb and forefinger about ten centimetres apart. "That long ago," he said.

"Twenty-five, thirty minutes ago," said Mr. Paunch.

"How do I find Harry? Where does he live?" Kennet glanced around the circle. "His family is really worried."

"Not bloody likely," said the young chap. "Not even after a million years."

"We can't really help you, sir," said Mr. Paunch. "He had a room in the Royal Alex for years, and when it closed, he moved across the street to an apartment block. Then he left. I personally haven't seen him for it must be three years."

"The Royal Alex. You mean, the Royal Alexander hotel at the bottom of Simpson Street?"

"Yessir. And then he took a room in Solly's place."

Kennet addressed Cornelius. "Did he say where he was going?"

Cornelius waved the bottle to the south, towards The Super Stack. "He just went. That way. He had to catch a train."

"To catch a train?"

"He was going to the railroad. He'd cross that bridge when he come to it." Cornelius lost his balance and sat down hard.

Kennet uttered a quiet thanks to the group, and walked away, leaving the grocery bags on the ground. "Enjoy," he said over his shoulder.

Kennet returned to his truck and drove south on Carrick Street and past the intersection with the Harbour Expressway. Carrick ran straight for a good half kilometre through a commercial/industrial area. There were no pedestrians. At the end he could see a grove of trees. A tall ethereal structure to the southwest rose out of the cityscape. He was reminded of the Devil's Tower National Monument he had once seen in Wyoming.

The street ended at the McIntyre River. Across the river, about forty metres away, trees intermingled with residential and industrial buildings. The dark tower, backlighted by the sun, looked more familiar. He remembered passing under it when he had visited the place on the river where he had bought his kayak two years ago. Close up, it had looked like an abandoned industrial structure.

Looking to his left, he observed an iron railway bridge spanning the river. Perhaps Harold had crossed it when he came to it.

Kennet drove to the old Royal Alex on the south end of Simpson Street. The ancient structure looked ready to crumble into the street. He parked across from it. He could see chains and padlocks on a pair of big double doors.

The apartment block on his side of the street consisted of two storefronts on the ground floor, and between them, a door, over which was the name S. Wisner's Apts. The door was locked. He walked through an empty lot to the rear. A sturdy preserved-lumber staircase climbed to the second floor. He took a deep breath and released it. He climbed. Names occurred on labels beneath buttons on a security panel. There was no "H" Somebody. Certainly no H. Elder. He pressed one button at random.

The exterior door lock clicked. He pushed it open and peered down the dim hallway. Closed doors led off it. He rapped on the first. No response. On the second, no response. On the third, someone peered at him from the eyehole, but did not open the door. On the fourth, a tired old man swung the door open to the width of the security chain. He eyed Kennet up and down without enthusiasm. "Yeah?" he said. He looked moldy. If someone sprinkled him with water, he'd sprout like a Chia pet.

"I'm looking for one of the former tenants."

The man did not move a muscle. "Yeah?"

Kennet called upon his overseas experiences and his knowledge of Raymond Chandler novels, and slid a five-spot through the crack. The man's eyes brightened momentarily. He snatched the bill.

"Yeah? How'd you get that eye?"

"Old war injury. You used to have a neighbour. Harold Elder."

"Elder? Not since I been here."

"How long have you been here?"

"Since March."

Kennet mentally kissed his five-spot goodbye. "Maybe another of your neighbours remembers him."

"Well, ask them then." He slammed the door shut. The other doors yielded no responses.

On the sidewalk Kennet looked up and down the street. In three or four blocks he spotted only three pedestrians. Across the street was a second-hand store, Golden Pond Antiques. He crossed and entered.

From the back area a man with bulging hips emerged and wormed his way through one of the two crowded aisles. The fat sacs around his eyes crinkled as he greeted Kennet: "Looking for something special, sir?"

"I'm looking for an old friend. He may have dealt here. Name of Harold Elder."

"I know many Harolds. Can you describe him?"

Kennet described the man he had seen in the photograph.

The proprietor stroked his chins. "Beardmore, you say? Sure, I know him. Not a customer any more. Seen him maybe once in two years."

"Did he say where he was living?"

"Nah. He's dropped a lot of weight. His clothes just hung on him. Just wanted to say hello. Sure you don't see something you like?"

Kennet looked around. The assortment of junk and clothing in the small space boggled the mind. Bric-a-brac crowded the wall shelves, including framed photographs. He moved over to the photos and picked up one of a fishing vessel. It looked vaguely familiar.

The proprietor held out his hand. "Let me see that," he said. With his fingers he wiped the dust from the glass. "I remember this. Harold brought it in, years ago. Maybe twenty years ago. It's never moved. Interested?"

"Yes. If you can help me."

"Let me wrap it up." He extracted a used plastic bag from under the counter and slipped the frame in. "Now let me see. He said sometimes he swept out a store. You know, a corner store, like a 7-Eleven."

"There are a lot of corner stores."

The man nibbled his lips.

Kennet took the hint. "How much for the picture?"

"Ten dollars?"

Kennet gave him five. It seemed the going rate in that neighbourhood.

"This one was close to the Exhibition Grounds. On May and Northern, as a matter of fact. I got the impression he lived in the neighbourhood."

Chapter 26

... Monday afternoon, later

The Blue Lite Variety store on the corner of Northern Avenue and May Street backed onto the Exhibition Grounds. Kennet picked up the same-day edition of the Toronto Globe and Mail and took it to the counter. A petite Oriental woman in her thirties served him with a smile.

"I wonder if you can help me?" he said.

"Sir?"

"I'm looking for an elderly fellow, may have done some work for you. Name of Harold."

"Mr. Elder? Of course! Comes in every morning, like clockwork. I usually have some small chores for him – unpacking boxes, washing windows, sweeping, you know. Maybe half-an-hour's work. And then he picks up his paper."

"He buys a *Lakehead Journal*?"

"I give him yesterday's paper. From the returns, you know? Ones where I've cut off the date?"

"Of course."

"And I give him a coupla bucks for helping, you know. Or

maybe something from stock."

Kennet used his standard opening: "Look, he has family looking for him. Can you tell me where he lives?"

"Not really. But he always comes and goes from there." She gestured up Northern Avenue towards the west. She paused. "He did say he enjoyed watching the birds. The big birds, like seagulls and eagles."

"Eagles?"

"Well, he didn't actually say 'eagle', but it's one of those kinds of bird. A hawk, maybe? Falcon? Yes, that's it. It had its nest on the cliff face, he said. Could see it from his window."

"That's what he said, a falcon's nest on a cliff?"

"That's what he said. Sounds weird, I know."

Kennet thanked her, and added: "In case I miss him, what time does he usually come in?"

"Twenty after nine, like clockwork. We're open 24-7, you know. I usually do four hours in the morning, and the same in the evening." She smiled. "Come back again."

Kennet sat in his truck and gave his next step some thought. He would not turn up on the man's doorstep empty-handed. He drove back to The Super Stack and picked up an assortment of fresh fruit. He returned to the Blue Lite Variety store and turned west on Northern Avenue. He looked north up each cross street. When he came to Vickers Street North, he spotted the tower, a perfect setting for a scene in *Lord of the Rings*. He turned down the street, crossed a railway track, and stopped across from Thunder Bay Iron Works.

It was a three-story yellow brick structure, chock-a-block with glazed windows. Vehicles in the yard confirmed that the welding shop or metal fabrication business was a going concern. Behind it rose the tower, the lower part of poured concrete, the upper stories of brick. A few widely spaced windows, all boarded up, indented the sheer face of the tower, rising to the top like foot- and handholds for a giant climber. Across the street, the side on which he was parked, a handful of residences faced the tower.

He drove slowly past the modest vintage houses, counting them: five. The last had been converted into a canoe shop, the place where he had bought his kayak when he had returned to the city. Beyond the store and fenced-in yard was the river.

The owner was puttering around the yard, canoes and kayaks stacked around him. Kennet walked through the open gate in the metal security fence. "You sell motorboats here?" he called out.

Without looking up the owner responded, "God gave you your own motors. Your arms." The middle-aged man looked up and then straightened up. "I know you," he said evenly.

"Hi, Geoff," said Kennet, sticking out his hand. "You sold me a river runner."

"I remember now," said the owner. He had pulled back his long dark hair, heavily streaked with gray, and tied it off with a band. Small gold rings hung from his ear lobes. "And I hope you're kidding. Ken, isn't it?"

"Kennet. And I am. I'm after information."

Kennet explained that he was tracking down an elderly gentleman who lived nearby. He described the man he had seen on campus. "A dedicated walker," said Kennet.

"Sure," said Geoff. "See him every day. If he's not walking up Vickers, he's headed for the river. I think he uses the railway bridge. Lives two doors down. So, you need a new boat yet? A sea kayak, maybe? Gonna try really big water?"

Kennet laughed. "I'll stick to what I know." At 860 Vickers St. North he knocked on the side door. He carried a large paper bag of groceries. The small domicile with yellow clapboard siding had a picture window facing the tower.

A man with a broad good-humoured face and clipped white hair opened the door. Kennet said, "Hello. I'm looking for Harold."

The man smiled as he opened the door wider. "Well, you got lucky. Harold's in. Come on in."

Kennet saw that a living room occupied the front of the house, from which came sounds of a TV. The man led Kennet down a short hallway to the rear. Looking back, he said, "Harold's just finishing his supper." Harold sat at a small table in a tiny spotless kitchen. The man said, "Harold, you got a visitor."

Harold was wiping out his bowl with a crust of toast. Kennet smelled chili con carne. Harold looked up and nodded. He had draped his suit jacket over the back of the chair. Thin shoulders poked through a tan-coloured shirt. He had loosened his tie.

The man turned to Kennet and held out his hand. "I'm Art," he said. "Short for Artritis." He laughed at his own joke. Kennet introduced himself. He offered the hand to Harold also, who held it limply for a second. Art said, "I'll be in the front room. My program's on." He left.

"Harold," said Kennet, "you don't know me, but I know people who know you." Harold nodded. Kennet pulled out a chair and sat down and placed the paper bag on the table. "I brought some fruit, all the way from California."

"You came from California?" queried Harold.

"From The Super Stack, actually. I talked to Cornelius." Harold nodded. "And a gentleman in a vest and polished shoes."

Harold nodded. "Dorian. Haven't seen him in three years." His long swarthy face looked at him stoically.

"I saw you at the university," Kennet continued. "You were looking for someone." Harold nodded.

Kennet took a deep breath. "You know she's dead."

Harold merely looked at him.

"You know that, don't you, Harold." After a moment, Harold's head dipped fractionally.

"Let me explain who I am." Kennet explained that he taught at TBU, that he had grown up in Geraldton, that the university had been examining some bones found near Beardmore, and that he had been asked to check around the community for clues to the victim's identity. He had met Mrs. Elder, he said, and Gracie.

At the mention of Gracie, Harold's eyes betrayed a flicker of interest.

Kennet exploited the opening: "Gracie misses her sister, Harold."

Harold's body shrank. The pupils in his gray irises shrank as he withdrew to a distant world and to another time. His head dropped suddenly to his chest and his shoulders shuddered. Great racking sobs tore from his throat. Art came rushing into the kitchen.

"What have you done?" he shouted. He put his hands on Harold's shoulders. "What's wrong, Harold! Tell me, what's wrong!" He glared at Kennet. "What did you do to him?"

Kennet said evenly, "There's been a family tragedy. It's hit him hard."

Harold was gasping now, taking deep, shuddering breaths. He clawed at one of Art's hands, removing it from his shoulder.

"Just leave him be," said Kennet. "I'll help him deal with it."

Art looked at him accusingly and stalked stiffly from the room. Kennet grabbed a tea towel from the railing of the gas stove and passed it to Harold. Harold wiped his face. He bunched the towel in his fist and dropped it to his lap. He stared hard at the tabletop, one arm lying across the flowered oilcloth. They sat that way for a long time.

Finally Harold mumbled something. Kennet reached over and rested his fingers lightly on his arm. "I didn't catch that," he murmured.

Harold spoke in a very subdued voice: "Thank you."

"I don't understand."

"Thank you," Harold repeated. He raised his eyes to Kennet's. "I never cried like that when she died. I just drank. I just drank and drank." He dropped his eyes again. "I had some tears, sure, but I never hurt like that. All at once. Thank you."

They sat quietly for a spell. Finally Kennet said, "I have something in the truck for you. I'll fetch it." He advised Art that he was just stepping outside. Art was sitting in front of the TV set, one leg crossed over the other and twitching spasmodically.

When he returned, Art was comforting Harold, one arm embracing his upper back. After a signal from Kennet, he left again.

Kennet passed over the framed picture of the boat. Harold touched the glass over the image of the boat. He spoke softly. "That's the Rainbow," he said. "My old boat."

"I thought so," said Kennet.

Harold looked up. "St. Clair's boy took that. I can't remember his name now."

"Cameron."

Harold nodded. "Cameron."

Harold returned his gaze to the photograph. "It started there," he said.

"What started there?"

"I got back – we got back late. Lake was rough. I missed her graduation."

"You mean Georgie's graduation."

Harold nodded. "I felt bad, I started drinking. I was feeling good, too, you know. It'd been a good trip, a good catch. We loaded the tubs into the van, and the young fellow – what's his name? – he took the truck to Thunder Bay, to Campbell Fisheries. And we kept drinking."

"You and who else?"

"Why, Mac, of course. He wasn't a regular fisher, but when he come, we always had a good time."

"Get to the part about Georgie."

"Well, the young fellow, before he left, he said the kids, the high school kids, were having a party to celebrate up at the camp road, and maybe Georgie was there by then. So after a while, we went lookin'." Harold kept his eyes fixed on the photograph.

"Who drove?"

"I drove. I was blotto by then, and that road from the harbour in them days, it was rough. Almost took the bush a coupla times, but we weren't gonna hurt nobody, that time of night, in the bush. And then we drove slow up and down that camp road, windows open, listening for the party. Them camps, you know, they're on the lake, a long ways from the road."

"I know. What happened?"

"We were driving along, you know, and we had our bottle with us, so we weren't soberin' up, and then there was this bump." Harold paused. He was still looking down.

"A bump."

"Yeah. We run over somethin'."

"Something."

"Yeah, so I got out." He started drawing deep breaths.

"You got out."

Harold raised his head and looked at Kennet. "I swear to God, I swear to God it was a accident!"

"What was, Harold?"

"Georgie. It was Georgie. She must've been layin' on the road. I didn't see her. Honest to God, I didn't see her!" Harold stared wildly at Kennet.

"I picked her up. She was breathing, she was still breathing. I got her in the truck. She was layin' on my lap. She was moanin'. She was trying to talk." His eyes teared up again. "I told Mac to drive. I told Mac to drive. Hard! Hard! We had to get her to hospital. She was bleeding from her head and her mouth and her nose."

Harold squirmed in his chair. He raised the arm that had been resting on the table and rotated his wrist aimlessly, palm open. Kennet pressed it down gently and held it there, squeezing his forearm. "What next, Harold?"

"She was barefoot."

"What?

"She had no shoes. Why was she laying there, under there, barefoot?"

"What next, Harold?"

Harold stopped fidgeting. He dropped his eyes to the table. "We never made it."

"What happened, Harold?"

"She stopped moving. I thought she was unconscious but I couldn't get a pulse. Mac pulled over and he couldn't get a pulse. She was gone."

"What next, Harold?"

"Mac took her someplace."

"That," said Kennet, "doesn't make any sense. What happened, Harold?"

Harold brought his moist eyes to bear on Kennet. "That's what she wanted. The last words out of her mouth. 'Not the graveyard!' she said. She didn't want to be buried in the graveyard. So Mac said he knew a place. I was outta my mind. I couldn't think. Couldn't do nothing. I was a mess."

"What happened next, Harold?"

"Mac took this old coat. He wrapped her in it. He was real gentle. He went away. And after a while, I heard this motor starting. A diesel. Then it drove off. I didn't hear no treads clanking. I stayed there. I must've zonked out. When I woke up it was pitch black. It was black before, but it was really black then. Like being in a mine. Underground. Next thing I know Mac's driving, the lights're on. The smell of shit. I shit myself." Harold slumped in the chair. He looked exhausted.

"What did Mac tell you?"

"He didn't tell me nothin'. Just clammed up. When I woke up it was daylight and I was on board the Rainbow. Laying on deck. With a cushion under my head. Lying there stinkin'. I had a change of clothes, I cleaned myself up, best I could. Then I drove home. Edith wasn't home, nobody was home, of course. That evening Mac phoned."

"So this all happened with Mac's truck."

"Yeah. Didn't I say that?"

"You said you were driving."

"Yeah, I was drivin'. Mac's truck. Mac give me the keys. He was too drunk."

"What did he say about Georgie, Harold? What did he do with her?"

"He said she was at peace. A nice sunny place, where she could see the lake. She loved the Rainbow Quest. That was her name, she give it that name. When she was younger."

"Where was she resting, Harold?"

"He wouldn't tell me. Said if I knew, I'd leave a trail there. Then there'd be questions. Said we'd have to make a story up. About how she'd left home. She'd caught the bus and gone west. I'm really tired now."

"The police will have to know all this, Harold."

Harold nodded.

"It'll be really tough."

Harold nodded. "Will I be able to see her now?"

"I don't think there'll be any question."

After a moment, Kennet continued: "I hope you can take some comfort in this, Harold. It wasn't your fault. Not entirely your fault. Georgie was high on drugs. She must've collapsed on the road, before you . . . hit her."

Harold looked uncomprehendingly at Kennet. "I got to go now. I'm really tired."

As he left, Kennet glimpsed Art in the living room, puffing furiously on a pipe.

Chapter 27

...Monday evening

When Kennet got home, the message light on his answering service was blinking.

Before he had left Harold's house, he had advised Art – Arthur Templeton was his name – to respect Harold's privacy. Art said that he hoped Kennet's visit hadn't set Harry back in his 12-step program. They both attended meetings. If Harry were to take to the booze again, he'd die. He had only one kidney now, and half a liver. He was doing so well. Eighteen months ago, he was a wreck.

Outside in the street Kennet had glanced up at the darkening tower, the setting sun licking around its edges. He could see no birds.

Robert Kenilworth had called – twice. The first message complained about his cell being switched off. The second was more profane, telling him to call him at home.

A young girl's voice came on the line. Kennet said, "May I speak to your father, please, dear?"

"My father's in Winnipeg," said the girl. A male voice called out in the background: "Who is it, Chérie?" Then Robert came on the line.

"Kennet here. I apologize. I got caught up –"

"Chr -!" Robert instantaneously switched vocabulary. "Uh, that was my granddaughter." He lowered his voice. "Jeez, Kennet, you ask for information, and then you switch off. Has your phone-free schedule kicked in again?"

"I'm calling you, aren't I? I apologize, but I was investigating. I was talking to people."

"Well, Kelly came through with a transcript, a partial one, anyway. I've e-mailed it to you. Take a look. What people?"

"It's a long story. Let me take a look and get back to you."

It was a single page, double-spaced, with D.C. Armitage interrogating Dunstan Ritchie:

Q: What business did you have there?

A: My business.

Q: Your business is now our business. A man is dead. You are a prime suspect. Answer the question.

A: A metal.

Q: What?

A: A metal. It's our goddamned metal. He took it. He had no business taking it.

Q: Are you saying that you had staked the claim? That Vanderhorst was a, a . . . claim-jumper?

A: We got a claim alright, on that metal. And the only jumping that Vander-who-zit was doing was up and down and heaving rocks at us. Wouldn't let us near him. Or talk to us. Even after we asked polite.

Q: You, being . . .?

A: Lanny and me. We asked him real polite.

Q: For the metal. It must have been precious metal. Was it?

A: Fucking right it was a precious metal. Real precious to us.

286

Q: Precious metal. What was it, gold? Silver?

A: How would I know? I ain't no prospector. But it was valuable. And that bastard had no right to it.

Q: You're saying that you're not a prospector, and that you never staked a claim there, but you had a right to that metal? And you don't know if the metal was gold or silver? Tell me, then, was it a relic? You had staked a claim, so to speak, to a relic?

A: It wasn't no relic. It was like, you know, that mess of potage. What do you call it? You know that story in the Bible? It was our . . . birth-something . . . . Birthright.

Q: We're getting nowhere here. Let me ask you about Henderson again. What time

Well, hell's bells, thought Kennet. It's so obvious. He punched the redial button.

"Robert," he said, "Fleming was talking about a medal. As in 'medallion'. When I talked to Al Cummings, he mentioned a badge, like a marshall's badge, he said, with points."

"That's not what he told us. He told us it might've been a nugget, but the manager at the mine, Nordstrom, he said that was highly unlikely. That the gold in that ore tended to be fine and widely dispersed."

"Read the transcript, Robert, and substitute 'medal' for 'metal'. And interview Ritchie again."

"So who's giving the orders now?" said Robert agreeably.

"I'm just excited. Bear with me. I talked to a key informant today, tonight, a man who may be the father of the dead girl – I'm referring to the bones in our forensics lab."

"Give me his name and address. We'll talk to him."

"Robert, give me some space. Please. He's an old man, and he's in a fragile state. He didn't entirely make sense. I want to re-interview him when he's pulled himself together."

"Well, the bones, as far as we know, offer no evidence of culpable homicide. Not yet, anyway. But we are getting flak from the university about the Vanderhorst case, and we have to move faster on that."

"I have an idea on that. I have to make some calls to Beardmore. I'll call you in the morning."

"Promise? Your communications regimen will allow that?"

"Fuck the regimen. Good night, Robert."

Kennet ran down to the truck and recovered the regional telephone directory he had picked up at The Hook'n Bullet. He found a number for H. Elder in the Beardmore section. Gracie answered.

"Gracie, this is Kennet Forbes. I have a question. I hope it's not too late for you."

She assured him it was not too late.

"Gracie, when I was visiting, I noticed a medal near your father's photograph. Can you tell me about it?"

It was a war medal, she said. She didn't really know anything about it.

"May I speak to your mother? Is she up?" Kennet glanced at the clock. Almost 9 o'clock.

Mrs. Elder came on the line immediately. "Yes, Mr. Forbes. Professor. I'm up. Harold served in Korea with the Princess Pats. He was awfully proud of that medal."

"Another question, Mrs. Elder. Did anyone else in Beardmore have a similar medal?"

"Another medal? I really don't know. Harold belonged to the Legion, you know. And he was friends with Rolfe Fleming. He said, Harold said, he served in Korea, too. If he had a medal from that war, I don't know. We didn't mix, you know, socially. When they – Harold and Rolfe – dressed up for ceremonies, they wore their ribbons and things, but I never looked that closely, you know."

"Thank you, Mrs. Elder. You've been a great help. I can't tell you how yet. And I'll be returning your photos this week."

288

After he hung up, he examined his motives. He had not mentioned he'd seen Harold. It was, he decided, the right decision at that point.

He looked up the Flemings' number. A rough male voice answered. Kennet said, "May I speak to Saxon, please?"

"Yeah, sure."

When Saxon answered, Kennet said, "Saxon, this is Kennet Forbes. Do you mind speaking to me?"

"No."

"It's a rather personal question. Your father served in Korea?"

There was a degree of surprise in Saxon's reply.

"And," said Kennet, "do you remember a medal he received for that service?"

"Yeah. What's this all about?"

"Just bear with me, Saxon. Do you remember seeing it lately?"

"Yeah. What about it?"

A querulous male voice rose in the background.

"Did you see it when you were growing up?"

"No. It just come to light now. Are you going to tell me what this is about?"

A rough male voice spoke inches from Saxon's mouthpiece. "Who the fuck are you talking to?" It sounded like Rawling.

Saxon said, "None of your fucking business. Do I meddle in your calls?"

Saxon spoke into the phone: "I want to talk to you. Private."

"I'm coming up tomorrow. I'll be at the motel."

Kennet dialed the number for the Regency Motel and got an answering machine. He requested a room for the following night, Tuesday. Mac Kueng had no phone. Mac had some hard questions to answer. Kennet recalled that the matter of the bones and a missing girl had never been raised between them.

He dug out the postcards that he had received from Mrs. Elder and examined them again. They were hand-printed. The first one, dated August 13th, 1983, had a Calgary postmark. There was a photograph of the Rockies. It read:

Dear Mom, Dad

I am fine. Don't worry about me. I found work and am all right. I need time on my own. Say hi to Elsie.

Love

Georgie

The second one, dated March 21st, 1984, had a postmark for Vancouver. The photo showed the Lion's Gate Bridge, and read:

Dear folks

Got to the West Coast. I am fine. Might stay here awhile or go South.

Love you

Georgie

Kennet thought. Someone was creating the illusion that Georgie lived. For whom? For Mrs. Elder. If Harold had gone travelling, his family – well, Mrs. Elder, for Gracie was not yet born – his wife would have remarked on the coincidence of the dated postcards and Harold's travels. It had to be Mac. After Georgie had died, Mac had phoned Harold from Thunder Bay. Why had he gone to Thunder Bay? To create a cover story for Georgie's disappearance, that was obvious. But had he returned to Beardmore, or had he gone travelling?

Kennet removed Elsie Newman's letter from the envelope with the return address of Mrs. E. Griffith, 238 Balmoral St., Thunder Bay, Ont. The letter was dated September 16th, 1989, and addressed to Georgie's parents:

Dear Mr. and Mrs. Elder,

Just wondering if you ever heard from Georgie, I was just thinking of her. I'm married now as you can tell by my name, and Derek and I have a beautiful little girl, with dark hair just like Georgie's. We have a two-story house in a quiet neighbourhood, there isn't much of a lawn in front but the back yard is huge and fenced in and it will make a good place for Darlene, that's our baby's name, to play.

If Georgie wanted to get in touch she wouldn't know my name so that's why I'm writing you Hope you folks are enjoying good health and little Gracie – she must be five now, isn't she – that you told me about Mrs. Elder, in a previous letter is also healthy. I would really like to hear from her, Georgie I mean.

Very sincerely yours,
Elsie (Newman) Griffith

The same Balmoral Street address appeared at the top of the page, and a telephone number beneath her signature.

There were six Griffiths in the phone book, none of whom had a Balmoral Street address or that phone number. He dialed the C. D. Griffith number, and when someone answered, he asked, "May I speak to Elsie Griffith, please?" Wrong number. There were two more D. Griffiths. He repeated the question for the first D. Griffith. Same response. For the second, D. R. Griffith, with an address in County Park, the male voice said, "Sure. Just a sec."

"Yes?" said a woman's voice.

Kennet responded with his name and said he had recently seen Mrs. Elder. Was she the Elsie Newman who used to live in Beardmore?

"Yes! Yes I am. Have you heard from Georgie? After all this time?"

"I'm afraid it's not good news, Mrs. Griffith. I don't want to talk over the phone. Can we meet somewhere in the morning and have a chat?"

"I work in the morning. What kind of news? You can't leave me hanging like that, I'd never get to sleep. Let's talk now."

He described himself. They arranged to meet in twenty minutes at the Tim Hortons near the County Fair Plaza.

Kennet was sitting at a window table when a white Toyota Lexus pulled into a parking space and a man and woman emerged.

291

In the lights from the overhead standards, Kennet noted the woman's reddish hair. She wore dress slacks and an embroidered vest. She walked briskly to keep up with her companion's golfer's stride.

As soon as she entered the coffee shop, she waved at Kennet. Kennet stood up. "My," she said, "you really do have that piratical look." She shook Kennet's hand, and her companion thrust out a manicured hand. It was tanned and strong. "This is my husband, Derek," she said. "He's a lawyer."

"You didn't need a lawyer, honest."

"No, but I needed a husband." She flashed strong white teeth at Derek. "At least, it was a good idea at the time."

Derek had tanned good-looking features beneath dark hair streaked stylishly with gray. He offered to help Kennet get their orders. Kennet ordered black coffee, Derek, a cappucino, and a juice for his wife. Kennet insisted on paying.

Back at the table, Elsie wiggled in her seat. "The suspense is killing me. Spill."

Kennet described the circumstances that had taken him to Beardmore, and the supplementary assignment of digging into – Sorry, he said. Poor choice of words – looking into the mystery bones. Elsie's face grew paler. He said that an encounter with Marcus Chambers – Elsie reacted to the name, asking where he had been all these years – and a conversation with Mrs. Elder had pretty well capped his conviction that the bones belonged to Georgie Elder, but that the university's Paleo-Forensics Lab had yet to confirm the victim's identity. Kennet asked Elsie what she remembered about the party at the lake.

"It was a wild party," she said, glancing sidelong at her husband. "But I remember everything that happened – to me – and I do remember that Georgie was out of it, really dozy. She got sick, I remember that, and I helped Marcus brush the, you know, vomit from his shirt." She made a face. "When we made the Mardi Gras parade – that's what we called it – at the cemetery, she was really freaked out. When Gron put her down, she just sort of melted into the darkness."

"Do you remember the Fleming boys?"

"Do I ever. Now, that Donny, the youngest of the tribe. He was a gentleman. Real sweet. He could have eaten crackers in my bed anytime." She glanced at Derek, smiling mischievously. "But Lanny? And that other?" She searched for a name.

"Rawling."

"Rawling." Her voice hardened. "Those sonsuvbitches. They put the make on every girl at the party. They tried it with me – one of them did. I gave him such a kick. Missed Lanny's groin, but he was limping when he left." Derek squeezed her arm.

"Notice anything about the way they were dressed?"

"That's a long time ago. But. I remember Lanny had a badge, which he pushed into my face, and said I was about to be interrogated. I said he was about to be castrated, and he backed off. Next time I saw Rawling, he had the badge, pinned to his t-shirt, under his khaki jacket, like an army surplus jacket. I heard he didn't like the way Lanny was using it."

"Can you describe the badge?"

"Not really. It was spiky, that's all. And shiny." She looked hard at Kennet. "Is this really helping? When will you know if it was Georgie that – those bones, and all."

"It's up to the lab now, Elsie. Do you remember seeing Georgie again?"

"No. Come to think of it, no. That was the last time. At the cemetery. There was no one at her house next day. And when I talked to Mr. Elder later, he said she had packed up and gone to Thunder Bay. Mrs. Elder wasn't home, then. He said Georgie had a summer job somewhere. And by Canada Day, I was gone myself. A job on a tobacco farm, near Thamesville, where I have family. I came back for a brief visit before I went to school. Mrs. Elder said they had a card from Georgie, from Calgary. And then my own family, mom and dad, they moved from Beardmore."

"Do you remember the Flemings leaving the party?"

"Oh yeah," she said dryly. "They were encouraged to leave."

"Donny too?"

"Donny left at the same time. Drove his brothers home, I believe." She smiled again at Derek, and patted his hand. "Too bad. He could've been the love of my life. But then I met you." She stood up. "Excuse me, gentlemen. I'll be right back." She headed for the washroom.

Kennet and Derek chatted in a relaxed way. Derek said that he thought he had recognized Kennet from television. The P.I., wasn't it? The Public Investigator. Exposing corruption and scandal and all that? And did Kennet golf? His handicap was four now, on the City's best course. Elsie returned, and the couple took their leave. Before they got out the door, Elsie returned, ostensibly to retrieve the purse she'd left on a chair, but really to slip him her business card, accompanied by a whisper: "Call me on my cell – at work." Kennet waved back at them through the window as they prepared to embark in the Lexus.

The card identified Elspeth Griffith as manager of The Home Makers, a boutique for high-end home décor and accessories at the Intercity Mall. In pen on the back she had written "After 9:00 a.m."

Chapter 28

Tuesday, August 18th . . .

Sheets of wind-driven rain obscured the great bay and the Sleeping Giant. Kennet copied the phone number for The Hook'n Bullet before he drove to the campus.

Just inside the doors of the Fermi Building, he stamped his feet and shook out the loose sections of his high-end Gore-Tex rain suit, colour red, before stripping it off. Melissa Sharpe crowded in behind him, wrestling with an umbrella.

"Why don't you buy an umbrella, like everybody else?" she jibed.

"I prefer dry to semi-dry," he said, glancing meaningfully at Melissa's glistening nylons. "In wine too. Melissa, it looks like I have to return to Beardmore."

"Whatever," she said, brushing by him with her folded umbrella.

In his office he dialed Walter Kellerman's shop. "Bull," he said, "I'm coming back tonight. Keep the coffee hot."

"It's just short of piping," said Kellerman, jovially. "Grows hair on your palms. Leastways, that's how I explain the hair on my palms."

"Bull, I can't talk to Mac - Mac Kueng; he has no phone. Tell me, what was he driving back in '83?"

"Mac Kueng drove a '53 Chevy pickup. Guess he figured he got his money's worth, 'cause when he returned from his trip, he was driving the '82 Silverado he's driving now. Must be close to trade-in time again. You know, that man's a master mechanic and artificer. But he preferred to putter around with trappin' and odd jobs all his life."

"Tell me about his trip, Bull."

"He never really talked about it. Left that summer, told nobody nothin', and returned a year later. Asked old man Carlson to pack up his library and keep it warm till he returned."

"Any idea where he picked up the new truck?"

"I saw a Thunder Bay dealership logo on it. Still there, as far as I know."

Kennet glanced at his watch. Too early to call Elsie Griffith. He responded to e-mails or relegated them to appropriate electronic folders for later attention. He tried to concentrate on the new book he was introducing to the course. At 9:03 he called Elsie's cell.

She answered immediately. "Yes, Kennet. Thanks for humouring me. There's – there's something I wanted to tell you but it was awkward with Derek there. It's about Donny. Donny Fleming."

"Yes?"

"After the party, I couldn't find Georgie. While I was killing time before I left for Thamesville, I couldn't find anyone to hang out with. Everyone was working. And I – I couldn't get that sweet guy out of my mind. So I went looking for him."

"And?"

"Not at his place, I didn't want to run into his brothers. I found out he was working at the mine, found out when his shift was over, and sort of hung around the tracks near his home. When he was dropped off by someone, he saw me. And we talked."

"By the mine, do you mean the Con Empire?"

"Yes, that's the name. He was in some sort of clean-up operation. They were mothballing the place."

"So, what was it you wanted to tell me, Elsie."

"It was just a school girl impulse, to talk to him. Nothing came of it. I expected nothing to come of it. But when I returned at the end of the summer, I looked him up again. And guess what."

"I heard he left town about that time."

"Yes. And no one could tell me where he'd gone to. I even got up the nerve to ask Rawling, and all he said was 'The little bugger did a runner. Didn't even say goodbye to his mother.' I thought it so queer at the time."

"When you last saw him, was there anything different?"

"No. Yes. He was wearing that badge – that badge Lanny was wearing at the party. That I thought was funny. Funny odd, not funny ha ha."

Something clicked in Kennet's mind. "Elsie, you're a doll!"

Elsie laughed. "Well, I don't know which of your buttons I pressed, but thanks for the compliment. I just thought it odd, thinking about it since, that both of them disappeared that same summer. I sometimes wondered if they ran away together. But I guess Georgie wasn't that lucky."

Elsie paused, then continued: "This is probably totally irrelevant, but . . . at the party, Georgie wasn't wearing a brassiere."

After he broke the connection, Kennet experienced a rush of euphoria. The story was coming together! He called Detective Inspector Robert Kenilworth at his office. Robert's first words were, "They picked up Dunstan Ritchie at 7:45 this morning, at the Fleming residence. When the ward office opened at 8:00, they sat him down and questioned him, taking the line you suggested. You were right. It was a medal, with a D, the Flemings were looking for. He was referring to a medal, a Korean war medal. It belonged to the father, Rolfe Fleming, long since deceased. What does it mean, Kennet?"

"It means we may have another body on our hands."

Robert swore. "This better be good," he said.

"Did he admit to having the medal now?"

"No. But if Vanderhorst didn't have it, or didn't admit to having it, that would give them motive to go after Henderson, which they're still denying in spite of Henderson's allegation. They were charged, of course – Lanny and Ritchie – with that assault before they were released yesterday. They're still looking good for Vanderhorst, though. What's this about another body?"

"In the summer of '83, the younger brother, Donny Fleming, disappeared without a trace. I have a witness who saw him wearing that medal, or something like it, the last time she saw him. That may or may not be close to the time he disappeared, but I have a hunch."

"I like your hunches. So if Vanderhorst picked up that medal in the mine the other day, there may be a body there. And," said Robert, half to himself, "his killer, or killers, may have been trying to cover their tracks."

"My hunch precisely." Kennet paused a moment, then said, "Did your people ever search Rawling's Dodge Ram for weapons? Rifles, to be exact?"

"Not that I'm aware of. Why?"

"I neglected to mention this, but someone shot at me. I was looking over the mine . . . on the sly."

Robert swore imaginatively for thirty-five seconds. "This is my punishment," he concluded, "for trusting a civilian. Why in God's name and in the name of His Holiness Joe 'The Rottweiler' Ratzinger did you not report this before?"

"Oops," said Kennet. "*Mea culpa.*"

Robert snarled something unprintable and hung up. The phone rang almost immediately. Kennet said, "Robert, I apologize. I took matters into my own hand, I –"

"Kennet," said Peter Sheridan. "Stop nattering. I have news for you. The lab has a match between the bones and hair sample you supplied. Subject to verification of the mitochrondrial DNA. Now you need to 'fess up. Who's the victim?"

Kennet gave up the name of Georgiana Florentine Elder, and disclosed Mrs. Elder's address. "Peter, I'm going to Beardmore today. And thanks, by the way, for your intervention with Melissa. But let me break the news to Mrs. Elder. Please. She suspects the worst, but hope springs eternal and all that."

"I can give you a few hours before I pass on your information, but after that, it's out of my hands. Good luck. So, you won't be attending the Vanderhorst funeral."

"Damn. It slipped my mind. But it can't be helped. There's a real lead on the motive for his murder. I have to go. Please, explain to Cindy."

There was a light rap on his door frame and Malcolm Stevens walked through the open door, grinning. "Malcolm!" said Kennet. "You've got it!"

Stevens passed him the cassette and a DVD case labeled like the cassette "GRAD PARTY '83". "I was expecting you to call this morning," he said, "but I had a few minutes to run it over. Time for coffee?"

"I wish. I'll buy you a bucketful next time."

Stevens wanted to chat, but Kennet steered him diplomatically out the door. On the Internet he found an image of a 1953 Chevy truck. It indeed had five windows. It was a restored model. Other trucks, both restored and junked, were offered for sale.

He looked up Murphy's Auto Body Shop in the directory and dialed, asking to speak to Franco Spadoni, mechanic. After some fussing by the secretary or manager or whoever she was, who claimed the phone was ringing off the hook and it wasn't company policy to take personal calls, and after she had asked someone to fetch Frank, he could hear her barking in the background and telephones ringing. As he heard her speaking into another phone, Frank came on the line.

"Frank, it's Kennet. Hear you and the guys are working on a '69 Swinger. But that's not why I called. This is rather urgent – I'll explain later. Here's the scenario: It's 1983, and I have '53 Chevy pickup, and I want to trade up. What do I do? The venue is Thunder Bay."

"Well," drawled Frank, and Kennet imagined Frank's shaved head smeared with grease and his lanky frame draped in coveralls. "First of all, no auto sales business would take a thirty-year-old truck in trade, or if they did, they would not hang on to it."

Kennet heard the manager in the background yell at Frank to pick up the pace.

"So where would the Chevy end up?"

"Today, in one of a dozen places," said Frank. "But only one has a memory dating back to '83. DND."

"DND. Oh, you mean D and D, that scrap yard in Westfort."

"Yes. David and Dermot Davidson. Talk to Dermot. He's the brains when it comes to classic auto parts."

As Kennet was hanging up, he heard the manager yelling, "About fucking time! We run a –"

The rain appeared to have slackened. Grabbing his rain suit, and clutching the cassette and DVD in the other hand, Kennet left the building, draping the jacket over his head when he encountered a misty rain. He checked that his cell was still on. He hoped Robert would call. He drove directly to the Blue Lite Variety on North May Street.

The lady proprietor of the variety store had not seen Mr. Elder that morning. That was not like him, she said. She hoped he was feeling well. Kennet drove to 860 Vickers St. North. The tower had lost its romantic aura. It was a relic of industrial decay, its windows staring blankly at a neighbourhood that the good times had abandoned ages past. When he stepped out of the truck, it was

10:11. The air was damp, a few droplets landing on his exposed face.

Arthur Templeton answered the door. He had a pipe gripped in his teeth. When he saw his visitor he stood there uncertainly. After a moment he opened the door wider and Kennet entered.

Art glared at him. He removed his pipe. "He had a bad night."

"What I thought."

"He tried to cut himself."

Kennet felt a rush of concern. "He's alright?"

"He wasn't serious, thank God. I put a band-aid on it."

He led Kennet to a tiny bedroom and flicked on a table lamp. "Harold," he said. "That p'fessor again."

Harold had pulled the covers of the single bed up to cover his mouth. His exposed fingers clutched the coverlet. An old-fashioned wallpaper smothered every square inch of every wall. Faded pink nondescript flowers drooped from washed-out green stems.

Kennet squatted quickly by the bedside and reached for Harold's left hand. He enfolded Harold's fingers in his. "Harold, I'm glad to see you."

Harold's eyes moved to engage his. His voice was muffled. With his free hand, Kennet moved the coverlet off Harold's lips.

"You still have a daughter who misses her father," said Kennet.

"How could she?" Harold turned his head away.

"That's what daughters do. They miss their fathers."

"I was never there," mumbled Harold.

"You were always there . . . in some sense." Kennet searched for words. "You remember your father?" Harold nodded once, looking at the wall beyond.

"You remember your grandfather?"

Harold nodded almost imperceptibly. In a small voice he said, "He died when I was little." After a silence he added, "I used to visit him."

"So you remember visiting him? You have memories of him?"

"No," said Harold, turning his eyes toward Kennet. "He died before I could remember him. But I visited him, where the family buried him."

Kennet squeezed his fingers and released them. "In that cemetery beside the lake. With the picket fence."

Harold looked at him now. "My father – he loved him. So I loved him. Though he was gone." He strained his neck to look at the bedside clock. "What time is it?" He pushed the bedclothes down to chest level. Kennet saw the band-aid on his right wrist.

"You don't have to get up," said Kennet.

Behind Kennet, Art spoke up, "You rest there, Harold. You take it easy."

Harold struggled to sit up. "Of course I have to get up. No one promised me easy." His frail shoulders strained at the striped pyjama top.

Art touched Kennet on the shoulder and motioned for him to leave. In the kitchen, Art poured Kennet a hot coffee. He put two slices into the toaster.

The toilet flushed. A radio, volume turned low, played tinnily on top of the cream-coloured china cabinet. Eventually Harold appeared, in tie and suit coat, freshly shaven. "I'm going to work," he said.

Art said, "Not without something in your stomach, you're not. Sit down." He put coffee in front of him. Harold added an inch of two-percent milk, and four teaspoons of sugar, and slopped raspberry jam on the toast.

As he chewed he looked at Kennet. "Why'd you come back?"

"I had a question."

Harold chewed and nodded.

"When those postcards came," Kennet said, "supposedly from Georgie, you knew Mac sent them."

Harold nodded.

"How long was Mac away, that time?"

302

"A few months. A long time." He resumed chewing. "There was one came," he said, "that I never showed Edith. I usually got the mail, from the post office, if I wasn't on the lake. I burned it."

"What did it say, Harold?"

Harold stopped chewing and teared up. " 'I miss you'." Harold gulped and began choking. Art leapt to his aid and began thumping him on the back. Harold coughed up the messy clump into the saucer. The sobbing convulsed his body. He covered his eyes, wiping away tears, and the sobs became long shuddering sighs. In minutes he was calm again, and dropped his hands.

He glanced at Art. "Thanks," he said. He looked at Kennet. "Thank you. Again."

Art removed the saucer and uneaten toast.

Harold said, "I miss her." He added, "I miss Gracie." After a pause: "What's she like?"

Kennet described Gracie's long hair and her job and lifestyle from his scanty store of knowledge. "She makes dream-catchers," he said.

"I have another question," Kennet continued. "You knew Rolfe Fleming. Did he have the same medal as you did for service in Korea?"

Harold nodded. "Yes. Poor Rolfe. Died before his time. Heart, you know. Left five boys for Karen to raise. They grew up wild. Except the second youngest one."

"Donny."

Harold nodded.

"Do you recall the last time you saw Donny?"

"Edith came back before Canada Day. There's always a good time on Canada Day. Parade. Barbecue at the park. I don't remember seeing him there. I don't remember ever seeing him after that. I remember the other two boys cuttin' up." Harold rose from the table. "I gotta go."

"I'll give you a ride."

"No. No. Thanks. It's good for me."

Outside, Harold looked up at the tower limned against the gray ceiling. "No birds today," he said. "There's a peregrine lives up there. I saw the babies this spring. Gone now, I expect."

Chapter 29

. . . Tuesday morning

The building that housed D & D Auto Supply dated to the same era as Thunder Bay Iron Works and the ancient tower. The shabby one-and-a-half-story building squatted beside a railway line in the industrial zone of Westfort, the suburb between the airport and the Kaministiquia River. Beside it, enclosed by a cyclone fence, sprawled a car graveyard.

Behind the counter, a young man with dirty blond hair was leafing through a *Playboy*. Kennet asked him for the owner. "Which one?" said the clerk.

"Dermot?"

"Ain't here. You can speak to David." The youth led him to a dingy, cramped office, shelves bulging with junk coated with dust and petroleum products. The occupant lifted his head from behind reams of paper. "Yeah?" David appeared to be in his late sixties, dressed like a labourer, his hairline having retreated halfway to the nape of his neck.

Kennet introduced himself. David shook his hand limply. "Something I can do for you?"

"I'm looking for a '53 Chevy pickup that may have been dropped off here in 1983."

"Good luck," said David, sweeping his arm towards the unseen graveyard beyond the wall. "Be my guest."

"I was told Dermot might remember."

"You might be right. He keeps that trash in his head. I got a business to run here."

"Is Dermot around?"

"Dermot is re-tired." David put emphasis on the first syllable. "'F you ask me, needs a whole new chassis, and a body, and a sludge-removal treatment."

"How do I contact him?"

David reached for a phone hitherto buried on his desk. Kennet heard the rotary dial spinning, and then David spoke into the black instrument. "Dermot. Get down here. Got a live one for you."

Kennet loitered in the outer office for a few minutes, inspecting old fly-specked calendars of muscle cars and busty bimbos. Then he walked out to the cinder-paved yard and surveyed the grim landscape of the neighbourhood.

Ten minutes later a sporty yellow coupe convertible braked sharply to a halt. A big heavy-set man with an irrepressible grin extricated himself from the car. He addressed Kennet: "You're the fish, are you?"

Kennet introduced himself. Dermot's grip left his fingers tingling.

"What can I do for you?"

Kennet explained his mission.

"I know exactly," said Dermot, grinning, "who and what you refer to, and when. I got a memory like a steel trap. What do you want to know?"

"I don't really know, exactly. I'm just following my nose."

"This handsome devil drove up on a Saturday, our busiest day, on June – June – I'll remember in a minute. I never caught his name, we did a lot of cash deals. Said he'd part with his baby -

like he was doing us a favour – said he'd sell it if we broke it up, cannibalized the parts. I had to promise. Just as well, because there was one horrible stench from the cab, like somebody shat in it. We shook on it. June 25th. My wife's birthday."

"Any damage to it? Front-end damage?"

"Yeah, the grille was bent, couldn't sell it. And the hood – the hood had a dent, a big dent. Said he'd bounced off a moose calf. Are we talking a hit-and-run here?"

"No. The calf died. And was buried. Still have any of those parts?"

"I should swear. Follow me." Kennet felt his six-foot stature diminish as he trailed the hulking man into the shop. Dermot said over his shoulder, "David tell you I was re-tired?" He used David's emphasis.

Kennet said yes.

"And that I needed a new chassis?" Dermot halted and turned around, grinning.

"Among other things."

"Thank God he keeps himself amused. I keep amused. What did you think of my new toy?" Dermot gestured toward the outdoors.

"Wow. What year?"

" '65. I got my own shop, at home. After fifty-one years of work time, it's playtime."

"Tell me more. About the car."

"MG. An MGB roadster, to be precise. That was first year of production. Swallows up my long legs like a boa constrictor. Did you notice the bumper?"

"No, sorry."

"Rubber."

"Wow. I'm a hobbyist too. You heard of Frank's Auto Dream Shop?"

"I should swear. What're you working on now?"

"I've been away, but I understand we're going to restore a '69 Dodge Dart Swinger."

"Lovely beast. Always wished I owned one. Come this way." Dermot led him behind the counter. He flipped a remark at the young man with the magazine: "Memorize those body parts, Dickie. Fondle 'em. You'll never touch the like on living makes and models." He walked through an aisle with parts stacked on shelving stretching up to the ceiling, and up rickety wooden stairs. He grinned back at Kennet, who was placing his feet carefully: "Welcome to *my* Little Shop of Dreams."

Shelving and used parts crammed the upper floor. Above the aisle several large parts – body, drive train, engine – hung from the ceiling on pulleys. "Chevies at the back, way back," said Dermot, "this side o' the Buicks. This is all organized, like my brain." Eventually he stopped and turned around and swept his arm in a showman's gesture: "*Wahla!*" he said, in fake French. "The '53 pickup."

At eye level a few parts occupied a section measuring about a metre square and a metre-and-a-half deep – in a swift scan Kennet picked out one intact headlight, a steering wheel, wipers, a bumper, radiator, and several other items.

Dermot scooped up a smudged sheet from the shelf and studied it. "Tranny, engine, front-end, steering – all sold. Rear axle and differential's up there." He pointed to the ceiling.

"May I have a closer look?"

"Help yourself." Kennet sorted through the junked parts on the shelf.

"Bumper – front one?"

"Nix. Just the rear one. What're you looking for?"

"Not sure yet. Hood ornament?"

"The '53 models never had one. Just a name plate. Got that." He reached into the shelf and pulled out a chrome piece about a foot long with the name "Chevrolet" prominently embossed. As with everything else, dust and grime coated it. A black substance lodged in the interstices between the letters.

"I'll take this."

As soon as he closed the door of the Sportage, his cell rang. It was Robert Kenilworth. Kennet said, "Good timing, Robert. Listen, I have a smart mouth. I apologize –"

"Forget it," said Robert. "So have I. I would like you to be at the Beardmore mine office at 4:00. Can you do that?"

"Yes, of course. What's up?"

"I've advised Nordstrom that I will be there with an investigative team. And, I had Kelly go straight to the Fleming residence and ask Rawling straight out. He produced certificates for the rifles. He had no problem showing her where he kept them – they belong to him and his brother and cousin – in the truck. But, my dear Kennet, he could produce only one of three. Claimed the other two were stolen recently."

"I heard that too. What did Kelly find?"

"A Winchester .300. Unloaded. Trigger-locked. Encased. All legal."

"That's not the rifle I heard when I ducked a bullet."

"What're you, a firearms expert?"

"No, but the rifle I heard, I heard growing up, on hunting trips with my father. And in Croatia and Lebanon and other places. And it wasn't a Winchester."

"What's interesting," said Robert, "is that Rawling declined to file a report of stolen property. Said the Flemings don't rat to the police. Should you be careful, Kennet?"

"Whose Winchester was it?"

"Rawling claimed it."

Kennet ruminated a moment, then said. "I'll meet you in Beardmore, Robert, but I want to do something first. If I talk to that Kyle Henderson, would I be tampering with a witness?"

"Be my guest. We've got our statement – well, our report – he's still not speaking – and we'll call him for the trial. Listen, what's the number of that motel? I have a feeling I won't get home tonight."

Kennet pulled off Golf Links Road into the visitor parking at Superior North College and strode briskly through the building to the library. He waved to the two librarians and found a free computer terminal. In the search engine he entered the terms. Within ten minutes he was looking at a sunburst Korean War medal. He printed off the image.

He continued north on Golf Links Road to the formidable complex of the new regional hospital. A nurse pointed out Kyle Henderson, who was dressed in civvies and seated in a chair near the nurses' station, leafing through a golfing magazine. She said he was waiting for his ride. He was being discharged.

Henderson looked up when he approached and accepted his hand. He was a stocky lad with a high forehead. A scab protected a long laceration on his forehead. A bruise dominated the left side of his face and bruises underlined his eye sockets. The fact that he did not smile or speak confirmed that his jaw was wired tight.

Kennet began hesitantly, not certain how to conduct the interview or how to interpret responses. Henderson produced a notebook and pen. An elastic bandage supported his right wrist.

"So this Inspector Kenilworth," continued Kennet, "gave me permission to interview you."

Henderson nodded slightly.

"How many times did the police talk to you?"

Henderson held up one finger. He scribbled: *Responded just once apparently.*

"I have a picture here. Does it mean anything?" Kennet held up the print-out.

Henderson nodded almost imperceptibly and scribbled again: *Thats the one – did you find it?*

"Not yet. Where was it?"

Henderson wrote: *V's gym bag.*

"Tell me, Kyle, how did they beat you?"

Henderson grasped an imaginary baseball bat and swung.

"A bat?"

Henderson nodded. He wrote: *The big sonofabitch – other used his boots.*

"I'm puzzled, Kyle. Why did you leave Vanderhorst? Why weren't you with him?"

Pain flickered in Henderson's eyes. He wrote a long message and thrust it at Kennet: *Was going back for him – needed a dump in real toilet – without fucken flies. Sat on bed, nodded off Woke up – poundng on door.*

Kennet thanked him and stood up to leave. Henderson held up his index finger and then scribbled furiously: *Police tht robbery – coulnt understd why wallet untouch Wasnt – I wasnt thinkg clearly Didn't explain.* The *I* was underlined twice.

Back in his apartment, Kennet packed swiftly. He changed into his bush outfit. If he was going to descend into the bowels of the earth, if he was going to brace the devil in his lair, he would dress for the campaign. He left word with Mrs. Sandberg, and after stowing his gear in the truck, he decided to leave the kayak in the garage.

The sky lightened up. Occasional sputters of raindrops required the activation of the windshield wipers. He stopped in Nipigon at the Husky Service Centre to grab a pre-packaged sandwich. A wind from the north raised whitecaps on Lake Helen and dried the freshly scrubbed faces of the weeping cliffs.

On satellite radio he found a song by The Eagles. It was *Hotel California*. He was wandering through the chambers, looking for the lovely face. When he found it, she was dancing, dancing with pretty boys, and sipping champagne, and he heard voices calling, calling from far away, and he had to find the passage back . . . Had to find the passage back . . . Had to leave . . . Forever.

He switched the radio off.

The teeming leaves of the long burn had been revived by the recent rains. In Beardmore he pulled into the Regency Motel. It was 3:37. His cell rang.

Chapter 30

. . . Tuesday afternoon

"Where are you now?" asked Robert Kenilworth.

Kennet spoke into his cell phone: "Just pulling into the motel."

"Okay. I'm at the tavern, waiting for the SOCOs. Both Greenstone detective constables are here. I couldn't get a room there – full up. Highway crews, apparently. Meet us here."

Alice was in process of closing the restaurant for the day. She said she had assigned Kennet his old room – none of the construction guys, she said, wanted the jinxed room. "That's what one of them called it," she said.

"In that case," said Kennet, "may I have two keys? A friend of mine will be staying with me, since there's more than one bed."

Kennet pulled into the parking area of Arlene's Tavern. There were two OPP vehicles and the Inspector's Chrysler. Robert was descending the staircase, followed by Detective Constables Armitage and Mueller, Staff-Sergeant Jillian Halvorsen, and another gentleman in a business suit. The scene-of-crime officers whom Kennet had encountered on his first day in Beardmore, exited their Chevy Suburban.

As his foot hit the bottom step, Robert stopped and made a round-up-the-herd gesture. "Okay, ladies and gentlemen. Listen up. This is my party. This gentleman here," said Robert, putting his hand on the shoulder of the business suit, "is Detective Staff-Sergeant Lockwood, assisting me." Silver-haired, with a salt-and-pepper moustache, Lockwood looked like Robert, a refugee from Bay Street, Toronto.

"And that gentleman," he said, pointing to Kennet, "is Mr. Forbes, also assisting. The mine office is just over there, so let's roll. And by that, I mean, let's stroll."

As the group moved toward the two-story clapboard building, Kelly Armitage threw Kennet a smile and a discreet hand wave. Mueller pointedly ignored him. Staff-Sergeant Jillian nodded and said, "Nice to see you again."

As everyone crowded into the office foyer, Ioanna Mallory glanced apprehensively at them and buried her nose in her monitor again. Dan Nordstrom emerged from his office.

"Which of you is Inspector Kenilworth?" he said.

"I am."

"Inspector," said Nordstrom, "I've been talking to my boss, Vice President of Operations, and he wonders if you have a warrant. This is private property, Inspector, and you'd be obstructing business."

"I have no warrant, sir. But if you want to see obstruction of business, just watch me."

"And I see," said Nordstrom, surveying the crowd, "you have a member of the press with you." His eyes settled on Kennet. "I thought this was strictly a police investigation."

"You have my assurance that it is. And Dr. Forbes, from the university, not the press, is assisting the police. Nothing that he sees or hears will reach the press."

Nordstrom set his jaw. "Still, Inspector, my boss would like to see a warrant. He has stockholders to answer to."

314

Robert took one step forward, looking down at Norstrom's five-foot ten from a distance of inches.

"Mr. Nordstrom, I can roust out a J.P., even if I have to go to the city. And, I will immediately advise Thunder Bay Action Television about the reluctance of Crown Resources to cooperate with police. They may wish to send a camera crew out. And I will do the same for local radio and *The Lakehead Journal*. And, in the meantime, the officers here," he gestured to the group, "will conduct an alcohol-detection program on the highway out front. And if anyone asks why the show of force, I am not forbidding any officer from explaining what we are doing here. By tomorrow morning, perhaps even tonight, Crown Resources will be headline news."

Nordstrom smiled wanly. "Of course we'll cooperate. The VP expressed a preference, not a requirement. You still haven't stated what you expect to find."

"Thank you," said Robert. "You may still make the news, but as a good corporate citizen. Now, what's the next step?"

Nordstrom said he would precede them to the custom mill, leaving the gate open.

When the fleet of vehicles stopped outside the mill, Kennet noted the skeletal headframe perched on the low ridge about fifty metres from the mill. Everyone crowded into a new-looking two-story building next to the mill, clad in yellow steel panels. A grumpy-looking individual in mud-stained working gear hovered at the far end of the passageway. He wore a white safety helmet, complete with miner's lamp, and yellow waterproofs. Gym-style lockers lined one wall. Nordstrom assumed a position facing the group.

"Gentlemen. And ladies too – my apologies. This is the dry. We must change clothes for the occasion. And this is where we're going." He turned sideways and pointed to a cross-section of the mine workings in a wall chart. He used a metre-stick as a pointer. "We can approach the workings from the decline, shown by this graphic, that descends to Level 2. We can drive down the ramp to Level 1." Nordstrom pointed to the right side of the chart. A drift, Level 1, ran horizontally east-west. It ran almost a kilometre west to the old shaft.

"Or," Norstrom continued, "we can approach from the manway and vertical shaft, which takes us to Level 1." He pointed to the left side of the chart. "So, depending on how much you want to walk, for the drifts do not accommodate vehicles, at which end would you like to start? Inspector?"

Robert stepped forward.

Norstrom continued, "What exactly do you want to investigate?"

Robert motioned to Kennet. "Dr. Forbes will explain."

Kennet moved to stand beside Nordstrom and the chart. "Dan, can you pinpoint for us where your crew was working last Thursday?"

Nordstrom motioned to the sour-looking workman. "Ferg, would you enlighten us, please?" To the group he said, "This is Ferg Christie, our foreman."

Ferg Christie moved ponderously up to the wall, his eyes flicking contemptuously over the group. His jowly cheeks supported a few days' growth of grey stubble. He stabbed a finger at Level 1, perhaps five hundred metres from the shaft, according to the chart scale.

"And," said Kennet, "where was Mr. Vanderhorst intercepted and turned around?"

Christie stabbed at a point closer to the shaft. "Here," he said, in a truculent tone, which was quite possibly his normal tone. "Cummings was signaling the cage – we have a bell and flashing light system – which the work crew used to get to Level 1, so I met him – I intercepted him. That tourist had no business underground, so I sent him, and Cummings, packing."

"Okay," said Kennet, turning to Dan, "that's what we want to see. This stretch." He pointed to the drift between the shaft and the point where Christie had accosted Vanderhorst.

"Alright," said Nordstrom, "there are certain safety precautions everyone must take, which I will explain, and safety gear everyone must wear. It's in the visitor lockers behind you. However," he added, "we cannot accommodate more than six people at a time. That's me and Ferg and four of you."

Twenty minutes later, a team of underground explorers emerged from the dry, outfitted in safety helmets and battery-operated lamps, heavy steel-toed rubber boots, and either yellow waterproofs or red coveralls. Kennet and Robert wore the coveralls.

The party waddled up the slope to the headframe, following Nordstrom. A cable ran over the enormous sheave wheel, one end down to the cage, the other to a small shack beside the headframe. Mueller and Lockwood and the two SOCOs, their wardrobes unchanged, remained outside the dry, looking disconsolate.

Nordstrom, in white hard hat and yellow waterproofs, waited at the collar until the party had gathered round him. "When we arrive at the station, Ferg will lead," he said, "and Kennet will be next. I will bring up the rear. The only real danger is the shaft. Step off the cage and into the station. You won't need your lamps because we keep Level 1 illuminated round the clock. It is, after all, an escape hatch." He turned around and slid back a wire-mesh safety door between pillars of the headframe, and then a wire-mesh door in the cage. "In the event we cannot use the cage to return, there is a ladderway in the other compartment." He gestured to the side of the cage. "This is a two-compartment shaft."

The six people jammed into the confined quarters of the cage. Nordstrom, last to enter, closed the doors and pressed buttons in a panel. Two bells clanged. The cage began descending. Bodies pressed against the sheet metal walls of the cage and against one another. All eyes focused on the mesh door, where Nordstrom's head lamp revealed the bare rock walls of the shaft rushing by.

Darkness enveloped them. The cage fell, gathering speed. Kelly's voice asked a question.

"What's under us? I mean, if we fall, what do we hit?"

Nordstrom replied over his shoulder: "Nothing but air. And then water. Hundreds of metres of water."

"I can't swim!" Jillian squeaked in mock terror. She and Kelly both broke into giggles.

"Don't matter," Christie grunted. "You'd be dead already."

"Ferguson!" Dan interjected. "Attention to business."

Immediately the cage slowed. Kennet swallowed, popping his ears. The cage creaked and swayed towards a halt. A brightly lit chamber appeared beyond the door. The cage stopped and gave a bounce. Nordstrom threw back the door, reached out, and slid back the shaft's safety door. He stepped out into the station, the others following, blinking their eyes.

Beyond the small chamber in the rock, a passageway stretched before them, three to four metres wide. Kennet followed Ferg Christie into the passageway. He glanced at his watch: almost 5 o'clock. The raw rock ceiling hovered half a metre above their heads. Naked incandescent lamps, linked by a electrical tubing, sprouted from the ceiling every fifteen to thirty metres. A large-diameter flexible tube hung from the ceiling where it met the right-hand wall. *Air*, thought Kennet. *I hope.* A whirling box fan soon validated his observation. From time to time the passageway curved gently to the right. Occasionally Kennet noted the broad tips of rock bolts in the ceiling or walls. He was surprised by the lack of timberwork, the lack of timbered arches to support the ceiling. He noticed occasional wooden patches in the walls, and deep dark clefts.

The explorers followed behind, Indian file, paralleling a narrow-gauge railway track on wooden ties. A tramway, Kennet guessed, would be the proper term. They proceeded in silence, the only sound the clomp of boots and splashing and the rasping of outerwear. The floor of the drift glistened with dampness. Boots splashed through a shallow stream, which ran back toward the shaft. Kennet spoke to Christie's back:

"These rails been here long?"

"Seventy, eighty years," came the muffled reply.

"They look in good shape."

"Steel don't rust underwater. Wood don't rot."

Kennet stepped closer to Christie, almost treading on his heels as he prepared more questions. They rounded a shallow corner of the drift and encountered a vista of perhaps fifty metres. Christie stopped abruptly, and Kennet trod on his heels. Christie turned about.

"You know where you're going?" he said.

"There's an ore car somewhere along here?" After Christie nodded, Kennet said, "Just this side of it. Where the stope is." He hoped that his grasp of mining terminology impressed the mining foreman.

"There's stopes all along here," said Christie. "There's one there." He pointed to a wooden patch built into the wall on their left. They moved up to it. It was about a metre-and-a-half square, seeming to plug a gap where the ceiling met the wall. It consisted of timbers aligned horizontally, and a short lip or chute on the bottom end.

"What's behind this?" asked Kennet.

"Broken ore, maybe. Maybe nothing. Maybe just air. It's a stope."

Jillian came up behind Kennet. "How did this all work?" she said.

Christie became more gracious. "The miners reamed out a cavern, ma'am. A big rock chamber. And the ore dropped down, gravity feed, you know, and this gate and chute channeled the broken ore into cars on the track. See the lever here?" He touched a metal mechanism. "The tram operator could control the feed."

"Is this gate still workable?" she asked.

"Don't see why not. But I ain't touching it, ma'am. Could be tons of loose rock behind there. Or just air. Three weeks ago, it was full up with water, till we drained this level. See? This stope is still draining." He pointed to the moisture patch on the wall beneath the gate.

Kennet asked, "How did the miners access the stope?"

Christie twisted his lips disdainfully. "There's a manway," he said, gesturing down the passageway. "Are we here on police business or what?" He faced about and trudged down the drift, the party following. As he passed a cleft in the wall, he pointed wordlessly to it. It was another passageway, pitch black, about the width of two men standing side by side. Kennet sensed a slight draft against his face. In another minute or two, they passed another dark passageway. Kennet detected a slight odour.

Christie stopped once again and faced around. "There's your bucket car," he said, "and a chute. This one's released some ore." Behind him a single rusty ore car, coming up to chest height, sat on the tracks. He kicked at a small pile of broken rock, about half a cubic metre in volume. "This what you're looking for?" There was now a distinctive odour, like pickled herring.

"You smell that?" said Kennet.

"Yeah," said Christie. "Maybe a dead rabbit. Or a rat. Sometimes an animal gets lost down here."

Kennet looked at the wooden gate. The bottom timber has been raised a few centimetres. He fumbled with the lamp on his helmet. "How do I turn this on?"

Christie reached over and flicked a switch. In the beam Kennet could see large chunks of rock behind the crack in the timbers. He squatted to examine the rock pile, consisting of crumbled rock and small shards. He picked up the largest shard and used it as a trowel.

Robert knelt down beside him, his light assisting in the search. The two women moved past and took positions near the ore car. Jillian took out a hanky and muffled her nose.

"Wait a minute," said Kennet. "What's this?" He fished out a saturated black rag. It measured about eight centimetres square.

"You hit the jackpot, son," said Christie. "A miner's hanky. You can wipe your nose."

Kennet drew the rag up to his face. "See this, Robert?" He passed it over.

"I see it," said Robert. "A hanky with a buttonhole. And it stinks to high heaven."

Christie leaned over. "Eh?"

Kennet stood up swiftly. "Where's that manway? We have to examine the stope."

"Fuck that," said Christie. "That's dangerous. The place hasn't been scaled for eighty years. A falling rock this size," he said, holding up his fist, "can put a hole in your skull, even with a hardhat."

Nordstrom intervened. "Ferg, take them up as far as you can. Just don't expose them to danger."

Christie protested. "But, boss –!"

Behind Christie came a shriek. The two women jumped away from the ore car. Jillian had her hand over her mouth. Christie whirled around. Jillian said, "It moved!"

"What?" asked Christie, glancing left and right.

"The car," she said. "The ore car. We were leaning on it. It moved."

"Sure," said Christie. "Why not? Has the same grease on its axles that it had when this drift was abandoned."

Christie turned about face. "You and you," he said, pointing to Kennet and Robert. "Red coveralls. You follow me. And," he said, with emphasis, "you stay behind me!" He switched on his lamp.

Christie retraced their footsteps up the drift, Kennet and Robert following. He turned into a dark narrow passageway where only their headlamps illumined the space. Kennet could touch the walls on either side by extending his arms. After a few paces, Christie stopped. He raised an arm and grasped the rung of an ancient wooden ladder leaning against the end wall, and tugged at it. He put a foot on the bottom rung and stomped hard on it, twice. He started climbing, tugging and stomping. The ladder rose into darkness. Christie climbed into the darkness. Soon he called down: "Okay, one at a time."

Kennet moved aside and motioned for Robert to proceed. Robert climbed rung by rung, gingerly. His feet disappeared, and a moment later there was a sharp crack and Robert cried out: "Jesus!" After a pause he called down in a flat voice: "Just the one rung, Kennet. Skip over it."

Kennet placed one foot on the bottom rung and prepared to climb. An overwhelming sense of dread stopped his breath. He shrugged his shoulders and drew in a lungful. He began climbing. Two headlamps shone in his face. He had several metres to go. He grasped the weakened rung, and released it, and reached for the next one. Then he was on a level with Robert and Christie, who were standing shoulder-to-shoulder on a ledge just to the right of the ladder. Beyond them the blackness gaped.

"As far as we go," said Christie.

Robert said, "There's a floor here, Kennet. Here, let me steady you." Robert sniffed and continued, "There *is* an odour here. And I've smelled *that* before."

The three explorers edged themselves around until they were looking into a vast low empty chamber. By turning their heads, the lights glanced off far rock walls. The lights even reached the ceiling. About thirty metres down the broken rock floor, the lights bounced off a timber structure.

"Unfinished stope," grunted Christie. "Probably lost the vein, so they abandoned it."

Kennet addressed Christie: "Ferg, take us to that timber. Isn't that where the chute begins?"

Christie plodded ahead, and reached a cribbing of timber about two metres square. He removed the lamp from his helmet, leaned over the topmost timber, which was about a metre off the floor, and shone the lamp downwards. Kennet managed to remove his own lamp and merged its beam with the beam from Christie's lamp. Robert adjusted his helmet and directed his beam to the same point.

"There's something there," said Robert.

"Looks like rags," said Christie. "Some miner discarded his shirt or something."

"And left his arm in them," said Kennet.

Christie did a double take. "Eh?"

"That," said Kennet, "looks like flesh to me. A wrist."

All three gazed hard at the bundle of rags. After a moment, Robert said, "I think you're right, Kennet."

Christie said, "Well, fuck."

Chapter 31

... Tuesday afternoon, later

Back in the drift, Robert Kenilworth described the gruesome discovery to Dan Nordstom and the two police officers. Nordstrom was appalled.

"You must be mistaken! It's not one of our crew."

"That I believe," said Robert. "It antedates your de-watering of the mine. And, we have to retrieve the remains." He turned to Ferg Christie: "Mr. Christie, can we erect some kind of protective roofing in the stope so that our scene-of-crime officers can work safely?"

Christie, as profane as ever, spoke in subdued tones. "Hell, I can't order any men to work in those conditions. Boss," he said, turning to Nordstrom, "even if I get the volunteers, it could take days to bring down fucken materials and construct scaffolding and every-fucken-thing else. And we'd be paying premium wages to work around *that* fucken thing."

Robert said, "We must retrieve the remains."

Kennet spoke up. "Can we go through the chute?"

Christie looked at him, and nodded slowly. "Yeh-us. We

could. That cribbing looked stable. There'd be very little ore in the chute. It shouldn't swamp us if we open the gate." He looked at Robert. "But you might get that *thing* only in pieces."

Robert nodded. "That's unlikely to be the scene of a crime. If it was a crime. We'll take it in pieces."

Robert and Christie and Nordstrom moved aside and spoke in low voices with a great deal of gesticulation.

Staff-Sergeant Jillian Halvorsen sidled up to Kennet. "Well, Kennet, you lead an interesting life. Your second body in less than a week. How did you know?"

Kennet felt faintly embarrassed. "A wild guess," he said. "I'm still putting the pieces together." Kennet winced after he said it. "Jillian, we need more information on the mine's operation back in the early eighties."

Jillian said, "That's a job I'll leave to our detectives. D.C. Armitage?"

Kelly, who had moved up to stand beside Jillian, said, "Right, Staff-Sergeant. I'm ready to start anytime."

Robert came over. "Okay, folks. We're leaving. This is a job for Hal and Andrew." He looked at Kennet. "The SOCOs," he said. "Let's get the hell out of here."

Back on surface, as they exited the cage, Kennet noted that everyone drew deep breaths of clean air. The sun was still high over the horizon. Robert strode quickly downhill to the group that had remained behind. Kennet's group came up as everyone was moving into the dry.

As one party stripped off its outerwear, the others suited up. Robert raised his voice: "Okay, listen up, everybody. Constables Marchand and Rutledge – that's Hal and Andrew – will assist in retrieving the remains. So will D.C. Mueller. Detective Staff-Sergeant Lockwood will be in charge. The forensics identification team will be arriving from Thunder Bay. The rest of us have assignments."

Ferg Christie returned from the nether regions. "Okay, I got two guys. Crazy bastards. I told them of the hazard, but they jumped at the chance. Work is scarce. And they get double time. Probably have to raise that to triple time when they see what they gotta do. I'll take respirators for everybody."

Mueller said, to no one in particular, "Are we going to eat first, or what? We could be gone for hours."

Robert responded, "Trust me, Con. You don't want to eat. Maybe not for a long time."

Jillian and Kelly's Tahoe truck followed Dan Nordstrom's white Ford F-250, headed for the mine office. Robert and Kennet left in their respective vehicles, having agreed to meet at the motel. Earlier, Kennet had advised Robert that there were two extra beds in his motel room.

Robert transferred both his overnight bag and Lockwood's to the room. Kennet assigned Robert to the master bed in the common area, and chose the single bed in the back room which was furthest from the door. He couldn't bring himself to sleep in the bed where Kyle Henderson had been found battered and comatose.

Robert said, "I haven't informed the family about the identification of Georgiana Elder's remains. I thought we'd do it together."

"Appreciate it," said Kennet. "Before we go there, there's something on this DVD that may shed some light on the body in the mine. It's a home movie, taken at a high school grad party out at Lake Nipigon, in June of '83. I haven't seen it yet myself."

"Okay," said Robert, "break out the popcorn. I suppose there's no chance of a stiff drink?"

"I'll dash over to the store and get us some cokes."

At Melody's Variety, he selected some soft drinks, some canned goods, bread, margarine, and packaged luncheon meat, and then asked the cashier, Barb, if Melody were home. She was. He

326

knocked on the frame of the open doorway at the rear, and entered when Melody sang out.

Melody rose from a collation on the kitchen table, her ample proportions disguised by a mou-mou. "Professor! How delightful! What can I do for you?"

"I'm at the motel, Melody. Got in too late to shop at the liquor store. Do you have a bottle of hard stuff that I can replace tomorrow? I'm entertaining."

"Oh?" she said, arching her eyebrows.

"Ontario's Finest." When she looked mystified, he added, "Officers of the law."

"Oh," she said. "Let me see." She turned to the cupboards and opened a door. "I rarely touch the stuff myself, but my husband, my late husband, Rudy, he liked a drink. To relax, you understand." She pulled out a bottle of rye whiskey, about half full. She held it out to Kennet. "You're welcome to it, professor. And don't worry about replacing it."

"I would worry, Melody. Thanks. See you tomorrow."

"So," she said, "what is going on there, at the mine? All those police."

"Sorry, Melody. Sworn to secrecy."

The video began at the lakeside camp in fading daylight. Cars with glaring headlights were arriving and competing for parking space. Then the lens, shooting from the interior, pointed to the camp door and greeted each laughing arrival. The video had no sound. Some flaunted the booze they had brought. Almost everyone wore casual clothes, having obviously changed after the graduation ceremonies at the high school. Many wore shorts. One hulking fellow ducked to enter the doorway.

"Gron Murdstone," said Kennet. "A gentle giant."

"Are you in this video, Kennet?"

"I graduated the year before . . . And this is Georgie Elder." A pretty girl, laughing vivaciously, entered the cabin. A brunette with bobbed hair, she wore jeans and a yellow shirt. She had a red belt and black boots. A young man was guiding her with his hand on her elbow.

"Who's she with?"

"I knew him only by sight. He was a couple years ahead of me, in school. That may be our victim in the mine."

Robert was flabbergasted. "The hell you say!" He looked wildly at Kennet. "What's the name? Roll that back!" Kennet rewound the disk to Georgie's entrance and paused it. The well-built youth had good looks and long black hair, rag cut.

"Donny Fleming," said Kennet.

"The Fleming we thought had broken with his family! What's your theory?"

"Still full of holes. I'm hoping this video will fill some blanks. Let's continue."

There was a sequence of interior shots as the gathering became more festive. There was a cameo of a young Marcus Chambers in tie and sports jacket. A glimpse of Georgie Elder dancing solo, trance-like. The camera moved to a window, shooting out a pane into the darkness. It focused on a bonfire on the rocky shore. It cut to the interior again, where now young men engaged in a tournament of Indian wrestling, one foot braced against an opponent's foot, and one hand grasping the opponent's hand and trying to push or jerk one another off balance. A guy in short sleeves and muscular arms appeared on screen for the first time. He tried to stomp his opponent's arch, and when his adversary protested and tried to break off the engagement, Mr. Muscles pushed him up against some furniture and boxed him in the ribs with his free hand. He broke off the contest and danced toward the camera, arms above his head in a boxer's victory salute. It was a young Lanny Fleming, in fighting trim, unlike the beefy man he had met recently.

"Recognize him?" asked Kennet.

"Yeah. Always the asshole."

"See that?" said Kennet. He stopped the DVD player and rewound and froze on Lanny. He walked up to the screen and tapped Lanny's chest. "That," he said, "is a medal. I believe it is a Korean war medal. We'll have to isolate that frame and blow it up."

He pressed Play on the machine. "And where there's Tweedledee, there's Tweedledumber. Rawling."

Rawling was sitting on a couch, entwined with a female, engaged in a deep-throated kiss. As the camera homed in on them, Rawling's head jerked up, and he mouthed the words "Fuck you!" at the unseen cameraman. The camera backed off. The girl availed of the opportunity to slip out of Rawling's grip. Rawling favoured long shaggy hair and wore a khaki army jacket, unbuttoned.

After a few more interior shots, the camera moved outside to the bonfire. Weiners and marshmallows roasted on long trimmed alder branches. Close-ups of individuals popping marshmallows into mouths and licking fingers and chomping wieners still spiked on the sticks. One guy removed his weiner, brought it to his lips, and sucked it in whole, and then expelled it, holding the tip in his teeth. He started clowning for the girls, thrusting his face into theirs, and sucking and blowing the weiner, to everyone's great merriment.

The next sequence took place in and around the sauna. The one interior shot was brief. A powerful light revealed tightly packed naked bodies and silent screams of protest and flapping hands from the girls. The exterior shots, lit only by the flickering flames of the bonfire, disclosed only a few suggestions of movements in the darkness.

The camera moved inside the cabin. Girls wrapped in large bath towels entered, shrieking, and headed for one of the two back bedrooms to change into their clothes. Boys apparently changed at the cars. The party resumed inside. Kennet recognized a girl with long red hair: Elsie Newman. The camera picked up Lanny

Fleming again, apparently at his insistence. He plucked at his shirt to display his badge. He thrust the badge at the camera, and it appeared on screen in extreme close up.

"That," said Kennet, "is a Korean war medal. Distinguished Service Star. I have a picture of it. It's the same kind of medal that Kyle Henderson said Vanderhorst picked up in the mine, at the muck pile under the chute. It may well be the same medal."

"Where is that medal now?"

"I have a lead on that. I'll follow it up tonight."

"Where are you going with this, Kennet?"

"I don't know – yet."

"Are the Flemings implicated in their brother's disappearance?"

"I don't know yet."

A few shots later, Rawling Fleming staggered into view, slugging back whiskey from a mickey. His khaki jacket swung open. Now there was a flash of metal from his shirt-front.

The next sequences showed a torch procession. Beacons of flame wove erratically across the head of the bay where figures were apparently wading through shallows. At the graveyard, makeshift torches poked at gravestones and wooden crosses in order to illuminate the inscriptions. Two or three clowns, their bodies hidden by gravestones, rose slowly until their heads perched on the top of the stones and grinned fiendishly for the camera. At one point a *danse macabre* occurred among the grave markers, torches aloft, the scene recorded dimly and incoherently by the camera.

The next shots showed a crowd milling in front of headlighted cars. There appeared to be a shoving match among the young men, Gron hovering above them head and shoulders. At one point Gron grabbed a figure in a bear hug and walked him back into the darkness between the cars. Three or four other guys crowded a lone belligerent backwards in the same direction.

"The Flemings are leaving," said Kennet.

"And you know this, how?" asked Robert.

"I talked to a participant in the melee the other day."

"What else haven't you told me?"

"Honestly, Robert, I'm just piecing things together. I don't know everything that's relevant, and that's not."

The video concluded with interior shots. Someone had produced a guitar, and a sing-song ensued. Some bon vivants had passed out on the furniture or the floor.

Robert rose to his feet. "We've got to talk to the Elders."

"I'll phone first." Gracie answered on the first ring. She assured Kennet that it was alright to come over. They'd heard he was in town. Yes, he could bring a friend.

They were seated, all four of them, at the kitchen table. Kennet accepted black coffee. Robert, his back to the living room, took milk in his. Gracie and Mrs. Elder took tea. The men helped themselves to biscuits.

"Maybe I'm getting my appetite back," said Robert.

"Can I fix you gentlemen a sandwich?"

Kennet said, "Thanks, Mrs. Elder. We'll manage. We have a forsenic report, Mrs. Elder, and you can guess why we're here."

"Yes, I knew when you came in. Such faces. But I've resigned myself." She glanced at Gracie. "We've resigned ourselves. Can you tell us how she died? And how she got there?"

"I believe it was an accident," said Kennet. "And she was buried with the best intentions."

Robert raised his voice. "That's news to me!"

"We haven't had a proper chance to talk, Robert. I'll catch you up later." He turned his attention to the women. "I'm still verifying the details. But Harold was there. When she died. She died with family in attendance."

Mrs. Elder nodded slowly.

"It was a vehicular accident. And Harold wasn't in his right mind. He was devastated."

Mrs. Elder said softly, "He was drinking, you mean." Her gaze wandered to the living room door and into the darkness beyond. "I always knew there was something wrong. Harold was never the same after that day – the day she left." Her gaze came back. "And I never trusted those postcards. Not really. They weren't Georgie. I know my own daughter."

Gracie let her fingers rest on her mother's hand.

Mrs. Elder looked directly at Kennet. "How did you know about Harold?"

"I've seen him, Mrs. Elder. In Thunder Bay. He told me. He's clean and sober. And he's a very sad man."

"We're all sad," she said. "Some," she added, "in more ways than one."

"Mrs. Elder, that graveyard, where Harold's grandfather is buried. You used to visit there, as a family. Georgie too."

She lifted her head and looked up into the corner where the ceiling met the wall. "Georgie hated it. The visits. She was afraid of the dead. She was spooked once, by a skull."

Nobody said anything.

She continued: "It was a Hallowe'en. Georgie was six then. Someone had found a real skull, a human skull, in shallow water, beneath a sand bank, in the lake. It had washed down from a grave, I guess. And that Hallowe'en, they put a candle inside it, and set it in the window to greet the trick-or-treaters. The Natives raised a real stink about it, next day. It would've been Native, of course, being where it was found. We're part Native, too, you know. Métis."

Kennet said, "Before she . . . she passed on, she said something to the effect of avoiding the graveyard. That's what Harold said. He took that as a death bed instruction. He was fulfilling her dying wish. But," Kennet continued, "when he sobered up, he was scared. He thought that no one would understand. And," he added, looking at Robert, "that the law wouldn't understand."

Robert offered his condolences. He had a question to ask, he said. Did the family want Georgie's remains? Of course, she said. He would see to it personally, that they were returned to

Beardmore. And yes, he said, he would arrange for the remains to be cremated, if that was the family's wish.

As they were leaving, Robert said, "Mrs. Elder, I'll also see to it that Georgie's personal effects are returned." She murmured her thanks.

Kennet said, "Those pictures you lent me, they're in that envelope. I'll be in touch. Good night. Good night, Gracie." Gracie nodded.

They had come in their respective vehicles. When they reached the street, Robert was fuming.

"So, that you solved the mystery of her demise, you didn't think important enough to tell me?"

"I haven't solved it – entirely. There are loose ends. There was another person involved. I'm going to see him now."

"Who is this person? And by the Lord Christ, no bullshit."

"His name is Mac Kueng. He and Harold were buddies."

"Kueng? The Beardmore Hermit? Let's go. Now. I want to interrogate his ass."

"And you'll strike out. He's a model of anti-sociality. At sight of you, he'll fill your britches with buckshot. Let me handle this, Robert. Please."

Robert threw up his arm and looked at his wristwatch. "Alright," he said, surprisingly agreeable. "You've done alright so far. And I've got to check with Halvorsen and Lockwood. Catch you later."

Chapter 32

. . . Tuesday evening

The sun was touching the bald hills when Kennet arrived at Kueng's property. The '82 Chevy pickup was parked in its usual place. He honked three times, and waited in his Sportage. After five minutes, he climbed down from the cab. He retrieved a white plastic grocery bag from under the front seat and proceeded down the path in the darkening woods.

Kueng's homestead was quiet. The windows dark. He rapped on the door. A raised voice informed him it was unlocked. He entered.

Mac Kueng sat at his oilcloth-covered table in the gloom. "I knew it was you," he said. "You know your way here, without help." He rose and fetched a gasoline lantern from the cupboard area. "I suppose you'll want light."

Kennet pulled out a chair and sat down, uninvited. The double-gong alarm clock ticked away on the table. After pumping up the lantern, Kueng struck a match and lit the mantle. A comfortable glow grew inside the cabin. Blankets had been thrown across the clothesline that ran across the room so that a

334

view of Kueng's bookshelves was effectively cut off. "I suppose," Kueng said, "you'll want a drink."

Kennet looked into the pale eyes in the dark sockets of the handsome face. "Just had coffee, thanks." He added, "At the Elders' residence."

Mac Kueng took his seat to face him. Kennet laid the white bag on the table. Kennet continued: "We have just informed Gracie and Edith that we have identified Georgie."

Kueng remained silent, staring at him. Kennet said, "You knew Georgie was missing." Kueng nodded almost imperceptibly.

"You knew where she was buried." Kueng remained immobile.

"I've talked to Harold, Mac. He told me everything, about that night, at the lake, and your jaunt in a rubber-tired skidder, up the Camp 72 Road."

"I figured it would be you," said Kueng, "who figured it out. You're an educated man. Not like the boneheads in uniform who police the drunks and the wife-beaters – at least that's what they did in my day, when I was a drinker."

"When did you quit, Mac?"

"After. You know."

"But not Harold. Harold had just begun."

"Yeah. After I got back from my vacation, he was a mess. And he was messing up his family. Little Gracie."

"And you treasure family, don't you, Mac." Kennet said this with an edge, with intent to wound.

"Yes. Yes, I do. I respect it. I don't understand it, never tried it myself, but I respect it. It's a mystery, to me, but there's something about it, something – oh, I don't know – I guess what you'd call . . . sacred."

Kennet was not prepared to grant Kueng any fine feelings. He leaned forward: "You were driving that night."

"Is that what Harold told you?"

"Harold was blotto. He didn't know the time of day. Or night. You ran down that girl."

Even in the pale yellow lamplight, Kennet could see the blood leaving Kueng's face. Kueng rose, his fists clenched, arms tense and trembling.

"I gave up profanity," he said, "when I went dry. But I'm saying this now: Fuck you!"

"You ran her down, and I have the proof. Harold thinks she was lying in the road, because that's the bullshit you fed him, but you struck her down, and you smashed her head in on your hood." Kennet rose and dug into the white plastic bag and removed the '53 Chevy name plate.

He held it out. The chrome gleamed sickly in the yellow light. "That's her blood there, Mac. That's her blood."

Kueng took a step back, unclenching his fists, raising them to his chest in a gesture to ward off evil.

"That's crazy! You're insane. That truck is in pieces – scattered to hell and gone."

"Then this is the proof from hell, Mac. I retrieved this from D & D Auto, Mac, and I have an affidavit, a sworn affidavit – " he felt the need to embellish – "from one of the owners, the one that bought your wreck, that this comes from your pickup on June 25th, 1983, the day after you killed her."

"Damn you! I did not kill her! She was alive after I – we hit her. She musta been spooked, ran into the road, we couldn't stop. It was an accident, I tell you. It was a goddamn accident."

Kennet lowered the name plate to the tabletop. Kueng's eyes followed it down. He said, "I can't believe you found that. After all this time."

Kennet sank into his chair. Kueng lifted the palms of his hands and ground them into his eye sockets. He took a step back and slumped against the cupboard. One hand dropped, the other moved up to his forehead and he pressed the heel of his hand there, as if plugging a leak.

"That was a good truck," he murmured.

"She was a good daughter!" said Kennet, savagely.

Kueng dropped his hand. "I didn't mean that. I meant – I was distraught, too. I watched her grow up."

"Harold raised her. Harold and Edith raised her. They had an investment – a huge emotional investment in that child. What did you have?"

Mac Kueng stared at him. Kennet thought he detected remorse there. But he wasn't prepared to grant him that noble emotion.

Kueng stuttered: "I . . . I –" He dropped his gaze to the floor.

"The police are in town."

"I heard," said Kueng dryly, still looking down. "Buddies of yours, I hear."

"Are you going to make things right?"

Kueng raised his head. "*Can* I make things right? A little late for that, isn't it?" The corner of his mouth twisted in the suggestion of a sneer.

"You know what I mean. They say confession is good for the soul."

Kueng gave a short laugh, more like a bark: "My soul . . . my soul –"

Kennet raised his voice. "Cut the crap, Mac! Are you going to man up?"

Mac Kueng pulled back his shoulders. He looked directly into Kennet's eyes. "I'll do," he said, "what a man does. I'll do . . . the right thing. You have no right to talk to me like that."

"I'm going back to the motel now. Same room I had before. The cops will be there, seven a.m. sharp. I'll expect you. Even give you coffee."

"I'll do the right thing. That's a promise." He added: "Tell me, are those Flemings going down for anything? Anything at all? A dirty licence plate? Looking cross-eyed at a cop?"

"There's an investigation – multiple inquiries. Several crimes to solve. It looks like some dirt will cling to them." Kennet replaced the name plate in the plastic bag. Mac Kueng's eyes followed his movements.

Kueng said sarcastically, "Well, that's some comfort then. Not just hard-working taxpayers being harassed. That's progress."

Kennet swung by The Hook'n Bullet, but it was closed up. The sun had dropped behind the hills. There was no one back at the room. He sent Susan an e-mail to let her know where he was. He assumed a meditative posture on the floor. "Diane," he murmured. "Miss you. We all miss you." After a moment: "Mom. We all miss you." The image of a girl sprawled at the bottom of a flight of stairs sprang into consciousness. "Liliana," he said softly, "good night. Good night. May choirs of angels sing thee to thy rest." He focused on clearing his mind, but images persisted. "You too, Georgiana. Sweet dreams. And Donny. Alfie. Alfred. Alfred, you died in the line of duty, no finer death, according to the ancients." He emptied his mind.

When the rap came on the door, he was at peace. It was a sharp, imperious rap. He returned to the real world immediately and sang out, "Coming!" He rose from his cross-legged position without aid of his hands. Lockwood, he thought. He has no key.

He swung the door open. Past his red Sportage a figure was standing, out in the dimly-lit parking lot, its back to him, a hood pulled over its head. A dark-hooded figure, like the grim reaper. Kennet stepped forward. As his leg swung over the doorsill, he sensed a movement to his left. Instinctively he leaned back. For that reason his skull did not crack wide open.

When he opened his eyes, his head was exploding. Pieces going everywhere. A voice was buzzing over him. He was flat on his back. He raised his hands to either side of his head. His skull was intact. Yet pieces were churning inside, waves of pain, fragments grinding one another. He pressed his hands together, to hold his skull together.

"Mr. Forbes!"

There was someone there. Someone in a black bomber jacket. Hoodless. A short-furred collar. An insignia on the right chest. A crown. Royalty was calling. Royalty was calling on him! He focused his eyes on the face.

"Mr. Forbes! Should I call the ambulance? No, don't move! Just rest." Saxon Fleming was kneeling over him. "Just a minute! Don't move." Saxon disappeared. A moment later he was raising his head, gently, and inserting a pillow beneath it. "Just lie back. You've been hurt. Took a blow to the forehead."

Red waves forced his eyes closed. He felt nauseous. Pain. Incredible pain. Throbbing. He moved a hand to his forehead. Agony.

"Don't touch!" said Saxon. "You're developing a goose egg. A fine, fine goose egg. No skin broken."

Kennet groaned and opened his eyes. Saxon was grinning.

"Make a fine omelet in the morning, sir!"

Kennet pushed the words out: "What happened?"

"I found you like this. I swung by. You said you'd be here."

"You saw nothing?" He closed his eyes again.

Saxon said nothing.

"Help me," said Kennet. He opened his eyes. "Help me sit up."

By degrees Saxon assisted him over to a padded chair, where Kennet leaned his head back, both hands pressing his skull. Saxon fussed in the kitchen area for a while, there was a chopping sound, and he returned with a tea towel wrapped around crushed ice.

Kennet thanked him. "I've got painkillers," he said, "in the side pocket, flight bag. Gimme three or four."

As Kennet nursed his injury, waiting for the analgesic to take effect, Saxon sat in another chair, staring at his feet. He had closed the outer door. After a long while he said something.

Kennet responded, "Eh?" He was squeezing his eyes shut.

"I'm taking her with me, when I leave. My mother."

"That's nice." The pain in his head had abated to barely tolerable proportions.

"That's why I came back."

"Eh?"

"That's my only family now. My mother."

"Okay."

"As far as I'm concerned, the rest can rot in hell." Kennet opened his eyes and looked across at Saxon. The black hair, the black leather jacket with the crest of the Princess Pats, the crisp-looking blue jeans sheathing the long legs, the western-style boots – Kennet took it all in. But it was the eyes that held him. The fury in Saxon's eyes.

Saxon continued: "I grew up without a father. I'm not complaining, mind you. But those brothers – Lanny, Storm – they made it hell for me. Rawl was rough, God knows, but he stuck up for me when the brothers from hell were on the point of doing me serious injury. I got my education and I left. But it always bothered me that I had to leave Mother behind. And when I came back last year, there was that Ritchie. Supposedly a cousin. And my mother was a slave to them – washing, ironing, cooking, keeping house, like always. This time," he said, leaning forward, "she's leaving with me."

"Okay." Kennet kept his eyes on him, still holding his skull.

"That boy that was beat up, in this room. He gonna be alright?"

"Yeah. His jaws're wired, and he can't talk, but he's recovering."

"He was a professor at the university?"

"A grad student. Might be professor some day. He could've been killed. Or had his brains addled. Permanently."

"I respect education. If I'd gone to college, I'd be an officer today. You can help me."

"Go to college?" Kennet was not sure he was hearing right. The throbbing had declined to manageable levels.

"Naw. Too late for me. I'll always be a grunt. Expendable."

"I have the highest respect for grunts. I've seen them operate, close up. You got a stripe?"

"Yeh. One."

"Corporal. Salt of the earth."

Saxon nodded slowly, but did not appear convinced. He said, "Storm's in jail another four months. With Lanny and Ritchie out of the way, I could put Mother on the bus. I've got a little house rented near the Edmonton base. She'd be so happy there. Dad's sister, my aunt, she's close by. And nieces and nephews, grand-nieces and -nephews."

"And Rawling?"

"I can handle Rawl. And it'll do him good to cut the apron strings. Maybe make a man outa him, before he collects the old age security."

"Sounds like a plan. But what can I do?"

"If the police was to call around the house tomorrow morning, and look at the work bench in the garage, they'd find a bat. A baseball bat. In plain sight. That's important, isn't it?"

Kennet said slowly, "I suppose so."

"And the police have got people who can find things, traces, on weapons used in crimes?"

"That bat is there now, on the bench?"

"It will be, tomorrow morning."

Kennet removed one hand from his skull. "Rawling has an alibi for the Henderson assault."

"I know. And so do I. Thanks in part to you." Saxon stared steadily at Kennet. "Tell me, how did you get that eye?"

"This?" Kennet gestured toward his right eye. "Panjawai District, August 23rd, '06. With "D" Company of the PPCLI."

"An I.E.D.?"

"Yes. An explosive device, under the floor of our LAV. I was sitting in the rear, driver's side, when the burst came up between me and the corporal on my right. We both got lucky. He just broke his arm."

Saxon reached into a pocket inside his jacket and stood up. He walked over to Kennet, holding out something in his hand. "You were interested in this."

It was the Korean medal.

Kennet turned it over in his hands. It had been polished recently. It gleamed dully in the lamplight.

"Where did this come from?"

"It was Father's. That's what Rawl says. It had one point bent, and an RF scratched on the back."

Kennet turned it over. There was the scratch. "When did it turn up?"

"I've never seen it before. But Rawl told me about it. Told me, as kids, he and my brothers used to wear it, when Father wasn't looking. It just turned up recently."

"How?"

"He didn't say."

After Saxon Fleming left, Kennet lay on the bed in the main room. He put the medal on the side table. Saxon had entrusted it to him. He replaced the ice in the tea towel twice. He had spread a bath towel over the pillow to catch the drips. Toward midnight both Lockwood and Robert Kenilworth came in. With barely a glance at him, Lockwood strode immediately to the back room. Robert sank into the chair that Saxon had been sitting in, and listened silently, grimly, as Kennet explained the tea towel pressed to his forehead. They could hear the shower running in the bathroom.

Finally Robert said quietly, concern in his voice, "Jeez, Kennet, I leave you for a coupla hours and –"

"There's more." Kennet explained about Saxon's invitation to the Fleming property in the morning.

"And these same guys did *this* to you?" Robert's voice was rising.

"Probably." Kennet sat up and moved over to the chair, tossing the tea towel into the sink. "But what's important, is to nail them for the Henderson assault. And, we have an opportunity here."

"What's that?"

"To search for a .303 rifle."

"Ah."

"And this may be the motive for the assault on Henderson." Kennet handed him the Korean medal. "Belonged to Rolfe Fleming, the old man. Just turned up recently in the Fleming family." Kennet explained how he had acquired it.

Robert weighed the object in the palm of his hand, and smiled thinly. "A medal made of metal. Interviewing can be a tricky business."

"You haven't told me what you've found."

Robert Kenilworth described the gruesome remains they had recovered from the ore chute. The body was wonderfully intact, said Robert. How could that be? After a quarter century?

Kennet said, "You heard of the Edmund Fitzgerald?"

"Everyone's heard of that – the freighter that sank in a storm in Lake Superior. The Gordon Lightfoot song? All hands lost."

"That was 1975, Robert. People have dived on it, in submersibles. There've been injunctions to protect the site, as a graveyard. But no one ever saw a body. Until 1994."

"I never heard that."

"There is film footage, which I've seen, of a body, caught in a whirlpool current, at the bottom of the sea, going round and round. There's been no attempt to recover it, and no one's ever seen it again."

"How could that body have remained intact?"

"Superior is the coldest lake in the world, outside the polar regions. It preserves everything. Even, apparently, drowned sailors."

"And those wooden timbers in the mine, there're like new. Not a sign of rot."

"Precisely. So exactly what did you recover?"

Robert explained that Hal and Andrew, the scene-of-crime officers, had photographed the body and the scene, and that the idents, when they had arrived, had conducted their investigation. The face was bloated, useless for identification. They had managed to transfer the remains into a body bag although the limbs were disarticulating. Boots they had recovered separately, and they were in the trunk of Robert's car. Also a loose belt buckle. And from the hip pocket of the jeans, a sodden wallet. The papers inside – cards, bills – were seriously deteriorated and indecipherable without lab work.

"Where's everyone now?"

Jillian and Kelly and Mueller had returned to Geraldton. The ambulance was transporting the body bag to Thunder Bay, and the idents team were following in their vehicle. In the morning, said Robert, he would show the items to Mrs. Fleming.

"Not too early, though. We'll have a visitor in the morning. Seven o'clock."

"Oh. You paid the Hermit a visit, didn't you."

"Let me back up a little." Kennet told him of spotting Harold Elder on campus the day before, as he inquired after his daughter's remains, and of tracking him across the city to his house on Vickers St. North.

"Good God, Kennet! You're like that actor, Paul Gross, he played that Mountie in that TV series, *Straight South*, or *Due South*, was it? He could track a car across Chicago when the trail was a day old! All you're missing is the wolf companion."

"Elementary, my dear Watson. Now, Elder's a recovering drunk. In the twelve-step program. He told me a story." Kennet described Harold's version of events. And then he explained how, earlier that morning, he had tracked down the name plate from Mac Kueng's '53 Chevy truck.

"I confronted Kueng tonight, and I held that blood-caked name plate under Kueng's nose, and he admitted to running down

Georgiana Elder the night of that party. He claims it was an accident, and I don't see it happening any other way. He'll report here in the morning."

"'Blood-caked plate'?"

"I may have exaggerated. If it comes to that, you may find trace evidence on it."

"And Kueng disposed of the body?"

Kennet explained that Kueng did not deny it. "I'll leave it to your detectives to elicit the finer details. Harold Elder *is* accessory after the fact, but I trust the quality of your mercy is not strained."

"Spare me the preaching, Kennet. And get the hell out of my bedroom. I'm beat."

Chapter 33

Wednesday, August 19th . . .

Inspector Robert Kenilworth of the Ontario Provincial Police stood on the creaky rotting boards of the Fleming porch and rapped on the door. Dirty white paint was peeling from the wooden door and door frame.

Robert had given Kennet a poke in the shoulder that morning to wake him up. It was 6:47 when he emerged from the bathroom. He dressed in casual clothes. Coffee was on. Lockworth was still snoring away, on his back, in an unconscious re-creation of the pose of the injured Henderson whom the maid had found a week ago.

Mac Kueng had not appeared by 7 o'clock, nor by 7:15. At 7:30 they had gone for breakfast, waking up Lockwood before they left. Alice said she had not seen Kueng yet – very unusual.

Kennet felt remarkably good as he stood in the cinder driveway beside D.C.s Armitage and Mueller. A small rain during the night had freshened the landscape. The sun glowed behind a light overcast. He noticed his head injury only when he inadvertently touched it or something brushed against it. Out on the street stood a black Tahoe , Robert's Chrysler, and a cruiser with two officers lolling in it.

When the door opened, a stooped woman, her cherubic face framed by silver hair, stood there with her mouth in an O. Kenilworth introduced himself, and invited himself in, gesturing for Kennet to follow. Rawling sat at the table in the cramped kitchen, nursing a coffee. The shabby kitchen was spotless.

Rawling's face registered shock. When he saw Kennet, his face twisted in fury.

Mrs. Fleming smiled angelically at her son. "Rawling, we've got company! Stand up, now." She might have been speaking to a seven-year-old.

Rawling struggled to his feet. "Mother!" he blurted. "They got no business in this house!"

"This is my house," said Mrs. Fleming, setting her jaw firmly, "and I rarely get company. So behave."

Rawling swept his coffee cup up and stalked from the kitchen. Mrs. Fleming invited Robert and Kennet to sit. She offered coffee. Both men declined. She remarked on the goose egg on Kennet's forehead, and asked if he needed some gauze and tape. Kennet declined, with thanks.

Robert maintained his grave expression. "Mrs. Fleming, we have some awkward questions to ask."

She sat down in Rawling's vacated chair and nodded. She said softly, barely audibly, "Trouble again?"

"Does this ring a bell?" Robert withdrew a transparent evidence bag from his jacket side pocket and handed it over. She gazed dumbly at the dark-coloured, nondescript wallet. She shook her head.

"Does this?" He passed over another bag with a decorative oversized belt buckle. It depicted a rider on a bucking bronco. Mrs. Fleming's eyes widened.

"Let me see that!" Rawling had reappeared in the doorway, propping himself up with an arm on the jamb. Robert handed the bag to him.

Rawling fingered it. "I've got one. Exactly like it. So has Lanny. And Storm. Where'd you get this?"

Robert replied, "In due time, I'll tell you. First, tell me how you got yours."

Rawling handed the bag back. "Father. Father gave us all one. When we graduated. Well, Lanny and me never quite got there, but when we started working for a living, he gave us one. Did you get this from Storm?"

Robert ignored the query. "Thank you. Now let me fetch something." He got up and stepped outside, returning immediately with a pair of warped cowboy boots. Mrs. Fleming sat there with tears in her eyes.

"These mean anything?" Rawling scowled. Mrs. Fleming said nothing. "Okay. Mrs. Fleming, let me ask you. When was the last time the lock on this door was changed?" Robert held the front door open.

Rawling responded: "It's never been changed. In my lifetime."

Robert whipped out a rubber glove and pulled it over his right hand. "Alright. Let's do an experiment." He retrieved the bag with the wallet. Looking at Kennet, he said, "Lock the door behind me." He stepped out, taking the wallet, and leaving the boots on the table. Kennet turned the brass handle so that the bolt shot home.

Someone came thumping down a staircase which was out of sight. Rawling glared at Kennet. "What the f—" Rawling caught himself. "What are *you* doing here?"

"I'm a witness." Lanny Fleming in deshabille had moved up behind Rawling.

"To what?" Someone else was tumbling down the stairs. That person landed with a thud.

"In due time."

There was a scatching at the door, the lock clicked, and Robert pushed the door open. His begloved hand grasped a key in the lock. Everyone looked disbelievingly at the door. Kennet noted rivulets of tears from Mrs. Fleming. Ritchie's head popped up over the heads of Rawling and Lanny.

Robert removed the key, shut the door, and took a seat again. "I'm sorry, Mrs. Fleming," he said.

"What's going on?" demanded Ritchie.

"Yeah," said Lanny. "What's happening? What's *he* doin' here?"

"He's a witness," said Rawling, sarcastically. Robert was tucking the key into the change pocket of the wallet.

"To what? A growth spurt on his forehead?" Lanny gave a short, ruthless laugh.

Robert looked at the three men standing in the doorway. "Gentlemen. Can't you see this woman? Can't you see she's distressed?" He stowed the wallet in the evidence bag and laid it on the table. He peeled off the glove.

Rawling stepped quickly forward and looked into his mother's face. "Mother! What's the matter? What have they done to you? By God –!"

"Calm down!" said Robert, firmly. "Maybe it's something you've done."

Rawling reared back. An expression of fright flashed across Lanny's face. Ritchie simply scowled.

Rawling shouted, "What the hell d'yuh mean by that?"

"Calm down," repeated Robert. He continued speaking, slowly and deliberately. He explained that the police had been recovering a body from the old workings of the Con Empire mine. That the remains had been taken to Thunder Bay in the middle of the night for analysis by the OPP lab.

Rawling was more restrained but still truculent: "What's that got to do with us?"

"We believe the body has been lying there for twenty-six years," said Robert.

Rawling pulled a chair back from the table and sank into it. Lanny said rudely, "Again, what's that got to do with us?"

"All these items," said Robert, gesturing to the tabletop, "came with the body."

Rawling turned his head slowly, moving his eyes from the tabletop to focus on Lanny's face. Lanny looked mean and uncomprehending.

Rawling said slowly, "It's Donny." Lanny flicked his eyes to Rawling, still uncomprehending. Rawling stabbed four fingers at the recovered evidence: "*That* is Donny!" Light dawned in Lanny's eyes.

Ritchie said impatiently, "Will someone tell me what's going on?"

Everyone ignored him. Rawling reached out his left hand to touch the elderly woman's shoulder. "Mother," he said, and dropped his hand.

"Well, fuck," said Lanny.

Rawling sprang to his feet, his face inches from Lanny's. "Watch your mouth!"

Lanny held up his hand, palm outward. "Okay, okay."

Rawling turned to Robert. "We thought he'd run away! That he couldn't take –" He clamped his jaws shut.

"What?" said Robert softly. "The abuse?" Rawling stood there, lips pressed. "Never mind," Robert continued. "We're here for another reason. Mrs. Fleming, let me offer you our sincerest condolences." The woman stared into the distance, her cheeks wet.

"We need to confirm the body's identity. We want to take swabs, for DNA purposes, to confirm the familial relationship." Mrs. Fleming did not move. Robert shifted his attention to Rawling. "How about you first?"

"Sure. What the h – heck," he finished, lamely.

"If you'll step outside, the detective constables will take a swab."

Lanny and Ritchie had retreated to another part of the house, probably the living room. Their muffled voices drifted into the kitchen. Rawling soon returned, and hollered to his brother to get the heck out there.

Lanny stalked out the door. When he returned, he was followed by D.C. Armitage. She said, "Mrs. Fleming, may I?" The woman nodded silently. Kelly instructed her gently to open her mouth. She inserted the swab, patted her inside cheek, and stored the wand in a protective tube.

Robert said, "What about your other son, Mrs. Fleming? Saxon?"

"I heard him leaving this morning," said Rawling. "'Bout six. He often takes a run early, out to the lake."

Robert said, "Mrs. Fleming, do you have any weapons in the house? Guns?"

Rawling interrupted. "We keep our rifles outside. In the truck. Used to, anyway." He glared at Kennet.

"Nothing in the house?" Robert still addressed the woman.

"Well," said Rawling. "There's Father's old rifle. Never been fired since he – he passed."

"May we look around, Mrs. Fleming?" She nodded, and weakly spoke her consent.

"I don't understand," said Rawling. "Was Donny – was he shot?"

"Still underdetermined," said Robert. "Just routine, that's all. Detective Armitage, would you ask Detective Mueller to come in? You know what to do next."

Mueller came in the door, a swagger to his walk. He was pulling on rubber gloves. Rawling said, "I'll show you."

Mueller responded, "You do that."

Kennet rose and stepped out on the rickety porch. He took a deep breath of the cool air. He saw Kelly coming from the workshop with a baseball bat in a large transparent evidence bag. She was grinning. "Right where you said it would be," she said.

"Well, where Saxon said it would be." Kennet stepped down to the cinder driveway as Kelly walked past, headed for the police truck parked on the road.

Mueller and Rawling emerged from the house. Mueller held a rifle case. Lanny and Ritchie poured out the door, almost tipping Mueller down the porch stairs.

Lanny hollered, "What's she got there?" He waved his arm wildly at Kelly Armitage's back. Mueller was descending the stairs, followed by Rawling.

Lanny was still yelling. "She can't do that! She can't just walk in here and –"

Robert said in his ear, "Yes, she can." Robert had stepped out of the house right behind Lanny. Lanny scrambled down the steps as though pushed, followed by Ritchie. Robert continued: "We have your mother's permission to search the premises. Mrs. Fleming is the registered owner of this property."

Lanny whirled to face the inspector. The blood had left his face. He said with barely contained fury, "*I* live here! This is our home. Where's your warrant? Let's see your warrant. Else, you and your dogs get the fuck off this property!"

Robert gazed down at him unperturbed. "We have the owner's permission."

Mueller had unzipped the case and lifted out the rifle. Rawling said quietly to Lanny, "Can it."

Lanny snapped back: "*You* can it!"

"Lanny," said Rawling evenly, "we have something to deal with a little more serious than your bat. Donny is dead."

"I had that since I was a kid!"

Robert chimed in, "So that's your bat?"

Lanny snarled. "Fucken right!"

Mueller had been fussing with the rifle, a .303 Lee-Enfield, as Kennet looked on. He had checked the breech and put his eye to the muzzle. He looked over to Robert.

"My guess is, sir, this hasn't been fired since the Korean War."

352

"Father used it for hunting," said Rawling. "He died in '86. No one's used it since. The last time he hunted, that must've been ten years before he passed. It was his gun. No one else touched it."

Mueller addressed Robert: "I'd believe that, sir."

"Nevertheless," said Robert, "we'll let the lab look at it."

Lanny said bitterly, "So now we shot our brother, did we?"

"We don't know that he was shot," said Robert. "Maybe someone cracked his skull."

Lanny's head jerked up. He looked thoughtful. He mumbled to no one in particular: "Son of a bitch."

"One more thing," said Robert, descending the steps and reaching into an inside jacket pocket. "You recognize this?"

He held out the Korean medal enclosed in an evidence bag. Rawling snatched at it. "Let me see that!"

Robert pinched the bag so that both he and Rawling were straining for possession of it. "Take it easy," said Robert.

Rawling bent over to peer at it. "Where'd you get this?" he demanded. "Turn it over." Robert allowed him to turn the bag over to examine the obverse. "That's ours! That's my father's service medal. What are you doing with it?"

"The question is," said Robert, calmly, "what were you doing with it?"

Rawling released his grip on the bag, reluctantly. "I lent it to Saxon. It's not his to give away."

"And where did you get it?"

"I —" he began. "We've always had it. It's a family keepsake." He could not prevent his eyes from flicking toward Lanny. Lanny's face remained immobile. He seemed to be scarcely breathing.

"But it went missing for a while, didn't it?"

"Yeah? Well, it turned up."

"After twenty-six years?"

Rawling's face blanched. "What the hell are you saying? Are you saying that Donny – that we – that someone –" Rawling sputtered into silence.

"I simply want to know the circumstances under which this item turned up. After twenty-six years."

Rawling looked desperately at his brother. "Lanny, for God's sake. Tell him how you found it. What you told me."

Lanny's face remained impassive. He spoke slowly. "I found it in the workshop. I was working on my bike. A nut fell off, and rolled under the bench. Lots of crap under there. When I was scrounging around, I found it."

Robert held a straight face. "You found it," he said, "when your nut fell off? That's your story?"

Kelly Armitage had returned to join the group assembled in the yard. Blood crept into Lanny's cheeks. "It's the truth!" he blurted.

"Show me."

"Eh?"

"Show me your nut."

Lanny's face reddened. His voice rose. "Are you jerking me around?"

Robert's voice hardened. "Not around and certainly not off. Now show me. Corroborate your story."

Lanny led the way to the workshop, his shoulders stiff. Everyone followed but Mueller, who retired to the police truck with the encased rifle. Lanny grabbed his trail bike by the handlebars, and turning to face the group, raised the front end as though showing off a thoroughbred. "This is my bike!"

"So," said Robert, "show me. Show me the nut."

Lanny glanced down uncertainly, his eyes sweeping the length of the machine. He settled for an area in front of the seat, near the gas tank. "Here," he said. He jabbed his finger at a nut. "This is stupid."

Robert bent down to examine the nut. "Yes. Something *is* stupid. This nut is frozen."

"Eh?"

"It's coated with rust."

Lanny's voice rose in exasperation. "Well, maybe it was another one!"

"Show me."

Lanny pointed to another nut. Again Robert leaned in.

"This one is dirty. Hasn't been touched in ages."

"Well, shit!" said Lanny. "Maybe it was somewhere's else."

"Show me."

"Find it yourself! I ain't your lapdog!"

"I will, then. I'm impounding this machine."

"What? You can't do that!"

"You just gave me permission. Besides, your mother has jurisdiction over this entire property, and I have her permission."

Kennet followed the police officers as they vacated the property. Kelly Armitage was wheeling the trail bike. Only Rawling trailed behind. Lanny and Ritchie had hung back in the workshop and appeared to be arguing.

As he passed the fence line, Kennet heard Rawling speak in an undertone.

"Hey, you."

Kennet stopped and faced about. Rawling came up close and stopped, hands on hips. "You found him, didn't you."

"Excuse me?"

"Donny. You found him." Pain flickered across his face. "You can't think," he said, "I had anything to do with it."

"No," said Kennet. "I don't think that. I think, if you could have, you would've protected him. That's what I think."

"Thank you for that." It was obvious that Rawling was making an effort to be civil. His eyes flicked up to Kennet's forehead. "And I'm not responsible for that."

"I believe you. It's not your style."

"Eh?"

"You would've hit me between the eyes, head on."

Rawling gave a quick smile. "You're right. I would've been facing you. I don't blindside a guy."

"Unless he happens to turn his head." Kennet flashed a smile in return.

"Well," Rawling drawled, "that's his lookout then. That's a failure to pay attention."

Chapter 34

. . . Wednesday morning

"He isn't here." Kennet addressed Robert Kenilworth. Robert had pulled up behind the Sportage and joined Kennet on the bush road.

"How do you know? Maybe he's hiding."

"His truck is gone. No one else would touch it."

"Maybe we should check anyway."

A police cruiser pulled up behind the Chrysler.

"You have no reasonable grounds to search his property."

Robert said wryly, "You sound like a judge."

"Look. I'll find him. He'll come in. He's a man of his word. What I'd really like to do now, is examine what the detectives found in the records of the Crown Resources office."

Robert agreed that Kennet could peruse whatever D.C. Armitage and Staff-Sergeant Halvorsen had uncovered. He would phone Jillian Halvorsen and get the okay for Kennet. Meanwhile he would return to the city and monitor the autopsy on the body recovered from the mine. He strolled over to the cruiser and, as Kennet listened with one ear, advised the officers to be on the lookout for Mac Kueng, but to approach with caution.

At Jellicoe, Kennet stopped at the Trading Post to pick up a bottle of water. The proprietor, a tall man, dark hair streaked with silver, and gray stubble complemented with a raggedy moustache, said business was slow that season. Tourists weren't coming north on account of the recession, he said. If it weren't for the few mining people and the occasional forest worker who dropped in, he'd be spending the summer at his cabin, fishing.

Where was his cabin? asked Kennet.

Did he know this country?

Used to, said Kennet.

Onaman Lake.

Spectacular fishing, said Kennet.

Not any more. Ruined by the commercial fishers, and the sledders. No lake was safe from the hundreds of sledders nowadays. They had come from a thousand miles away. He damned them to hell.

Before the turn-off to Geraldton, Kennet turned into the OPP detachment office. A few puffy cumulus drifted in the blue vault.

He negotiated the tiny foyer and tiny lobby and addressed a woman behind a glass-wall barrier. Yes, the Staff-Sergeant was expecting him. Just a moment, please.

Jillian came from the inner sanctum and opened the solid metal door into the lobby. She greeted him warmly, and they retired to her office, which overlooked the parking lot where Kennet had left the Sportage.

When Kennet was seated, she gestured to her own forehead. "I feel guilty about that. You're so involved in this – in *these* investigations, we should've given you better protection."

"Water under the bridge. I've moved on. Inspector Robert told you what I would like?"

"Yes, yes. Of course. Let's get to it." She pushed a file folder across her desk. "There are some print-outs in here, and some files on this stick." She held up a computer memory stick.

The folder held a couple dozen documents, some with multiple pages. Kennet sifted through them. There was a computer-generated longtitudinal section of the Continental Empire mine's underground workings, oriented east-west. The main shaft descended to 2,460 feet, or 750 metres. Every hundred and fifty feet down, a drift stretched horizontally, a few hundred metres to the west of the shaft, and longer distances to the east. Above and below each drift, colour-coded areas identified stopes, areas from which ore had been removed. On the first level, 150 feet or 45 metres from surface, Kennet thought he could identify the stope from which the body had been recovered. A narrow shaft of colour extended to the surface.

Other documents described the de-watering of the mine in 1979 for a small high-grading operation between the first and second levels. Sometime in 1980 or '81, underground operations had been suspended, and also, presumably, the de-watering process. The old workings would have filled again. By 1981 another company had entered the picture and focused on the aboveground ore piles and waste dumps left over from operations in the 1930s and '40s. A mill had been constructed on site to process the rock.

By 1982 the mill was in full swing, but government ministries had mandated the clean-up and security of the property, addressing open adits, areas of subsidence (collapses of stopes that left depressions on surface), manways (narrow shafts to surface with ladders to provide emergency escape routes for underground workers), and industrial waste such as scrap metal and explosives containers. The documents explained some terms that a layman or an underpaid bureaucrat would have had difficulty with.

There were reports on the geology of the property, on rock types and structures and mineral occurrences and gold valuations, most of which Kennet skipped over as so much gobbledegook.

Kennet looked up. "I need more of the day-to-day detail," he said.

Jillian inserted the memory stick into her computer and brought up the files on screen. "There's a lot of detail here, but I didn't know what I was looking for. Okay. You sit here. I have to stay in the room, so that I can vouch that you did not breach the secure files of the OPP." She smiled disarmingly.

Kennet scrolled through the menu. They consisted primarily of PDF files – images of documents – of a company called Mining Teck Ltd. There were plans for the mill, specifications, power consumption, details about the construction of a settling pond, daily ore runs through the mill, metal recoveries, time sheets of mill workers, time sheets of casual labourers . . . Kennet clicked on a list for 1983.

He scrolled down to June of '83. There were three names listed, one of which looked familiar: D.R. Fleming. Another name cropped up on different days of the week: M. C. Kueng. All the workers put in a five-day week, except Kueng. Kueng had worked one day a week, sometimes two days. Then on June 27th, which had been a Monday, another name had been added: C. C. St. Clair. St. Clair had also worked five days a week, Monday to Friday. Fleming had worked only three days that week, and then disappeared from the roll.

Kennet scrolled down to July. C. C. St. Clair and the others continued to draw pay. Except, after the second week of July, Kueng dropped off the roll. Well, Mac *had* gone "on vacation".

"May I print off a couple of pages?" asked Kennet.

"Certainly. What have you found?"

"I believe I've found Donny Fleming's record of employment, in June of '83. And possibly a lead. I'd like to follow it up."

"Well," said Staff-Sergeant Jillian, "Robert has let you run with the bit in your teeth, so who am I to challenge success? But I'll keep copies too, if you don't mind."

When Kennet passed the Jellicoe Trading Post, he noted a truck camper taking on gas at the pumps, and a white Ford F-150 pickup with the name Buffalo Grass on the door.

As he crossed the railway track, he put his foot down again. His mind raced along with his engine. So much had happened in twenty-four hours. So much information to process. He needed to govern his runaway thoughts. When he spotted the railway bridge over the Blackwater on his left, he braked suddenly, and turned into the track that led to the ghost town of Nezah.

Wes Carlson's Silverado sat outside his door. Kennet steered toward the river until he ran out of trail. He turned the engine off. A footpath melted into the green forest. It descended the high ground until it was paralleling the river a few metres away, beyond a tangle of alders and tree trunks. He realized he had been hearing the rapids long before he saw them. A faint side trail led to the river bank, and he emerged at a cascade of dark, white-streaked water.

The river, just a few canoe-lengths across, descended in a series of low-rise steps. The water was low. He removed his shoes and socks and found a shelf that allowed him to wade out to mid stream, the water calf-deep in places. In front of him, the main stream hurried by, the bottom hidden by the dark flood. He stopped and reached down. With his hands he scooped up the cool clear liquid and dashed it over his head – his hair, his face, his neck. He paused there, eyes closed, and let the sun's heat dry him.

After a while he returned to the river bank and found a large boulder to sit on, feet immersed in water. Eyes closed, he let the river wash away the tangle of thoughts.

When he returned to the Sportage, he found a note tucked under the windshield wiper. It read: *Water's boiled.*

As he approached the chocolate house, the door opened. Carlson stepped into the doorway and grinned: "You're getting to be a regular."

"Eh?"

"Two visits in one week. To what do I owe the pleasure?"

As Kennet stepped into the shady, cool interior, he said, "Just passing by. Thought I'd check out your waterfalls."

Two mugs had been set out on the table. "No one owns a waterfall," Carlson said, "though the folks at Ontario Hydro pretend to. They'd soon discover that, if they tried to put a leash on it." He glanced at Kennet's forehead. "You didn't knock your noggin on a mining timber, did you?"

"Nothing like that."

Sipping his coffee, Kennet glanced around. Several cardboard boxes sat scattered around the floor, some open to reveal books. There were hundreds of books.

Kennet looked across at Carlson. "Starting a library?"

Carlson laughed. "I could, couldn't I. No, these were donated. I'm going to pick them over, and pass them on. Maybe to the fly-in communities up north. You know – the reserves, like Fort Hope and Marten Falls. I started reading this one."

From the seat of an empty chair next to him, he plucked a volume and slid it across the table. It was Ayn Rand's *Atlas Shrugged*.

"Ever read it? That bloke, Hank Rearden, he's got talent and brains and good looks. He could be me." Carlson's eyes glinted with amusement. "And he doesn't suffer fools." He tapped the book cover. "Well, that's where we part company. I'm tolerant. Too tolerant for my own good."

Kennet asked a few questions, and then left, thanking him for coffee.

Back in Beardmore, he observed the helicopter dropping down into the sports field with the dream-catcher apparatus. He stopped by St. Clair's Hardware. There was no customer in the store. Gerald St. Clair made his way from the back, greeting him warmly.

"Gerry, here's one cassette I borrowed. I have another favour to ask. How can I reach Cameron?"

"Right now?"

"Yes."

Gerry rummaged in a drawer under the counter and came up with a business card. "I'll write his home number on the back," he said.

"One more thing, Gerry. The year he graduated, did Cameron work at the old Con Empire that summer?"

"As a matter of fact, he did. On surface, mind you. He even took his camera to work. No wonder he turned professional."

When Kennet exited the store, he walked across the street to the offices of Ombabika Bay First Nation. He told the girl at the desk he wanted to see the chief.

"Chief isn't here," said a voice behind him. A slim Aboriginal with stylish black hair was lounging on the leather couch. He was, he said, the economic development officer. Kennet explained that he wished to report a desecrated cemetery. By whom? asked the young man.

"The Beardmore Fire."

"So. Mother Nature is the desecrator, eh? Where?"

Kennet described the location. The young man said to wait a minute. He left, and returned with an elder, a distinguished-looking man with gray hair streaked with black. Charlie Lesperance, he introduced himself. Was there anything left there?

"I found a partial headstone. The name of A. Fraser. Died 1937."

"Alexander. Alex. David's grandfather. David Elder. And Harold's. Did you report it?"

"Just to you."

"We'll take care of it."

"Sure."

"*We*'ll take care of it."

"Sure. That's all I wanted."

When Kennet walked into his room at the motel, the beds were made. He sat down and looked over the card carefully. *Cameron C. St. Clair*, it read. *CCL Studios. Cinematography and*

Production Services. There was a New York address, and two phone numbers. He decided to try the cell phone.

A male voice answered immediately: "Cameron St. Clair. Who is this?"

Kennet explained that he'd just finished talking to his father, that he taught at TBU, and that he had been looking into the death of a colleague in Beardmore.

"I recognized the area code," said Cameron, "otherwise, I wouldn't have answered. How is Dad?"

"In fine form. He let me look over some of your early work."

"Just a sec," said Cameron. "I need some privacy here." Kennet heard him issuing some orders through the muffled transmitter. Cameron came back on the line. "Continue."

"I viewed the video of the grad party out at the lake."

"Whatever for? Amateurish."

"My inquiries took me to that time and place. You remember the Fleming brothers?"

"Up till now, I'd succeeded in forgetting. They were brutes. They were at the party. They were so obnoxious, we guys got together and gave them marching orders. They were so drunk, their brother, Donny was his name, he drove them home. After what they did to him."

"Please explain."

"That muscled bastard – not Rawling, the other one –"

"Lanny."

"Lanny. He gave Donny a black eye. That's after Donny pulled him off a girl he was assaulting. They're both about the same build, both strong, but Lanny was mean. Just pure meanness. Is this helping?"

"Yes. Thank you. One more question. When did you last see Donny?"

"The beginning of the next week, I went to work at the mine, next to Beardmore. Worked all summer. Donny was on the payroll when I started, but he didn't stay long. Just took off one day."

"Do you remember the day?"

"Sure. Three days after I started work. I remember commiserating with him, about his eye. It was a real shiner by that time. When I turned up to work Thursday, no Donny. Never saw him again."

"Do you remember the names of the other guys working on surface?"

"Sure. Alan Greenbank and Martin Frost. Worked with them all summer."

"Do you remember a guy named Kueng?"

"Mac? Sure. But he worked only the odd day. Prospector. They used him on the ore dumps and mill loading bin and in the assaying office. Also employed him as a mechanic."

After a few moments, Kennet thanked him and hung up.

Now he had to track down Mac Kueng.

Chapter 35

. . . Wednesday mid-day

Mac Kueng's parking space was still vacant.

Kennet had checked with Alice at the restaurant when he grabbed a bite, and with Bull Kellerman at The Hook'n Bullet, and with Melody Mallory at the store. No one had seen Kueng that morning. When he drove by the Community Centre, the pilot, in a red cap, seemed to be engaged in disconnecting the dream-catcher apparatus from his helicopter. The gigantic ring lay on the grass, with the network of cables collapsed and streaming toward the machine.

As he approached the log cabin, he saw a scrap of white paper spiked to the door. The handwritten note was brief: *Meet me there – alone.*

Kennet met no one on the Camp 72 Road. At the fork just past the bridge, fresh tire tracks in the moist ground signified that a vehicle had recently taken the road to the Brennan-Kenty property. At times when the vehicle had emerged from one of the many scattered puddles, a set of tread marks pointed westward.

He was bearing down on a black blob on the bush road. The

blob grew larger. Suddenly it raised its head and stared at him, ears pointed. The bear galvanized into action, scrambling for the cover of the bush. As Kennet passed it, he noted the limbs working furiously as it melted into the woods. It had been scavenging some small carrion on the road.

When he hit the burn he spotted another black bear poised on a hillock at the side of the road. This bear did not spook. It stared hard at Kennet as he whizzed by. He saw two smaller black forms in the brush behind it.

He passed through the open gate and paused at the top of the hill to survey the sweep of burnscape and the rocky ridge about a kilometre away. A few vapoury clouds hung in the blue vault.

Soon the ridge towered above him. He swept around the south side and, switching to four-wheel drive, scrabbled up the sixty-degree incline to the top of the trenches. The '82 Silverado sat there alone.

He disembarked and changed swiftly into bush clothes and hiking boots and jammed the safari hat on his head. He belted on his hunting knife. In his first steps up the trail he saw a fresh boot print paralleled by a distinct bear paw print, also fresh. As he climbed the trail, he glimpsed the odd boot print and paw print. Once he stooped to examine a paw print superimposed on a boot print.

When he reached the stripped zone at the top of the ridge, he spotted a bulky backpack sitting on the exposed rock. He turned his head to look west, following the line of bare rock until it fell off into space. Far beyond, the great lake glimmered in the sunlight. At the edge of the ridge a lone figure stood rigid, gazing at the lake. A stick projected up from its right shoulder. A rifle slung on its shoulder.

Kennet made his way to the lone figure. Kueng was wearing khaki-coloured clothing and a brown slouch hat. When Kennet was a few steps away, Kueng half-turned, gave him a wry smile, and then returned his gaze to the lake.

"I climbed faster than that," he said. "I heard you arrive thirty minutes ago.

"Did you see the bear?"

"What bear?"

"What's going on? Why are we here?"

"This is the last stop I wanted to make. Before . . ."

"Before what?"

Kueng turned back to him. "What the hell happened to you?"

"What? Oh, you mean this." Kennet gestured to his forehead. "I wish I could say I incurred it in the line of duty. But, it's retribution for my foolishness. You haven't answered my question. You said you'd report to the motel this morning."

Kueng returned his gaze to the lake. "No. No, I didn't."

"You said you'd own up to the accident. To your role in Georgie's death."

"No. No, I didn't." Kueng unslung his rifle and stood its butt on the rock in front of him, both hands on the barrel. "I said . . . I'd make things right." He lowered his haunches slowly until he was sitting on the rock.

"You have a Lee-Enfield, I see. A .303."

"Best rifle I ever owned. Have a seat."

"You shot at me."

"I shot *near* you. I warned you about the mine. A dangerous place."

"You could've missed."

"Hardly likely. I'm a trained marksman. I was a sniper in the forgotten war. This was my talisman." He patted the rifle. "Sit down. Stay a while."

"What are you saying?" Kennet moved closer, stopped three metres away, and sank to the rock, facing the lake.

"Kap'yong. The 38th Parallel. Korea. I was there. I never told anyone. Except Harry. Swore him to secrecy. My medals, I threw away. I don't get nostalgic about war. War is the dirtiest business there is."

"Dirtier than murder?"

"Immeasurably. War is wholesale murder." He turned his head to look at Kennet. "*You* must have seen some things."

The bodies of mutiliated civilians stacked in the Rwandan brush.

"A soldier," said Kennet, "a real soldier, is not a murderer. And does not become one. Did Harry?"

Mac Kueng looked away. "Harry," he said, "did not know what hardship was."

"And you did?"

"I was a prisoner," said Kueng, looking at him again. "I spent nine months in a Red Chinese open-air prison. I was interrogated every day. It was not your run-of-the-mill browbeating that your Canadian policeman engages in. These interrogators were experts – in terror and psychology and brutality. Far superior to those amateur thugs in that Iraqi military prison – Abu Ghraib, or something. If they'd had any idea – the merest inkling – that I was a sniper, I'd have got a slug in the back of the head. I never cracked. But that wasn't the hardship, professor."

"I'm guessing you'll tell me."

"It was my homecoming. To my compatriots, to my Canadian brothers-in-arms, I was a piece of shit. I was a traitor. I had been captured. I had survived. So I must have been weak. I must have broken under pressure, and betrayed my unit and my country. Shit!"

He turned away. He was twitching in odd places. There was now a tremor in his voice. "*They* would have. *They* would have buckled. So they assumed that I did. And the other 30-odd Canadian POWs got the same reception. From a grateful nation!"

"I've heard things to that effect."

Kueng turned back to him. "I worked alone! I knew the name of my lieutenant – his last name – never knew nor wanted to know his first name. I never talked to the other guys. What possible information could I betray?"

Kennet remained silent.

"I cannot abide disrespect. If we had taken Georgie – if we had taken Georgie to the hospital or a clinic, even when it was too late, there would have been questions. Some jerk would have found something wrong in what we did, in running her over, when she had been flushed like a deer, into our path! How could we prove that? It would've turned into a donnybrook. I might've killed someone right there and then."

After a moment, Kennet said, "But you knew, or thought you knew, who did it."

"Damn right."

Kennet said, "You never told me where your trapline is, Mac. I asked Kellerman this morning, when I was looking for you. Seems it covers the Warneford Road area."

"So? You have a question for me?"

"Did you kill Vanderhorst?"

Kueng turned his head to look at Kennet, then turned away. "I batted a fly. I squashed an insect. No one tells me to go to hell."

"You killed a man, for God's sake!"

"No one pisses on my leg and tells me it's raining. That's my territory. I've run that line for near fifty years."

"But why, man! Why?"

Kueng threw a glance at him. "You know why. You figured it out."

"It was the medal, wasn't it. You knew it would stir up the past."

Kueng turned to look at him. "I knew it would be you. You're smart, educated. Been through the mill. You stood up to the Flemings. I knew you wouldn't let go. Just like a bulldog. Once you had the case in your teeth, you'd shake it and worry it till something fell out. We're not too different."

"How can you say that?"

"If you'd been in my shoes, you'd have stepped on that little shit."

"What are we talking about? I've never killed anyone – that you know of."

"You're capable. We're all capable. Sometimes it just takes a government to sanctify it. The killing. I learned that."

"You killed Donny. Donny Fleming."

"Did I?"

Kennet looked around. A few metres behind them, to their left, was the bulldozed area where Conrad had uncovered the remains of Georgiana Elder. He swung his gaze back to Kueng, who sat immobile, staring ahead, and then he focused his gaze on the great lake. It lay almost perfectly calm in a blue haze. Here and there the sunlight shimmered on the surface where some errant breeze stirred the waters. He could not see the far side. *Did anyone ever see the far side?* As his eyes probed the haze, it became mist or fog or cloud on the horizon. He could see the dark suggestions of land stretching north and south, the islands of mid lake. Closer to the near shore, in the mouth of the crescent bay that bellied towards the ridge upon which they sat, a small archipelago rose out of the lake off one of the horns, like something out of a Lawren Harris painting.

Kennet spoke quietly. "How did you do it, Mac? Did you have to lure him to the pit? Was it just before quitting time, and you claimed you needed a hand with something? And when his back was turned, you hit him. Was it with a spade, as with Vanderhorst? You were hired for your prospecting skills, so maybe it was a hammer. Your rock hammer."

Kueng glanced at him. "As I said, smart."

Kennet continued quietly. "That boy you saw, on the road that night, in your spotlight, that wasn't Donny Fleming."

Kueng whipped his head around. "The hell it wasn't! I know a Fleming when I see one."

"She *was* being chased, Mac. She must have jumped in front of the truck, like a deer. You couldn't react in time."

Kueng glared at him.

"And Harry was passed out, or half conscious, whatever. The collision jolted him awake."

Kueng stared at him, face twisted, bitter.

"And you both got out, didn't you, Mac?"

Kueng released a hollow laugh. "Harry fell out. He couldn't get that door open fast enough. He thought we'd hit a rock. Thought we were back on the fishing tug."

"But he picked her up, didn't he." Kennet was making a statement, not a question.

"He was around the front in a flash, to check the damage. And he saw her lying there, on her back, under the truck, only her head sticking out, and he was looking into her face. Blood streaming down her face."

Mac Kueng was trembling. A frisson had gripped his whole body. Kennet said softly, "Horrible."

"And when I come up, he was pulling her out, her eyes were open, wide open, and he cradled her, and lifted her up. I could do nothing. Nothing!"

"She needed medical assistance."

"Didn't I know that!" said Kueng, fiercely. His whole frame had become rigid again.

"And then you trained the spotlight on those figures. Those were Flemings, Mac. But neither of them was Donny Fleming."

"The hell you say! I saw the star." Kueng swung his head away, his features contorted.

Kennet let the silence build. Then, "Why are we here, Mac?"

Kueng refused to look at him. "You know why!" he said, furiously.

Kennet glanced back at the bulldozed area. "You brought her here," he said, "to stuff her in a hole in the ground?"

Kueng sprang to his feet with a roar. He raised his arms and threw his head back. His rifle, gripped in his right hand, looked as lightweight as a toy. His whole body shook. He screamed into the blue nothingness above.

Kennet found himself on his feet. His heart froze, or maybe it was his breath. He watched as Mac Kueng whipped around, gripping the rifle with both hands. He thrust the muzzle towards Kennet. It was a bayonet thrust. It must have been a reflex action, for he immediately withdrew the weapon and hugged the stock to his hip.

"You!" he shouted. "*You*, of all people, *you* must understand! This is what *she* would have wanted!" His chest heaved, and after a moment, the muzzle of the rifle drooped.

Kennet took breath. "I understand," said Kennet, carefully, "that she had a fear of graveyards. But *here*, Mac? Where she could be scavenged by bears? *Here*, Mac?"

Kueng's voice dropped to a whisper. "I thought," he said, "we had an understanding. I thought . . . you would understand."

"I'm trying to understand, Mac."

"Look at this," he said. He made a panoramic sweep with his free hand. It took in the great lake and the big sky and the land, the land that swept to the horizons. "Look at all of this." There was awe in his voice.

Kennet looked. Kennet looked at the green verdure thrusting itself out of the tortured soil and the cobalt blue of the heavens with its scattered linen handerchiefs hanging on invisible threads and the deep, deep sea in the west, throwing back shafts of sunlight so brilliant they hurt the eyes. His father had buried his mother in a quiet country churchyard in a rural village in Quebec. *She'll find peace here,* he had said. And Kennet's most vivid memory of that spot was the sound of dirt hitting the coffin lid. Every handful of dirt, striking the coffin lid. He had never returned there, to that cemetery of aging tombstones and peeling wooden crosses and prickly weeds.

And that had been the last time he had seen Jamie, his brother. Jamie did keep in touch, loosely speaking. He always phoned at Christmastime, from some different outpost on some frontier. He seemed happy.

Diane, his own dear wife, he had buried in Mountainview Cemetery. He had placed the urn on the sunrise side of the headstone, facing the big mountain that dominated the city of Thunder Bay. Mount McKay looked down on the inland port and across the great bay to the distant rock giant in repose, feet thrust into the ever restless waters of Lake Superior. He had never consciously thought this before, but he thought it now: The mountain took it all in. To the mountain it was all one. Each clod of earth and drop of water and breath of air. And in a hundred years, in a thousand years, the city, and he, and Diane, would be clods of earth, and water, and air, all one.

Diane had said, *I want a piece of me to lie in your country, forever, dearest.* And she had made him promise to take a portion of her ashes to her own country. She had wanted, she said, to embrace the world. He had not made that journey overseas. Not yet. Now he would. Now he would give her peace.

Mac Kueng stood facing the lake, the butt of the Lee-Enfield resting on the ground, shoulders thrown back, straining at the khaki jacket. It was a pose reminiscent of those old legionnaires, the aging veterans, as they paid their respects on the 11th of every November at the local cenotaph. There was a new sound in the air, a faint sound that Kennet could not place.

Kennet addressed the stoical features, viewed in profile. "Maybe I understand."

Kueng, still looking at the lake, said, "She was my daughter too."

"What!"

Kueng twisted his head around. "She was my daughter. I fathered her. Harry always suspected, but he raised her as his own."

"Of course! You were a lady-killer then, weren't you. And when Harry was in a drunken stupor, you took advantage."

"Something like that. It never happened again."

Kennet lapsed into silence. Harry and Edith Elder had raised Georgiana for eighteen years, for better and for worse, and then in her eighteenth year, she had reeled out of their control. Kennet said, "You told her, didn't you."

Kueng said nothing.

"You watched her grow up, never contributed a cent to her upbringing, never offered advice, never suffered rejection, never enjoyed her affection, never got her respect – and then you told her. When she turned eighteen. Did you do it on her birthday?"

Kueng said, "I gave her a locket."

"I've seen the locket."

"It was a cameo of my mother."

"And you told her, it was her grandmother."

"She had good blood in her."

"I'm not so sure."

Kueng smiled grimly. "You are trying to hurt me. You can't. Experts have tried." Kueng changed the subject: "You took your sweet time getting here," he said. "I could have been gone."

"Gone? Where would you go? Besides," said Kennet, "you said you would own – you would make things right."

Kueng broke his stance. He lifted the rifle by the barrel and swung around. He came towards Kennet and planted his feet two paces away. In the shadow of his hat brim, his pale eyes gleamed.

"I am. I am making things right. And you will help me."

"Help you? God, Mac!" Something tugged at Kennet's awareness. "You killed two men! And those were not casualties of any war. Those were victims of malice." Something was thrashing the air.

Kennet swung his head around and studied the way he had come, down the gentle slope of the ridge. It was a motor sound.

He swung his head back. "What's going on, Mac?"

"You think that 'victims of war', as you call them, were not casualties of malice? Think again, professor!" He hefted the Lee-

Enfield, gripping it where the stock met the hardware, and started up the slope. "Come on."

Kennet followed him, keeping to his left, and matching his long stride. "This professor knows bullshit where he hears it," he said.

Kueng studied the ground as he walked. The thrashing grew louder, and a gleaming red machine materialized above the ridge top a hundred fifty metres away.

Kueng said, "No need for vulgarisms, professor. The term is 'casuistry'. That's what my Jesuit teachers taught me, centuries ago. Now listen up. You have to return to my shack before five o'clock. Sharp! You understand?"

"No." Kennet was stretching his legs to keep up.

"There are letters there. Failing that, check the bank." He added, "Whatever you do, do not be in my shack after five o'clock."

"Whatever. So, you're running away."

Mac Kueng stopped dead and straight-armed him in his right shoulder. They faced each other as blasts of air from the helicopter blades raised dust and forest floor debris and plucked leaves from the shrubs.

"I am serious!" He had to raise his voice above the racket. "Pick up those letters and get the hell out! Before five."

"Okay."

"And I am *not* running away! If anything, I'm running *to*."

"Either way, you're running. You're not coming back. That's why you've given your library – your whole library – to Wes Carlson.

Kueng also had to shout now: "I going to . . . embrace –" he was struggling for words "– my destiny."

Kennet took a pace toward him. He was shouting. "Whatever you're doing, it's easier than spending the rest of your life in a cell – in a hole in the wall. But I'm not going to make it easy for you."

Kennet stepped closer and grasped his upper arm with his right hand. "You killed an innocent man! Two innocent men. Rawl Fleming, in the dark that night, was indistinguishable from his brother Donny. Rawl gave the medal to Donny, the next day maybe. The brothers did that then – still do – they take turns wearing that medal. They're honouring their father, a soldier! You killed the wrong man, Mac."

Kueng shrugged off Kennet's hand with a violent movement. He stepped back. The whirling blades of the chopper, only thirty metres away, were ramping down. The pilot cracked open his door, which faced them. Kueng's normally fair features dissolved into paste.

He started a stumbling walk toward the chopper, hunched over, looking back at Kennet. He flung out his last words: "You lie!"

Kennet pulled back his shoulders and placed his hands on his hips. He shouted back: *"You know I do not!"*

Kueng gained the helicopter where the pilot in his red cap was stuffing the enormous packsack into the rear compartment. Kueng ducked around the front end, bending low, still grasping the rifle, and opened the door on the far side. His face was ghastly.

Kennet retreated a few paces down the hillside. The pilot at the controls, the blades ramped up. With a roar the machine ripped itself from the hilltop. Kennet saw plainly the words WiniskAir, embossed in white on the red fuselage. The aircraft tilted its nose to the north and moved off, twenty metres above the stunted trees.

Kennet ran after it. A grassy trail, overhung with brush, opened up, and he plunged down it. A few moments later, he arrived at a rock outcrop that overlooked the vast burnscape below and beyond.

The insect shrank as it arrowed north. It emitted a momentary pulse of red.

Chapter 36

...Wednesday afternoon

He was approaching his truck when the bear materialized. In the clearing above the trench, not five metres from his truck, a huge black hulk was swinging its head from side to side, about sixty metres away. It made a gargling sound, almost like a whinny. Kennet stopped dead.

His mind raced. *Fight*, he thought. *Or flight.* Neither was an option. His right hand moved to the hunting knife at his waist. A puny weapon at most, against an adversary equipped with fangs and claws and several hundred pounds of muscled fury. Still, if it came to close-quarters combat, he was not utterly defenceless.

The head-swinging became violent. The animal was snorting and gargling. The bear's forelegs raised a few inches and descended, rhythmically, its paws stamping the ground stiffly and with such force he could hear the thuds. Kennet raised his left arm carefully and lifted his hat straight up and flapped it. Perhaps he would seem taller. *So it was to be fight.* His right hand fumbled at the knife on his belt. He released a grunt. Much too weak. He gulped down air and forced out a barbaric yawp.

Abruptly the bear charged. Kennet began dancing, waving the hat in wide sweeps. He found himself screaming gibberish. The black death hurtled toward him. Immediately Kennet gave up on the knife and dropped his hand to the large pocket of his cargo pants and clawed at the flap. He had wished fervently for his bear banger and then there it was – *that's* where he had stored it!

He dropped the hat and, with both hands, frantically cocked the slim, pencil-like launcher. When he looked up the bear was twenty metres away and closing. He aimed for a point mid-way between them and released the spring. The banger fired and bucked. He saw the cartridge kick up dirt and then explode a metre or two above the animal's muzzle. The monster veered with incredible agility and shot away to its left, running uphill and melting instantly into the brush. He followed its progress with his ears for a good minute and a half. Meanwhile he screwed in another cartridge.

In the silence that ensued he gently explored the seat of his pants. No dampness or evidence of premature evacuation. *Well, that was something.*

He closed the gap to the Sportage, experiencing a hollowness in his stomach. When he put his hand on the door handle, he heard a whimper. *It was not he.* He bent down and peered under the truck. A large wolf-sized animal moved its tail tentatively.

It took several minutes of Here boy, here boy, and That's a good chap, and Come on, now, to coax the dog out. It appeared to be a husky mix, crossed with some breed that gave its gray coat black streaks. It inched its way out with a series of whimpers. Once it was out it was reluctant to stand. Kennet examined the animal gingerly, discovered a spot of blood on its upper right foreleg. When he pressed around the spot, the dog reacted with a yelp. Perhaps it was a bear claw puncture. Perhaps he had stolen the bear's lunch. Kennet patted the great gray head, walked around to the passenger side and opened the door. He spread his good rain jacket on the seat, impermeable side up. He put both arms under the dog, lifted it, and carried it around to the seat. He continued to croon to the animal.

Once behind the wheel, he continued crooning: You're a lucky chap, aren't you, What's your name, boy, Are you hurting there? That's a good doggy, That's a good chap. He got his cell from the pocket of the shirt he had left in the truck, but he could get no signal. From time to time he reached over and stroked the head.

He met no traffic on the Brennan-Kenty road, nor did he expect to. Once across the bridge and into the red pine plantation, he saw a pickup coming. It looked familiar. He flagged it down. It was Bill Meyers in his '97 Ranger.

They spoke through their respective open windows. He had found a dog, said Kennet.

Well, good for him, said Meyers, noncommittally.

It was hurt.

Well, let them have a look. Meyers climbed down and walked around to look at the dog. He fingered the wound gently. Looked like a bullet wound, he said. Maybe a .22.

Who would do that? asked Kennet.

He'd be surprised. Did he get lucky?

Eh?

Any fish? Walleye? Meyers sounded exasperated.

He wasn't fishing.

Well, what the hell was he doing in the bush then?

He'd be surprised, said Kennet.

Take it to the clinic, he said.

Eh?

There was no vet. He should take the dog to the clinic, to Yvette. And let her check himself out too. That was quite a goose egg he had.

When Kennet reached Highway 11, he glanced at his watch: 4:49 p.m. He should have tried his cell sooner, he thought. He should have reported to Robert or the OPP. There was no time left. He had to check Mac Kueng's cabin immediately.

He parked the truck and cracked the windows, cautioning the dog to stay. The cabin door was unlocked, he pushed it open. The room was dark, as usual, only the sunlight filtering through dusty panes. There were no books left. No personal belongings. Some stuff on the kitchen counter. On the table, two white envelopes, the copy of the last book Kueng had been reading, and the clunky alarm clock. The hands indicated 5:01. He picked up the envelope marked *Forbes*.

It was unsealed. He slipped out a single sheet of paper. The message was handwritten.

Professor, it began. *I suggest you step outside. Immediately. Don't come back.*

Kennet scooped up the other envelope and the book and left quickly. He headed for the forge and placed the book and unopened envelope on the work bench and resumed reading. Kueng used a neat, precise script, very much like calligraphy:

I hereby appoint you executor of my estate. The other envelope is a copy of my holographic will, my signature witnessed, my affairs in order. I apologize that I could not offer you any more of my library, but Carlson will oblige you, if that is your wish. I won't see you again – not in this world anyway. I'm going on the tramp. I want to see new country. Fresh, virgin territory. When I see an iceberg, I'll know I've gone far enough. I'll end it there. Or maybe a white bear will end it for me. It was a pleasure talking to you, even if our time was short. I feel young again, as if I'm starting out.

It was signed *M.C. Kueng*.

Kennet reached for the other envelope. He never touched it, as far as he could remember.

When he opened his eyes, he heard voices. For some reason there was a weight on his back. It was an oppressive weight, for he could not rise. His fingers clawed at the ground. He was clawing dirt and cinders. Some had entered his mouth and he spat it out.

He heard a voice saying, Jeez, there's someone laying there, in the old forge! When he opened his eyes again a pair of heavy black rubber boots blocked his view. It's the professor! someone was saying. And his eyes are open.

Kennet ordered the man to help him. Rubber Boots knelt down. Rubber Boots was wearing very heavy khaki rain pants. Kennet! the man was saying. Say something. Talk to me.

Get this timber off me! said Kennet.

He's not talking, the voice said. But his lips are moving.

"Something on my back," said Kennet.

"Okay," said the voice. "He's trying to say something now. Just lie still, Kennet. This is Conrad. We've just called the ambulance."

Kennet twisted his head to look up. It was Conrad. It was Conrad Parker in a fireman's suit. "I can't –," said Kennet. "Can you move it?"

"Move what?" said Conrad.

"Something on my back."

Conrad's arm reached out. When his heavily gloved hand reappeared, it clutched a sliver of two-by-four. "Nothing on your back, Kennet. You've had a shock. Must have been the force of the blast. Lifted the roof off the forge, but the corrugated metal walls stood, for the most part."

"Help me," said Kennet. "Just lift my shoulder there, to see if I can move."

Conrad raised his shoulder, and somehow Kennet got his arm under his chest and rolled over on his side. Conrad helped raise him to a sitting position.

"You've got a knot on your forehead," said Conrad.

"I'm alright, I'm alright," said Kennet. "No pain – except a headache. But it feels as though there's a timber lying across my back."

Conrad gestured to the two-by-four framing in the wall. "Some of the lumber missing," he said. "Maybe something hit you."

There was indeed no roof. The hardware of the forge had collapsed into the back wall, parts of which were blown out. Conrad helped him the few short steps to the opening, where khaki-suited firemen in black helmets scurried about, arranging hoses. He thought he recognized Gerald St. Clair and Al Cummings.

"I can handle it from here," said Kennet, and Conrad released him.

"Some flames on the edge of the bush there," said Conrad. "I have to help." And then he was gone.

One stream of water was already directed into the wreckage that had been Kueng's cabin. Only the foundation logs remained, and a few logs tilted askew here and there. Where the kitchen had been, flames shot up a few metres, and black smoke coiled up above the treetops.

The envelope, thought Kennet. The workbench had collapsed, and he could spot no paper anywhere. He made his way to the path through the confusion of hoses and shouting firemen. Hoses had been strung along the path. He found himself walking reasonably well, although his back was almighty stiff. He heard the siren of the ambulance before he saw it.

A large yellow fire engine blocked the road. Pickups and cars were parked helter-skelter along the sides of the road. Two fellows leapt from the white ambulance and ran toward him.

"Where's the casualty?" shouted the tall one.

"That would be me."

"What's the matter with you?"

"You tell me."

The tall one grabbed his right arm and the short one his left arm. They looked him up and down, front and back.

"Can't see nothing," said the short one. "Better take him in anyway."

"I have a wolf – excuse me – a dog in my truck. He needs medical attention."

"Sure," said the tall one. "We're making the trip anyway. Garth, you get it."

Garth, the short one, said, "Is it friendly?"

"Is to me. It's hurt in the right shoulder." Garth asked for the keys, and Kennet turned them over, and as he was walking to the ambulance, he realized he'd left the doors open.

When Kennet was seated in the back and the gray dog stretched on the floor, the ambulance drove with siren wailing. After a few turns, unnecessarily sharp, in Kennet's opinion, the ambulance stopped.

The tall one led him by the arm into the Beardmore Health Clinic. Garth carried the dog. The receptionist, a blonde matron, said, "Right this way," and led them to a private office, past several geriatrics in the reception area and at least one expectant mother.

No one objected to the triage that assigned the dog priority treatment.

Kennet noted that the back of his aching head was now sore. When he touched that area, he winced. When the medical attendant entered, she almost tripped over the dog, which was lying on the floor.

"Okay," she said, "who's the first patient."

Kennet drew in his breath and held it a moment. "The dog's been shot," he said. The nurse practitioner was smiling. She was a tall brunette with shoulder-length hair, long eyelashes, dusky skin, and dressed in pastel slacks and a tan smock that was open to reveal her full-breasted chassis. *She's beautiful!* Kennet's eyes dropped to the ring on her finger. *She's married.*

"Has it? Let's take a look." She knelt down and zeroed in on the wound immediately. She manipulated the foreleg gently. "Nothing broken," she said. "I'll clean it, but you'll have to see a vet."

Kennet mumbled something.

"Excuse me?" she said.

"Not my dog," he said.

"Ah," she said. "But you've assumed responsibility, I take it." Whenever she turned her eyes on him, she looked right into him. She set about cleaning the gunshot wound and applying a dressing on both sides of the shoulder. The dog never moved. "It's a through-and-through. I never thought I'd say that."

"Excuse me?"

She turned her attention to Kennet. "My first GSW. Thank you."

"You're welcome."

"Now, you. That's a nasty." She put her fingers on his forehead. They were cool, and soothing.

"Oh. That's old. I have a fresh one on the back of my head."

She brought her face down to the back of his neck and probed with gentle fingers. "Tell me the circumstances." She wore a subtle scent.

Kennet explained about the explosion. She had heard it, she said. Everyone in town had heard it. And then the sirens.

"Better take off your shirt," she said. "Better safe than sorry."

She watched with keen, dancing eyes as Kennet removed his shirt. He felt a twinge across his shoulder blades as he contorted his arms. She made him turn around.

"Yes. I see a long, broad red mark. You'll probably have a large bruise."

"And my head?"

"Concussion, most likely. A mild one. Minor bleeding, which has stopped. I'll put a patch on it. But I'd recommend seeing a specialist."

She insisted on putting a patch on his forehead too. She cleaned it first, and applied antiseptic. The skin was sensitive, abraded, she said, and susceptible to infection. He was obliged to sit there, bare-chested, and to stare at her chest as she applied the bandage. *He couldn't help himself. It was part of the treatment.*

Kennet carried the dog outside. He set it on the ground and encouraged it to pee. It limped around a bit and then managed to urinate, unable to cock a leg in true masculine fashion.

Kennet found the Sportage in a parking space. Someone had delivered it and left the keys in the unlocked vehicle. He drove to The Hook'n Bullet. It was busy.

Bull Kellerman broke off a conversation with a customer as soon as he saw Kennet. He asked the fellow named Ambrose, who was loitering about, to help Marta, and took Kennet outside.

"Tell me what the hell's going on!" he said, when they had separated themselves from the crowd. Kennet quickly summarized the events of the past twenty-four hours.

"And you don't know where he's run off to."

"He flew north. That's all I know."

"And you're sure he's your man. Responsible for two murders. And Georgie's death."

"Without a doubt. But I can't *prove* it beyond a reasonable doubt. I have yet to tell the police. I came to you first because I need your assistance." He explained that he had lost Mac Kueng's holographic will in the explosion, but that Kueng had intimated there was a copy at the bank. Could Kellerman induce the manager to retrieve it for him?

"No problem. Have a seat." He gestured toward The Grouch's Chair. "You look a bit shaky."

Kennet moved towards the chair. He did feel faint. "By the way, you'll be happy to know," he said, "your bear banger worked." He described the bear's charge.

"Good work! Some damn fools don't know how to use those things. They fire right at the bear."

"Oh?"

"Yeah. And then the cartridge explodes behind the animal, and drives it into their arms." He disappeared into his shop. Customers emerged and drove off. In the next ten minutes two more vehicles pulled up and disgorged customers. A harried-looking gentleman in shorts and a sports shirt draped over an incipient paunch scurried up from the direction of the bank. He was carrying a large manila envelope.

"You Mr. Forbes?" he asked.

Kennet acknowledged his name.

"Then this is for you. I'll have to have you sign." He thrust an official-looking receipt book at Kennet.

After he handed the envelope over, he said, "Mac told me what he's giving you power of attorney. He's a very wealthy man, you know. Has assets in seven figures. You remember the Bre-X mining scandal?"

Kennet nodded.

"He told me that he sold his investment when that penny stock reached $269. He figured there was something fishy about it."

"He had a good sense of smell."

Before he left, the manager gestured to The Grouch's Chair. "Bull never lets anyone sit there. Better watch out."

Kennet tore open the envelope. There was a single handwritten sheet, dated the previous Sunday, and signed, and witnessed by Wes Carlson. If no one heard from him, Maximilian Cornelius Kueng. resident of Greenstone, municipal tax number such-and-such, after one year from the above date, he should be presumed dead. He left all his worldly goods – and at this point the writer listed financial institutions and account numbers – to the following: fully one half to Edith and Gracie Elder, residents of 282 Walker Street East, Beardmore, Ontario; $1,000,000 cash to "the immediate family of the archaeologist who died on my trapline in August , 2009,"; and the remaining assets to be distributed to charities of his choice by the executor of the estate, Kennet Forbes, resident of Thunder Bay. The Municipality of Greenstone was authorized to offer up for sale the deceased's property on the Blackwater River in lieu of taxes accumulated. The deceased would leave this world, he wrote, "beholden to nobody".

Kennet looked inside the envelope. There was another sheet, folded. It was Kennet's power of attorney over Kueng's assets, effective as of Monday, two days ago.

Kellerman poked his head out the door. "Need to use a phone?"

"Let me check if mine works," said Kennet. He fished his cell out of his shirt pocket. It lit up. Kellerman nodded and ducked back inside. He speed-dialed Detective Inspector Robert Kenilworth. Robert answered. He was at home, he said. What was up?

Robert listened, without speaking. Without cursing. When Kennet was done, Robert said he would issue an APB for Maximilian Cornelius Kueng, aka Mac Kueng. And he would check with the manager of the WiniskAir office in Thunder Bay. His last words: "Come home, boy. Come home. I'll have a large whiskey for you."

In his room at the motel, Kennet packed swiftly. He left a hundred dollars cash in an envelope that he found in a drawer, and addressed it to Jennifer. He asked her to pay his bill and keep the change. As he was pulling the door shut, Conrad Parker drove up in his pickup. He still wore his fireman's protective gear, sans helmet, the khaki-coloured suit trimmed with yellow stripes on the cuffs.

"We found these," said Conrad, proferring some paper through the open window. One item was Mac Kueng's note to Kennet, mostly intact. The other was an envelope, still sealed. "We were checking the perimeter of the property for smoke or flames, and came upon these."

"Thanks, Conrad." He could hear a drone emanating from the north.

"I couldn't help but read the note."

"That's alright, Conrad. It won't be a secret long."

"Leaving?"

"Yes." He could hear the helicopter coming in.

"Keep in touch."

"I will. I most certainly will." Kennet shook his hand.

The WiniskAir LongRanger helicopter sat on the playing field, its blades quivering to a stop. Kennet parked and stepped over the low fence and approached Red Cap the pilot, who was preparing to stick a fuel hose in the chopper's tank. He had light red hair and a brushy moustache.

Where had he been? asked Kennet.

Depended who was asking.

Kennet gave his name.

Ah. He was authorized to give that information. Tashota.

Tashota?

An old mining camp on the CNR mainline. He'd taken old Mac there before. But this time, Mac made him fly over it. Flew until the point of no return. Set the machine down on bare rock in a burn. Mac waved when he left.

Arrangements for pickup?

Not with him. He must've made other arrangements.

What's up there?

Nothin'. Purely nothin'. All the way to Hudson Bay.

As he drove south to the city, the sun dropped in the west. It was a golden disk. When it touched the horizon beyond the darkening burn, a redness drained out of its lower reaches and spread north and south beyond the distant rim of earth. He imagined the sun sinking into the great sea and cleansing itself. In the morning it would spring up and leap over the Giant and illuminate the land. Illuminate his life.

He switched on the satellite radio. He scanned the channels until he found a classic rock station. He tapped the steering wheel in time with the beat. After a few tunes, the DJ announced the next hit, *Following the River*, a Rolling Stones oldie. As the music and the voice carried him along and the volume intensified, he found himself stamping his left foot and beating the sides of the steering wheel with both hands. *She* was laughing. Diane was laughing in an out-of-town café. The phone was ringing but she wouldn't take his call. She couldn't take his call. So *he* was following the river, following it to the sea. He was shouting pieces of the lyrics as he recalled them, and other times he was repeating the vocalist's lines. And in the end he was whispering I'll be dreamin' of ya. I'll be dreaming all about you. I'll be dreaming . . .

He was gulping, and squeezing out great sobs.

Chapter 37

Sunday, September 13th . . .

He had never been up there before, Curtis Mallory said. Wow, he said. What a view!

They were standing at the overlook built of treated timber on the ridge above High Hill Harbour. Ioanna was leaning on his arm. Kennet cast his eye back along the walking trail, but the others were not in sight yet. Before them spread the magnificent blue sea of Lake Nipigon as far as eye could see, and all around them the riotous green and gold bushes of the old burn dropped down to the dancing waters.

"Are they coming?" asked Ioanna, glancing down the trail.

"If they're much longer, I'll go back," said Kennet.

The rising hill and the vigorous vegetation behind them, dappled and streaked with orange and red, cut off the view to the harbour basin. To their right the shore stretched north to the distant postage-stamp beach of Poplar Lodge Park, and far beyond the park, the shining white sand cliffs where the invisible cottage subdivision sat. Between the park and the cliffs lay the ancient cemetery.

The Elders had decided against the graveyard, to respect the memory of Georgiana Elder. They had decided to give her ashes to the wind. To the wind and to the water and to the earth.

Almost a month ago, Kennet had returned to the city. He had accepted Detective Inspector Robert Kenilworth's offer of a large whiskey that night, and the next day, his doctor had checked his cranium and declared him fit for service. The North West Regional Office of the Ontario Provincial Police had officially debriefed him. The all points bulletin on Maximilian Cornelius Kueng had yielded no results. It was not long before the OPP released the bones of the daughter to her father, Harold Elder, who had been asking every day. Long before that point, Kennet had paid a visit to Cindy Vanderhorst and commiserated with her for an hour. And then one day Dr. Peter Sheridan had called him down to the anthropology lab.

Peter told him that he, Kennet Forbes, had a gift for the science.

How did he work that out? asked Kennet.

Bones migrated to him, said Peter. The police had dropped off another package – bones unearthed near Lake Nipigon, a scant three hundred metres from the old bear's den where the young woman's body had been cached.

"You know Conrad Parker?" asked Peter.

"Yes! Of course."

"He told the scene-of-crime officers that you had to know. That you'd solve the mystery." Conrad had been stripping a new stretch of ground on the infamous ridge when he encountered a jumble of boulders near a cliff edge. Boulders with jagged edges. So he had climbed down to investigate. He concluded that they had been blasted. That some prospector long ago had examined that ground. The site overlooked the north face of the ridge, in a confusion of brambles and windfall. He began removing boulders with his backhoe, and that's when he found the bones.

Peter led him to a corner of the lab where he had been laying out the bones in the pattern of a human skeleton. "Almost everything's here," he said. "Do you notice anything amiss?"

"My God! The left side – the whole left side. It's been . . . crushed." Gaps in the skull. Left clavicle and scapula splintered. Ribs on that side collapsed. Pelvis broken. Left arm and leg shattered. The hand and foot disintegrated. Multiples pieces of unsorted small bones bunched together at the foot of the skeleton.

"And something else," said Peter.

Kennet studied the remains. The living specimen had been a tall individual. He said to Peter, "Male?"

Peter nodded.

Kennet's eyes traveled over the right side of the skeleton and fastened on the tibia and fibula, the lower leg bones. "That," he said, pointing to it, "is the only real damage to the right side."

"You have a knack for this, Kennet. That's a perimortem fracture. Under a glass, you can see no evidence of healing. It may antedate the poor guy's death by mere days. Or hours. And my experienced eyes have spotted a healed fracture higher up, in the femur, and some pieces of the right pelvic girdle chipped and hosting embedded metal. And there's one more thing, which I didn't expect you to see, given the state of the skull, but the extreme tip of the upper spine has been pulverized. And I have more goodies."

He whipped back the flaps of a long cardboard box on an adjoining table. He extracted a rusty rifle barrel attached to remnants of a wooden stock. "This came with it."

Kennet recognized it immediately. "A Lee-Enfield .303. Let me see that." He scrutinized the metal parts. "An early model. A very early model."

"There's more. Bits of clothing. Strong leather boots. Cartridges, which I ain't touchin'. The ammunition will be unstable. A hammer – two hammers – and two odd chisels. A metal canteen. The remains of a haversack. Various small items.

And this." Peter handed him a small object. "I cleaned it, using a high-tech method. I soaked it overnight in a glass of coke. You can make out the markings now."

Kennet turned the object over and over in his fingers. "It's a regimental badge, a cap badge. I recognize the insignia. PPCLI."

"What?"

"Princess Patricia's Canadian Light Infantry. Once upon a time, our victim was a soldier."

"I gathered that, from the shrapnel in the hip. World War II?"

"The rifle is older than that. More likely the Great War. With a little research, I can probably figure out when the badge was issued."

"Something else I have concluded. This soldier died by his own hand."

"What?"

Peter pointed to the head bones. "See this nick under the mandible? And this fragment missing from the basal edge of the occipital bone at the back of the skull? And the atlas, the cervical vertebra that fuses with the skull, has been pulverized. I believe the poor guy held the muzzle under his chin, and pulled the trigger."

"Makes some kind of sense," said Kennet. "With a broken leg, he wasn't going to get off that mountain. There was no road there earlier than the 1950's. No means of communicating his distress. Hell, my cell phone didn't work up there. And I might have wanted an ambulance. Or a hearse."

Kennet described his encounter with the raging bear. Peter had looked appropriately interested, and then he had held up an index finger. One more piece of news, he said.

He had turned over the debris from the Vanderhorst dig to colleagues in the Physical Sciences Department. They had been delighted with the dating challenge for the metal fragments. They had conducted metallurgical analyses. Most of the fragments were centuries old. The composition suggested iron that had been smelted and forged to manufacture articles such as swords and bucklers. Perhaps the late Alfie had been on to something. Peter would be sourcing funds to conduct an official examination of the site next season.

Fortunately, the police had collected the paraphernalia from the crime scene and turned them over to Cindy, who had turned over the camera and notebook to the Anthropology Department. So they had some records from Vanderhorst's project.

The day after returning to Thunder Bay, Kennet had left the injured dog with a veterinary service. He checked on it daily. When he finally came to collect the animal, the size of the bill floored him. And, the supervising vet insisted that the dog get all its shots. And the dog should have a name, he said ponderously. Kennet thought the vet officious. He looked him in the eye and said, "What do you suggest, chum?" So, Chum it was.

When he went to work, Kennet tethered Chum outside, leaving the man-door of the garage ajar so that he could duck inside out of the weather. After Mrs. Sandberg complained, he made a practice of gathering up Chum's excretions on a daily basis. Evenings, and early mornings, they went for a walk to Hillcrest Park, climbing a little higher every day. Nights, they spent together upstairs in the apartment.

Robert Kenilworth told him that Lancelot Fleming and Dunstan Ritchie had been charged with the assault on Kyle Henderson, which would likely get them two years in penitentiary, and they had been detained in custody. If Kennet were to agree to testify, they could add an attempted murder charge. Kennet demurred. There were no charges against Rawling Fleming, but he had not stood bail for his brother and cousin. An autopsy on the body of Donally Rolfe Fleming had determined that the upper spine and several other bones had been fractured, possibly sustained in the fall down the manway. The proximate cause of death had been asphyxiation by drowning. In the case of Georgiana Elder, the coroner issued a ruling of death by misadventure, and the police had closed the file. There was an arrest warrant for Maximilian Cornelius Kueng for the murder of Alfred Vanderhorst. Kueng was still at large.

Kennet kept in touch with Harry Elder. Harry made the trek every morning to the Thunder Bay OPP Detachment. He clung to the belief that they held the key to the remains of his daughter. After putting in his time at the Blue Lite Variety, he had caught the Memorial bus to the Brodie Street Terminal, and then he had transferred to the Mainline, which took him to Westfort in time to catch the Neebing bus. The Neebing pursued a rural route, past scattered houses and fields and thick groves, where he luxuriated in the colours and scents of the countryside. At its furthest point west, it dropped him off on the 25th Side Road. Then he walked north, until he hit busy Highway 17, and then he walked the shoulder west, until he reached the OPP Headquarters located in the middle of nowhere. It was an eight-kilometre round trip on foot. One morning a cruiser gave him a lift to the university's Paleo-Forensics Lab, where he signed a release and received a box of remains. Kennet helped him arrange the cremation. On one of his trips to Vickers St. North, he cut a deal with the canoe shop for a new kayak.

And Kennet kept in touch with Edith and Gracie Elder. Sometimes his daily phone call routine included Conrad or Ioanna or Curtis or the Kellermans or, when she was home, Crystal. He would casually comment on the progress of his healing and of the dog's healing and offhandedly suggest that Yvette the nurse practitioner might like to know. He also asked some cleverly disguised questions about Yvette, the nurse practitioner. Her name was Yvette Desrochers. She was a lifelong resident of Beardmore. She had attended Geraldton District High School and graduated five years behind him. Had a teenage daughter named Yvonne. Was a widow. Her husband, Armand, had been working in the tar sands in northern Alberta, returning home for a visit every three

396

months. Had expired of injuries sustained three years ago in a vehicular accident on his way to Edmonton airport.

One day he had phoned D.C. Armitage. He told her that he had referred the abandoned lakeside cemetery to Ombabika Bay First Nation. Kelly agreed that was a wise course of action.

Now it was an autumn weekend, and he was back in the Greenstone region. He and Harry Elder had left the city early that Sunday morning under a blue sky laced with sketchy clouds. Harry had been silent, dressed in a dark suit and white shirt but no tie as a concession to the warm weather, and gazing out the windows. When they skirted the shore of Lake Helen, he showed interest in the birds – ducks and seagulls and ravens. "Eagles," he said, pointing to a flock of ravens on the mud flats. Kennet looked hard, and he did distinguish a large white-headed adult, and two other large dark-coloured birds that he assumed were young bald eagles. Four or five ravens strutted and fluttered about, apparently harassing the trio of raptors.

Harry diligently scrutinized the cliffs of the Pijitawabik Pallisades. Kennet asked him for the pronunciation: *pee-jee-tuh-WAW-bik*. He displayed interest in the burnscape, asking several questions. In Beardmore Kennet stopped at The Hook'n Bullet, and Kellerman gave Harry Elder a warm welcome. Kellerman told Kennet that Bill Meyers wanted a few words with him, gesturing to the derelict garage across the street. He, Kellerman, had some catching up to do with Harry.

Meyers was puttering around a car up on blocks.

"I wanted to thank you," said Meyers.

"For what?"

"For removing two of the blights on this community – the Flemings, and the Hermit. And I made a nice packet on them." The day Kennet had left, the police had detained Lanny and Ritchie, and Rawling had disappeared for a spell. Meyers explained that Saxon Fleming had commissioned Meyers to demolish all structures on the Fleming property, including the house with all its contents. Mrs. Fleming had stood by, nodding her head, and had signed a release for Meyers. Then Saxon had put his mother on the bus and followed on his bike. Meyers had been instructed to group together all the boys' recreational toys around the battered green pickup – the boats, motors, bikes, and sleds – and cover them with polyethylene. Everything else he had carted to the landfill. Saxon had paid him cash money. He had driven by the empty property the day after the job had been done, and had found Rawling standing on the cinder driveway, in a state of shock.

Rawling accepted that his mother had ordered the demolition. He had climbed into his truck and driven off.

"And then Martinson, the manager from the bank? He dropped by, and gave me Kueng's handwritten instructions to clean up his property, and two thousand dollars down. I got another three thousand when the job was done. Nothing there now but a clearing. And I found this."

Meyers walked into the hole he called an office and came back with a book. "I was cleaning up the old forge. Where the firemen found you. I figured you dropped this." He handed him the book *Dark Journey*. Kennet looked more closely at the book cover. Blocks of arctic ice gripped a ghostly full-rigged sailing ship, its bare masts pointing to a blue heaven. And beneath the keel, a black abyss.

"Yours?" asked Meyers.

"Yes. Thank you."

Kennet and Harold had lunched at the home of Edith and Gracie Elder, the meal prepared by Crystal Mallory. Conrad Parker and Curtis and Ioanna Mallory had attended. By unspoken agreement, neither Kennet nor Conrad raised the issue the newly discovered bones. The Elders had been very shy with one another. At one point, Gracie had passed a dream-catcher to her father, without words, and he had accepted it. From his jacket side pocket he had produced the framed picture of the Rainbow Quest and passed it to her. They had a whispered conversation.

And then they had taken three vehicles to High Hill Harbour. On the walking path, Crystal and Conrad had trailed the Elders, prepared to assist the older man and woman, but Harold needed no assistance. He had kept up with Kennet and Curtis and Ioanna until he noticed Edith struggling along with the assistance of her daughter, Gracie. He had dropped back.

Kennet and his two companions arrived at the furthermost overlook in close to twenty minutes. The first overlook had had the view obscured by tall shrubbery. On the trail they spooked a rabbit still in its summer brown, and a partridge. After waiting ten minutes, Kennet walked back along the trail. Fall flowers embroidered the trail – fireweed and asters and goldenrod and pearly everlasting. Occasionally a vista opened up to the north, along the eastern shore of the great lake. A crescent of sand stretched between the bottom of the ridge and the distant park. He found the stragglers sitting on the benches of the first overlook. A lone mosquito flew erratically by. Perhaps the last fly of summer.

Edith flashed him a dazzling smile. "We're coming! We're in no rush. This is a great adventure."

Harold sat by, beaming. "There was a time," he said, "when Edith was a sailor. The only thing I didn't make her do, was scramble up the antenna mast."

Everyone was in high spirits. Gracie kept glancing at her father, a sense of wonder growing in her eyes. Her hand rested on a bulky item in her shoulder bag. They started off again, Kennet trailing in their wake. When the trail dipped, Harry gave Edith his arm, and when the trail rose, he pulled her by the hand.

They joined Curtis and Ioanna at the overlook, and everyone looked out to sea, far out, to the land masses on the horizon, dissolving into mist. After a time, someone spoke. "Is that the far side?" asked Edith. "Are we really seeing the far side?"

Harold answered. "We never see the far side. You know that, Edith. To see the far side, you have to go there."

A gentle southern breeze picked up the ashes and scattered them over the hillside and some flakes reached the water. No one spoke. Harold removed a small pouch from his suit jacket and extracted a pinch of tobacco and released the strands into the breeze.

He smiled shyly. "My father used to do that," he said, addressing Gracie. "I got this from my friend Art."

On the return trip, Kennet stepped out ahead. He thought the group was abominably slow. Crystal called to him, "Kennet, you catch us up at suppertime. You go ahead."

"For what?" he asked.

Conrad grinned broadly. "You know what. You brought two boats. You do what you gotta do."

Kennet imagined that everyone was smiling. Harold Elder added his two cents.

"Don't be too late, eh, professor? I got to work in the morning."

Kennet forged ahead. After the northernmost overlook, the trail dropped rapidly. The last drop was a flight of timber-and-dirt stairs. He paused on the bottom step. He felt the same way he had when he had climbed the stairs. He felt a lightness of being. An incredible lightness of being.

The trip into Beardmore passed in a blur. He felt a sudden urge to see the Fleming property. When he drove up, the painted wagon stood in the cinder driveway, facing the lot. An elbow poked out the driver's side window, and a face peered at him in the side-view mirror as he walked up.

Rawling Fleming turned his head to look at him. He hadn't shaved for days. Kennet said, "Do you mind my being here?"

"Be my guest. It's a free country." Rawling looked to the front.

"This is not my doing, you know."

Rawling's voice was flat. Emotionless. "Maybe. Maybe not. It's somebody's doing. Enjoy it. Everybody else is."

"A lot of it is your doing, Fleming." Kennet broke away from the truck and advanced further into the yard and stopped, looking around the near empty lot. Only the boys' recreational toys remained, bunched around the green Chevy. Meyers had done an excellent job. He heard the door slam and he turned to confront Fleming.

Fleming stopped an arm's length away. He lifted his hands to his hips. "Just what are you getting at?" Now there was an edge to his voice. "Are you trying to provoke me?"

"Maybe. Maybe not." Kennet raised his hands to his own hips. "Twenty-six years ago, someone supplied a high school girl with drugs, here in Beardmore, and she died."

"Fuck you," said Rawling, equitably. "No one ever died of an overdose here."

"At the grad party in '83, out at the lake, Georgiana Elder was high, probably on ecstasy, and two local yobs were stalking her."

"Fuck you."

"They chased her up a trail to the road, in the dark."

"So?"

"She was run down. The driver didn't see her."

"We didn't see nothin'. Just a truck, idlin'. And the sonuvabitch spotlighted us, and we turned around. I know what they're sayin' now, that she died, and that maniac buried her in the bush. So what? We weren't drivin'."

"No snowflake in an avalanche ever feels responsible."

"What the hell does that mean?"

"It's a wise man's observation. The driver saw your father's Korean medal, Rawling. The Distinguished Service Star. You were wearing it."

"So what? A couple hours before, Lanny was wearing it. We took turns. He was a hero, our father. We respected him.

Tremendously. Come to think of it, I've never respected anyone else as much in my life."

"Yes. He was a hero. The last in his line. If you discount Saxon. And Donny. Donny might have carried on that line."

"What the fuck do you mean by that?" Rawling showed some heat.

"When the driver saw that star again, Donny was wearing it."

Rawling had no comeback. His jaw slackened. As Kennet gazed into his eyes, he could see the machinery whirring. Rawling dropped the hand from his right hip. He staggered slightly.

"You mean –" he said hoarsely, "– that Donny died . . . because – " He could not finish the thought.

"Because of your doing."

Kennet walked past him, brushing his jutting elbow lightly. When he looked back, Rawling was kneeling on the ground, both hands jammed into his temples.

Kennet drove around to Kellerman's shop and asked to look at the phone directory. Marta spoke up first. She said it was 344 Garnet Drive. Kennet asked what was? Bull said, You know who. Did everyone know his business? said Kennet petulantly. Pretty much, said Bull. Both he and Marta smiled. And he should approach it from Walker Street West, said Bull, not from Laroque's direction. That was a dead end there. And that was Walker St. West, he said, far west of Walker St. East, because Walker St. Central did not exist. She lived below the rapids.

He parked in front of a pretty bungalow facing the river. There were no houses on the riverside. It featured medium blue clapboard siding with white shutters and trim. He rapped on the door. A slim teenage girl with streaky blonde hair answered. Yes? she said. Her gaze lingered on his bad eye.

"Is your mother home?"

She turned her head and shouted, "Mom!"

When Yvette arrived, the girl said in a stage whisper, "Is this the guy?", and disappeared into the interior.

Yvette wore a brilliant white short-sleeved shirt and short purple shorts and her raven black hair framed her dusky face and she looked beautiful.

"Dr. Yvette, I presume?"

Her eyes twinkled. "Are you a reporter?"

"I am an explorer. I have eluded the talons of eagles and chased off a fierce rabbit and a partridge and fought off wild flowers to find you here."

"Did you now, professor."

"I'm no professor."

"I'm no doctor." Her whole face laughed. "Why are you here? Are you looking for a body again?"

"In a manner of speaking."

Her expression changed. "Oh! Of course." Her hand flew to her mouth. "How insensitive of me! You came for Georgiana's memorial ceremony."

"That's part of the reason."

"You came about the prospector's bones that Conrad found."

"No. I came about a live body."

"Really?" Her cheeks started to colour.

"Yes. I wanted you to examine me again. To verify that I'm perfectly healthy."

"Oh."

"And Chum thanks you. Chum is my dog."

"I know."

"How do you know that? Oh, of course. Everyone here knows my business. I must look silly."

"You *look* good, investigator. Good and healthy. I know a lot about you."

"I guess as an investigator, I'm not too suave."

"I don't like my investigators suave. I checked you out too."

"You checked *me* out?"

"Sure. You're all over the Internet. I put your name into Google and got ten billion hits. It appears you own several Fortune 500 companies, have mistresses in Belize and Dubai and Milan, and you are wanted for questioning by the secret police in Croatia. And, as a sideline, you file stories and read the news on TV and teach aspiring journalists from Beardmore."

"That's me. The last bit, anyway."

"Oh my gosh!" Her hand flew to her mouth again. "Here I've kept you waiting on my doorstep. Come on in!"

"Actually, I came to ask you to go on a trip with me."

"Oh, Kennet!" she said, tapping his shoulder lightly. "This is so sudden! Is this a proposal?"

"I propose we go paddling." He stepped back and gestured towards his truck on which perched two apparently identical kayaks. "But I'll marry you first, if that's what you want."

"I've never been. Kayaking, I mean. It looks scary."

"It's fun."

"They look tippy."

"I'll tip you back up."

"I'm not dressed for it. I have no wet suit."

"Your birthday suit is the ultimate wet suit."

"Are you proposing we go *au naturel*?"

"I'm willing if you are. No, I'm saying we'll go as we are."

"I have guests for supper in a couple hours."

There was a wail from the interior of the house. "Oh God, mother! Go already! Go!"

"We won't go far. The first time." Kennet gestured towards the river across the road. "We can just paddle in circles, if you wish."

She grabbed his hand and pulled him toward the kayaks.

"What fun would that be? I prefer getting somewhere."

"We could follow the river."

"Sure. Just get me back in time for supper."

Epilogue

Our Father . . . Who art is heaven.
Our Father . . . Who art in heaven.
Our Father . . . Who art in heaven.
The short prayer helped him cope with the pain. After a while, after a very long while, he grasped his right knee with both hands, and held them there for a long while, and then he edged his hands downward, down, down, until he felt what he feared. He felt an enormous lump on the inside of his calf. Both leg bones threatened to break the skin.

He had little tobacco. He had been preserving the little he had for one early morning smoke and one late evening smoke. In his excitement to get away he had skipped his smoke this morning. He would smoke now. He deserved it now.

When he focused on breathing in the smoke, and focused on breathing out the smoke, the pain did not go away. But it was a more bearable pain. And it allowed him to size up his situation.

He had food. He had water. He had no appetite. And he

could stretch the water for days. In days he could figure out something. He could figure out something in hours. He could figure out. His mind worked. It always worked for him. Thank you, Father. Thank you.

He could, with considerable pain, he could, with indescribable agony, straighten his leg, and push the bones back in, and force them into alignment, and then bind his leg, maybe using his rifle as a splint, or using the branches nearby, that he could reach if he had to, if he levered his body toward them, and dragged his bad leg along with him. And then what?

He was not going to walk out of here.

He was not going to get off the mountain.

And if he got off the mountain, if by the grace of God and all that's holy he got off the mountain, and he found his blazes, well, then, he might be walking, he might be hobbling with a makeshift crutch, and he would be falling, he would be falling, many times, many, many times, and would inevitably lose the blazes at some point, after he had clawed himself back up to a standing position, and disoriented himself, and started for the next blaze, where he imagined it to be, and was just a few degrees off. Unless, of course, he consulted his compass.

His compass. He fumbled for his compass. He was not going to use his compass. It was smashed. The glass had broken. Needle destroyed.

So he must depend on the blazes.

He would never find his canoe.

When he found his canoe, he must drag it downstream until it floated freely. That was no mean chore.

And when it floated, and he reached the bay, and the wind was right, and the sky clear, with no threat of storm or tempest, he would paddle, all day he would paddle, all night, if necessary, and he would not stop at the Indian encampment, because they could do nothing for his leg, so he must paddle, through calm seas and under serene skies. As his leg festered.

The festering might have already started. He knocked the dottle from his pipe and stowed it away. Very carefully he pulled up the leg of his trousers, and when it started to bind, he worked his knife out of its sheath and poked a hole in the trousers just above the knee and slit the material, down, down, to the cuff. The material fell away. And he saw that one bone had broken the skin. So the festering had started.

When he reached the fishing village of Macdiarmid, the inhabitants would help him to the train, if the train were there, or perhaps it had already left, for it ran every day, one day travelling north, and the next day travelling south, and he wanted to travel south, to the nearest city. So he might have to wait a day. Two days at most.

He had no money. But the jolly conductor had been very friendly. The jolly conductor would stake him to a ticket. A ticket to the doctor. To the hospital. To the healing hands of science and the comforts of home. If the conductor were on that run. He didn't work seven days a week, did he? And always travel south?

Whatever. He would figure it out. When he got to Macdiarmid.

Meanwhile. He had found the holy grail. He had found the dream of every prospector.

His mind told him to prospect. He was a prospector. And when a prospector found a showing, he wanted to know everything about it. He needed to dig. And besides. He needed a display sample. He needed to show the jolly conductor that he was, sure, needy, but he was also rich. Very, very rich.

He removed his railroad watch and draped it over the face of the ledge by its chain from a tiny knob, near his face. The single jack – the small sledge – and the drill steels – the ten-inch rod with the chisel point, and the twenty-four-inch rod – he still had them. They were under him, and by virtue of squirming, and shifting his body by degrees, he retrieved them.

He studied the rock face. The greenstone protruded beyond his back another good nine-and-a-half, ten feet, and rose the same distance, and extended in front of him another eleven, twelve feet, before it fused with the sloping terrain. Before he had stumbled, he had had an impression of its thickness. It was a few inches deep at the top, and perhaps four, four-and-a-half, five feet towards the bottom.

With the fingers of his left hand he explored a seam that ran almost parallel to the ground on which he sat, a few inches above the ground, and above that seam he discovered some smaller cracks, also parallel, but discontinuous. He would start with the bottom-most seam. He pulled on his Texas gloves.

He placed the cutting edge of the ten-inch steel in the seam near his left foot, just above the foot, and he tapped the head lightly, several times, rotating the steel in his left fist and striking with the single jack in his right hand, until he had collared the bore hole. Then he positioned the wedge of the sharp tempered bit in the round notch, and then he swung the sledge hard, and after impact, his left hand automatically gave the steel an eighth-of-an-inch turn, and he swung again, and turned, and swung again, and turned, and swung again . . .

After a quarter hour he stopped. Rock powder dusted his left boot and lower pant leg. The drill bit had sunk a good four inches. Good. Very darn good. Especially because he could get no leverage from his right leg, the injured leg. But it was now difficult to rotate the steel in the bore hole. He took a sip from the canteen. The merest sip. He must preserve his water.

He dug into the haversack and found his powder spoon. He did not have the water supply to wash out the rock chips, the finely ground powder, so he must spoon it out. Most miner's spoons consisted of a metal rod up to thirty inches in length, the last few inches of which had been flattened by a blacksmith, and the tip curved. The whole affair did not exceed three-quarters of an inch *in width, to fit into the hole bored with a seven-eighths-inch-diameter steel.*

He himself preferred to carry a modified version in the field. He carried a four-inch spoon with a slim six-inch handle which terminated in a four-sided spike. He could first carve a groove into the tip of a straight branch, lay the spike in it, and then drive it up into the shaft of the branch, and then lash it securely with fishing line. He gritted his teeth. He inched himself and his useless leg to a nearby clump of birch saplings and selected a likely handle. He inched himself back. In another quarter hour, he had the powder spoon ready, and he fished out the rock dust, spoonful by spoonful.

He resumed the swings and turns, finding his rhythm again.

By ten o'clock the light had faded to such an extent that he feared if he swung and missed, he might injure himself, hit his left wrist, or strike his thumb or fingers, or God forbid, get clumsy, and slam the sledge into his right foot, so he stopped. He lay back slowly. The light would persist in the west until close to midnight. He deserved a pipe, so he had one.

It would be eight o'clock in Saskatchewan. Martha would be penning the cows up in the barn and by coal-oil lamp she would be sitting down at the seldom-used dining table and drawing toward her the last letters he had written. Her father would be outside on the veranda, smoking, and her mother finding some last-minute things to do in the kitchen and she, Martha, she would read his last letter and then set to writing. Dear Archibald, *she would begin. Or* My dear Archie. *Or perhaps tonight, she would begin,* My dearest love.

My dearest love, *he would write back to her.* Our troubles are over. I have found it. Give the good news to your mother and your father. Tell them we will be getting married this fall. And tell my father too. I am writing Dad tonight but you might get this letter before he learns of my good fortune – our good fortune! And he'll want to tell my

brothers right away. He will be chuffed to learn that his
eldest son can now be happy, can get that job in town now
. . .

Dear father . . . who art in heaven.
Dear father . . . who art in Saskatchewan.
Dear father . . .

When he awoke the dawn light was filtering through the trees.
His pipe was dead, cold, lying on his chest, and he knocked the
ashes out. He discovered he was damp. It must have rained
during the night, a light rain, a gentle rain. He struggled to a
sitting position. So long as he did not disturb it, he could bear the
throbs of pain that worked themselves up his leg and up his torso
and into his brain. He felt an urgent need to urinate. That would
be difficult.

He could not roll over on his side. Either side. He must stand
up. Like a man. Urinate like a man. His fingers sought out seams
in the rock face, knobs, ridges . . . anything. It was a chore. He
levered himself up with his fingers, his wrists, his shoulders, his
chest muscles . . . Two fingernails broke. He was on his feet. His
foot, rather. His left foot. Blood rushing down into his right leg
brought waves of pain flooding up. But he managed the job. And
he buttoned up. And somehow . . . he eased himself down. And
both legs now lay on the urine-soaked ground.

He must keep up his strength. He rummaged in the haversack
and came up with a larded biscuit and he topped it with strips of
cold bacon and he forced it down, choked it down, bit by bit. He
needed two swallows of water to clear his throat.

He examined his handiwork. Four bore holes. Twenty-and-a-
half inches deep, 21 ½, 21, and 20 ½. At the end of each drilling,
he had marked the hole depth with his thumb, and then measured
the steel against his big knife. His knife was exactly 13 inches
long, and the handle was 5¼ inches long. He would have
preferred a full 22 inches for each hole. But time was his enemy.

He was always impatient to move on to the next hole. And he could always come back. If he had time.

The four holes spanned a distance of 48 inches, from right to left, along the seam at the bottom of the rock face. He needed another row now, above the first, about two feet above the first. He had all day. He would get it done.

After he had finished each hole, he had lifted his hips by pressing on the ground, arms straight down, with his knuckles, and pushing off with his left foot, and dragging the broken leg backward, until he had displaced himself about sixteen inches. Then he had collared the next hole.

For the second row of holes, he would strike the steel, and rest the face of the sledge on the steel for a moment, the merest moment, and then he would draw the hammer back. He had it figured. He collared the first hole, exactly between the last two holes in the first row, only two feet higher.

At noon he paused to take another swig. He had wet his whistle now four times that morning. He had collared the eighth hole, the first hole in the third row. Before the sixth hole in the second row, he had manoevred his whole body frontward, sixteen inches, to reach the spot that he must bore. He had lifted his hips and shoved them, and his left leg, three or four inches frontward. Then he had lifted his injured leg with both hands and extended it forward the three or four inches. He had repeated that maneuver for the seventh hole.

He deserved a pipe. He smoked a pipe. He lay back as he puffed, and looked up at the blue vault. When he awoke, it was almost one-thirty. He struggled frantically to sit up. He sat up. He was losing strength. He felt the strength draining from him. He applied himself to the eighth hole. Then three more to go.

The last row of holes, the third row, required reaching above his head almost the full extent of his left arm. The four holes of the last row would match the bottom row of four holes. He had to modify his hammer.

He took a piece of rawhide string, a boot lace that was attached to the strap of the haversack, and he threaded it through the pre-bored hole at the end of the single jack handle, and he tied a knot in it. He slipped the thong over his right hand and wrist, and he raised the ten-inch steel up to third-row height.

And then he swung, he swung hard, releasing the handle at the end of the backswing, and then gripping it again, hard, and bringing it forward to strike the head of the steel, releasing it momentarily as it struck, and then he gripped the handle firmly, and swung it back again. He had gained extra leverage in his swing, and he could rest his grip twice in every swing, rest it for a fraction of a second each time, but it was a relief twice in every swing.

The depth of the upright slab decreased as it drew nearer the top, so he would shorten the holes. He should not penetrate the slab more than half-way through in order for his plan to work. He decreased the borehole depth to a maximum of 18 inches.

He struck the last blow at ten minutes after eight. For five minutes he spooned out the powder. He examined his handiwork. Beautiful. A work of art. No two jobs were ever the same. He had never before fixed to bring a rock slab down. But he had experience. And he had listened to other prospectors discuss their work. And he felt that his strategy had been correct.

Now for the dynamite.

He extracted one stick from the haversack. He extracted a coil of powder fuse. He stretched the coil out on the handle of the single jack, and using his knife, measured off 30 inches. He made a clean cut, pressing through the fuse into the wood. From his shirt pocket he took a small aluminium tin, a snuff box, really, and removed the lid, and set the tin on the ground near his right leg. Cotton batting kept the caps from rattling or moving about.

He folded back the brown paper from one end of the dynamite stick. He removed the metal spoon from its handle, and with its spiked tip, he created a pocket in the explosive. He took one cap, a

412

slim metal cylinder about an inch long, and inserted one end of the cut fuse into the cylinder, until it touched the closed end, where the percussive material was packed. From his haversack he took his crimping tool, slipped it over the cap, and started pressing the cap down over the fuse, taking care to stop short of the percussive material hidden inside the cap. He turned the cap and fuse as he crimped.

He inserted the cap, percussive end first, into the pocket in the stick. Reaching into his haversack again, he found the fishing line. He cut off a few inches with his teeth, gathered up the paper at the end of the stick, and tied the paper tightly around the fuse. The cap would not fall out. Nor would it admit dampness.

He put the stick, fuse hanging out, into the last hole he had made, Hole No. 11, on the extreme left of the third row, and carefully pushed it with the small end of the wooden spoon handle to meet the bottom of the hole. About 20 inches of the fuse dangled out of the hole.

For the second row of holes, he cut the fuses two inches shorter. And for the bottom row, he cut the fuses four inches shorter, so that the fuses sprouted from the holes and stretched a short distance on the ground.

Before it got too dark, he had stuffed every hole. He would finish the job in the morning. Then he would be away.

He stored everything away. He dared not smoke. The smallest ember, the merest hot ash could ignite one of the dangling fuses. And he might not even notice. Sleep did not come easily. He had to plan the future. When he returned from the war, in the fall of 1919, it was to a house of mourning. His mother had succumbed to the influenza. The pandemic had swept the world, and millions had died. Many died in their own beds, far from the battlefields of Europe. Many felt it was a judgement.

He found he could not follow a plow. Although the horse did most of the labour, he had to command the plow to stay upright and to dig deep. He had to put tremendous strain on his bad leg when he heaved sheaves and stacked hay. He was no good anymore as a farmer. When a prospector offered to apprentice him, he gladly accepted.

They started in the Northwest Territories, and then put time in northern Quebec and Ontario. After two years they parted company, the prospector deciding that farming was less work and more rewarding. He had learned to walk long distances over rough terrain on his gimpy leg. He could paddle all day. All night, too. He eked out a living, selling gold that he dry panned, and selling claims, and conjuring up grubstakes. If he and Martha were to marry, he had to get a stake and find a town job. In real estate, maybe. Or insurance. He could run his own store.

The explosion woke him up. The ground shook. It shuddered. Flashes of light in the heavens. He crushed his hat to his face. The shell had missed him. The deadly shards would be raining down now. He thought of his Father. His father was always there in times like this. His father always offered comfort in his letters. This too shall pass, *he was fond of saying.* Fear no evil. *He sensed his heartbeat returning to normal.* Lie down beside still waters.

When he awoke in the gray light he discovered that he had moved his bowels. Disgusting. But it had to happen sometime. He had to urinate too, but he held it. It had rained during the night; he was soaked; the ground was soaked. Good. Very good. Thank you, father. When he had pulled himself into a sitting position, he pushed one stick back that had advanced one inch towards freedom. He was shivering. He shivered himself warm.

Now he took the spoon and began scratching the ground between his thighs. He took the butt of his rifle and pushed back the leaf litter and the black organic soil and exposed the lighter-coloured silt, the mixture of sand and clay. The silt was damp. He excavated a shallow basin and fumbled with his trouser buttons and emptied his burning bladder into the basin and with the spoon he loosened clumps of silt and conveyed it to the basin and soon he

414

had a mess of mud which he continued to feed with more silt until a handful of that mud caked in his hand, clung together, like potter's clay.

He began packing the bore holes. With the small end of the wooden spoon handle he packed the mud in, taking care not to disturb the fuse. He was not worried about the fuse getting damp. Once lit, it would burn through anything. Even water.

The voices bothered him. It was not his bad leg which bothered him. After twenty-four hours the ache had become part of his environment. As long as he did not move his leg, did not jolt it, he was okay. But his chums always felt they could do something better, and were prepared to give him the benefit of their opinions. For the last three holes, he emptied his canteen into the basin of mud. Careless, the voices said. But there was plenty of water in the lake. And today the lake would be calm. Still.

Sometimes he could not hear them for the birds. It was turning out a beautiful day. The spacing was wrong, they said. Holes should be closer together. And the mud. The mud would dry up and fall out. He should work faster. You'll never do it, said the Boche. He knew it was a Boche because of the spike on its helmet. The skull sat on the bank in front of him and it grinned at him. And to his right an arm extruded from the wall of the trench. The flesh was gray. And the flesh inside the boot, it would be gray too. The foot was detached from the leg. And over all the stench of shit. Of piss. And decay.

You can do it, son. Thank you, Father. You can do it, son. Soon you'll be away. From all this. Back home. Thank you, Dad. I need a match. A long match. I have paper. Waxed paper. Wrapped my bacon in it. You should have shared, said the voices. We shared with you. We shared our dugouts with you. Not this one, he replied. You don't want to share this one.

He took the crumpled sheet of waxed paper from his haversack and folded it longtitudinally and then rolled it into a wand. Chappie nuzzled his cheek. What are we doing? Chappie said.

415

We're getting out of here, he replied. He set the butt of the .303 in the empty basin and leaned the barrel on his left shoulder. He would have to grab it fast. And run. In his mind he was already running.

He tucked the cap box back in his shirt pocket. He fingered the metal badge under the pocket flap. He was never without it. It identified his unit and nationality. Even if there were nothing left of him, they would know he served his country. This magnificent country. This green country.

He flicked the head of the wooden match with his thumbnail and it flared. He ignited the wand and quickly touched it to each fuse. First the two centre fuses in the top row, and then the outer fuses. Next the centre row, centre fuse first. And last, the bottom row, centre fuses first. He had mere seconds now.

He placed the muzzle under his chin.

Bless you, Martha. Learn to be happy.

THE BEARDMORE RELICS

ABOUT THE AUTHOR

Edgar J. Lavoie pursued a teaching career in Ontario schools for 35 years. He married Olga, his first and current wife, and their two children have families of their own. The author has solid credentials in writing and publishing, ranging from little magazines, news articles, and short stories to local history books. He and Olga live in the boreal forest north of Thunder Bay, in a big cabin on a big lake. This is his debut novel.

CPSIA information can be obtained at www.ICGtesting.com
Printed in the USA
LVOW060445221111

255970LV00002B/1/P